Drugs and Alcohol in Perspective

Mary Grimm

Drugs and Alcohol in Perspective

Richard Fields, Ph.D.

Director, FACES
Family and Addiction Conferences and Educational/Counseling Services

Bellevue, Washington

Wm. C. Brown Publishers

Book Team

Editor *Chris Rogers*
Developmental Editor *Susan McCormick*
Production Editor *Jane Matthews*
Designer *Jeff Storm*
Art Editor *Carla Marie Heathcote*
Photo Editor *Carrie Burger*
Permissions Editor *Mavis Oeth*
Visuals Processor *Andréa Lopez-Meyer*

Wm. C. Brown Publishers

President *G. Franklin Lewis*
Vice President, Publisher *Thomas E. Doran*
Vice President, Operations and Production *Beverly Kolz*
National Sales Manager *Virginia S. Moffat*
Group Sales Manager *Eric Ziegler*
Executive Editor *Edgar J. Laube*
Director of Marketing *Kathy Law Laube*
Marketing Manager *Pamela Cooper*
Managing Editor, Production *Colleen A. Yonda*
Manager of Visuals and Design *Faye M. Schilling*
Production Editorial Manager *Julie A. Kennedy*
Production Editorial Manager *Ann Fuerste*
Publishing Services Manager *Karen J. Slaght*

WCB Group

President and Chief Executive Officer *Mark C. Falb*
Chairman of the Board *Wm. C. Brown*

Cover photo © Frank Pedrick/The Image Works

Photo Researcher Kathy Husemann

Copyeditor Clare Wulker

The credits section for this book begins on page 369, and is considered an extension of the copyright page.

Library of Congress Catalog Card Number: 91-73710

ISBN 0-697-12071-6

Printed in the United States of America by Wm. C. Brown Publishers, 2460 Kerper Boulevard, Dubuque, IA 52001

10 9 8 7 6 5 4 3 2 1

Dedication

■

This book is dedicated to the memory of my younger brother, Barry, who died of another deadly disease, AIDS, in November of 1989.

CONTENTS

PREFACE

The eleven chapters in this book are designed to give readers as full an understanding of the dynamics of chemical dependency as possible. Each chapter is developed to integrate concepts that build on each other. The goal of the book is to help readers develop their own perspectives on the multifaceted aspects of drug/alcohol dependence and addiction. Each chapter contains tables and illustrations that are easy to understand. All chapters answer common questions readers may have and conclude with a chapter summary. Throughout the textbook case studies are interwoven into the chapter to bring clarity and definition to each topic. In addition, some chapters have worksheets that help readers to formulate their own viewpoint (perspective) about drugs/alcohol.

The book's major emphasis is on family dynamics as opposed to the traditional pharmacological textbook. Thus, we do not focus exclusively on drugs and alcohol without considering the individual and each individual's family system. Within the last decade we have seen an emerging awareness of the impact of dysfunctional or imbalanced family systems on individuals and their use of chemicals. This book explores those dynamics giving a more structured perspective of the use and abuse of drugs and alcohol.

The introduction to this book explains the reality that drug/alcohol problems are not going to be solved by simple solutions. The failure of previous approaches has been due to this simplistic solution thinking.

The one arena that may have the greatest impact on the drug/alcohol problem is the family. Yet, many societal problems contribute to the drug/alcohol epidemic. Some of the biggest problems today involve the use of crack cocaine by people of color, and the use of drugs/alcohol by young addict mothers.

Although we have seen a reduction in the use of marijuana and cocaine by young people, the extent of use, abuse, and addiction is still too high. Alcohol is still the number one drug used by young people. Alcohol is especially problematic as evidenced by the high incidence of traffic fatalities of youth under the influence of alcohol and the binge patterns of alcohol use by college students.

Chapter 1 explores the reasons for drug/alcohol use, the functions and meanings of drugs, different models of dependence and addiction, and at-risk factors.

Chapter 2 focuses on the assessment of various stages of drug/alcohol use, while emphasizing our current behavioral definition of addiction. At the end of the chapter a worksheet assists readers in identifying their own perspective or viewpoint of drug/alcohol use/abuse.

Chapter 3 describes all types of drugs. The format is designed to give the necessary background information about drugs, while not being too technical or too pharmacological.

Chapter 4 begins to explore the arena of family systems and the many aspects of family life that make individuals at risk for drug/alcohol dependence and addiction.

Chapter 5 continues with the theme of family, with specific focus on the issues of shame, abandonment, and rejection, including case studies.

Chapter 6 focuses on family in its description of children who grew up in alcoholic families, and the developmental difficulty they experience as adults (adult children of alcoholics).

Chapter 7 shifts the focus to prevention of drug/alcohol problems. We explore the positive proactive aspect of preventive efforts with examples of school curricula, alternative activities, and other prevention efforts.

Chapter 8 explores intervention, an approach that helps the family of those people who deny and do not seek help for problems with drugs/alcohol. The process of intervention is developed in a case study to give readers the sense of empowerment the family feels in taking action.

Chapter 9 deals with a new emerging issue—the combined problem or double trouble of individuals who have both a psychiatric and drug/alcohol problem. Case studies give a better understanding of these dual disorders.

Chapter 10 is an important chapter in its discussion of drug/alcohol recovery and relapse prevention.

Chapter 11 summarizes the many problems explored in the previous chapters of the book, and outlines some possible reforms and solutions.

This textbook may not answer all of the readers' questions. In fact, it may cause readers to have more questions after reading it. These are the questions readers need to ask to develop their own perspective of drugs and alcohol.

Acknowledgment

This book would not have been possible without the patience and support of my wife Deborah and my son Matthew, who are both the source of great emotional energy that touches my heart so deeply.

There have been many students, clients, and patients who have taught me a great deal about human growth, especially those people I have had the good fortune to get to know in individual and group therapy, both in California and the state of Washington.

A special thanks to my old friends Michael Leeds, Allan "Kip" Flock, Richard Rawson, and Michael Meyers. Many thanks to Michael Meyers, M.D., and Russell Vandenbelt, M.D., for their assistance on chapters 3 and 9, and thanks to Nancy Sutherland of the University of Washington, Alcohol and Drug Abuse Institute, for her help with researching this book.

Thanks to R. J. Petershagen for facilitating the start of this project, Chris Rogers for his faith in the project, the editors Susie McCormick and Sue Pulvermacher-Alt, the reviewers, and all the staff at Wm. C. Brown Publishers, who made this project a reality.

INTRODUCTION

The Myth of the Simple, Magical Solution

Too often people search for that simple solution to an epidemic problem. Philosopher H. L. Mencken remarked that "any solution to a big problem that is simple, is usually wrong." The Just Say No approach to preventing drug use is helpful for children three through twelve years of age; however, it is a present-day example of this simplistic approach. The reality is that the drug/alcohol problem is multifaceted, involving efforts in many arenas. We need to work on all aspects of this problem *in an in-depth manner.* We need to further develop prevention, intervention, and treatment programs for all segments of society—young children, adolescents, adults, and seniors.

Approaches to the Drug/Alcohol Epidemic

From the 1930s to the 1960s, public and private responses to the drug/alcohol problem failed dramatically, causing tremendous damage that we are still trying to overcome. These approaches were riddled with emotional and political biases that denied the real dimensions of the problem. Scare tactics—a politically biased approach that alienated young people—began in 1937 and continued for the next thirty years in a variety of forms. For example, this marijuana scare story appeared in the July 1937 issue of *American* magazine:

> An entire family was murdered by a youthful marijuana addict in Florida. When officers arrived at the home, they found the youth staggering about in a human slaughterhouse. He had ax murdered his father, mother, two brothers, and a sister. He seemed to be in a daze. He had no recollection of having committed the multiple crime. The officers knew him ordinarily as a sane, rather quiet young man, now he was pitifully crazed. They sought the reason. The boy said he had been in the habit of smoking something with youthful friends called "muggles," a childish name for marijuana.

The coauthor of this article was Henry J. Anslinger, then commissioner of the Federal Bureau of Narcotics and Dangerous Drugs. After reviewing this single case and a study of the paranoid schizophrenic reactions of heavy hashish smokers in India, Anslinger expounded on the evils of marijuana. He described marijuana as a drug that would consistently result in violent, aggressive, paranoid behavior, as evidenced in the Florida case.

Another scare-tactic example is the 1936 movie *Reefer Madness.* This movie's serious intent to discourage marijuana use backfired because the situations were so absurd that audiences viewed it as a humorous farce.

Those using scare tactics assumed that if young people were frightened by adverse reactions to drug use, they would be too frightened to use the drug. For those young people who perceived drug use as incongruent with their values, their goals, and their style of life, scare tactics were effective. For most young people, however, scare tactics proved to be an ineffective approach because much of the information was either exaggerated, overgeneralized, or sensationalized. As a result, young people did not perceive the source of such information as credible or trustworthy. What young people heard did not bear any resemblance to what the majority of users experienced. All in all scare tactics alienated young people, heightened their curiosity, and increased rather than decreased experimentation with drugs.

In the late 1960s and early 1970s, President Richard Nixon declared his famous war on drugs. Even though an all out, warlike effort was needed and money was readily available to fight drug/alcohol addiction, no one knew how to tactically fight this war on drugs/alcohol. Drug/alcohol use had spread to epidemic proportions. Also, President Nixon was not the ideal general for this war, as he had already alienated young people during another war in Vietnam.

Unfortunately, the government was duped by treatment program directors; some mismanaged funds and others didn't know what to do with the money. At that time there were few experts and little, if any, clear direction to the battle. The failure of Nixon's war on drugs left a bitter taste in the mouths of government funding sources. Money for treatment programs was cut each year thereafter and the focus shifted to prevention. Realizing that the war was being lost, the government developed this new, more positive approach: If we can reach the kids before they become dependent on drugs, we will prevent a future generation of drug/alcohol casualties. Recognizing at last that scare tactics were ineffective, they focused on drug-specific educational approaches.

These programs provided information about drugs such as the often prescribed brand names, the physical and psychological reactions to the drugs, drug effects, toxic and lethal doses, tolerance, routes of administration, withdrawal symptoms, and physical and psychological dependence. In August 1977 under the Carter administration, the Drug Enforcement Administration (DEA) published a very colorful brochure entitled *Drugs of Abuse.* Unfortunately, *Drugs of Abuse* became a how-to manual for some young people. The DEA assumed that if young people received credible drug-specific information, they would then wisely decide not to use drugs. Unfortunately, this was a rather large assumption. The result was that *drug-specific approaches heightened curiosity and alleviated the fears associated with drug use.* Researchers soon found that exposure to drug-specific information had indeed increased drug experimentation by young people.

All of these approaches did do some good and we certainly learned from them. No programs, however, were effectively using our resources to address the multifaceted dimensions of the drug/alcohol problem.

The current U.S. administration emphasizes the supply side of the drug/alcohol problem but neglects the demand side of the problem. The facts are clear: *The drug/alcohol epidemic is a family disease that is bred from generation to generation.* Developing in-depth prevention, intervention, and treatment programs for the family should be an essential component of our war on drugs/alcohol.

The Family System as the Arena

Although school systems are responding to the problem, their inherent problems prevent systems from meeting individual needs. Teachers have a difficult job, and they can support—but not take the full responsibility for—efforts to stop the drug/alcohol epidemic.

The criminal justice system and law enforcement have become the panacea to this drug epidemic. Even though the criminal justice system can be a deterrent to drug use, reducing availability is only one element. Our society's *demand* for drugs has caused dealers to develop more sophisticated methods of distribution to meet that profitable market.

Physicians can be the first primary care gatekeepers to assess drug/alcohol problems. Yet, they need more training in drug/alcohol assessment, referral, and treatment. Some family therapists, social workers, psychologists, and mental health practitioners are developing their skills in drug/alcohol treatment. A larger percentage need more training and can work on their biases about drug/alcohol treatment.

Our society is riddled with drug/alcohol messages. Our cultural values lean toward power, money, pleasure and self-absorption while neglecting more traditional values of commitment to family and community. Families have become isolated, scattered, blended, and broken. Friendships, neighborhoods, and trust have diminished. We hear and read of sexual violations, physical and emotional abuse, homicide, and even the kidnapping of our children. These stressors have made family members more vulnerable to psychological breakdowns, physical diseases and illnesses, and suicide. All of these changes result in a society more vulnerable to the disease of drug and alcohol addiction.

There is no simple solution. Perhaps the problem may have to get worse, or as we say in the field of alcohol and drugs, perhaps our society must hit bottom, before change can occur. A major goal of this book is to expand awareness and assist readers in developing their perspective of drugs/alcohol as a contribution to this change.

Family Response

The family can be a major factor in combating drug/alcohol dependence. Families must develop their capabilities, skills, and resources to work on prevention with their children, early intervention with adolescents and young adults, and drug/alcohol treatment for those in the family who need it.

During the last fifteen years while working in the drug/alcohol field with individuals and their families, I have heard a wide range of parental, spouse and family members' reactions to drug/alcohol dependence and addiction. Some deny the problems of drug/alcohol use and minimize their impact. The vast majority are concerned, anxious, and fearful. We all recognize the prevalence of alcohol and drugs in our society and are aware of the pressures that may lead to use and abuse. I understand and empathize with the confusion, fear, and pain of family members dealing with drug/alcohol dependence; I have helped them work through the pain of denial, the grief of ruined lives, and the death of loved ones.

Although this book can help students, health professionals, parents, and families understand drugs/alcohol, it is not the magical solution. It is a resource book used to address the problems of drug/alcohol dependence and addiction.

What Is the Extent of Drug/Alcohol Use?

The 1988 National Household Survey on Drug Abuse is the ninth in a series of surveys conducted under the auspices of the National Commission on Marijuana and Drug Abuse since 1971. This survey has been sponsored by the National Institute on Drug Abuse in Rockville, Maryland, since 1974. The three major age groups sampled are

Youth—ages 12 to 17
Young adults—ages 18 to 25
Older adults—ages 25 and over

The results of the 1988 survey were based on personal interviews with 8,814 respondents including an oversampling of blacks, Hispanics, and young people. The survey is a probability-based sample, representative of the United States population aged 12 and over.

The most significant results of the 1988 survey concern marijuana and cocaine. The positive news is a statistically significant decrease in the use of marijuana, suggesting a general change in attitude about marijuana. Based on the 1988 survey, however, Charles R. Schuster, director of the National Institute on Drug Abuse, stated that "over the past few years, the abuse of cocaine and its freebase derivative, crack, has become the number one drug problem of concern."

The survey reported decreases in illicit drug use since the 1985 survey. In 1985 an estimated 37 million Americans used marijuana, cocaine, or other illicit drugs at least once in the past year. In 1988, this figure was down to 28 million. In 1985, 23 million were classified as current users who used illicit drugs in the past month. In 1988 this number was down

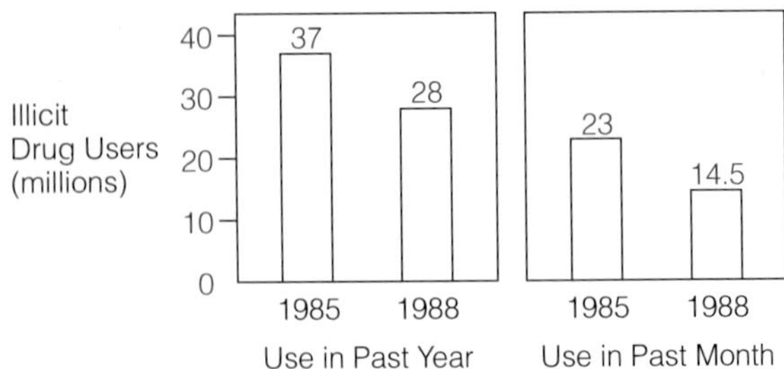

Figure I.1

Extent of illicit drug use, 1985–1988

From *1988 National Household Survey on Drug Abuse*. National Institute on Drug Abuse; U.S. Department of Health and Human Services.

to 14.5 million (see *figure I.1*). Alcohol use in both the past month and past year categories has also shown a statistically significant decrease when compared to 1985. There were 105.8 million current drinkers of alcohol in 1988, compared with 113.1 million in 1985.

Despite these positive alcohol-use trends, which began decreasing in 1979 and continued to do so between 1985 and 1988, the population of alcohol users is still significant, as evidenced by the 105.8 million current users of alcohol in 1988. Of the 135 million who drank alcohol in the past year, more than one-third, or 47 million, drank once a week or more often.

The statistics on cocaine, especially crack cocaine, are more alarming. First, among the 8 million cocaine users, once-a-week use of any form of cocaine increased dramatically and daily use of cocaine also increased (see *figure I.2*). A second troublesome statistical trend was that more than 600,000 young people aged 12–17 had used cocaine within the past year. The highest rates of cocaine use were among young adults aged 18–25, the unemployed, and those from large metropolitan areas.

A third very serious problem is the increasing number of newborn babies who suffer from the consequences of their mothers' drug addiction. The 1988 survey found that of the nearly 60 million women in the childbearing years of 15–44, more than 5 million (9 percent) had used illicit drugs in the past month.

While tracking medical emergencies and deaths related to drugs, the Drug Abuse Warning Network (DAWN) has found a fivefold increase in medical emergencies due to cocaine abuse: In 1984 there were 8,831 cocaine medical emergencies; in 1988, 46,000 emergencies. Their statistics are even more frightening for crack and freebase cocaine: crack or freebase cocaine emergency room episodes totaled 549 in 1984 and escalated to 15,000 in 1988.

	Weekly	Daily
1985	647,000	246,000
1988	862,000	292,000

Figure I.2

Persons using any form of cocaine

From *1988 National Household Survey on Drug Abuse*. National Institute on Drug Abuse; U.S. Department of Health and Human Services.

These figures underscore the seriousness of our current situation. As William Bennett, former director of the Office of National Drug Control Policy, commented in July of 1989: "Drug crime is up, drug trafficking is up, drug [overdose] deaths are up, drug emergencies in our hospitals are up—all since 1985. And much of this can be explained in one word: crack."

Marijuana

Marijuana is the most widely abused illicit drug. The survey found that current use of marijuana decreased from 18 million in 1985 to 12 million in 1988. Marijuana led the decline in illicit drug use since 1979, especially among youth and young adults where the rates are at the lowest level since the survey began in 1971.

Despite this decreasing trend, the 1988 survey shows that many of the people who have tried marijuana have used the drug extensively. For instance, 21 million Americans had used marijuana in the past year. In July 1989, Director Charles R. Schuster commented: "When we look at the frequency of use for these marijuana smokers, we see that almost one-third used once a week or more, and almost one-fifth used the drug daily or almost daily."

Summary

The 1988 National Household Survey on Drug Abuse clearly indicates some positive trends: Progress in *changing attitudes about illicit drug use,* especially marijuana and cocaine. Among youth only 37 percent saw great risk in smoking marijuana regularly in 1985, as compared to 44 percent three years later. In 1988, 53 percent of youth believed that trying cocaine posed a great risk, compared to 31 percent of youth in 1985.

Overall, illicit drug use has declined; especially significant is the decline in marijuana use. Yet, cocaine—specifically crack—presents a new and escalating problem especially in the inner city. In addition, Schuster identified populations that are not being reached: chronic users, the children of substance abusers, the poorly educated, the unemployed. We can add the homeless, people of color, women, and the newborn infants of addicts.

Again we remind you, alcohol is still the primary drug of use and abuse in the United States.

Women and alcoholism: an ever-increasing awareness

References

Bennett, William J. *1988 National Household Survey on Drug Abuse,* press conference written remarks, July 31, 1989.

Drug Enforcement Administration. *Drugs of Abuse* (pamphlet). Washington, D.C.: Superintendent of Documents, U.S. Government Printing Office, 1977.

National Institute of Drug Abuse. *1988 National Household Survey on Drug Abuse.* Rockville, Md.: U.S. Department of Health and Human Services, 1989.

Schuster, Charles R. *1988 National Household Survey on Drug Abuse,* press conference written remarks, July 31, 1989.

CHAPTER

1

Why People Use Drugs and Alcohol

It's peer pressure. . . . No, it's poor self-concept. . . . It's just because it's fun and pleasurable. . . . It's the hopelessness of our society. . . . It's due to the dishonesty and hypocrisy of our institutions. . . . No, it's our inability to connect with each other and establish effective relationships. . . . It's the parents. . . . It's the media that promote instant pleasure, short-term goals, and alcohol use. . . . It's the ineffectiveness of the school system and other institutions. . . . It's the avoidance of pain and the hedonism of modern society. . . . It's the lack of caring for our fellow humans. . . . It's stress, pressure, and the breakdown of the family. . . . It's just available. . . . Why not?

Chapter Goals

1. Explain drugs/alcohol as a drive to alter one's state of consciousness.
2. Describe drug/alcohol use as a passive activity.
3. Explain the symbolic meanings and functions of drug/alcohol use.
4. Identify the three criteria that establish alcoholism as a disease.
5. Cite the research that supports the genetic or biological etiology of drug/alcohol addiction including twin studies and adoption studies.
6. Identify various personality traits that may contribute to psychological vulnerability to drugs/alcohol.
7. Explain the psychoanalytical models of drug/alcohol abuse.
8. Define stress and tension and explain their roles in alcohol/drug use.
9. Explain the effects of alcohol in relation to stress and tension.
10. Describe sociocultural factors and influences on drug/alcohol abuse.
11. Identify the three criteria for developing a positive sense of self.
12. Explain and describe adolescent developmental tasks and their relationship to drug/alcohol problems.
13. Describe at-risk factors for adolescent drug/alcohol problems.
14. Explain the relationship of academic failure and drug/alcohol problems in adolescents.
15. Explain the impact of family on the development of drug/alcohol problems.
16. Describe the impact of parental alcoholism/drug addiction on the development of drug/alcohol problems in their children.
17. Explain the role risk taking and antisocial behavior plays in drug/alcohol abuse.
18. Explain why no one is immune from the disease of alcoholism and drug addiction.

This section provides important background information about drugs/alcohol by explaining some basic underlying reasons why people use them. The three major reasons outlined in this chapter are

1. the innate human drive to alter consciousness
2. drug/alcohol use as a passive activity
3. drug/alcohol use and abuse have specific functions and meanings

By recognizing and understanding these features of drug/alcohol use, we can better address the problems of drug/alcohol dependence and addiction.

Our Innate Drive to Alter Consciousness

We all recognize the innate drives of hunger, thirst, and sexuality. Our needs for water, food, and shelter are inherent parts of our physical and psychological well-being and part of our innate drive to survive. Our sex drive leads to sexual activity and procreation. We have another less familiar but very important innate drive—the drive to alter our consciousness.

In *The Natural Mind,* Andrew Weil (1972) states "every human being is born with an innate drive to experience altered states of consciousness periodically to learn how to get away from ordinary ego-centered consciousness." Thus, the fact that drugs/alcohol can shortcut altering one's state of consciousness is one of the primary reasons for drug/alcohol use.

For instance, young children twirl around and around to get dizzy and alter their consciousness. The goal of daydreaming is to alter consciousness when the day dreamer is bored. Concentration may drift in a classroom when a student is preoccupied with thoughts more interesting than the subject being taught. Dreaming is a specialized altered state of consciousness, an outlet for unconscious content symbolically communicated during the period between light sleep and waking. Meditative activities, exercise, reading, and even sunbathing are methods of altering one's consciousness.

"It's unsettling to have the TV on the blink, isn't it, Miles?"

Reprinted with special permission of King Features Syndicate, Inc.

Altered states of consciousness

In *Intoxication,* Ronald K. Siegal (1989) describes drugs/alcohol as the fourth primary drive, after hunger, thirst, and sex. Siegal believes this drive has made drugs/alcohol attractive throughout history; he believes this drive will continue to make drugs/alcohol an attractive alternative in the future.

Weil identifies drugs as potential keys to unconscious issues, conflicts, and even an awareness or new perceptions of life. However, drugs can easily become potential traps that can keep us from using our minds in better ways. Weil defines addiction as using drugs in an unrealistic, neurotic fashion. Thus, when individuals use drugs, they react in a destructive, passive, dependent manner. They are less free to use their nervous systems in constructive, interesting, active ways. Our society is becoming more aware of positive ways to alter consciousness while avoiding addictions to drugs/alcohol, food, gambling, television, work, and many other activities.

TABLE 1.1
Drugs and Their Functions

Drug Category	Function
Narcotic analgesic or opiates	Kill pain
CNS depressants	Decrease activity
CNS stimulants	Increase activity
Hallucinogens, marijuana	Change the user's view of the world

Drug/Alcohol Use as a Passive Activity

Many people are passive procrastinators and conflict avoiders. In my private counseling practice, I often see clients who deny the painful issues that initially brought them to counseling. Once they get some immediate relief, they avoid the real issues. Nonetheless, growth involves working through painful conflicts. Our search for the magic pill or cure for the pain of the human condition has created a modern marketplace for drug and alcohol elixirs.

Drug and alcohol use is a passive activity; individuals take pills, powders, or liquids and wait for the desired effect—an alteration of their consciousness. Users of opiates (heroin, morphine, and others) take them to kill physical and emotional pain; they want to just be numb to life. Users of central nervous system (CNS) depressants (alcohol, tranquilizers, and barbiturates) take them to decrease activity. Or they may use stimulants (cocaine, amphetamines, and others) to increase activity. The hallucinogens change the way users view the world and distort and manipulate their perception of reality. Whatever the desired effect, a drug exists to serve that function (see table 1.1). This powerful combination of individuals seeking altered states of consciousness, the passive natures of many people, and the vast array of drugs that can almost immediately provide various desired effects has resulted in many individuals developing problems with drugs and alcohol.

Cocaine—a highly addictive drug

The individual's choice of a particular drug is related to the meaning that drug has both consciously and unconsciously for that person. As we explain in the next section, the drug also has a symbolic meaning.

Functions and Meanings of Drug/Alcohol Use

Drugs/Alcohol as Power

Drugs/alcohol frequently denote power or feeling powerful to users. The expression *getting high* symbolizes feeling above others or above one's usual sense of self. Ironically, despite the original reason for using drugs/alcohol to feel powerful, the ultimate state in the cycle of addiction makes the individual powerless. Cocaine is a drug that has a symbolic meaning of power. As a power drug, cocaine is attractive because of its status as well as its physical and psychological effects. An energizing stimulant, cocaine produces a sublime feeling of well-being; users describe being on top of the world, in control, able to accomplish a great deal, able to have tremendous capabilities and insights, and able to stimulate sexual arousal and performance. Yet, the reality today is that cocaine is the most addicting drug and takes the least time to develop an addiction that ultimately renders users powerless.

TABLE 1.2
Aspects of Life Experience Adult Daily Users Most Frequently Described as Positively Affected by Marijuana

- ability to relax and enjoy life
- enjoyment of food
- ability to overcome worry and anxiety
- ability to sleep well
- ability to avoid feeling bored
- enjoyment of sex
- understanding of others
- creativity
- ability to avoid feeling angry
- ability to enjoy varied activities
- self-understanding
- overall happiness
- ability to avoid feeling depressed
- ability to be tolerant and considerate of others

From Herbert Hendin, et al., *Living High: Daily Marijuana Use by Adults.* Copyright © 1987 Human Sciences Press, New York. Reprinted by permission.

Other drugs and alcohol symbolize power in the forms of sensuality and sexuality; potency; feeling supernatural, pleasure, sensitivity, insensitivity or not feeling pain; productivity; rebelliousness; high energy; and so forth. Our review of the research on why adolescents initially used marijuana indicated the following reasons:

- for pleasure, contentment, the joy of being high, relaxation, and recreation
- to facilitate social interactions; to achieve status in one's peer group, friendship leading to better understanding
- to defy authority, seek thrills and flirt with danger
- for curiosity and excitement, escapism, enhancement of activity
- to enhance aesthetic appreciation or sexual stimulation
- to alleviate a sense of alienation, make life better and more tolerable
- to understand or find oneself, expand the mind for religious insights, to improve oneself

Herbert Hendin's (1987) studies on daily marijuana use among adults report similar reasons for marijuana use, as shown in table 1.2.

Case Study
A Drug's Meaning
Lyn

A female patient of mine successfully stopped her dependence on marijuana for ten months. During a party, a male acquaintance was flirting with Lyn. He established eye contact across the proverbial crowded room; she was very interested so she returned the seductive eye contact. When they eventually found themselves in the same part of the room, they began talking and he invited her out to the balcony. Even though Lyn had not smoked marijuana in over ten months and was determined not to start again, she accepted and smoked the marijuana he offered. The symbolic meaning of her accepting the marijuana was that she was available and open to his seduction.

Drugs/Alcohol as Self-Destruction

Drugs/alcohol can also have a powerful meaning as weapons of self-destruction and ultimately death. In *Family Therapy of Drug Abuse and Addiction,* M. Duncan Stanton and associates (1982) describe the addict "as part of a continuum of self-destruction." Stanton reports that when compared to the general public addicts have a higher death rate, shorter-than-average life expectancies, and greater-than-normal incidence of sudden deaths. Addicts also view death as more positive and potent than their peers and are more likely to express a wish for death.

A number of clinicians have described drug/alcohol addiction as an unconscious death wish. Self-destructiveness is the failure of ego functions involving self-care and self-protection. "We are all subject to our instincts, drives, and impulses, and if they are expressed indiscriminately, we are subject to hazard and danger" (Gottheil 1983).

The psychoanalytical interpretation sees addicts as fundamentally suicidal. According to this viewpoint, addicts are trying to destroy the bad, depriving mothers with whom they have identified. They use drugs/alcohol to repress underlying feelings of depression, guilt, and anxiety generated by their bad feelings about their mothers.

Drugs in Seduction and Sexuality

Drugs/alcohol have important symbolic seduction and sexuality meanings. Practically all drugs and alcohol have been described at some time as aphrodisiacs. Unfortunately, no drug is truly an aphrodisiac. Drugs/alcohol may reduce inhibitions and stimulate sexual arousal at low-dose levels; however, drugs and alcohol impair sexual performance especially with prolonged use.

The symbolic seduction and sexuality meanings of drugs/alcohol are exploited in advertisements for tobacco and alcohol products. If such advertising were legal, it would probably be used to advertise illicit drugs, too.

Whether celebrating an important event with a traditional toast of wine, champagne, or alcohol; or passing around a pipe filled with marijuana; or sharing cocaine, heroin, or other drugs, the symbolic meaning is a common, shared, altered state of consciousness.

Drugs/Alcohol as Reinforcers

A strong reinforcing factor to drug/alcohol use is the memorable feeling attached to the first use of drugs and/or alcohol. A first-time experience with a drug or alcohol-induced altered state of consciousness is a new and unforgettable awareness. This first or early experience with drugs and/or alcohol is so reinforcing that time after time the individual attempts to reproduce or recapture that original memorable experience. Those smoking heroin describe it as "chasing the dragon." This can be similar to one's first romantic involvement or to the extremely pleasurable yet painful romantic associations of unrequited love. Drugs/alcohol can become that first love, like no other experience ever felt before. Unfortunately, it is impossible to duplicate that feeling. The cycle of addiction has then begun: The individual tries to repeat an experience that cannot be recaptured because by definition it was the first. This is the reason addicts continue using drugs/alcohol even though the feeling and behavioral experiences are clearly negative and unpleasant. They hope that somehow the next time will be different.

Frequently addicts and alcoholics have **euphoric recall** of their pleasant experiences during earlier excessive uses of drugs/alcohol. They forget the negative consequences and dangerous situations that they barely escaped. The human mind defends against the overwhelming fear and shock of these negative experiences and instead recalls the positive good times. Thus, addicts and alcoholics forget how destructive and dangerous their experiences with drugs/alcohol can be.

All of the preceding functions and characteristics perpetuate the use of drugs/alcohol. If they were legal, imagine the unlimited advertising campaigns that could be developed for the sale of drugs based on these characteristics:

> Feeling down and depressed? Lack the energy to do even the most basic things? Suffer from lowered sex drive, sleep disturbances, or have difficulty with interpersonal relationships? Not making the kind of money you would like to; need a vacation, a general lift? Wondering what life is all about or if it is even worth it? Try Zippy, the new nonnarcotic wonder medication brought to you by the What's Happening Now, Don't Worry, Be Happy Institute of Living Life.

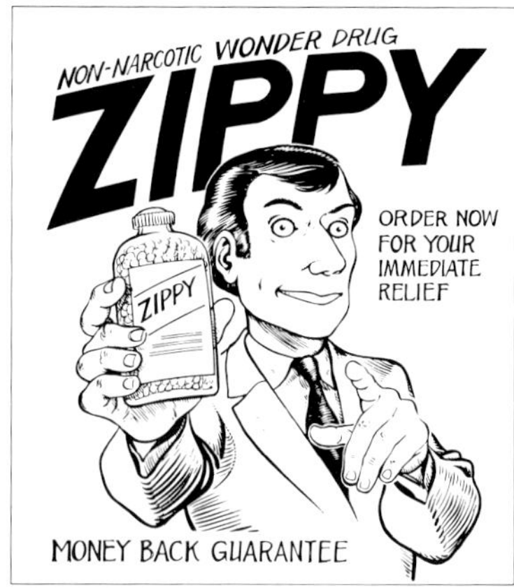

Advertisement for Zippy, the new nonnarcotic wonder drug

Models of Drug/ Alcohol Dependence and Addiction

We cannot isolate one specific cause of alcoholism and drug addiction. There are often multiple, confounding reasons for addiction, just as there are numerous causes for cancer or other medical diseases. Many theories and models of causality exist. Early alcoholism models labeled alcoholics as inherently weak, or unable to control or tolerate their consumption of alcohol. One test of manliness was the ability to "really hold his liquor." Other early models focused on the individual as psychologically pathological. Alcoholics used alcohol in a pathological manner to block out memories of unpleasant, traumatic personal experiences that brought with them unmanageable feelings. As time went on, a physiological model of alcoholism developed as scientists searched for a biochemical link or genetic marker of alcoholism.

Today, those of us in the drug/alcohol field generally accept the fact that alcoholism and drug addiction have multiple causes or etiologies. Clearly, a matrix of both genetic and environmental factors can cause an individual to develop problems with alcohol and drugs. "Evidence has accumulated to indicate that alcoholism is a heterogenous entity arising from multiple etiologies" (Tabakoff and Hoffman 1988). We discuss some of the causality models in the next section.

The Disease Concept of Alcoholism

In 1957 the American Medical Association declared alcoholism a disease on the basis of three criteria: Alcoholism is (1) a known etiology (cause) with (2) a known progression of symptoms that get worse over time, and (3) a known outcome. The outcome of alcoholism is dependence, physical symptoms, and eventual death. For more than 30 years, research has indicated an increasingly strong case for a genetic component of alcoholism; this validates the disease model.

The disease model is the foundation of Alcoholics Anonymous and other self-help programs. The increased acceptance of this disease model is due to continuing research linking alcoholism to genetic markers, the model's effectiveness as a recovery tool, and its reduction of the shame-based stigma associated with problems of drug/alcohol dependence and addiction. (See chapter 10 for more information on the advantages and disadvantages of Alcoholics Anonymous.)

Genetic Model of Alcoholism

In January 1990, researchers at the University of California, Los Angeles, and University of Texas, San Antonio, identified a link between the receptor gene for the neurotransmitter dopamine and alcoholism (Blum, Noble et al. 1990). Although these findings need to be replicated with a larger sample, they establish more clearly the significance of a genetic factor in predisposing people to alcoholism. Ernest Noble of U.C.L.A. said that this research "more firmly establishes alcoholism as a disease, and adds to evidence that genetic factors are as important as environmental factors in predisposing people to the disease." The general opinion is that alcoholism is related to several genes, however, and no one gene can be a genetic marker to identify individuals at risk for alcoholism.

The implications of these findings may lead to the development of a blood test to detect the presence of genes associated with alcoholism within five years, as well as a drug that would block the action of the gene within ten years (Nazarte 1990).

Adoption Studies

Donald W. Goodwin (1971) conducted a series of adoption studies in Denmark indicating that sons of alcoholics were four times more likely to become alcoholics than sons of nonalcoholics. The results held true whether the sons were raised by nonalcoholic foster parents or their own biological parents, thus supporting the genetic component of alcoholism.

C. R. Cloninger, M. Bohman, and S. Sigvardsson (1981) conducted the most detailed and extensive adoption studies. Their work confirmed the earlier work of Goodwin in demonstrating that:

1. Adopted sons of alcoholic biological parents are four times more likely to become alcoholics than adoptees whose biological parents were not alcoholics.
2. Sons of alcoholic biological parents are more likely to be classified as alcoholics at an earlier age than their peers.
3. Daughters of alcoholic fathers, although not demonstrating a greater incidence of alcoholism, exhibit a high incidence of somatic anxiety and frequent physical complaints.

Twin Studies

Studies of identical (monozygotic, or MZ) and fraternal (dizygotic, or DZ) twins have supported a genetic factor. Because identical twins share 100 percent of their genes, while fraternal twins share only 50 percent, research should show a higher rate of alcoholism in MZ twins than DZ twins. L. Kaij (1960) examined 174 sets of twins and demonstrated that indeed MZ twins had a 71 percent concordance rate, and DZ twins had only a 32 percent concordance rate. In 1981, Z. Hrubec and G. S. Omenn again demonstrated a higher concordance rate in MZ twins (26 percent) than DZ twins (12 percent). A more recent study by Gurling and associates (1984), however, did not support the previous studies' results.

Currently no significant genetic research is exploring drug abuse due to the many research design problems with illicit drugs. The assumption is that the genetic factors for drug addiction are comparable to the genetic research findings on alcoholism.

Psychological Models and Psychological Vulnerability

For quite some time, various counselors have emphasized the concept of an **addictive personality.** This simplistic approach makes the mistake of labeling all alcoholics and addicts as somehow possessing particular personalities that made them weak, and therefore, vulnerable to drugs/alcohol. Psychological factors certainly can make an individual vulnerable to the disease of alcoholism and drug addiction, but to conclude there is an addictive personality is beyond the scope of modern medicine. Psychological vulnerability is defined as some prior psychological factor that makes a pattern of drug/alcohol dependence more likely to develop (Jellinek 1960).

Affective and personality disorders are more common in the relatives of alcoholics than they are in the control population (Winokur et al. 1971). Disturbances in mood, mood disorders, and depression are common causes of abuse and addiction to medical and nonmedical psychoactive substances, especially in women (Whitcock, Lowrey et al., 1967). Personality disordered individuals may be attracted to drugs/alcohol to self-medicate feelings of discomfort, anxiety, depression, anger, grief, and even shyness. V. M. Hesselbrook and associates (1983) reported that 52 percent of a sample of male alcoholics had a current or lifetime diagnosis of antisocial personality disorder.

Many researchers and clinicians have described various personality traits of alcoholics/addicts. These personality traits include:

- high emotionality, anxiety, and overreactivity
- immaturity in interpersonal relationships
- low frustration tolerance
- inability to express anger adequately
- anger over dependence and ambivalence to authority
- low self-esteem with grandiose behavior
- perfectionism
- compulsiveness
- feelings of isolation
- sex role confusion
- depression
- dependence in interpersonal relationships
- hostility
- sexual immaturity
- rigidity and inability to adapt to changing circumstances
- simplistic, black and white thinking

Psychoanalytic Models

The traditional psychoanalytic view of drug/alcohol dependence focused on a fixation at the oral stage of development, resulting in an oral and narcissistic premorbid personality.

Otto Fenichel (1945) theorized that individuals used psychoactive drugs "to satisfy the archaic oral longing which is a sexual longing, a need for security, and need for the maintenance of self-esteem simultaneously." K. Menninger (1963) believed that alcohol may function as a coping device to alleviate stress and that the primary psychoanalytic root was a mother's denial of milk (security) in infancy. Other psychoanalytic theories suggest drinking as a strategy for allaying anxiety over masculine inadequacy (Machover 1959). Analytical theories also suggest that abusers use drugs/alcohol to suppress latent homosexuality and ego-dystonic feelings of homosexuality (i.e., the person's ego is not compatible with the possibility of being homosexual.)

The major psychoanalytic theory today is "a structural deficit in object relations." This means that individuals have a hard time establishing effective interpersonal relationships due to their difficulty in managing their affect (feeling) and impulse controls. They often establish their defense mechanism of denial by defensive grandiosity. In his 1986 article, "An Etiologic Model of Alcoholism," James Donovan outlined psychoanalytic descriptions used by various researchers in identifying this difficulty in object relations:

H. Krystal and H. A. Raskin (1970)—indicated a defective stimulus barrier and an inability to desomatize emotions.

L. Wursmer (1974)—emphasized the maladaptive narcissism of the addict, a defensive stance against the potentially overwhelming feelings of rage and loneliness.

E. J. Khantzian (1978)—pointed to the impoverished self-esteem, the lack of capacity for self-care, and the poor emotional regulation of the alcoholic.

Tension and Stress Models

Tension has been defined as a variety of states that are aversive sources of motivation, causing feelings of fear, anxiety (vague fear), conflict, and frustration due to blocked goals. Stress is just a modern version of the same description. Webster's dictionary defines stress as "a physical, chemical, or emotional factor that causes bodily or mental tension and may be a factor in disease causation." The tension reduction theory has two major assumptions: alcohol reduces tension, and individuals drink alcohol for its tension-reducing properties (Blane and Leonard 1988).

A noted authority on drugs/alcohol, Stanley Gitlow, emphasizes an etiological model that focuses on discomfort and tolerance to stress as a major factor in the decision to use drugs/alcohol. Gitlow believes that we have biological variations in our levels of tolerance to stress and stimulation. "The initiating stimulus could well be perceived by one individual as minimally inconvenient, while another individual would perceive that same stimulus as agonizingly urgent. The overriding determinant and major variable of appetite regulation is most likely the intensity of the individual's perception of need for relief" (Gitlow 1985).

A. Petrie (1960) identified three basic classifications in dealing with stimuli: *Stimulus reducers* perceive and react to a stimulus as if that stimulus is less than it is. *Stimulus moderaters* perceive and react to the stimulus as it is. *Stimulus augmenters* perceive and react as if that stimulus is more than it is.

"A perceptual characteristic, such as stimulus augmenting, leading to an overly sensitive need for relief from any discomfort, appeared to be a possible and intriguing genetically determined CNS factor" (Gitlow 1985). In 1984 Lynne Hennecke reported a significantly higher incidence of stimulus augmenters in the sons of alcoholic fathers than sons of the nonalcoholic fathers. Hennecke suggests that alcohol is used to shut down the stimulation overload from the environment in stimulus augmentors.

Gitlow (1972) describes alcoholism as a biochemical defect. The individual possessing this defect is easily agitated by stimuli, becomes uncomfortable and, therefore, uses alcohol for its sedating effect. Unfortunately, withdrawal from alcohol creates an agitating effect and the individual must drink again to relieve this discomfort.

In *Stress without Distress* (1975), Hans Selye encouraged individuals to evaluate their optimal stress levels. See *figure 1.1* which depicts each individual's average tension level with the normal ups and downs, or stress, of daily living. Selye described some persons as turtles and others as race horses when it comes to stress tolerance. Too little stress leads to lethargy and depression, whereas too much stress leads to mania and anxiety.

People often use drugs/alcohol to self-medicate or adjust imbalances of stress tolerance regardless of whether they face too little or too much stress. This is evidenced by

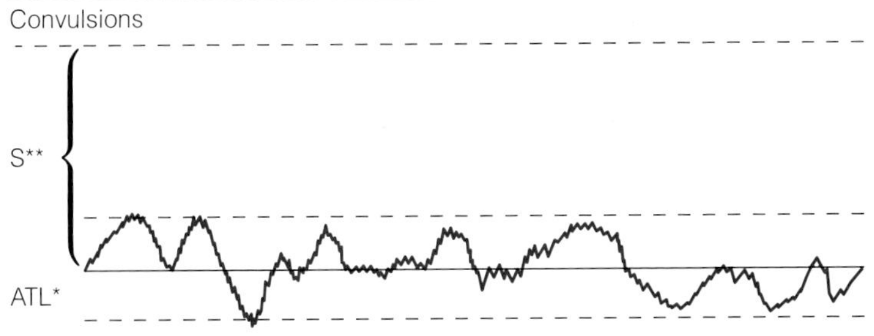

Comatose

Hours ➔ 0 1 2 3 4 5 6 7 8 9 10 11 12 13 14

**Average tension level* (ATL) varies with each individual.
**Average amount of *stimulation(s)* required to produce convulsion.

Figure 1.1

Average tension level

From *Facts About Drug Abuse*, 1975. National Institute on Drug Abuse; U.S. Department of Health and Human Services.

DEATH
Convulsions
Delirium Tremens
Hangover
Anxious Aggressive
Normal
Range
Reduced Inhibitions
Loss of Motor Control
Loss of Coordination
Passing Out
Comatose
DEATH

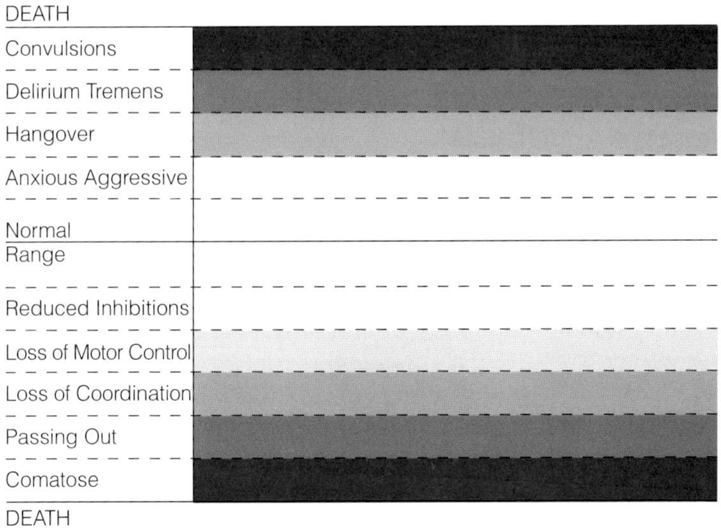

Figure 1.2

Reaction to sedative hypnotics (particularly alcohol)

From *Facts About Drug Abuse*, 1975. National Institute on Drug Abuse; U.S. Department of Health and Human Services.

the traditional cocktail or marijuana joint at the end of the day to unwind; or the ingestion of cocaine, coffee, or other stimulants to increase performance.

Figure 1.2 shows various reactions to alcohol and their relationships to stress. Anyone ingesting alcohol or other sedative hypnotics goes from the normal level of functioning to a level of reduced inhibitions. As that person continues to

Figure 1.3

Tension changes due to alcohol consumption

From *Facts About Drug Abuse*, 1975. National Institute on Drug Abuse; U.S. Department of Health and Human Services.

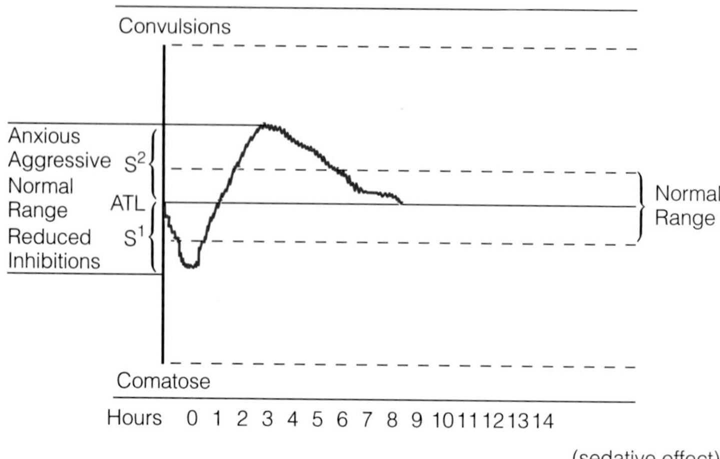

(sedative effect)

S^1 Reduced tension level due to sedative/hypnotic consumption.
S^2 Increased tension due to psychomotor stimulation.

consume alcohol, the effect becomes more pronounced as indicated by loss of motor control and loss of coordination. Excessive levels of alcohol ingestion can cause alcoholics to pass out, become comatose, and die. As an alcoholic stops using alcohol, the withdrawal symptoms follow the same progression. At low ingestion levels, the withdrawal may be minor anxiety or aggressive behavior. *Figure 1.3* describes the changes after approximately an hour of alcohol consumption. There is a reduced inhibition (change S^1) followed by anxious/aggressive behavior from withdrawal (change S^2). After one hour of alcohol consumption, the human body takes from six to eight hours to get back to its normal average tension level.

When more alcohol is consumed, the withdrawal symptoms are stronger—hangovers, delirium tremens, convulsions, and death. *Figure 1.4* shows that after five to seven hours of alcohol consumption, the human body takes sixteen to twenty hours to get back to its average tension level. *Figure 1.5* describes a forty-eight-hour binge pattern of alcohol consumption, which requires a recovery time of approximately 600 hours or twenty-five days.

Withdrawal from alcohol is far more dangerous than withdrawal from other drugs (see chapter 3). As *figure 1.6* illustrates, each time the drinker is about to go to the normal

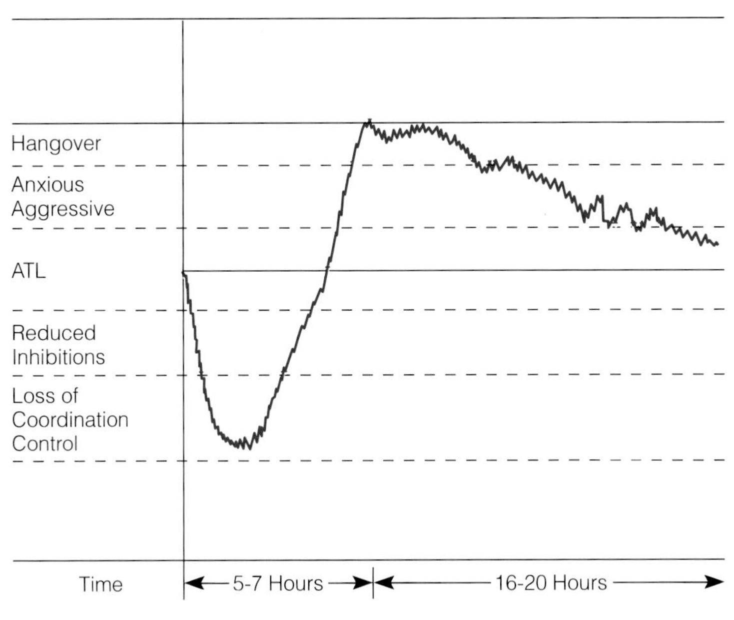

Figure 1.4

Effects of higher dosages

From *Facts About Drug Abuse*, 1975. National Institute on Drug Abuse; U.S. Department of Health and Human Services.

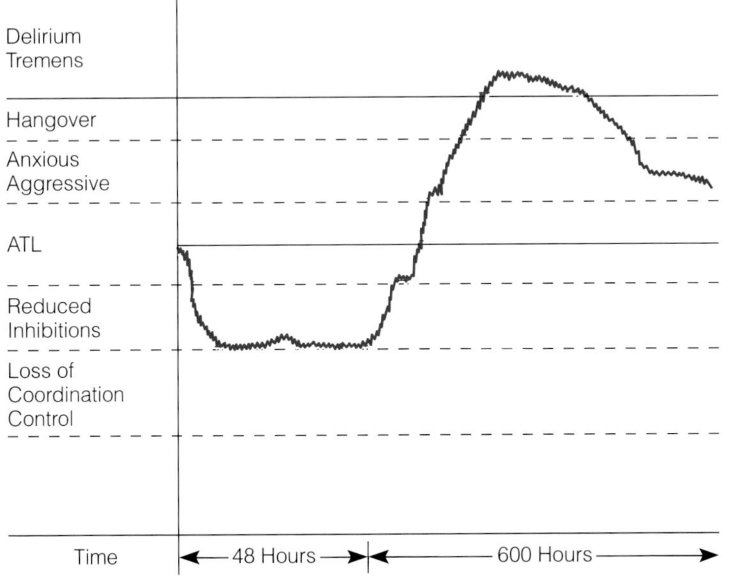

Figure 1.5

Tension levels produced by forty-eight hours of high-level alcohol consumption

From *Facts About Drug Abuse*, 1975. National Institute on Drug Abuse; U.S. Department of Health and Human Services.

Figure 1.6

The built-up effects of additional alcohol consumption

From *Facts About Drug Abuse*, 1975. National Institute on Drug Abuse; U.S. Department of Health and Human Services.

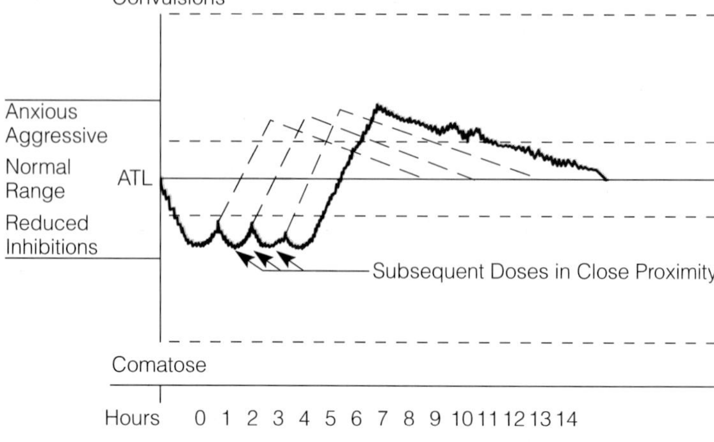

Figure 1.7

Hair-of-the-dog effect

From *Facts Abouts Drug Abuse*, 1975. National Institute on Drug Abuse; U.S. Department of Health and Human Services.

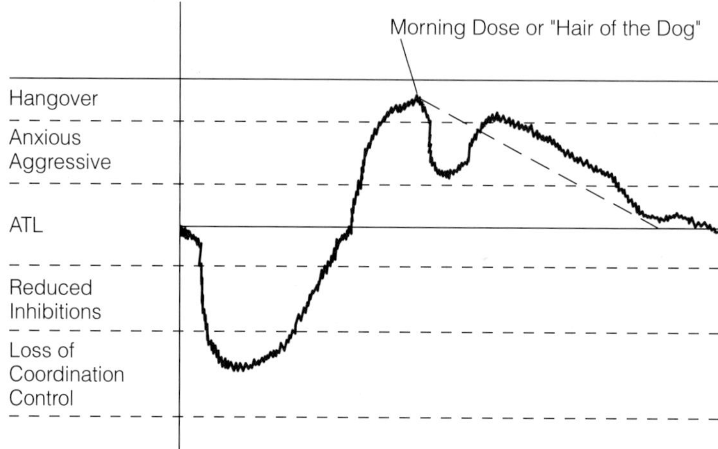

*The term *hair of the dog* refers to the colloquial expression, "to recover, take a hair of the dog that bit you."

range and suffer withdrawal, he or she consumes more alcohol to avoid experiencing withdrawal. To ward off withdrawal, alcoholics often resort to the "hair of the dog." *Figure 1.7* shows how after an entire evening of alcohol consumption, drinking the traditional Bloody Mary the next morning temporarily takes the edge off a hangover. We could develop similar figures for stimulants, hallucinogens, marijuana, and a variety of other drugs to illustrate the effects on an individual's stress levels and normal functioning.

Sociocultural Models

In his review of cultural and cross-cultural studies, R. Bales (1946) identified the following ways culture and sociological organization influence rates of alcoholism:

1. the degree to which a culture causes acute needs for adjustment of inner tension in its members
2. the attitudes toward drinking which the culture produces in its members
3. the degree to which the culture provides substitute means of satisfaction

Societies, cultures, communities, socioeconomic groups, and even neighborhoods offering few or limited alternatives to drinking and drugging as tension relievers are more susceptible to addiction. The more these groups produce acute inner tensions (shame), suppressed or acted-out aggression, extreme conflict, dilemmas, mixed messages, sexual tensions, and condoning attitudes about drugs/alcohol as the normal accepted way of relieving these tensions, the more prone individuals are to develop drug/alcohol dependence. When there is no limit on supply and distribution, attitudes are liberal, and cost is relative, the incidence of alcohol and drug abuse is high.

The attitude of the culture and ethnic customs may also facilitate patterns of drug/alcohol use. "The Irish and the American Indian groups positively sanction men's drinking to intoxication away from home; in these cultures the rates of alcoholism are high. Drug/alcohol dependence and addiction are influenced by sociological factors such as age, occupation, social class and subculture, and religious affiliation. In the United States, for example, young, single, unemployed urban men have a high incidence of abuse" (Donovan 1986).

Individuals who feel alienated from larger society and have no sense of belonging may feel that society's rules and values about drugs and alcohol don't apply to them. This feeling of alienation from a larger social body may result in more favorable attitudes about drugs/alcohol. The application of this social model of drug/alcohol use is evidenced by the crack cocaine epidemic.

The lack of opportunity or hope that one can achieve the American Dream can contribute to feelings of despair that lead to drug addiction and/or alcoholism. This despair is most prevalent in the ghettos in America's inner cities. Yet, this sense of despair can occur in any locale, in any socioeconomic setting. From the blue-collar bars, to the shooting galleries in abandoned buildings, to middle-class suburban high schools, to the plush boardrooms of major corporations, drugs and alcohol infest our society.

At-Risk Factors for Drug and Alcohol Problems

Biological, psychological, and environmental factors make an individual at risk for developing problems with drugs/alcohol. This section explores some specific at-risk factors: self-concept (sense of self), adolescence, academic failure, family and parenting, and risk-taking behavior.

Self-Concept

The most frequently generalized at-risk factor for problems with drugs/alcohol is a poor self-concept. Parents and schools talk about children's general underachievement, shyness, and aggressive or antisocial behavior as being a result of this lack of self-concept. Report cards and progress reports include comments such as "does not work up to his/her potential," "has difficulty finishing assignments and staying on task," "fails to participate in class, daydreams," or "more concerned with peers than teacher." It should be no surprise that the same evaluations occur for adults who have difficulty with work relationships and general achievement.

There are so many different definitions of self-concept that isolating this variable as a causative factor for drug/alcohol problems is impossible. While exploring all of these definitions of self-concept, we developed a more workable behavioral definition that better explains what we are talking about. Instead of using the label *self-concept* that implies something one gets from outside of one's self and is, therefore, beyond one's internal ability to develop, I relabeled it as **a sense of self.** A sense of self is less static than self-concept, involves more choices by the individual, and is active rather than passive. A sense of self comes from within to the outside world, rather than the outside world defining who the individual is. This important point has implications for those individuals who develop codependent relationships with addicts and alcoholics (see chapter 6).

Under my definition, a person with a sense of self is

1. a unique, worthwhile individual with emerging talents and skills

2. an individual who can accomplish things (i.e., develop, prioritize, and achieve goals; solve problems; resolve conflicts; accept and carry out responsibilities; and have the maturity to develop and grow)
3. an individual who can trust and be trusted; one who sets appropriate boundaries for intimacy in relationships

In his article, "Beyond Drug Education," Paul Robinson (1975) believes the goal is "not to convince people not to do drugs," but to empower them to enhance their development of self. Robinson suggests that we need to emphasize educational programs that help students acquire this sense of self, by developing the skills to

- control their destructive impulses
- understand their values, needs, and desires
- make wise decisions
- resist peer pressure when it endangers their welfare or inhibits their growth
- find nonchemical means of fulfillment and satisfaction
- think intelligently and rationally

By focusing on programs that teach children and adults to develop and enhance a sense of self, we make them less at risk for drug and alcohol problems.

Encouraging potential addicts and alcoholics to develop a sense of self is just one aspect of the problem; other factors must also be addressed. Even children and adults who possess a wonderful and creative sense of self are still at risk. Improving the sense of self is a preventive inoculation but neither a cure nor guarantee against having drug/alcohol problems (see chapter 7).

Adolescence

As kids enter adolescence they are at risk for drug/alcohol problems. Adolescence is a time of developmental changes, hormonal and growth changes, peer influences, identity formation, and differentiation from one's parents. The allure of drugs/alcohol that can alter one's state of consciousness to explore these developmental issues—especially issues of identity, control, and testing of boundaries—often entraps young people. Despite their feelings of immortality, as table 1.3 indicates, teens who drink and drive too frequently injure themselves or others.

TABLE 1.3
Teenage Drinking and Driving

1. The leading single cause of death among fifteen to twenty-four-year olds is drunk driving.
2. Close to 9,000 teenagers from fifteen to nineteen are killed in motor vehicle accidents each year.
3. Approximately fourteen teenagers die each day in drunk driving accidents.
4. Close to 130,000 teenagers are injured per year in drunk driving accidents.
5. Of all fatal crashes involving young drivers, 40 percent are alcohol related.
6. For all traffic crashes, young drivers are more likely to have been drinking than older drivers.
7. Of the 25,000 people who die each year in drunk driving accidents, 5,000 of the victims are teenagers.
8. One year after the state of Michigan raised its drinking age from eighteen to twenty-one, research showed a 31 percent reduction in alcohol-related car accidents. (National Council on Alcoholism 1988)

Excerpted with permission from *NCADD Fact Sheet: Youth and Alcohol.* National Council on Alcoholism and Drug Dependence, Inc.

Our goal is to help young people work through the developmental tasks of adolescence and assist them in making wise decisions about their lives. Too many adolescents get stuck and do not successfully accomplish these tasks. Some get stuck at this stage as a result of being under the influence of drugs/alcohol.

Academic Failure

Academic failure, especially in late elementary grades, highly correlates with early antisocial behavior and drug/alcohol abuse (Robins 1978; Johnston et al. 1978; Kandel 1978). Frequently these children fail to develop the skills to learn, integrate concepts, and succeed in school. Often they exhibit learning disabilities, emotional problems, and attention-deficit disorders. Parents are frequently in denial of these emotional and learning disabilities and the school system may not adequately address these problems, resulting in educational failure for children.

Some kids do well during adolescence, some barely escape drug/alcohol problems, some develop addictions, and some die.

Young adult contemplating a drink

TABLE 1.4 At Risk for Alcoholism/Addiction	
Parents	**Probability of Becoming Alcoholic/Addict**
One alcoholic/addict	Four times higher
Two alcoholics/addicts	Eight times higher

Family

Drug and alcohol dependence and addiction are **family diseases.** The genetic predisposition to alcoholism is well documented. The probability of developing the disease of alcoholism and drug addiction is four times higher for those individuals who have one alcoholic or drug addicted parent. The probability increases to eight times higher if both parents are alcoholics or addicts (see table 1.4).

Children from alcoholic, dysfunctional, and shame-based family systems are at greater risk for developing problems with drugs/alcohol. The modeling of family members who use alcohol/drugs also greatly influences the development of drug/alcohol dependence. Exhibiting poor communication, the alcoholic/addict family has specific "no talk, no feel, no trust" rules (see chapter 6). Such a family system breeds childhood traumas of fear, rejection, abandonment, and sometimes violation (see chapters 4 and 5).

Parents with drug/alcohol problems have extreme difficulty in being effective parents. "Parenting is a difficult, time-consuming, complicated task. Staying on top of the situation requires quick, sensitive, and intuitive judgment of that which works best" (Kempher 1987). Parents with drug/alcohol problems are ill equipped to provide the kind of patient, dedicated care necessary for children to develop and grow. Their parenting styles tend to be inflexible, rigid, and insensitive to the needs of children. These parents tend not to be nurturing and available. They often use coercive, or abusive parenting techniques learned from their parents (see chapters 4 and 5). Breaking the cycle of this family disease from generation to generation is our goal.

Risk-Taking Behavior

Drug/alcohol use involves taking the risk of use. There have always been individuals who when told "no," are curious and perhaps contrary and translate that "no" means "yes." This is especially true for adolescents. Drug/alcohol use affects each individual's physical and emotional balance; for some that balance may be very delicate even before they start to use drugs/alcohol. We know that because some individuals have a need to be in control, when they use drugs/alcohol the result is usually a negative reaction. Others who enjoy losing control and are looking for an altered state of consciousness that approaches their outer limits of effective functioning, become more involved in drug/alcohol use. Some thrill seekers may go further and progress to drug/alcohol dependence and addiction.

The drug addict/alcoholic life-style, subculture, and environment are often the most alluring feature of addiction for some. Scoring drugs, hanging out in bars, associating with users, stealing, and other antisocial behaviors, all reinforce the actual use of drugs/alcohol. The risk-taking behavior itself serves the function of rebellion, aggression, rage, self-destructiveness, and feeling alive (i.e., the adrenaline rush accompanying danger and fear).

The vicious cycle of problems that result from these risk-taking behaviors then leads to more abuse of drugs/alcohol to alleviate the feelings of pain, anxiety, and depression. This debilitating cycle continues until individuals recognize their own powerlessness and destructive behavior, or until they are in jail, or dead.

Tightrope walk of drugs/alcohol

No One Is Immune from Developing Drug/Alcohol Dependence and Addiction

What about the individual who has it all? One who has

- no genetic or family history of drug/alcohol dependence or addiction
- a strong sense of self
- a functional family system
- successfully coped with adolescent and/or adult issues
- good interpersonal relationships and a support system
- achieved success and avoided high-risk behavior

Why does this individual have drug/alcohol problems?

Being human—having experienced the traumas of life, the feelings, pleasures, and pains of the human condition—makes us all at risk for problems with drugs/alcohol. No one is immune to the disease of alcoholism and drug addiction or the accompanying devastation of the individual and the family. Individuals with strong constitutions; learned men and women; powerful men and women; talented and creative people; every socioeconomic, religious, and cultural group is at risk for the disease of alcohol and drug addiction.

Summary

This chapter explored the many reasons for drug/alcohol use and abuse, the models that help us understand drug/alcohol addiction, and at-risk factors for developing drug/alcohol dependence.

The three basic reasons outlined in this chapter for drug/alcohol use are (1) the innate human drive to alter one's sense of consciousness; (2) the passive activity of drug/alcohol use; and (3) the variety of functions and meanings that drugs/alcohol have in serving people.

The innate drive to alter consciousness is one of several natural human drives such as hunger and thirst and the drive to survive, as well as the sex drive with the goal of procreation. The reason for using drugs/alcohol is often an attempt to alleviate feelings of boredom, melancholia and sadness, fatigue, or just something to do to break up the monotony of everyday activities.

Drug/alcohol use is a passive activity in that the individual takes the chemical in and waits for the physiological and psychological reaction. The person is not actively involved in changing anything but instead looks to the drug as a means of changing feelings, observations, and interactions.

The variety of functions and meanings of drugs/alcohol include power, self-destruction, seduction, sexuality, and positive reinforcers.

Several models of drug/alcohol addiction explain the dynamics of addiction. The most widely accepted is the disease model of addiction. The American Medical Association in 1957 recognized alcoholism as a disease based on three criteria: Alcoholism has (1) a known etiology (cause), (2) the progression of symptoms that get worse over time, and (3) a known outcome.

The genetic model of alcoholism has been supported in adoption and twin studies. Twins from alcoholic parents raised in nonalcoholic families have a higher rate of alcoholism than normal, and children adopted from alcoholic families have a higher incidence of alcoholism than the adopted child from the nonalcoholic home.

Other models of addiction include psychological, psychoanalytic, tension and stress reduction, and sociocultural models.

The chapter concludes with a discussion of some key factors that may make individuals at risk for problems with drugs/alcohol. A person's self-concept is often identified as a key factor in being at risk for problems with drugs/alcohol. An individual who has a healthy self-concept or sense of self (1) feels unique, worthwhile; has emerging talents and skills; (2) can accomplish things with good decision making, problem solving and conflict resolution skills; and (3) can trust and be trusted while setting appropriate boundaries in relationships.

Adolescence is an at-risk time for the development of drug/alcohol problems. The adolescent developmental tasks of identity, independence, social and interpersonal relationship skills, sexual identity, and other developmental decisions of this stage make adolescence particularly vulnerable to drugs/alcohol. Academic failure often contributes to antisocial behavior and problems with drugs/alcohol.

Drug and alcohol dependence and addiction are family diseases. Dysfunctional and imbalanced family systems are the breeding ground for problems with drugs/ alcohol. We discuss family systems in chapters 4 and 5.

Another factor often associated with drug/alcohol problems is risk-taking behavior. The addict/alcoholic often enjoys taking risks and may negate the physical, criminal-justice, and interpersonal risks involved with drug/alcohol abuse, as well as the potential harm to others.

Finally, this chapter emphasizes that "No one is immune from developing drug/alcohol problems." Despite a healthy, functional family system, good academic performance, the attainment of adolescent and adult developmental skills, every individual is still at risk for developing the disease of alcoholism or drug addiction. This is part of the price of being human.

References

Bales, R. "Cultural Differences in Rates of Alcoholism." *Quarterly Journal of Studies of Alcohol* 6 (1946): 480–99.

Blane, Howard T., and Kenneth E. Leonard, eds. *Psychological Theories of Drinking and Alcoholism.* New York: Guilford Press, 1988.

Blum, Kenneth, Ernest Noble, et al. "Allelic Association of Human Dopamine D2 Receptor Gene in Alcoholism." *Journal of American Medical Association* 263, no. 15 (April 1990): 2055–60.

Cadoret, R. J., E. Troughton, T. W. O'Gorman. "Genetic and Environmental Factors in Alcohol Abuse and Antisocial Personality." *Journal Studies of Alcohol* 48 (January 1987): 1–8.

Cloninger, C. R., M. Bohman, and S. Sigvardsson. "Inheritance of Alcohol Abuse." *Archives of General Psychiatry* 38 (1981): 861–68.

Donovan, James M. "Etiological Model of Alcoholism." *American Journal of Psychiatry,* 143 (1986): 1–11.

Fenichel, Otto. *The Psychoanalytic Theory of Neurosis.* New York: W. W. Norton, 1945.

Gitlow, S. E. "The Pharmacological Approach to Alcoholism." *Journal of Drug Issues 2,* no. 3 (1972): 32–41.

Gitlow, S. E. "Considerations on the Evaluation and Treatment of Substance Dependency." *Journal of Substance Abuse Treatment* 2 (1985): 175–79.

Goodwin, D. W. "High-Risk Studies of Alcoholism." *In Recent Developments in Alcohol* 3, Mark Galanter, ed. (1985): 3–9.

Goodwin, D. W. "Is Alcoholism Hereditary: A Review and Critique." *Archives of General Psychiatry* 25 (1971): 545–49.

Gottheil, Edward, ed. *Etiological Aspects of Alcohol/Drug Abuse.* Springfield, Ill.: Charles C. Thomas, 1983.

Gurling, H. M. et al. "Genetic Epidemiology in Medicine—Recent Twin Research." *British Medical Journal* 288 (1984): 3–5.

Hendin, Herbert, et al. *Living High: Daily Marijuana Use by Adults.* New York: Science Press, 1987.

Hennecke, Lynne. "Stimulus Augmenting and Field Dependence in Children of Alcoholic Fathers." *Journal of Studies on Alcoholism* 45 (1984): 486–92.

Hesselbrook, V. M., E. G. Shaskan, R. E. Meyer. "Summary of Bio/Genetic Factors in Alcoholism." *NIAAA Research Monograph Series* 9 (1983): 159–66.

Hruber, Z., and G. S. Omenn. "Evidence of Genetic Predisposition to Alcoholic Cirrhosis and Psychosis Twin Concordance for Alcoholism and Its End Points by Zygosity among Male Veterans." *Alcoholism* 5 (1981): 207–15.

Jellinek, E. M. *The Disease Concept of Alcoholism.* New Haven, Conn.: Hillhouse Press, 1960.

Johnston, L. O., et al. "Drugs and Delinquency: A Search for Causal Connections." In *Longitudinal Research on Drug Use,* D. B. Kandel, ed. Washington, D.C.: Hemisphere Publishing Co., 1978.

Kaij, L. *Alcoholism in Twins. Studies in the Etiology and Sequelae of Abuse of Alcohol.* Stockholm: Alonquist and Winkell Publishers, 1960, p. 24.

Kandel, D. B., R. Kessler, and R. Margulies. "Antecedents of Adolescent Initiation into Stages of Drug Use: A Developmental Analysis." In *Longitudinal Research on Drug Use,* D. B. Kandel, ed. Washington, D.C.: Hemisphere Publishing Co., 1978.

Kempher, Carol. "Special Populations: Etiology and Prevention of Vulnerability to Chemical Dependency in Children of Substance Abusers." In *Youth at High Risk for Substance Abuse.* Washington, D.C.: U.S. Dept. of Human Services, 1987.

Khantzian, E. J. "The Ego, the Self and Opiate Addiction: Theoretical and Treatment Considerations." *International Review of Psychoanalysis* 5 (1978): 189–98.

Krystal, H., and H. A. Raskin. *Drug Dependence: Aspects of Ego Functions.* Detroit: Wayne State University Press, 1970.

Machover, S., et al. "Clinical and Objective Studies of Personality Variables in Alcoholism. An Objective Study of Homosexuality in Alcoholics." *Quarterly Journal of Studies in Alcohol* 20 (1959): 528–42.

Menninger, K. *The Vital Balance.* New York: Viking Press, 1963.

Nazarte, Sonia L. "Alcoholism Is Linked to a Gene." *Wall Street Journal,* April 18, 1990.

Petrie, A. "Some Psychological Aspects of Pain and the Relief of Suffering." *Annals of the New York Academy of Sciences* 86 (1960): 13–27.

Pickens, Roy W., and Dace S. Svikis, eds. *Biological Vulnerability to Drug Abuse,* NIDA Research Monograph 89. Rockville, Md.: U.S. Department of Health and Human Services, 1988.

Robins, L. W. "Sturdy Childhood Predictors of Adult Antisocial Behavior: Replication from Longitudinal Studies. *Psychology Medicine* 8 (1978): 617–22.

Robinson, Paul E. "Beyond Drug Education." *Journal of Drug Education* 5, no. 1 (1975): 183–91.

Schuckit, M., D. Goodwin, G. Winokur. "A Study of Alcoholism in Half Siblings." *American Journal of Psychiatry* 128 (1972): 122–26.

Schuckit, Mark B., E. Gold, C. Risch. "Plasma Cortisol Levels following Ethanol in Sons of Alcoholics and Controls." *Archives of General Psychiatry* 44, no. 1 (November 1987): 942–45.

Selye, Hans. *Stress without Distress.* New York: J. B. Lippincott, 1975.

Siegal, Ronald K. *Intoxication, Life in Pursuit of Artificial Paradise.* New York: E. P. Dutton, 1989.

Stanton, M. Duncan, Thomas C. Todd, and associates. *The Family Therapy of Drug Abuse and Addiction.* New York: Guilford Press, 1982.

Tabakoff, Boris, and Paula L. Hoffman. "Genetics and Biological Markers of Risk for Alcoholism." *Public Health Report* 103, no. 6 (1988): 690–98.

Weil, Andrew. *The Natural Mind, a New Way of Looking at Drugs and the Higher Consciousness.* Boston: Houghton Mifflin, 1972.

Whitlock, F. A., J. M. Lowrey, et al. "Drug Dependence in Psychiatric Patients." *Medical Journal of Australia* 1 (1967): 11–57.

Winokur, G., J. Rimmer, and T. Reich. "Alcoholism IV: Is There More Than One Type of Alcoholism?" *British Journal of Psychiatry* 118 (1971): 523–31.

Wurmser, L. "Psychoanalytic Considerations of the Etiology of Compulsive Drug Use." *Journal of American Psychoanalytic Association* 22 (1974): 820–43.

Perceptions and Perspectives: Do You Have a Problem with Drugs or Alcohol?

The most difficult assessment question is differentiating those individuals who fall in the gray area between occasional or nonproblematic use of drugs/alcohol and those who use excessively and/or have a drug/alcohol problem. Assessment is also complicated by the fact that people strongly deny problems with drugs/alcohol. Individual, family, and societal perceptions of drugs/alcohol are distorted by this denial system.

This chapter defines addiction and describes the stages of drug/alcohol use and stages of recovery. The major goal of this chapter is to help the reader develop a more focused perception of chemical dependency.

We all have a perspective or viewpoint about drug/alcohol use. Personal experiences, family patterns, even community, cultural, and societal values influence our perspectives. This chapter describes the four major perspectives of drugs/alcohol use: the moral-legal, medical-public health, psychosocial, and social-cultural perspectives. These perspectives give readers various angles by which to view the issue. At the end of the chapter a Fifth Perspective Worksheet can help readers further explore their own perspectives of drug/alcohol use.

Chapter Goals

1. Identify the three elements in the behavioral definition of *addiction.*
2. Establish guidelines for parents in trying to discourage initial use of drugs/alcohol by their children.
3. Describe factors that can decrease drug/alcohol use by adolescents.
4. Define and describe the impact of set and setting on drug/alcohol use.
5. Describe the stages and progressive cycle of drug/alcohol use: initial contact, experimentation, integrated use, excessive use, and addiction.
6. Explain the different types of alcoholism Jellinek identified and the behavioral characteristics of the progression of the disease.
7. Outline the stages of drug/alcohol recovery.
8. Describe some examples of denial that lead to problems in recognizing and perceiving drug/alcohol addiction.
9. Identify some physical, psychological, and emotional responses that might indicate a problem with the use of marijuana.
10. Identify some physical, psychological, and emotional responses that might indicate a problem with the use of cocaine.
11. List some assessment questions that can help in identifying a problem with drugs/alcohol.
12. Describe individual, family, and societal problems in developing an accurate perception of drug/alcohol abuse.
13. Describe the four major perspectives of drug/alcohol use.
14. Describe your own perspective on drug/alcohol use by completing the Fifth Perspective Worksheet.

Definition of Addiction

In the early 1980s, the rise in cocaine use challenged the basic framework of our definition of drug/alcohol addiction. Cocaine was previously thought to be a drug that incurred psychological dependence with no physical dependence. At that time, we defined addiction as a physical dependence measured by a significant and noticeable medical withdrawal symptom. Although cocaine had no significant medically noticeable withdrawal symptoms, users reported a severe addiction to it. David Smith (1988) was aware of this discrepancy and proposed a more behavioral definition of addiction. Because it is more functional, counselors in the fields of drug/alcohol treatment and addictionology use this definition.

Alcoholism and drug addiction are best described as "the dragon in the corner eating its own tail." (See chapter 3 for more information on the definition of addiction.) In fact, counselors now apply these concepts of addiction to codependency and various disorders involving eating, gambling, sex, workaholism, television, smoking, video games, spending/consumerism, and other activities.

The three basic components of the definition of addiction are

1. **Obsessive-compulsive behavior** with drugs/alcohol. Users think about drugs and alcohol in a vicious negative cycle; their obsessive concern and preoccupation follows incessant use of drugs/alcohol in a continuous pattern and compulsive life-style.
2. **Inability to stop** using the substances. Users cannot stop using drugs/alcohol for at least three months and/or make feeble attempts to cut back in a progression of stop-then-start patterns. They are unable to refuse readily available drugs/alcohol.
3. **Continued use despite adverse consequences.** Users are caught up in their addictions, illustrating the pervasive defense mechanisms of denial (rationalization and minimization). Eventually the addict/alcoholic suffers family, social and interpersonal, economic, and spiritual bankruptcy.

Dragon in the corner eating its own tail

Stages of Alcohol and Drug Use

Defining addiction is a challenge; however, defining the stages and patterns of drug/alcohol use that precede addiction is even more challenging.

Nonuse of Drugs/ Alcohol by Children

The most successful preventive approach is not to use drugs and alcohol, especially at early ages. Not smoking cigarettes at early ages highly correlates with not developing addictions later in life. Children are less likely to develop drug/alcohol dependencies later in life, if parents

1. do not model drug/alcohol use and encourage a healthy approach to life
2. encourage children to participate in activities that enhance the development of a strong sense of self
3. promote positive alternative activities to drug/alcohol use (see chapter 7)
4. are sensitive to what children feel while setting appropriate boundaries
5. provide structure, discipline, and consistency
6. develop a climate of discussion that facilitates an effective exploration of values and the development of skills in goal setting, decision making, and conflict resolution.

Parents can establish nonuse of drugs and alcohol in early childhood by teaching children to make positive life-style choices that they can maintain throughout adult life. Although the drive or desire to alter one's consciousness is innate, learning to alter one's consciousness with alternatives other than drugs/alcohol is a developmental task of childhood. Children can be encouraged to be more active in

TABLE 2.1
Annual Prevalence of Drug/Alcohol Use by High School Seniors

	Percent		
	Alcohol	*Marijuana*	*Cocaine*
1975	84.8%	45.0%	5.6%
1976	85.7	48.1	6.0
1977	87.0	51.1	7.2
1978	87.7	53.8	9.0
1979	88.1	54.2	12.0
1980	87.9	53.1	12.3
1981	87.0	52.1	12.4
1982	86.8	50.8	11.5
1983	87.3	49.1	11.4
1984	86.0	45.8	11.6
1985	85.6	46.3	13.1
1986	84.5	44.3	12.7
1987	85.7	41.7	10.3
1988	85.3	38.5	7.9

choosing things to do that change their mood and develop their sense of self, instead of choosing a passive solution, drugs/alcohol.

Nonuse of Drugs/ Alcohol by Adolescents

Encouraging nonuse of drugs/alcohol by adolescents is a difficult task. As outlined in chapter 1, simply being an adolescent is an at-risk factor for alcohol/drug problems.

The U.S. Department of Public Health and Human Services report, *National Trends in Drug Use and Related Factors among American High School Students and Young Adults 1975–88,* stated that alcohol is the number one drug of use by high school seniors (see table 2.1).

Marijuana and cocaine use by high school seniors has decreased dramatically. Marijuana use has decreased steadily from a high of 54.2 percent in 1979, to a low of 38.5 percent in 1988, and cocaine use has decreased from a high of 13.1 percent in 1985 to a dramatic low of 7.9 percent in 1988. Despite these decreases in marijuana and cocaine use by adolescents, many still continue to use alcohol. Initial use of alcohol by high school seniors has remained relatively stable as table 2.1 shows.

Some young people are able to use alcohol and drugs and not suffer any significant problems. For others, especially those who have family histories of alcoholism and drug addiction, such a trial could be the beginning of a lifelong pattern of addiction.

To help their at-risk adolescents, parents should

1. establish clear, consistent guidelines for drugs/alcohol
2. model nonuse of drugs/alcohol
3. establish clear, consistent communication of the hazards and potential harm of drugs/alcohol, especially at early ages
4. encourage the development of alternative activities to alleviate feelings of boredom, depression, and isolation, and to promote the development of a strong sense of self
5. promote active involvement in school, athletics, social situations, church, and other activities
6. encourage active development of skills and talents
7. promote trust and establish healthy boundaries in relationships
8. support adolescents in their perseverence through their developmental tasks

Initial Contact with Drugs/Alcohol

The initial contact stage is defined as the first time one tries drugs/alcohol. Usually this stage is thought to be relatively harmless; yet, there are potential hazards from initial contact, such as

- anaphylactic (allergic) reactions that can cause death
- toxic and lethal doses
- loss of control, emotional overreactions
- physical and psychological problems
- accidents and/or dangerous situations

Set and Setting

The three major components of drug and alcohol use are the individual, the drug, and the set and setting in which the drug is taken. Set and setting often determine the individual's reaction to drugs/alcohol.

Set refers to the psychological and emotional frame of mind of a person when using drugs/alcohol. Those who are relaxed, comfortable, and secure in the knowledge that they can handle possibly losing control usually have less trouble with the initial use of drugs/alcohol. Individuals who have a set that can be described as anxious, extremely nervous, or overly concerned with maintaining control are more prone to a negative drug/alcohol reaction. If a person is not emotionally stable and/or has psychiatric problems, drug/alcohol use can exacerbate those problems (see chapter 9). This is especially true for hallucinogens and marijuana.

Set can also be influenced by the person's mood or emotional state at the time of drug/alcohol use. The individual who has just received some bad news or had a negative experience, might be feeling down or depressed; this may result in a negative set and a negative experience with drugs/alcohol. Significant trauma, shame, and embarrassment can also contribute to a negative experience with drugs/alcohol.

Setting involves not only the physical environment but also the social and interpersonal environment. Negative drug reactions may be the result of being in an uncomfortable setting, with unknown people who are not trusted.

The importance of set and setting is dramatically illustrated with the use of hallucinogens. A bad trip can often result from a negative set and setting, and a good trip can result from trust and comfort in set and setting. This sense of trust and comfort often involves trusting someone more experienced with hallucinogens, a person who could provide the necessary support during times of discomfort resulting from the distortion of reality caused by hallucinogens. The drug revolution of the 1950s and 1960s taught us a great deal about the impact of set and setting and the differences in individual reactions to drugs. For some it was a time of self-exploration, for others a negative experience, and for still others a significantly traumatic experience.

Drug/Alcohol Use—A Progressive Disease

Certainly, the beginning of drug/alcohol use starts with initial contact. Because drug/alcohol use is a progressive disease, individuals get more involved as they progress through the stages. A positive initial contact usually leads to the next stage of drug use—experimentation. Experimentation may lead to the subsequent stages that end in addiction. Richard Rawson (1989) has written about his outpatient treatment of cocaine addicts. He describes the progressive themes at various stages of cocaine addiction, as shown in table 2.2. This model also applies to other drugs and alcohol and illustrates the progressive nature of addiction.

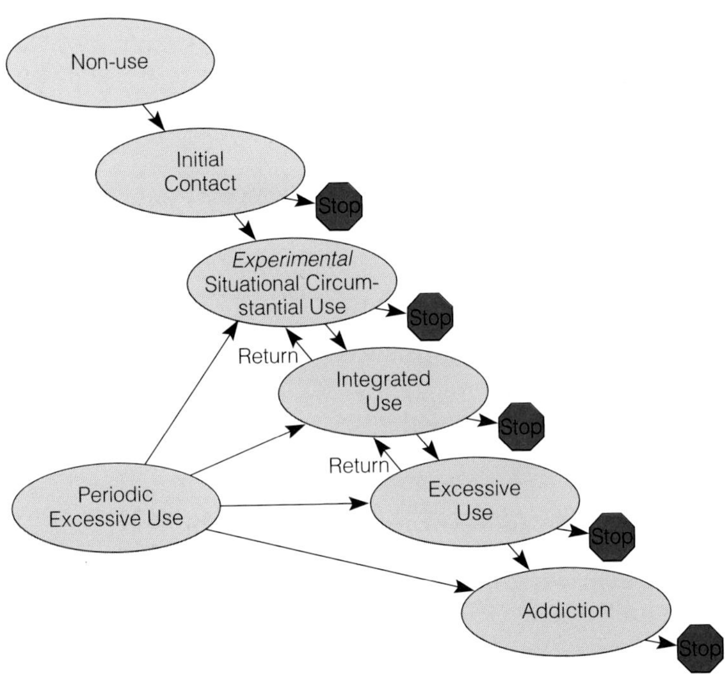

Stages of drug/alcohol use

© Richard Fields, Ph.D., 1986, REVISED 1988

TABLE 2.2
Phases of Cocaine Addiction

Initial contact	"Isn't this a great drug!"
Experimentation	"It's sure expensive, but it's worth it."
Excessive use	"I really should cut down."
Addicted	"I know I have to stop, but I can't."

As we stated earlier, a positive initial contact may be the beginning of a progressive cycle to addiction. This is especially true for those who grew up in alcoholic/addict and/or dysfunctional family systems.

Experimentation

Experimentation is the stage of using drug/alcohol in different situations and circumstances. People explore and experiment with a drug, testing their own capacity to use drugs/alcohol in different situations and circumstances. Users learn about drugs/alcohol by experimenting with various doses, frequencies of use, methods of ingestion, and sometimes by

Drug effects

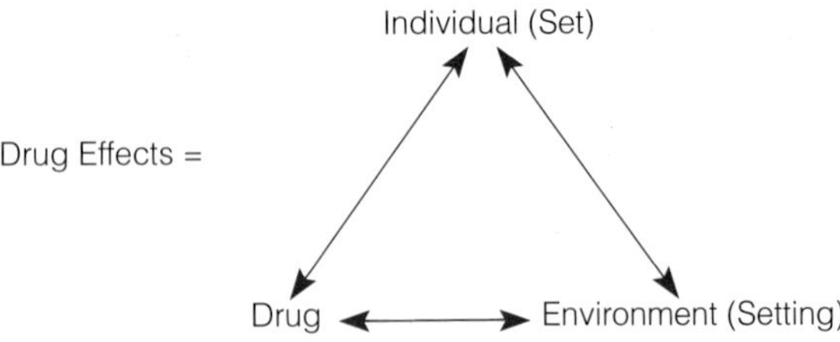

using drugs/alcohol in combination (polydrug use). Each individual's reaction to a drug is also affected by physiological, psychological, and emotional factors. Some factors might be not eating prior to use, fatigue, and levels of physical and emotional well-being. During experimentation, individuals change and adjust the drug, the set and the setting, and then determine their reaction.

Experimenters use drugs during this stage in different settings, with different people, and in different frames of mind or set. A triangular relationship exists between the individual (set), the drug/alcohol, and the environment (setting). During the experimentation stage, the user adjusts the three elements of this equation to determine the drug's effect.

Many systems that classify the stages of drug/alcohol use often call the experimental stage a recreational or social use stage. These terms tend to put drugs/alcohol in a more positive, emotion-laden frame of reference. The implication of the term *recreational* is that drug/alcohol use is no more than harmless recreational/social fun. This view overlooks the potential hazards or problems that may occur.

Parental guidelines during the experimental stage should include

1. talking with other parents and exchanging information about their children's behavior in the neighborhood, at neighboring homes, at school, or in the general community
2. knowing where children are, who their friends are, and meeting the parents of their friends
3. developing initiative, responsibility, and appropriate consequences for behavior
4. evaluating the dynamics of the family and seeking professional help for early drug/alcohol educational advice and assessment
5. being aware that a child is at risk and seeking family counseling for drug/alcohol education, prevention, and treatment if there is a history of alcohol/drug problems in the family

Integrated Use

At the integrated stage of drug/alcohol use, the person spends more time, thought, and energy in the use of drugs/alcohol. It has become an integrated part of the individual's life. Whether adolescent or adult, the person begins to associate with others who use the same drug. At parties the marijuana smokers congregate together, the alcohol users belly up to the bar, and the polydrug users are the life of the party, drinking at the bar and smoking dope in the backyard.

The individual at the integrated stage buys the drug to make sure that the drug is available. For example, at this stage a person must have the drug/alcohol available when away from home for a vacation or a business trip. Obviously, drugs/alcohol are well integrated into the user's style of life.

Excessive Use

Even for experts, the excessive use stage is difficult to describe because there are different kinds of excessive use. Some people call this stage drug abuse; however, drug abuse is very arbitrary, emotion laden, and difficult to define. The second Commission on Marijuana (1973) found that the term *drug abuse* had "no functional utility" and "had become no more than an arbitrary code word for that drug use which is presently considered wrong." The commission concluded that the facts of actual drug use are often not distinguished from feelings and opinions. The commission recommended that the term *drug abuse* be discontinued because of the emotion-laden subjective interpretation of the term.

Excessive use is an increase in drug/alcohol use that results in significant problems or negative consequences. Users are putting increased time, thought, and energy into buying—perhaps selling—and certainly using drugs/alcohol.

Periodic Excessive Use

Some people use drugs/alcohol excessively in a periodic pattern, sometimes in the form of binges, which are excessive drug use within a period of 24–72 hours. Periodic excessive drug/alcohol use can occur just on weekends, every other week, once in a month, even as infrequently as once every three months. When all the criteria for addiction are met, periodic excessive use is also defined as addiction.

Alcoholic's arm sinking into a glass of booze

Addiction

Addiction is the last stage. Based on our definition of addiction and the disease model, an addict cannot return to any of the previous stages of drug/alcohol use. The best recovery strategy is to abstain from drug/alcohol use and to participate in a twelve-step recovery program. This usually involves an inpatient program; strong development in self-help support groups such as Alcoholics Anonymous, Narcotics Anonymous, Cocaine Anonymous, and others; a relationship with a sponsor; and an aftercare treatment program on completion of the inpatient program (see chapter 10).

Chronic Addiction

Chronic alcoholics and drug addicts spend major portions of their lives addicted to drugs/alcohol. In this late stage of chronic addiction, they are extremely difficult to treat (see table 2.3). Some new approaches are required for this population. Such programs provide basic needs for shelter, food, and other health-related services, and educational and counseling services. These programs for chronic alcoholics have an emphasis on maintaining the individual's dignity while providing access to recovery services.

Alcoholic trapped in a shot glass

TABLE 2.3 Early and Late Stages of Drug/Alcohol Use	
Early Stages of Drug/Alcohol Use	**Later Stages of Drug/Alcohol Use**
More freedom	Lack of freedom
Fewer risks and less damage	More damage
Abuse possible	Abuse present
No illness	State of illness
Operating factors linear	Vicious cycles

Jellinek's Theory of Alcoholism

E. M. Jellinek (1960) believed that persons with certain types of alcoholism suffer through declining stages of functioning. He described five distinct types of alcoholism:

1. Alpha alcoholism
   a. psychological dependence in which alcoholics use drinking increasingly to help with their problems

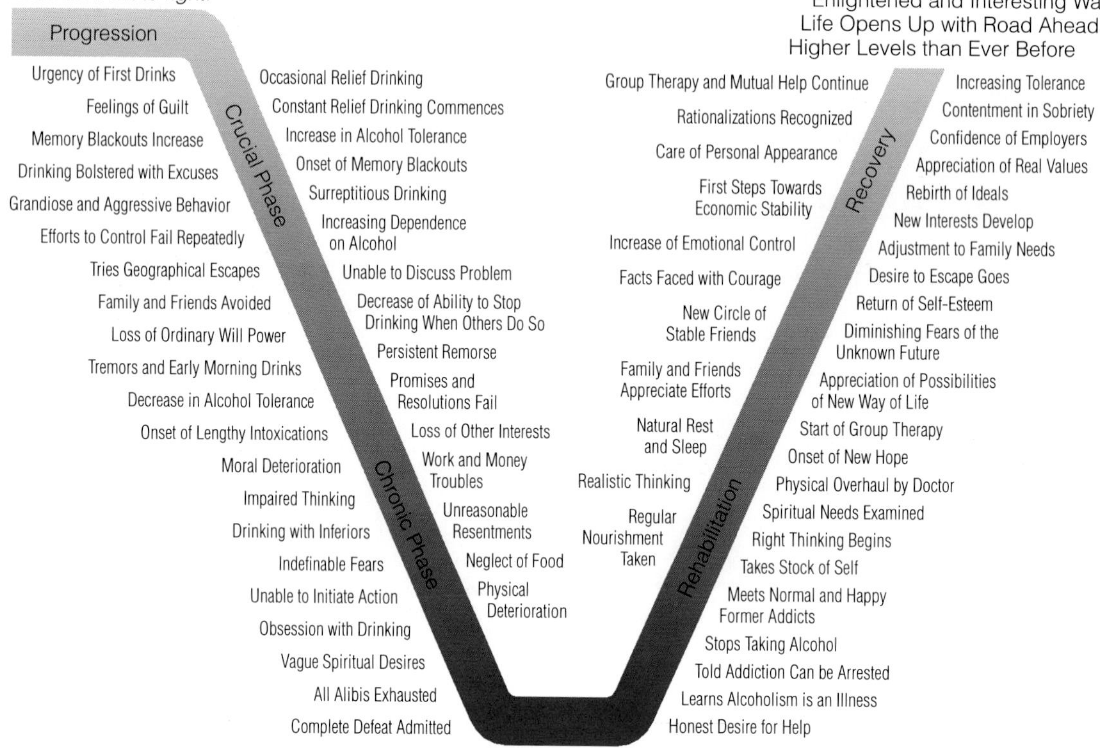

The progression and recovery of the alcoholic in the disease of alcoholism

2. Beta alcoholism
   a. physical problems such as cirrhosis of the liver or stomach problems resulting from the consumption of alcohol
   b. no physical or psychological dependence
3. Gamma alcoholism
   a. physical addiction with withdrawal symptoms occurring whenever drinking is stopped
   b. loss of control to regulate alcohol use
   c. severe damage to health, financial, social, and interpersonal functioning
   d. periods of abstinence (going on the wagon)
4. Delta alcoholism
   a. similar to gamma; however, the individual can control intake in given situations
   b. high degree of physical and psychological dependence making abstinence, even for brief periods, impossible
5. Epsilon alcoholism
   a. periodic, unpredictable drinking binges

The progression and recovery symptoms listed are based on the *most repeated experiences* of family members in the disease of alcoholism or other chemical dependencies. While every symptom in the chart does not occur in every member of every family, or in the same sequence, it does portray an *average* chain reaction. The entire process may take years or it may occur in a very short time.

The progression and recovery of the family in the disease of alcoholism

Stages of Drug/ Alcohol Recovery

Once a drug/alcohol problem is identified, the next step is recovery. Richard Rawson (1989) described a model for the stages of cocaine recovery, as seen in table 2.4. This model also applies to alcohol or other drugs, although the time periods for each stage can be different and variable. Each stage of recovery is fully explained in chapter 10.

TABLE 2.4
Stages of Recovery

Stage	Time Course*
Withdrawal	0–15 days
Honeymoon	15–45 days
The Wall	45–120 days
Adjustment	120–180 days
Resolution	180–360 days

*These generalized categories are rough estimates for periods of time when drugs/alcohol are not used. The actual time course for each stage of recovery may be quite different for each individual and drug or alcohol used.

Vulnerability to Relapse

At each of the stages of recovery, individuals are vulnerable to relapse or a return to drug/alcohol abuse or addiction. Therefore, all drug/alcohol treatment programs must address issues of relapse. Many experts agree that a longer-term inpatient or residential program is much needed (although financially impossible due to limitations in insurance reimbursement). Experts agree that a six to nine-month inpatient program would be most effective considering the high relapse rates. In addition, a one-year outpatient aftercare program would further enhance the probability of recovery without relapse. It is not surprising that the relapse statistics are high following the traditional twenty-eight-day inpatient stay, making it even more important to counsel patients in relapse prevention (see chapter 10).

Many people find it extremely difficult to stop using drugs/alcohol. B. G. Danaher and E. Lichtenstein (1978) describe the natural cycle of smoking, which is similar to the cycle of drug/alcohol use.

Family and Recovery

Recovery from drugs/alcohol also involves the family of the addict/alcoholic. The family system has been an integral part in the development of the disease. The most difficult work in recovery is dealing with family issues and relationships to help family members recover from dysfunctional patterns in the family system (see chapter 4).

Natural Cycle of Cigarette Smoking

Reasons for starting

- availability
- curiosity
- rebelliousness
- anticipation of adulthood
- social confidence
- modeling of peers, siblings, parents
- other reasons in the psychosocial domain

Reasons for continuing

- nicotine addiction
- immediate positive consequences
- signals (cues) in the environment
- avoiding negative effects (withdrawal)
- other reasons in the physiological and psychosocial domains

Reasons for stopping

- health
- expense
- social pressure
- self-mastery
- aesthetics (feeling that it is bad, ugly, and/or unbecoming)
- example to others
- other reasons in the psychosocial domain

Reasons for resuming

- stress
- social pressure
- abstinence violation effect
- alcohol consumption
- other reasons in the psychosocial domain

Assessment of Drug/Alcohol Problems

The most important question in assessing the potential for problems with drugs/alcohol is determining if there is a family history of drug or alcohol abuse and addiction. Family members may deny the extent of drug/alcohol use in their family. It might take additional questioning to clarify the true dimensions of family use of drugs/alcohol. Some education also might be necessary to establish a clear perception of the dimensions of drug/alcohol use and addiction. To assess an individual's drug/alcohol problem, counselors need the following information:

Drug/Alcohol History

- age of initial drug and alcohol use
- frequency of use, amounts used, set and setting of use
- patterns of use, binges, periods of nonuse
- stage of current use—experimentation, integrated, excessive, addiction
- history of negative consequences—physical, psychological, financial, familial, and spiritual
- medical history—conditions that might affect use of drugs/alcohol
- use of coffee, cigarettes, and medication

Individual Vulnerability to Drugs/Alcohol

What evidence is there of individual vulnerability?

- primary alcoholism/drug addiction in the family system of origin
- inherited or acquired mood disorder
- psychosis
- rejection or insensitivity to norms of behavior

What is the individual's attitude toward drug/alcohol use?

- favorable, unfavorable, nonexistent

Environmental Factors

- family, other

Availability of drugs

- legally available, readily available illegally
- individual has the necessary finances for drugs (Rankin 1978)

Counselors should also identify any other significant problems, especially other compulsive behaviors in the family.

Family history of

- drug/alcohol problems, gambling, workaholism
- eating disorders—anorexia, bulimia, obesity
- employment and financial problems
- marital problems
- and psychiatric disorders—depression, anxiety, affective (feeling) disorders, and others

Additional problems of

- neglect; emotional, physical or sexual abuse
- loss—death, trauma, divorce, separation
- numerous relocations and unstable home environment
- parental dysfunction creating feelings of parental unavailability and/or feelings of abandonment, rejection, or shame

Another key assessment issue with drugs/alcohol is the potential for suicide. Judith Landau-Stanton and M. Duncan Stanton (1985) state that the "recognition of substance abuse as a suicidal endeavor stems from as far back as 1938 when Menninger likened addiction to chronic suicide." Others have since concluded that the high rate of deaths among addicts "is more than a result of living in dangerous environments and is to a great extent—if not primarily—a suicidal phenomena" (Stanton and Coleman, 1980). The following assessment tool highlights key questions related to drugs/alcohol and suicide.

Drugs/Alcohol and Suicide

1. Is there a family history of drug/alcohol problems, suicide, or depression?
2. Do you use drugs/alcohol to
   a. overcome bad/shameful feelings
   b. deal with sleeping problems, depression, or stress
   c. quiet suicidal or self-destructive thoughts
3. Do you have suicidal thoughts?
4. How will you do it? Do you have a plan? (Assess the availability or means to commit suicide and the lethality of the means.)
5. Have you previously had suicidal thoughts and have you attempted suicide before? How frequently do these thoughts occur?
6. What role does drugs/alcohol use have in relation to suicide? Does it make you more likely or less likely to follow through?
7. On a scale of one to ten, how likely are you to kill yourself?
8. How much do you want to die? to live?
9. What would prevent you from committing suicide?
10. What might occur to make life worth living?

Marijuana and Cocaine Assessment Questionnaires

The questionnaires on pages 53–54 are designed to sensitize individuals to symptoms that might indicate they have problems with either marijuana or cocaine. I ask individuals to check those items that might apply to their use of either marijuana or cocaine. Individuals who answer "yes" to several questions may have problems requiring further assessment by a professional trained in drug/alcohol treatment. These questionnaires are available in my waiting room so that patients, especially family members, can pick them up and use them at their convenience.

Perceptions of Drug/Alcohol Use

Part of the problem in identifying drug/alcohol dependence and addiction is the black or white perception many people have about drugs/alcohol. People tend to put drugs into simplistic categories of good drugs versus bad drugs, licit drugs versus illicit drugs, and soft drugs versus hard drugs (Nowlis 1975). Public perceptions of drugs/alcohol are based on limited information and personal, often emotional, viewpoints.

Denial

Denial of drug/alcohol problems is another major reason for perceptual problems. There is widespread denial not only by individuals who have drug problems but also by family and friends as well as our society at large. It is often difficult to break through denial and have the courage to admit a problem with drugs/alcohol. Family members often experience a sense of shame or embarrassment or feelings of responsibility for the drug/alcohol problem.

The two major defense mechanisms used to deny problems with drugs and alcohol are minimization and rationalization. Common examples of minimizations and rationalizations of drug/alcohol problems follow:

Minimizations

Now if I drank and drugged like Shawn, then I would really have a problem.

I only use drugs and alcohol on weekends, a person with a problem uses everyday.

I never miss work, no matter how much (drugs/alcohol) I've used.

The media is just trying to get you scared.

I don't have a problem. Now Tiffany has a problem. Why don't you get her into treatment?

Marijuana Assessment Questionnaire

Denial of marijuana dependence and addiction stems from misconceptions of the harmlessness of this drug. Current research clearly documents the physical, psychological, and emotional harm of marijuana in the 1990s.

This questionnaire is a tool to help those who might have a problem, or those individuals and family members concerned with others who might have a problem with marijuana. Check the box before any question to which you would answer yes.

☐ 1. Are you smoking marijuana
- ☐ in the morning
- ☐ on a daily basis
- ☐ during work/school time

(one or more checks is a yes answer)

☐ 2. While under the influence of marijuana, do you experience any of the following symptoms:
- ☐ irritability
- ☐ anxiety
- ☐ tremors
- ☐ insomnia
- ☐ restlessness
- ☐ sweating
- ☐ feeling loss of control
- ☐ nausea, vomiting

☐ 3. As a result of marijuana use, do you experience a loss of initiative and ambition and/or a withdrawal from customary interests and interpersonal relationships?

☐ 4. After using marijuana have you experienced:
- ☐ a clouding of mental processes
- ☐ flashbacks
- ☐ delusions
- ☐ impaired thinking and confusion
- ☐ fear of brain damage

☐ 5. Have others commented on your poor driving skills while under the influence of marijuana, and/or have you noticed impairment in perceptual motor skills, driving decision making, and/or tracking and reaction time?

☐ 6. As a result of using marijuana, have you experienced any adverse negative consequences? (e.g., problems at work/school, accidents, difficulty in relationships, or mood swings)

☐ 7. Do you think about using marijuana often? (i.e., Do events, time of day, or particular daily situations trigger the desire to use marijuana?)

☐ 8. Have you been unable to stop using marijuana for 3 months or longer without substituting other drugs, alcohol, or medication?

☐ 9. Do you use marijuana with cocaine, alcohol, and/or other drugs?

☐ 10. Do other members of your family have problems with marijuana, alcohol, and/or other drugs?

☐ 11. Do you use marijuana to alleviate stress, loneliness, depression, boredom, and/or problems in relationships?

☐ 12. Did you start using marijuana at a young age and/or have you been using marijuana regularly for several years?

If you checked three or more of these questions, consult a specialist in drug and alcohol assessment and treatment for further evaluation.

Cocaine Assessment Questionnaire

Check the box before any question to which you would answer yes.

☐ 1. Are you using more cocaine than you plan to use and do you find that you are enjoying it less? That is, your tolerance is developing and despite not feeling very well, you continue to use.

☐ 2. Are you experiencing three or more of the following physical signs?

- ☐ Excessive periods of fatigue
- ☐ Sinus problems and nose bleeds
- ☐ Chest pains and palpitations
- ☐ Tremors and poor coordination
- ☐ Light spots on the periphery of your vision
- ☐ Sleep disturbances, sleepiness, or excessive sleeping
- ☐ Itching, scratching, and/or skin lesions
- ☐ Trouble breathing and/or catching your breath
- ☐ Decreased appetite or weight loss
- ☐ Headaches
- ☐ Hoarseness

☐ 3. Do you feel apathetic, disinterested, depressed; have you lost the ability to concentrate?

☐ 4. Do you experience mood swings, irritability, short temperedness, emotional outbursts, rage or excessive sadness, paranoid and/or frantic bizarre behavior?

☐ 5. As a result of cocaine use, have you been absent, late, or exhibited inappropriate behavior at work?

☐ 6. Are family members and friends suggesting that you have a problem with cocaine and/or are you lying about your frequency of cocaine use?

☐ 7. Are you reducing outside interests, withdrawing from, or in conflict with friends and family members?

☐ 8. Are you experiencing financial and/or legal problems as a direct or indirect result of cocaine use?

☐ 9. Are you injecting or freebasing cocaine?

☐ 10. The morning after cocaine use are you feeling depressed, remorseful, guilty, and/or shameful about your behavior the night before?

If you checked the boxes before two or more of these questions you may have a potentially serious cocaine problem. Pursue further evaluation with a chemical dependency professional.

Rationalizations

People use hundreds of rationalizations to explain away drug/alcohol problems. Some of them are quite bizarre, inventive, and so unbelievable that they illustrate the depth of denial. For example,

> Oh, Mama always said a little bit of alcohol once in a while stimulates the system.
> Doesn't everyone from our neighborhood drink/drug like me? Well, that's normal behavior.
> My grandfather drank every day of his life and lived to 102.
> It doesn't hurt anyone but me.
> Marijuana is a natural herb, so why not take it in?

Individual Perceptions

Perceptions of drug/alcohol use varies from one individual to another. One individual might think that drinking a six pack of beer each night is normal behavior; others might believe using any illegal drug once might be defined as an addiction problem. Individual's emotional and sometimes moral-ethical biases determine their perception of drug/alcohol dependence and addiction.

On the positive side, most people now recognize that drug and alcohol dependence and addiction are no longer limited to skid row alcoholics and street drug addicts. Media coverage has increased our awareness that a wide range of individuals have problems with drugs/alcohol.

Family Perceptions

Families are best understood as systems. The alcoholic/addictive family is a dysfunctional family system whose perception of drug/alcohol problems is distorted by denial. (See chapter 4 for more about dysfunctional family systems.)

Despite the daily reality of problems with drugs/alcohol, the dysfunctional family denies the true dimensions of the problem by minimizing and rationalizing. Parents, spouses, and family members may disregard, or blind themselves to obvious signs of alcoholism and drug addiction; often they are embarrassed, preferring not to talk about the problem.

The reality is there is hope for recovery, once the individual and family can admit that they are unable to manage the addiction. With luck this admission can occur before the lives of the individual and family members are devastated by great pain as the disease of alcoholism/drug addiction progresses.

Societal Perceptions

Just as the family has maintained denial, we as a nation have denied the existence of drug/alcohol problems for many generations. The current problems our nation is experiencing are a result of this societal denial. Alcohol and tobacco use have been imbedded in the core of our social habits. The popularity of alcohol and tobacco is evidenced by the growth of both of these industries over the years and reformers' inability to sustain the prohibition of alcohol. The use of alcohol and tobacco was so common that the nation tolerated the known negative and addictive nature of these substances. Only in the last decade have we seriously attempted to address these issues on a societal level. Only in the last few years has the collective unconscious of our society recognized that alcohol and tobacco are problems for America.

Four Perspectives on Drugs/Alcohol

In *Drugs Demystified,* Helen Nowlis (1975) described the major perspectives of drug use. These are (1) the moral-legal perspective, (2) the medical-health perspective, (3) the psychosocial perspective, and (4) the social-cultural perspective.

Moral-Legal Perspective

The moral-legal perspective is primarily the viewpoint of law enforcement and the criminal justice system. The major focus of this perspective is to keep specific drugs away from people, and people away from specific drugs. This approach reduces the availability of drugs and uses punishment as a deterrent in addressing the supply side of drugs and not the demand side.

The agencies in this perspective have not been able to significantly affect the availability of drugs. Although they are doing their best with limited resources, these agencies are unable to substantially affect the price of drugs by reducing their availability. The criminal justice system is a deterrent for some people, but few people stop drug use and drug dealing because they fear criminal-justice interventions. The antisocial personality of the people caught by the system makes rehabilitation difficult. The weak rehabilitative components of the criminal-justice system have resulted in minimal changes in the attitudes of those convicted or caught by the system.

The moral-legal perspective is the one emphasized by most presidential administrations. Yet, this perspective alone cannot be effective. Unless we address the demand side, the moral-legal perspective is ineffective. With so many buyers in the marketplace, sellers are motivated to deal despite the risks. (See chapter 11.)

Medical-Health Perspective

The medical-health perspective is held by physicians, nurses, and the medical and health treatment fields. In this perspective drug and alcohol use is a public health problem. Treatment focuses on the physical damage related to drug/alcohol use, abuse, and dependence.

The medical-health perspective assumes people seek good health. The perspective is also based on the assumption that health information influences attitudes and behaviors. However, we know that information alone does not change attitudes about the use of drugs/alcohol.

Psychosocial Perspective

The psychosocial perspective is a common viewpoint shared by a variety of drug/alcohol agencies that specialize in addressing the demand side of drugs/alcohol. The services they provide are

- recovery from drugs/alcohol
- intervention and treatment services
- early intervention approaches with adolescents
- prevention services for young children, adolescents, adults, and seniors

The goals of this perspective are to prevent, intervene, and treat drug/alcohol problems. Inadequate funding for drug/alcohol treatment programs and drug/alcohol prevention programs has created problems in obtaining treatment services and in maintaining prevention programs long enough to see conclusive results (see chapter 11).

Social-Cultural Perspective

The social-cultural perspective is held by most social agencies and institutions. The basic goal of this perspective is to adapt the environment to meet the individual's needs. The underlying assumption of this perspective is that drug use is due to the frustration and hopelessness of people's lives. If users had any hope that they could attain the American Dream, they would be motivated to achieve and establish a constructive place in society.

Unfortunately most social agencies are impersonal, bureaucratic, and rigid in dealing with their clients' needs. Such agencies are poorly funded and, therefore, poorly staffed; their employees are overworked, underappreciated, and underpaid. As a result, the agencies are reticent to change, change too slowly, or may even lack a mechanism to change.

The renowned author, Edward Brecher, *Licit and Illicit Drugs* (1972), believes we should "stop viewing the drug problem as primarily a national problem to be solved on a national scale. In fact . . . the drug problem is a collection of local problems." By supporting neighborhood and community efforts, we could provide an environment that could prevent the development of drug/alcohol problems.

Summary

The new behavioral definition of addiction was developed by David Smith to better classify addiction to cocaine. Currently counselors use this behaviorial definition in assessing an addiction to drugs/alcohol. The three basic components of the definition of addiction are (1) obsessive-compulsive behavior with drugs/alcohol; (2) an inability to stop using chemicals; and (3) continued use despite negative or adverse consequences.

The first of several key points in describing this stage model of drug/alcohol use is that at early stages of use, set and setting greatly influence the individual's reaction to the chemicals used; throughout use these factors continue to be dominant.

Set refers to the psychological and emotional frame of mind of the individual when using drugs/alcohol.

Setting involves not only the physical environment, but also the social and interpersonal environment at the time of taking drugs/alcohol.

Second, drug/alcohol use is progressive; individuals get more involved as they progress through the stages. Third, the drug/alcohol effect is based-on the drugs used, the individual (set), and the environment (setting). Fourth, the experimental stage is using drugs/alcohol in different situations, and under different circumstances (situational or circumstantial use). Referring to drug use as recreational during the experimental is misleading and minimizes the hazards of use at this stage. Fifth, the term *drug abuse* has limited functional utility and is often no more than an arbitrary code word for that drug use which is presently considered wrong.

Jellinek defines five distinct types of alcoholism, ranging from psychological dependence to periodic, unpredictable drinking binges. The popular Jellinek charts in this section emphasize the progressive nature of the disease of alcoholism.

Assessment involves not only taking a good drug/alcohol history, but also assessing the individual's vulnerability to drugs/alcohol, and suicide potential. During recovery, denial is the major perceptual problem due to users' minimizations and rationalizations of their involvement with drugs/alcohol.

The stages of cocaine recovery are fairly similar to other drug/alcohol recovery periods. They include

withdrawal (0 to 15 days),
honeymoon (15 to 45 days),
the Wall (45 to 120 days),
adjustment (120 to 180 days), and
resolution (180 to 360 days).

The length of each stage of recovery, however, could be quite variable for alcohol and other drugs.

> If the challenge is to keep drugs away from people, laws and law enforcement will be given a major role; if it is to keep man away from drugs, the responsibility will be that of those skilled in the behavioral sciences; if it is to create an environment in which the needs that drug use serves are better served by behavior involving less risk, less potential harm to the individual and the society, every institution and the individuals who have roles in each institution have a role to play. (Helen Nowlis 1975)

These perspectives are a bleak reality to the multifaceted problems of alcoholism and drug addiction. Ideally, if all of these perspectives worked cooperatively and had the necessary support, we might be better able to address the drug/alcohol epidemic.

The Fifth Perspective Is Yours

What is your perspective on drugs/alcohol? Complete the Fifth Perspective Worksheet to further clarify your perspective on drugs/alcohol.

The Fifth Perspective Worksheet

Moral-Legal Perspective

1. Should drugs be legalized? Explain ____________

2. Is the supply-side approach to the drug problem an effective approach? Explain ____________

3. Is alcoholism/drug addiction a defense for irresponsible and/or criminal behavior? Explain. ____________

Medical-Public Health Perspective

1. Is alcoholism/drug addiction a disease? Explain. ____________

2. Describe the physician's role in making a patient aware of problems with drugs/alcohol. ____________

3. Do people need more information about the health risks of drug/alcohol use? Does this information change attitudes? Explain. ____________

Psychosocial Perspective

1. What role does parenting play in the development of drug/alcohol problems? ____________

2. Is it important for the entire family system to be involved in drug/alcohol treatment? Explain. ____________

3. How can drug/alcohol treatment be more effective? ____________

Personal Perspective

Circle true or false and explain the reasoning supporting your answer to each question.

1. Illicit drugs are not necessary, and drug use is harmful. True False

   ____

   ____

2. Illicit drugs can play a role in enhancing life experiences. True False

   ____

   ____

3. Alcohol is a drug with great abuse potential. True False

   ____

   ____

4. My family history does not make me at risk for developing problems with alcohol/drugs. True False

   ____

   ____

5. If a family member or close friend had an alcohol/drug problem, I could either suggest the person get help or participate in an intervention. True False

   ____

   ____

6. Persons with drug/alcohol problems have to break through their own denial. True False

   ____

   ____

7. Alcoholism and drug addiction is a family disease. True False

   ____

   ____

8. Parent modeling of drug/alcohol use is an important influence on the child's use of drugs/alcohol. True False

   ____

   ____

Other personal views ______________________________

____

____

____

____

____

____

References

Brecher, Edward M. *Licit and Illicit Drugs.* Boston: Little, Brown, 1972.

Danaher, B. G. and E. Lichtenstein. *Becoming an Ex-Smoker.* Englewood Cliffs, N.J.: Prentice-Hall, 1978.

Jellinek, E. M. *The Disease Concept of Alcoholism.* New Haven, Conn: Hillhouse Press, 1960.

Menninger, K. *Man against Himself.* New York: Harcourt, 1938.

National Trends in Drug Use and Related Factors among High School Students and Young Adults 1975–1988. Washington, D.C.: U.S. Department of Public Health and Human Services, 1989.

Nowlis, Helen. *Drugs Demystified.* Paris: UNESCO Press, 1975.

Rankin, James G. *Core Knowledge of the Drug Field: A Basic Manual for Trainers.* Toronto: Addiction Research Foundation, 1978.

Rawson, Richard. *Cocaine Recovery Issues: The Neurobehavioral Model.* Beverly Hills, Calif.: Matrix Institute on Addictions, 1989.

Smith, David, and Donald Wesson. *Treating Cocaine Dependence.* Center City, Minn.: Hazeldon Foundation, 1988.

Stanton, M. D. and S. B. Coleman. "The Participatory Aspects of Indirect Self-Destructive Behavior." In *The Many Faces of Suicide.* Ed. N. L. Farberow. New York: McGraw-Hill, 1980.

Stanton, M. D. and Judith Landau-Stanton. "Treating Suicidal Adolescents and their Families." In *Handbook of Adolescents and Family Therapy.* Eds. Marsha Pravder Mirkin and Stuart L. Koman. New York: Gardner Press, Inc., 1985.

Drugs on the Street Where You Live*

This chapter brings home the point that every neighborhood and community is affected in some way by problems with drugs/alcohol. No house, farm, tenement, high rise, or alley way is immune from drugs/alcohol. Many streets of inner cities are infected with crack cocaine and other streets are contaminated by heroin. Perhaps families on your own block have problems with alcohol, cocaine, hallucinogens, or marijuana. Perhaps people who live down the street are mixing the highly explosive chemicals to produce methamphetamine. Even in rural areas kids might be inhaling the fumes of gasoline to get high or growing marijuana in secluded areas. Every family is vulnerable to the problems associated with drugs/alcohol.

Chapter Goals

1. Define and appropriately apply the following terms: *(physical) dependence, withdrawal, (psychological) dependence, metabolism, absorption, routes of administration, excretion, set and setting, tolerance, cross-tolerance, synergism, antagonism, toxicity, effective, toxic and lethal dose, placebo effect, and half-life.*
2. Define and outline the various aspects of our behavioral definition of addiction.
3. Explain the difference between psychoactive and nonpsychoactive drugs.
4. Outline the basic classification system of drugs.
5. Classify the drugs in the narcotic analgesics (painkillers) category
   - identify some common street names for these drugs
   - outline some important historical developments
   - describe major effects, routes of administration, hazards to use, tolerance, stages of withdrawal, and withdrawal symptoms for each
   - identify the special problem of opiates and pregnancy

*Michael Meyers, M.D., wrote this chapter with my assistance.

6. For the central nervous system depressants (alcohol, barbiturates, and tranquilizers):

   a. Alcohol
   - describe the major effects on the brain, peripheral nerves, gastrointestinal tract, heart and blood vessels, and lungs
   - describe tolerance, stages of withdrawal, and withdrawal symptoms
   - describe alcohol-related illnesses and fetal alcohol syndrome
   - explain how Antabuse works and its role in alcohol recovery

   b. Barbiturates
   - outline the classification of barbiturates
   - identify some common street names for barbiturates
   - describe medical uses, routes of administration, major effects (especially on sleep and pregnancy), tolerance and withdrawal
   - identify signs and symptoms of overdose
   - describe the interaction of barbiturates and other drugs
   - describe estimates and patterns of barbiturate use
   - classify nonbarbiturates with barbiturate-like action
   - describe the major effects and adverse reactions of methaqualone, a nonbarbiturate with barbiturate-like action

   c. Tranquilizers
   - classify the major and minor tranquilizers
   - for the minor tranquilizers, describe routes of administration, medical uses, major effects, tolerance, dependence, and withdrawal
   - explain the addiction potential of minor tranquilizers in the addict/alcoholic population
   - outline the estimates of use

7. Classify the central nervous system (CNS) stimulants:
   - identify some common street names for stimulants
   - describe routes of administration, major effects, adverse effects, dependence, and withdrawal
   - explain the phenomenon of bootlegged amphetamines
   - outline the estimates of amphetamine use
   - for cocaine, clarify the kinds of cocaine used and their routes of administration; briefly describe the history of cocaine; describe cocaine's major effects, clinical syndromes, tolerance, and withdrawal

8. Classify the drugs in the hallucinogens category
   - identify some common street names for hallucinogens
   - describe routes of administration, brief history, major and adverse effects, tolerance, and dependence
   - outline estimates of hallucinogen use

9. Classify the drugs in the cannabis sativa category:
   - identify some common street names for these drugs
   - describe routes of administration, brief history, major effects, negative effects on the body, dependence, adverse reactions, impairment of maturational process, and marijuana's effect on driving
   - identify the major medical applications of marijuana
   - outline estimates of marijuana use and trends

10. Classify the various inhalants and their available forms
    - explain how the inhalants are used
    - outline the various signs and symptoms of inhalant use
    - describe reasons for use, major effects, tolerance and dependence, acute adverse reactions, long-term effects
    - outline estimates of inhalant use and trends

11. Explain the problems in classifying phencyclidine (PCP)
    - identify some common street names for PCP
    - describe routes of administration, major effects, adverse effects, accidents and violence with PCP use, tolerance, and dependence
    - outline estimates and patterns of PCP use

12. Explain the various uses of drugs in sports and athletics, to include discussion of caffeine, tobacco products, amphetamines, steroids, cocaine and other drugs.

Definition of Terms

It is imperative to understand the definitions and terminology used in the chemical dependency field before addressing the individual drugs of abuse.

The Basics

Physical dependence

The altered state that develops when a person cannot stop taking a certain drug without suffering from withdrawal is physical dependence.

Withdrawal

Withdrawal symptoms are physical symptoms resulting from stopping the use of a drug. These vary according to the specific drug, the amount used, and the length of time over which it has been used. Because the body has actually adapted metabolically to the presence of the drug, when it is withdrawn (or even tapered too rapidly), the reactions may vary from mild flulike symptoms for a person coming off of opiates to a severe, potentially life-threatening situation when withdrawing from alcohol or other sedative hypnotics.

Psychological dependence (formerly habituation)

A user with a profound emotional or mental need for the repetitive use of a drug or a class of drugs is psychologically dependent. The user becomes so preoccupied with taking the drug to achieve the optimal level of functioning or to maintain a sense of well-being, that it becomes extremely difficult to abstain. Psychological dependence is a subjective state that is almost impossible to quantify; therefore it is of limited usefulness in establishing a diagnosis of chemical dependency.

Metabolism

The metabolism is the process by which an active substance such as a drug is transformed into an inactive substance more easily excreted by the body. Four reactions are generally involved in drug metabolism: oxidation, reduction, hydrolysis, and conjugation. One or more of these reactions may occur in the metabolism of a given drug. The rate of metabolism affects the intensity and duration of the drug's action. Although most drug metabolism takes place in the liver, the body has other sites where specific enzymes metabolize a given drug.

Absorption

For a drug to act, it must reach the site in the body where its specific action occurs. The exceptions to this rule are the topically applied drugs. Absorption of the drug depends on its solubility. Thus, drugs in solution are more readily absorbed than those administered in solid form.

Routes of Administration

The route of administration is the method by which the drug/alcohol is ingested. Ingestion may be oral, through the skin, by injection, by smoking, or through other orifices (i.e., suppositories). The most rapid reaction occurs after inhalation while smoking a drug; injection is the next most rapid route. Oral administration and absorption through the skin are the slowest routes.

Excretion

Drugs are mostly excreted through the kidneys. This can either be an active process, with the drug transported through the glomular wall to the urine, or a passive filtration. Excretion also occurs through the feces, with the drug being transported through the bile to the intestine. Small amounts of the drug are also excreted from the lungs and by the sweat glands.

Set and Setting

Set refers to the user's state of mind at the time of use. Setting refers to the physical environment or environmental factors surrounding drug/alcohol use. (See chapter 2.)

Tolerance

Tolerance to a drug develops when the individual requires increasingly larger doses to achieve the desired optimal effect. In other words, users require larger doses to achieve the same high produced previously by a smaller dose of the same drug.

Cross-Tolerance

Cross-tolerance is a diminished or reduced response to the effect of a psychoactive drug. This response is due to prior use of other psychoactive drugs, usually in the same drug category.

Synergism

In a synergistic process, one chemical enhances or adds power to the effect of another. The combined effect of two or more drugs is greater therefore than the effect of each agent added together (i.e., 1 + 1 = 3 or more).

Antagonism

The opposite of synergism, antagonism occurs when the combined effect of two drugs is less than the sum of the drugs effects acting separately (i.e., 1 + 1 = less than 2). For example, the depressant effects of alcohol are counteracted by the stimulant effects of cocaine.

Toxicity

Toxicity is any drug-induced effect that is either temporarily or permanently deleterious to any of the body's organ systems. Toxicity includes relatively minor to serious side effects.

Doses

Median Effective Dose

The median effective dose is the required amount of a drug over a specific time period that achieves the desired therapeutic effect in one-half of the sample subjects.

Toxic Dose

A user can receive a toxic dose due to an inappropriate amount of a drug or inappropriate timing in taking the drug or use with other drugs/alcohol that produces toxicity. Any drug-induced effect that is either temporary or permanently deleterious to any organ system is a toxic dose. This includes relatively minor side effects as well as more serious manifestations.

Lethal Dose

A user can receive a lethal dose due to an inappropriate amount, timing, or use of a drug with other drugs/alcohol. A lethal dose produces death in one-half of the cases.

Placebo Effect

In Latin *placebo* means "I shall please." Therefore, the effect is related to the act of taking a drug rather than the chemical properties of the drug.

Half-Life

A drug's half-life is the time it takes for one-half of it to be metabolized or broken down to an inactive form, usually to one more easily excreted by the body.

Definitions of Addiction

Historically, there have been a wide range of definitions of addiction. For example:

> A chronic, progressive and potentially fatal disease. It is characterized by tolerance, psychological and physical dependence, pathogenic organ changes, or both, all of which are the direct or indirect consequence of the alcohol ingested.
>
> *(National Council on Alcoholism)*

> An illness characterized by preoccupation with alcohol and loss of control over its consequences, which usually leads to intoxication if drinking is begun; by chronicity; by progression; and by the tendency to relapse. Typically associated with physical disability and impaired emotional, occupational and/or social adjustments as a direct consequence.
>
> *(American Medical Association)*

As described throughout this textbook, the current definition of addiction used in the drug/alcohol field is the one developed by David Smith. An expanded version of that definition of addiction follows:

1. Compulsion and obsession
   a. the compulsive use of the chemical despite it no longer having the desired effect
   b. the fear of being without the substance
   c. the compulsion to substitute other drugs if that particular substance is unavailable
   d. thinking about the drug as a dominant theme or integral part of one's life
2. Loss of control or inability to stop
   a. the inability to limit the amount of use
   b. the inability to refuse the substance if available
   c. the inability to stop using the substance for three months or longer
   d. binge patterns of use
3. Continued use despite known adverse consequences
   a. medical complications
   b. psychiatric complications ranging from mood swings and anxiety to depression, panic disorders, and paranoid-schizophrenic reactions, or other psychoses
   c. social consequences, deterioration of family and other significant relationships, work status, and legal complications.

Classification of Drugs

A drug may be most simply defined as a nonfood substance intended to affect the structure and function of the body, most often to diagnose, cure, mitigate, treat, or prevent disease.

There are many different ways to classify drugs such as by chemical structure or specific effects on particular organ systems. Most frequently, drugs are classified as psychoactive and nonpsychoactive. **Nonpsychoactive drugs** are substances which in normal doses do not directly affect the brain, such as vitamins, antibiotics, topical skin preparations, and so forth. **Psychoactive drugs** affect brain functions, mood, and behavior and are subdivided primarily on the basis of physiological and psychological effects. The psychoactive drug classification includes:

1. Narcotic analgesics: painkillers and designer drugs (fentanyl)
2. Central nervous system depressants: sedative hypnotics, alcohol, tranquilizers, and barbiturates
3. Central nervous system stimulants: amphetamine, cocaine, nicotine, and caffeine
4. Hallucinogens
5. Cannabis sativa: marijuana and hashish
6. Inhalants: volatile solvents
7. Phencyclodine (PCP)

Narcotic Analgesics

The term *narcotic* comes from the Greek word *narkosis,* which means to numb or to be in a stupor. Analgesia means to relieve pain, without producing unconsciousness.

The narcotic analgesics (morphine, codeine, and heroin) are substances that come from the poppy plant (papaver somniferum). The narcotic analgesic category also includes synthetic and semisynthetic drugs that have morphinelike action such as meperidine (Demerol) methadone, Dilaudid, and Percodan.

The term *narcotic* was often incorrectly applied to a wide variety of drugs, including marijuana, alcohol, and cocaine. This was the result of a legal classification system rather than a medical classification. The emotional overtone of narcotic was frequently misapplied to those drugs considered dangerous by the legislators and policymakers.

The term *narcotic* has a variety of meanings: Its scientific meaning is drugs related botanically to the opium poppy and pharmacologically to opium, morphine, and heroin. Its medical meaning is synthetic drugs having morphinelike effects on a user. Its legal meaning is anything the legislature of a state wants to classify. Its public meaning is anything the general public wants to label as belonging to a particular drug category. In some states, this includes all drugs having morphinelike action. Elsewhere the term may also be applied to drugs chemically unrelated to narcotics (e.g., cocaine and marijuana).

Additional analgesics are nonnarcotic and satisfy other functions, such as reducing fever (antipyretic) and reducing inflammation (anti-inflammatory). Other nonnarcotic analgesics include aspirin, phenacetin, and Darvon. Nonsteroidal anti-inflammatory drugs (NSAID) include Naprosyn and Motrin.

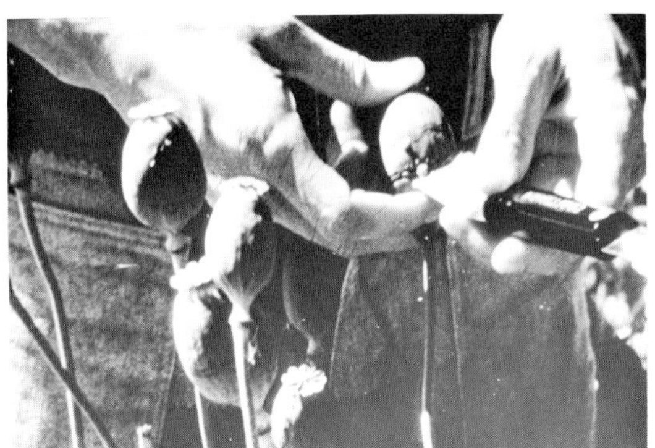

The poppy (*papaver somniferum*)

Narcotic Analgesics Classification			
Natural Opiods	*Synthetic*	*Semisynthetic*	*Antagonists*
Morphine	Demerol	Dilaudid	Narcan
Codeine	Meperidine	Percodan	Naloxone
Opium		Talwin	

Natural, semisynthetic, and synthetic narcotics

Narcotics of Natural Origin

Semisynthetic Narcotics

Morphine (illicit)

Heroin (illicit)

Morphine

Hydromorphone

Codeine

Oxycodone

Thebaine

Diprenorphine and Etorphine

Synthetic Narcotics

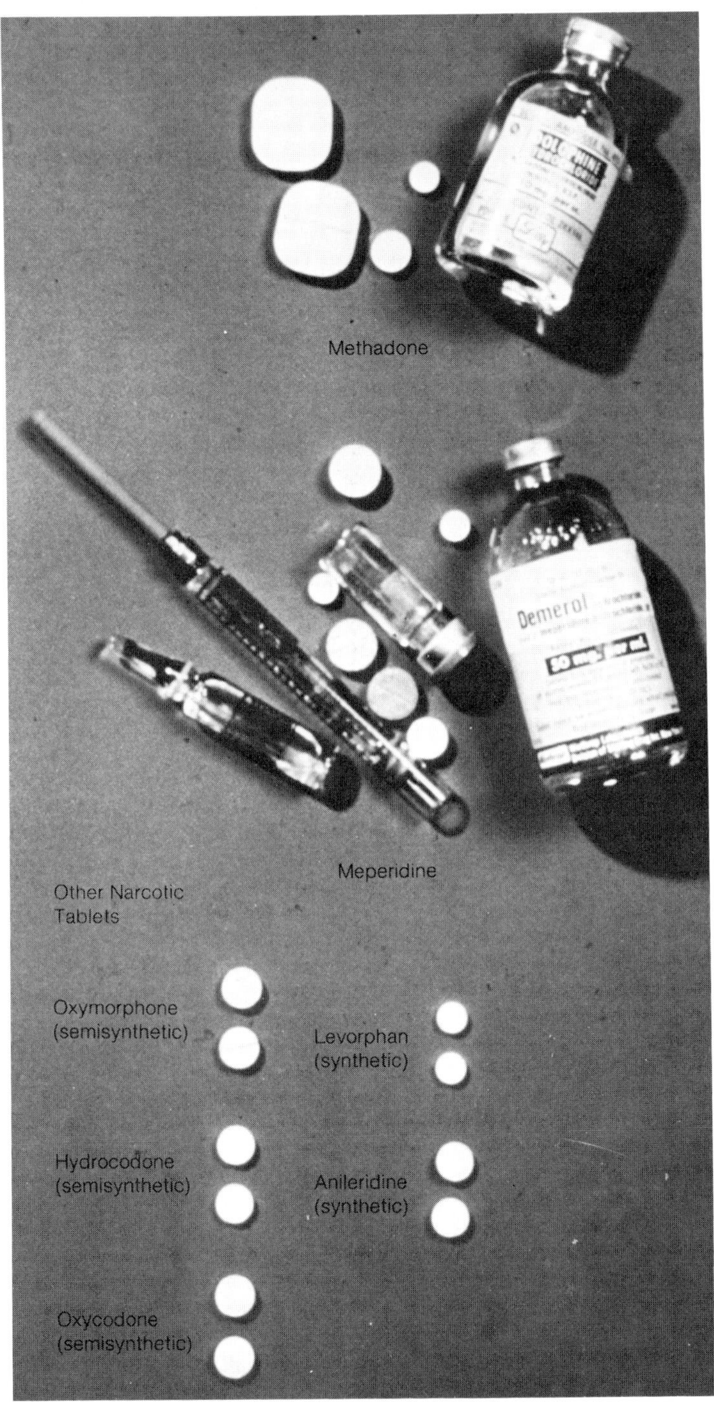

Street Names for Heroin

Big bag, big H, blanco, bomb, boy, brother, brown, brown rocks, brown sugar, caballo, cat, chich, Chinese red, Chinese white, chiva, crap, dogie, doojee, dope, duji, dust, eighth, flea powder, garbage, good stuff, H, hard stuff, harry, H-caps, henry, him, horse, hombre, jones, joy powder, junk, Mexican mud, mojo, muzzle, pack, poison, powder, pure, red chicken, red rock, rock, scag, schmeck, smack, stuff, tecata, thing, white boy, white junk, white stuff

Brief History of the Narcotic Analgesics

The opiates have been used for medicinal purposes and pleasure since prehistoric times. Opium eating has been known in Asia for thousands of years.

1806: Friedrich Wilhelm Adam Serturner, a German chemist, isolated morphine from opium.
1832: Codeine was isolated.
1845: Alexander Wood invented the hypodermic syringe.
1861–65: Approximately 45,000 Civil War soldiers were addicted to morphine.
1874: Alder Wright, a London chemist, first synthesized heroin from morphine.
1875: A San Francisco ordinance prohibited the smoking of opium in public houses or opium dens.
1906: Pure Food and Drug Act required all medicines containing opiates and certain other drugs to list them on the labels.
1914: Harrison Narcotics Act required licensure of drug manufacturers, importers, pharmacists, and physicians marketing or prescribing narcotics. Patent medicine manufacturers were exempt from the act providing that their products did not contain more than two grains of opium, or one-eighth grain heroin per ounce.
1942–43: During World War II, a German chemist, Aschenbrenner, synthesized methadone and named it after Adolph Hitler, Dolophine.
1970s: Most addicted soldiers returning from Vietnam withdrew from heroin on the trip back to the United States or shortly thereafter. The anticipated need for heroin treatment was not realized.

1978: Scientists discovered endorphines; these proteins play an important role in the body's pain suppression system.

Chemists first isolated morphine in the early nineteenth century. During the Civil War, doctors widely used morphine in injectable form. Addiction to morphine was very common at that time resulting in a significant addict population. Fortunately, society attached no stigma to the soldiers' addiction to morphine; it was commonly referred to as "soldiers' disease." Most soldiers withdrew from morphine on their own or under medical supervision, and there was minimal social impact.

Around the 1870s manufacturers added tincture of opium to many patent medicines sold over the counter for treatment of diarrhea in infants and children. When first introduced at the end of the nineteenth century, heroin was thought to cure opium dependence and morphinism.

Estimates of Addiction

Current estimates of addiction to narcotic analgesics range from 400,000 to 750,000 addicts in this country alone (NIDA 1989).

Routes of Administration

Users may inject narcotics either intravenously, subcutaneously (under the surface of the skin—known as skin popping) or deep within the muscle. They can also snort narcotics intranasally, smoke it affecting the lungs, or absorb it into their bodies via the mucous membrane of the mouth or rectum (using suppositories).

The route of administration determines how quickly the drug affects the brain: A drug that is smoked reaches the brain in 5 seconds. A drug injected intravenously reaches the brain 14 seconds later. A drug taken by mouth doesn't hit the brain until 30 to 45 minutes later.

The intensity of the drug effect, and the complications are also influenced by the route of administration. Intravenous use can lead to infection, local abscesses, disseminated infections (HIV, hepatitis B, pulmonary emboli) and local damage to the lungs and the lining of the nose.

Major Effects of Narcotic Analgesics

1. Pain relief (analgesia)
2. Euphoria (sense of well-being)
3. Cough suppressant (antitussive)
4. Respiratory depression
5. Sedation or drowsiness
6. Constriction of the pupils (pinpoint pupils)

7. Nausea and vomiting
8. Itching
9. Decrease in gastrointestinal activity (constipation)

Hazards

Even while using low to moderate doses, users face many hazards related to the circumstances of illicit use such as drug impurities, infection, and the consequences of the addict lifestyle. By using dirty and shared needles they contract infections (AIDS, hepatitis, and tetanus) and all other blood-borne infections (septicemia) leading to endocarditis, liver, brain, and skin abscesses.

Other hazards include allergic (anaphylactic) reactions to the narcotic or substances used to cut or dilute the narcotic. Overdosing causes cardiac arrest, lung reaction, and the narcotic's direct actions on the brain leading to coma, shock, respiratory arrest, and death.

Tolerance

Tolerance develops to a rapid degree with the effects of analgesia, respiratory depression, sedation, and feelings of euphoria. In effect, users must take more and more of the narcotic to get the original effect.

The rate of tolerance depends on the pattern of use, route of administration, and physical aspects of each individual. Even though some addicts build to phenomenally high doses, inevitably there is always a final dose that can produce death from respiratory depression.

Tolerance often returns to normal after withdrawal. Many narcotic addicts have fatally overdosed by returning to their normal and customary doses after detoxification.

Cross-tolerance exists between even chemically dissimilar opiods.

Withdrawal

Withdrawal symptoms and their severity depend on the specifics of the drug being used. With low doses of intermittent narcotic use, withdrawal symptoms may be negligible or perhaps resemble mild flulike symptoms. Anyone who has ever been seasick can identify with these feelings. Withdrawal symptoms include

- appetite suppression
- nausea and vomiting
- dilated pupils
- gooseflesh, or increased pylomotor activity, skin resembles a plucked turkey, hence the expression *going cold turkey*

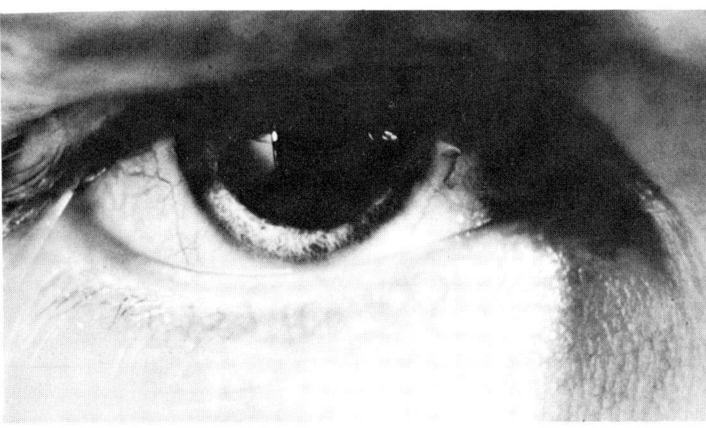

Dilated pupils

- restlessness
- intestinal spasms
- abdominal pain
- muscle spasms
- kicking movements, hence the expession *kicking the habit*
- occasional diarrhea
- increased heart rate and blood pressure
- chills alternating with flushing and sweating
- irritability
- insomnia
- violent yawning
- severe sneezing and runny nose (rhinorhea)
- crying and tearing, and nasal inflammation
- depressive mood, and tremor

The peak intensity of withdrawal occurs at forty-eight to seventy-two hours (two to three days) for heroin, but for methadone the peak withdrawal is from five to seven days.

Despite these symptoms, the management of withdrawal from opiates is far less dangerous than the management of alcohol withdrawal. The effects of the withdrawal are not life threatening but may need medical attention. The medical conditions worthy of attention may be excessive weight loss, dehydration, body chemistry disturbances, and stress on the cardiovascular system. Without treatment, symptoms usually disappear in seven to ten days for heroin, but may last two to three weeks for methadone.

Opiates and Pregnancy

Chronic use of opiates, especially heroin, results in a variety of obstetrical compromises. Because withdrawal in an addicted mother may lead to spontaneous miscarriage, the consensus of the medical community to date is to stabilize the heroin-addicted mother on methadone during the pregnancy. However, these babies tend to be born prematurely with a lower birth weight. Born addicted, these babies may display withdrawal symptoms and have significant neonatal difficulties, with more recent evidence indicating lifelong negative effects on psychomotor development.

Central Nervous System Depressants

The Central Nervous System (CNS) depressant category commonly refers to drugs that are sedative hypnotics. The basic sedative-hypnotic category includes alcohol, tranquilizers, and barbiturates.

Alcohol

Alcohol acts as a depressant to the central nervous system. Once absorbed, it is distributed throughout the body, enters the brain easily, and is uniformly found in all body fluids. In pregnant women alcohol crosses the placental barrier into the fetus.

A blood alcohol level of 0.05 percent or higher produces some driving impairment. Remember that in most states anyone driving with a 0.10 percent blood alcohol level is driving under the influence. Alcohol is metabolized at a relatively constant rate which depends primarily on the body weight of the drinker. A 150-pound man metabolizes approximately three-quarters to an ounce of alcohol in an hour.

Estimates of Alcoholism

Other than tobacco products containing nicotine, beverage alcohol (ethanol) is the most widely used psychoactive drug known to humanity. Currently there are an estimated 12 million alcoholics in the United States, and 10 million problem drinkers or persons for whom alcohol somehow interferes with normal social functioning (NIDA 1989).

Major Effects

The range of physical reactions to varying doses of alcohol is vast. The effects depend on the amount consumed, the circumstances of consumption (set and setting), body size, and the experience of the drinker. Someone unaccustomed to alcohol use is more likely to show signs of impairment than a conditioned drinker who has learned to compensate for impaired behavior.

One or two alcoholic drinks may induce talkativeness in one individual along with slight flushing and reduce the drinker's inhibitions so he or she appears more expansive and more animated, perhaps grandiose at times. The same amount of alcohol in another individual may induce drowsiness and lethargy.

Alcohol in even moderate doses generally reduces one's performance in tasks that require physical coordination or mental agility, such as driving a car. Larger doses can alter perception and cause staggering, blurred vision, and the manifestations of drunkenness. Yet, one person may become emotional or amorous, while another becomes aggressive and hostile. Extremely high doses—so typical during binges—can knock out a drinker, even kill the person, if the central nervous system is depressed to the point that body functions, such as breathing, cease altogether.

Alcohol is a toxic drug with irritating as well as sedative properties. It can have a negative effect on every tissue in the human body, as shown in the following section:

Alcohol is a CNS depressant.

1. Brain
   a. Amnesia—most commonly called blackouts—causes partial, or sometimes temporary, loss of memory often following binge patterns of alcohol use. Blackouts can occur even after low-dose alcohol consumption, or first-time alcohol consumption by someone who has a history of alcoholism in the family. Blackouts may be a significant early indicator of a diagnosis of alcoholism.
   b. Permanent loss of memory and mental confusion as in Wernicke-Korsakoff's syndrome.
   c. Damage to the cerebellum affecting balance and coordination.

2. Peripheral nerves
   a. Usually in the legs and sometimes other extremities, alcoholics experience pain, loss of sensation, and general weakness.
   b. Optic nerves are damaged causing blurred or dim vision.

3. Gastrointestinal tract
   a. Gastritis and esophagitis, irritation of the lining of the esophagus and stomach causing mild to severe pain. May aggravate an ulcer.
   b. Peptic ulcer at the outlet of the stomach (duodenal).
   c. Fatty liver, hepatitis, or cirrhosis (a scarring of the liver that destroys the tissue and is a leading cause of death from alcohol).
   d. Pancreatitis, in which muscle spasms block the duct from the pancreas, causes the acidic

These alcoholic beverages contain equal amounts of alcohol.

juices to back up and start digesting the pancreas. This is often very painful and can also cause death.

4. Heart and blood vessels
   a. Heart muscle becomes weaker, and heart expands because it is working harder. Alcohol complicates problems with heart disease.
   b. Peripheral blood vessels are dilated by alcohol. Initially this causes a sensation of warmth, followed by serious heat loss in the cold. The old habit of drinking alcohol to fend off the cold actually makes the person more susceptible to the cold.
   c. High blood pressure is often associated with alcoholism, but the relationship is not clearly established.

5. Lungs
   a. Emphysema occurs most frequently in the alcoholic who also smokes. Alcohol seems to have a direct toxic effect on the cells lining the alveoli, or small air sacs in the lungs, as the alcohol is excreted into the air.

Sobering Up

Contrary to much public opinion, steam baths, vigorous exercise, black coffee, and other sobering up agents have no

WINGTIPS **by Michael Goodman**

Alcoholic blackouts

effect on the rate at which alcohol is metabolized. Time is the only thing that works.

Tolerance

Tolerance to most of the immediate effects of alcohol develops with frequent use. Regular heavy drinkers may be able to consume two to three times as much alcohol as novice drinkers. Heavy drinkers have to drink more and more to achieve the desired effect.

Withdrawal Symptoms

Stage One Withdrawal Symptoms Withdrawal from alcohol usually begins six to twelve hours after the last drink, and may even begin in the presence of significant blood alcohol levels. Table 3.1 lists the stage one withdrawal symptoms. These symptoms, in varying degrees, may last anywhere from three to five days and are relieved by drinking more alcohol.

Stage Two Withdrawal Symptoms The onset of stage two withdrawal symptoms is usually within twenty-four hours after the last drink, but may occur as long as three days later.

TABLE 3.1
Stage One Alcohol Withdrawal Symptoms

1. psychomotor agitation
2. anxiety
3. insomnia
4. appetite supression
5. gastrointestinal disturbances
6. elevated heart rate, blood pressure, sweating, and tremors

Illustration of delirium tremens as a result of withdrawal from acute alcoholism

The Bettman Archive.

Stage two consists of the symptoms in stage one, plus hallucinations. These may be visual, auditory, tactile, olfactory (smell), or mixed. Although the visual hallucinations usually predominate, olfactory hallucinations are a particularly more ominous sign and may be accompanied by seizures. The delirium tremens—disorientation to person, place, or time—also can be life threatening: this is a true medical emergency with a 15 percent mortality rate if untreated.

Related Illnesses

Alcoholics have twice the chance of experiencing premature deaths as nonalcoholic persons. Liver disease of varying types is one of the most prominent manifestations of alcoholism. Among young males twenty to forty years of age, liver cirrhosis was the third fastest growing cause of death, after heart disease and lung cancer. Alcoholics also show higher than normal rates of peptic ulcers, pneumonia, cancer of the upper digestive and respiratory tracts, heart and artery disease, tuberculosis, and suicide.

Many heavy drinkers also suffer vitamin deficiencies, gastritis, sexual impotence, and infections. The more serious alcohol-related neurological disorders include peripheral neuritis (loss of sensation), Korsakoff's psychosis (loss of memory), and Wernicke's encephalopathy (mental confusion).

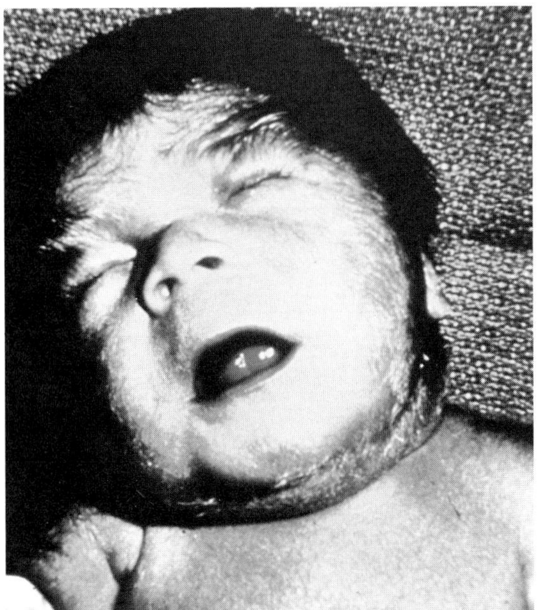

Fetal alcohol syndrome baby

Fetal Alcohol Syndrome

Alcohol use and abuse by pregnant women is the third leading cause of birth defects, exceeded only by Down's syndrome and spinabifida. The four basic abnormalities characteristic of fetal alcohol syndrome are

1. Distorted facial features. A FAS baby has short fissures in the eyelids, a small or underdeveloped upper lip with thinned vermilion, and a diminished philtrum, the line running between the upper lip and nose.
2. Prenatal onset growth deficiency. FAS babies are usually two standard deviations below normal in weight and height; they exhibit little or no indication of growth spurts to catch up after birth.
3. Reduced central nervous system performance. As a result, FAS babies have mild to moderate mental retardation, microcephaly or disproportionately small heads, poor coordination, irritability in infancy, and hyperactivity in childhood.
4. Increased frequency of major abnormalities. Such disorders range from gross cardiovascular abnormalities and congenital heart disease to abnormal and malformed limbs.

Alcohol use during the first trimester is often responsible for still births. Research further supports the position that even small doses of alcohol affect the development of the fetus, especially in the first trimester. The only safe dose of alcohol during pregnancy is no alcohol at all.

Antabuse

Some alcoholics have extreme difficulty in abstaining from alcohol. Usually, they choose Antabuse when other methods to stop drinking have failed. At early stages of recovery alcoholics may use Antabuse as a deterrent to drinking alcohol, but it must not be viewed as the only modality (see chapter 10).

How does it work? Alcohol is metabolized by a liver enzyme (aldehyde dehydrogenose) to form acetaldehyde. Normally acetaldehyde is rapidly metabolized by another enzyme which breaks it into inert substances, eventually becoming carbon dioxide and water. Antabuse (disulfiram) interferes with the enzyme that breaks down acetaldehyde. A person taking Antabuse and drinking alcohol would have a sharp increase in acetaldehyde, resulting in extreme feelings of discomfort that include nausea and vomiting, flushing, sweating, palpitations, increased heart rate, breathing difficulty, and anxiety. Blood pressure may first rise and then fall making the person appear to be in shock. Feelings of drowsiness may occur later. People rarely die from an alcohol-Antabuse reaction, but they feel so sick they think they will die. Nevertheless, some people continue to drink alcohol while on Antabuse.

Barbiturates

Barbiturates also belong to the sedative-hypnotic class of drugs and are widely prescribed to decrease central nervous system activity (i.e., induce sleep, relax the nervous system). Barbiturates and barbituratelike drugs seem to affect the cortex of the brain or those areas related to sleep more than other sedative hypnotics.

Medical Uses

In low doses of twenty-five to fifty milligrams the short or intermediate-acting compounds such as amobarbital (Amytal), pentobarbital (Nembutal), secobarbital (Seconal), and butabarbital (Butisol) treat or prevent acute convulsions associated with tetanus, control of epilepsy, overdose of stimulants such as strychnine, nicotine, or cocaine, and withdrawal symptoms associated with alcoholism and other sedative drug dependence.

Classification of Barbiturates and Street Names

Short acting

Amobarbital (Amytal)—known as blues, blue angels, bluebirds, blue devils, blue bullets
Pentobarbital (Nembutal)—known as yellows, yellow jackets, yellow bullets, nembies
Butabarbital (Butisol)

Intermediate acting

Phenobarbital (Luminal, Eskabarb)—known as phennies
Secobarbital (Seconal)—known as reds, pinks, red birds, red bullets, red dolls, seccies, F–40s

Long acting

Pento-secobarbital (Tuinal)—known as trees, tootsies, double trouble, gorilla pills, rainbows

For years doctors have prescribed barbiturates in the treatment of asthma, premenstrual tension, motion sickness, nausea and vomiting, peptic ulcer and other gastrointestinal disturbances, hyperthyroidism, high blood pressure, and other cardiovascular diseases. Now doctors can prescribe many newer drugs that have fewer side effects and less potential for abuse.

Estimates of Use and Addiction

After minor tranquilizers, barbiturates are prescribed more than any other psychoactive drug in the United States. Most individuals are introduced to barbiturates by physicians, who prescribe them as mild tranquilizers or sleeping pills.

Many individuals find barbiturates make coping with life easier. As tolerance to the tranquilizing and sedating effects set in, individuals increase their doses, often without their physicians' knowledge. Teenagers and young adults take enough barbiturates orally to produce highs the same way as alcohol might be taken. The sources of the supply for these young people are often the black market, the family medicine cabinet, and sometimes through manipulation of otherwise legitimate prescriptions.

Illicit use of barbiturates has been on the decline for the past several years in North America. Because they are still prescribed so often for a variety of medical conditions, however, their pharmaceutical use remains widespread, as well as their abuse by those who have obtained legitimate prescriptions.

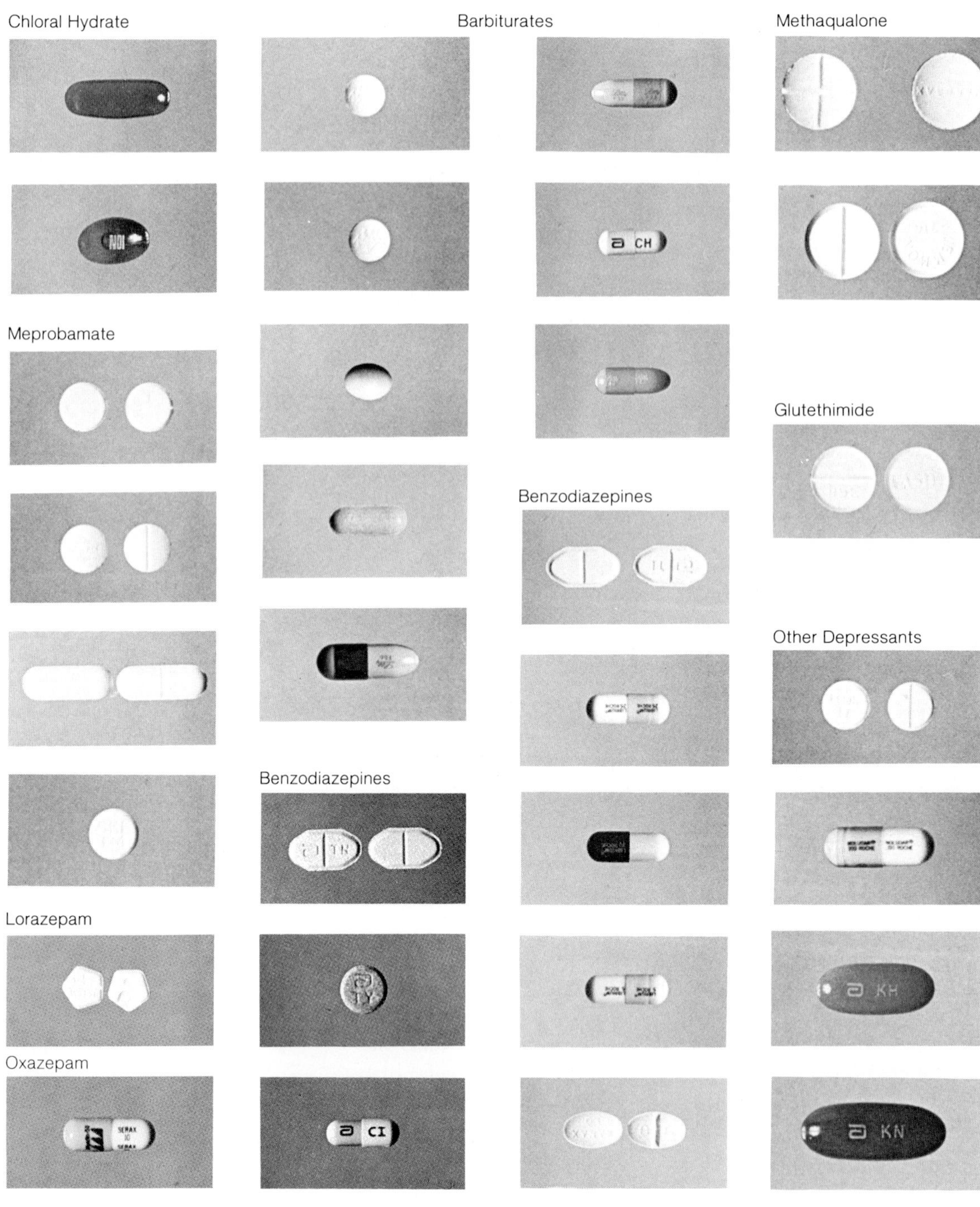

Barbiturates, methaqualone, and other CNS depressants

Routes of Administration

Usually taken orally, barbiturates are readily absorbed by the stomach and small intestine. Absorption into the bloodstream can be most rapid, especially on an empty stomach. Most barbiturates are white powders, odorless but with a slightly bitter taste. Most often packed in capsules and tablets of varying colors, they are also available as liquids, injectable solutions, and suppositories.

Major Effects

Short-term effects of barbiturates are very similar to those of alcohol. At low doses barbiturates tend to induce relaxation, a sense of well-being, and drowsiness. At higher doses the drug reduces the individual's ability to react quickly and to perform skilled precise tasks. Often there is a feeling of sedation and the individual may alternate between feelings of euphoria on the one hand, and hostility and aggressivenesss on the other. This is very similar to the high-dose reactions under the influence of alcohol.

At still higher doses, the symptoms may be similar to those of drunkenness, with confusion and difficulty communicating. The person may fall into a stupor or sleep. If the dose is high enough, it may impair the respiratory function so severely that the individual stops breathing and dies.

Barbiturates and Sleep Barbiturates are generally considered by the public as sleep medication. However, long-term barbiturate use can interfere with the rapid eye movement (REM) phase of sleep. REM sleep is associated with an essential feature of healthy sleep, that is dreaming. Normal functioning is further disturbed with the disruption of REM sleep. When the individual stops taking barbiturates, there is often a rebound effect and more REM sleep occurs. But the dreaming is more intense and frequently turns into a nightmare. The user interprets this as poor sleeping and again takes sleeping pills often escalating the dose and a vicious cycle is put into play.

Barbiturates and Pregnancy Barbiturates should never be taken during pregnancy, unless advised by a physician, because they could cause birth defects. Also the baby may be born addicted to barbiturates and have potentially dangerous withdrawal symptoms.

Tolerance

Barbiturates used repeatedly over a long period can induce tolerance and physical and psychological dependence. Tolerance to the euphoric effects of the drug develops quickly in many users, so larger and larger amounts of the drug must be taken to achieve the same high.

TABLE 3.2
Barbiturate Withdrawal

The withdrawal symptoms may include	From the third to seventh day of withdrawal, the user may experience
1. physical weakness	1. delirium
2. dizziness	2. delusions
3. anxiety	3. hallucinations
4. tremors	
5. sleeplessness	
6. nausea	
7. abdominal cramps and vomiting	

The lethal dose is usually only ten to fifteen times the therapeutic dose, so the margin of safety is low. As tolerance develops, the difference between the amount needed to get high may be only one or two pills away from an overdose; such an amount is also potentially lethal in combination with alcohol use.

Table 3.2 lists the withdrawal symptoms of barbiturates; these and other symptoms may last for days or even months. Anyone greatly addicted to barbiturates also runs a risk of having a grand mal seizure. Grand mal seizures can occur up to two weeks after the barbiturates are withdrawn and can be fatal. This is why it is essential that barbiturate addicts withdraw under a doctor's supervision, preferably in a medical facility.

Overdose Signs and Symptoms

1. Mood alteration ranges from depression to euphoria.
2. Sedation or drowsiness proceeds to stupor and coma with increasing doses. Paradoxical excitement rather than drowsiness may occur, especially in the young or the old.
3. Confusion and disorientation.
4. Slurred speech (dysarthria).
5. Staggering gait (ataxia) indicates motor coordination is impaired.
6. Nystagmus or involuntary rapid eye movement from side to side.
7. Pupils constrict a little at first, later as the level of unconsciousness deepens they dilate.
8. Respiratory depression occurs decreasing the oxygen supply to the brain; this can cause death.

Nonbarbiturates with Barbituratelike Action

- Chloral hydrate (Noctec)—known as Mickey Finn, or knock out drops when used with alcohol
- Methaqualone (Quaalude, Sopor)
- Flurazepam (Dalmane)
- Glutethimide (Doriden)—known as goofers
- Ethchlorvynol (Placidyl)
- Methyprylon (Noludar)
- Paraldehyde

Barbiturates Used with Other Drugs

Barbiturates are often used in conjunction with stimulants. Amphetamine users often use barbiturates to come down after a prolonged period of amphetamine use. Barbiturates are also used by heroin addicts when their drug of choice is not available.

Barbiturates plus other central nervous system depressants can have a synergistic effect when taken together (i.e., potentiate each other). People who drink alcohol and use barbiturates run the risk of accidental overdose. Overdoses on barbiturates plus alcohol are more common than on barbiturates alone.

Methaqualone

Methaqualone was introduced to the American medical market in the mid-1960s for the treatment of insomnia and anxiety. It was originally believed to have none of the abuse potential of short-acting barbiturates. It was alleged to be a safe, nonaddictive sedative; however, this drug has an extremely high abuse potential.

The popularity of methaqualone grew swiftly given its enthusiastic medical use and street use. Among its most enthusiastic users were college students in the 1970s. Since then, methaqualone has spread to not only high school and college campuses throughout the United States but also adult populations. Methaqualone use has also become popular among methadone maintenance patients because of the additive high the drug produces in combination with methadone.

Street Names of Methaqualone

Sopors, ludes, love drug, and others.

Estimates of Use and Addiction

Principally younger age groups use this illicit drug, with heaviest concentration of use between high school and the mid-thirties. The cost of illicit methaqualone ranges from four to eight dollars per tablet.

Route of Administration

Methaqualone is usually taken orally in pill form. Since 1984, pharmaceutical companies can no longer legally produce methaqualone in the United States. The drug is most often found on the street in bootlegged forms that look real but may or may not contain actual methaqualone.

Major Effects

Following its ingestion, methaqualone is readily absorbed from the gastrointestinal tract. Once transported into the blood plasma, it is distributed in body fat, the liver, and brain tissue.

Relatively low doses (75 milligrams four times a day) produce sedation; larger doses of 150 to 300 milligrams lead to sleep. Those who use the drug to get high often take far larger doses, sometimes 600–900 milligrams and much more if they have been using the drug steadily enough to develop a tolerance.

Users describe the sensation produced by methaqualone as "a peaceful calm, a rush, a drunk." Some describe it as a love drug due to methaqualone's alcohol-like symptoms (i.e., loss of motor and muscle control, loss of inhibitions, etc.), although just as with alcohol, actual sexual performance is reduced.

Adverse Reactions

Basically, intoxication with methaqualone is similar to intoxication with barbiturates or alcohol and subjects the individual to similar risks: death by overdose and accidents due to confusion and impaired motor coordination.

Methaqualone has induced headaches, hangovers, fatigue, dizziness, drowsiness, torpor (extreme sluggishness, apathy, dullness), menstrual disturbances, dry mouth, nosebleeds, diarrhea, skin eruptions, lack of appetite, numbness, and pain in the extremities. Researchers have found a coma occurs following 2.4 grams of Quaalude. Eight to twenty grams have produced severe toxicity and death.

Methaqualone overdoses are less often associated with cardiac and respiratory depression than are overdoses of the oral barbiturates. However, shock and respiratory arrests may occasionally occur. Methaqualone overdose can also result in delirium, restlessness, hypertonia (excessive tension), and muscle spasms leading to convulsions.

Tolerance and Withdrawal

As with barbiturates, tolerance to the intoxicating effects of methaqualone develops more rapidly than does tolerance to the lethal dose. Withdrawal from methaqualone dependence carries approximately the same risks as withdrawal from the short-acting barbiturates and can be quite severe for a large addiction.

Classification of Major Tranquilizers (Antipsychotic Agents)

Phenotiazines	Butyrophenones	Thioxanthenes	Other
• Thorazine (chlorpromazine) • Mellaril (thioridazine) • Stelazine (trifluoperazine) • Compazine (prochlorperazine) • Trilafon (perphenzaine) • Prolixin (fluphenazine)	• Haldol (haloperidol)	• Navane (thiothixene) • Taractan (chlorprothixene)	• Serpasil (reserpine) • Moban (molindone hydrochloride) • Loxitane

Japanese researchers have provided a good deal of the information about methaqualone's addiction potential. In Japan, where this drug was once available over the counter, it was widely abused by young people (Tamura 1989).

During 1963 to 1966 a survey of drug addicts in Japan found 176 out of 411 (41.8 percent) were addicted to methaqualone. Withdrawal convulsions occurred in 7 percent of methaqualone addicts and 9 percent developed delirium tremens symptoms. Subsequent studies in England and in the United States have documented cases of physical dependence as manifested by a withdrawal syndrome. The symptoms include insomnia, abdominal cramps, headaches, anorexia, and nightmares.

Research conducted in Philadelphia and at the Haight-Ashbury Clinic in San Francisco has also documented the high abuse potential and dependence producing properties of methaqualone, as well as its cross-tolerance with the short-acting barbiturates.

Tranquilizers

Minor tranquilizers are those drugs that act primarily as antianxiety agents. They reduce anxiety and tension. Major tranquilizers are those drugs used over the long term in the treatment of mental illnesses such as schizophrenia. They are antipsychotic agents.

Major Tranquilizers

All of the antipsychotic drugs can produce Parkinsonlike signs and symptoms with tremor, rigidity, and shuffling gait. To counteract these side effects, one of the following anti-Parkinsonism drugs is often prescribed along with the antipsychotic drug: Artane, Cogentin, Kemadrin, Benadryl.

Classification of Minor Tranquilizers (Antianxiety Agents)

Benzodiazepines	Meprobamate	Sedating Antihistamines
• Valium (diazepam) • Librium (chlordiazepoxide) • Serax (oxazepam) • Tranxene (chlorazepate) • Ativan (lorazepam) • Xanax (alprazolam) • Halcion (triazolam)	• Equanil • Miltown	• Atarax, Vistaril (hydroxyzine) • Benadryl (diphenhydramine) • Sleep-Eze, Sominex, Nytol

Because the major tranquilizers do not produce pleasant psychological effects, they are rarely used nonmedically and have no illicit attraction. The focus of this section is on the minor tranquilizers that do have an abuse and dependence potential.

Minor Tranquilizers

Medical Uses

Doctors prescribe the minor tranquilizers mainly for treatment of tension, insomnia, behavioral excitement, and anxiety. Some treat convulsive disorders, symptoms of barbiturate-alcohol dependence, and the anxiety and panic that sometimes results from the use of hallucinogenic drugs. Although fairly high doses are necessary, some minor tranquilizers are also effective muscle relaxants (e.g., Valium may be used in injectable form for this purpose).

Estimates of Use

Most Americans are introduced to minor tranquilizers by physicians and most use them according to prescription, but there are large numbers who do not stay within the physician's guidelines. Recent statistics show that the prescribing of tranquilizers is on a downward trend, and some authorities believe this trend may continue.

Routes of Administration

Most minor tranquilizers are usually taken orally as tablets, capsules, or liquids. Occasionally they are injected for both medical and nonmedical purposes.

Major Effects

With normal therapeutic doses, individuals usually feel well, relaxed, and may lose some of their inhibitions. They feel a lessening of anxiety, tension, and agitation.

As the dosage is increased, patients usually feel more sedated and may have a sensation of floating. Many individuals at this dosage level experience some depression of nervous and muscular activity, mental confusion, and physical unsteadiness. High doses may produce

- drowsiness
- loss of muscle coordination
- lethargy
- disorientation and confusion
- low blood pressure
- memory impairment
- rage reactions
- moodiness and personality alterations
- symptoms resembling drunkenness

Obviously, the ability to drive a car under high-dose levels is also impaired. Other side effects may include skin rashes, nausea, loss of sex drive, or menstrual and ovulatory irregularities.

The margin of safety of minor tranquilizers is so wide that death rarely results from use of these drugs alone, with the lethal dose being 100 or more times the effective dose. Where death has occurred, it has often been due to an interaction between the tranquilizer and other drugs such as alcohol.

Tolerance

With regular use, tolerance can develop to most of the effects of these sedatives. This means that the user has to take increased doses to get the desired effect.

Dependence and Withdrawal

Even though physical dependence and withdrawal can occur with most tranquilizers, these effects are infrequent in relation to the large number of people who take these drugs. On a therapeutic dosage level, addiction may still occur. Escalation of the amount and frequency of the dose without a doctor's orders increases the chance of physical dependence.

Withdrawal from a large habit may involve anxiety states, apprehension, tremors, insomnia, rapid pulse, fever, loss of appetite, nausea, vomiting, stomach cramps, sweating, fainting, and other symptoms. Withdrawal from high-dose tranquilizer dependence is often done gradually as the individual is tapered off of the medication. A quick withdrawal can produce life-threatening withdrawal symptoms.

Addiction Potential with Addicts/Alcoholics

Physicians should not prescribe minor tranquilizers for patients who are addiction prone. Pharmaceutical manufacturers warn physicians through medical journal ads and the *Physicians' Desk Reference* that tranquilizers are capable of abuse and dependence especially when prescribed to addiction-prone individuals. Many patients deny or are unaware of their problems with drugs and/or alcohol, however, and fail to report this to their physicians. A thorough assessment for drug/alcohol problems is necessary before prescribing minor tranquilizers. "Nonmedical use of benzodiazepines in the general population is rare and of little or no consequence; on the other hand, benzodiazepines are used with some frequency among populations with histories of drug abuse" (Woods et al. 1988).

Central Nervous System Stimulants

Amphetamines are central nervous system stimulants that—until recent years—have been widely prescribed by physicians for conditions such as: obesity, depression, and narcolepsy (uncontrolled fits of sleep). For certain kinds of hyperactive behavior in children, Ritalin is most commonly prescribed.

Doctors also prescribed amphetamines for Parkinson's disease, epilepsy, nausea during pregnancy, bed-wetting, asthma, sedative overdoses, and hypotensive states associated with anesthesia. Because amphetamines relieve sleepiness and fatigue, they are widely used nonmedically by students cramming for exams, long-distance truck drivers, nightshift workers, and individuals seeking general stimulation.

In the mid-1960s, a phenomenon new to North America emerged: intravenous use of massive doses of amphetamines (usually methamphetamines) by chronic abusers, or speed freaks. This abuse pattern had been common in Japan and some parts of Europe following World War II, when stockpiles of amphetamines used by the military were diverted to more general use.

As a result of their abuse potential, physicians have sharply restricted their use of amphetamines. Now, they prescribe amphetamines primarily for narcolepsy, hyperkinetic syndrome in children, certain mental conditions, and usually for short-term weight control. David Smith and Donald Wesson (1973) note that in 1972 when the U.S. government put federal control over stimulants in the same category as narcotic control, legitimate production of stimulants was reduced by 80 percent.

Amphetamines

Street Names of Amphetamines

A, AMT, bam, beans, bennies, black beauties, black mollies, brain ticklers, brownies, bumblebees, cartwheels, chalk, chicken powder, crank, Christmas trees, crossroads, cross tops, crystal, dexies, diet pills, dolls, double cross, eye openers, fives, footballs, forwards, hearts, jam, jellybeans, leapers, lid poppers, lightning, meth, pep pills, purple hearts, rippers, sparkle plenties, sparklers, speed, splash, sweets, tens, thrusters, truck drivers, turnabouts, uppers, uppie, ups, wake-ups, water, white crosses.

Estimates of Use

The Domestic Council Drug Abuse Task Force estimates that close to 500,000 American adults are now using stimulant drugs (primarily amphetamines regularly and nonmedically. A new and emerging population of methamphetamine users is developing in the adolescent and young adults (fifteen to thirty years of age) (NIDA 1989).

Routes of Administration

Amphetamines are available in a variety of forms; tablets and capsules are the most common. Amphetamines are usually taken orally or injected intravenously.

Methamphetamine (speed) is usually in powder or crystal form and is illicitly made. The new solid form of methamphetamine with the street name, ice, was first cooked up in Hawaii. Ice is smoked much like freebase or crack cocaine.

Major Effects

Typical therapeutic doses of amphetamines stimulate the central nervous system, increase blood pressure, widen the pupils, increase the respiration rate, depress the appetite, relieve sleepiness, and decrease fatigue and boredom. Other effects include increased awareness and alertness, slight euphoria, elevation of mood and self-confidence (although the ability to perform complex tasks is usually diminished), increased talkativeness and excitement, reduced nausea and gastrointestinal upset, and dry mouth.

Adverse Effects

In some individuals, even a moderate dose of amphetamines can have adverse effects such as agitation, an inability to concentrate, anxiety, confusion, blurred vision, tremors, and heart palpitations. Higher doses of amphetamines can produce quite severe adverse reactions that include

- tremors, palpitations
- dilated pupil (mydriasis)
- sweating and flushing, abdominal cramps, nausea
- tachycardia (rapid heartbeat), heart abnormalities
- hypertension (later hypotension), circulatory collapse
- anxiety, agitation, and panic
- aggression and violent behavior often associated with paranoia
- rapid breathing, respiratory collapse
- hallucination (visual and auditory) delirium
- extremely high fevers
- convulsions and seizures

Although death reports from amphetamine use are rare, some individuals who are unusually sensitive to these drugs have died as a result of burst blood vessels in the brain,

Classification of Stimulants		
Amphetamines	Cocaine (Benzoylmethylecognine)	Other Stimulants
• Benzedrine (amphetamine) • Dexedrine (dextroamphetamine) • Methedrine, Desoxyn (methamphetamine)		• Ritalin (methylphenidate) • Preludin (phenmetrazine) • Tenuate (diethylpropion) • INH (isoniazid) • Coffee, colas, tea (caffeine) • Tobacco (nicotine)

heart failure, or high fever. Amphetamine psychoses, a mental disturbance similar to paranoid schizophrenia, is sometimes associated with high-dose amphetamine use but many of its symptoms have been observed with moderate dose levels.

Injecting amphetamines causes other complications: Unsterile and shared needles cause problems with tetanus, AIDS, abscesses, and hepatitis. The injection of insoluble particles in street speed also causes many problems.

Dependence and Withdrawal

Abruptly stopping amphetamines after chronic heavy use is often followed by symptoms such as fatigue, brain wave abnormalities, prolonged sleep, voracious appetite, stomach cramps, muscle pains, lethargy, and severe emotional depression. Some of these symptoms seem just as dramatic as withdrawal symptoms form depressant drugs.

Withdrawing amphetamines from chronic users does not seem as physically distressing as withdrawal from depressant drugs. There is little evidence of any physical dependence on moderate doses of amphetamines, but researchers frequently report psychological dependence on even low doses.

Prolonged use of amphetamines leads to a broad range of illnesses. Chronic users suffer dehydration, weight loss, and vitamin deficiency. Their reduced resistance to disease allows sores, nonhealing ulcers, and chronic chest infections. Users have a higher than normal rate of liver and cardiovascular disease, hypertensive disorders, and psychiatric problems.

Bootlegged Amphetamines

The newer, tighter regulations imposed on the legitimate prescribing of amphetamines have caused widespread bootlegging of amphetamines and substituting of other substances to mimic the amphetamine rush or high. The most common substitutes include ephedrine—a mild stimulant found in some over-the-counter asthma remedies—and phenylpropanolamine, or PPA, the ingredients in most legal

Stimulants

Coca Leaves and Cocaine

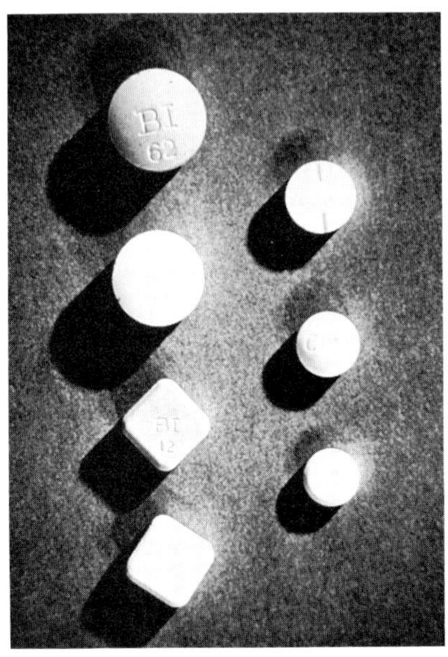

Phenmetrazine (left) and
Methylphenidate (right)

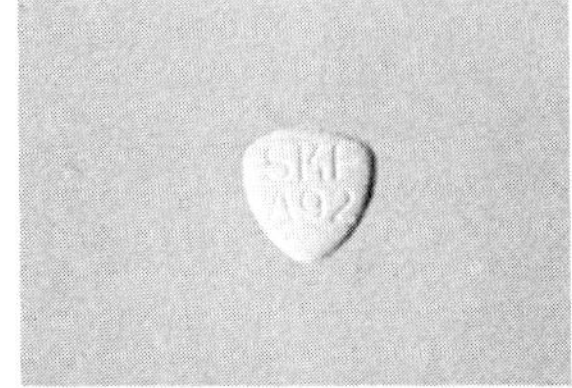

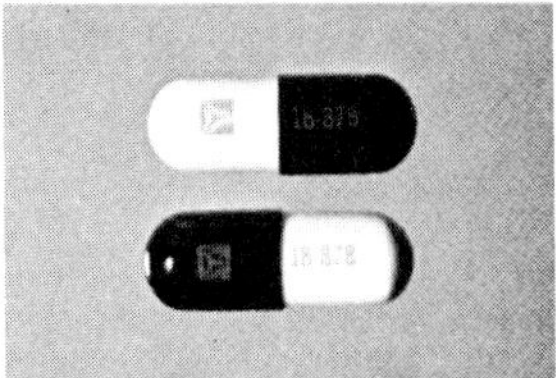

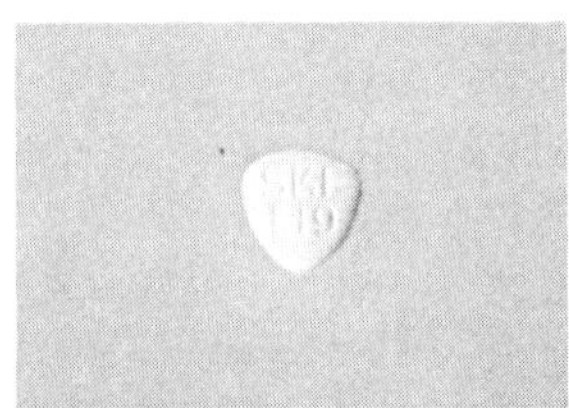

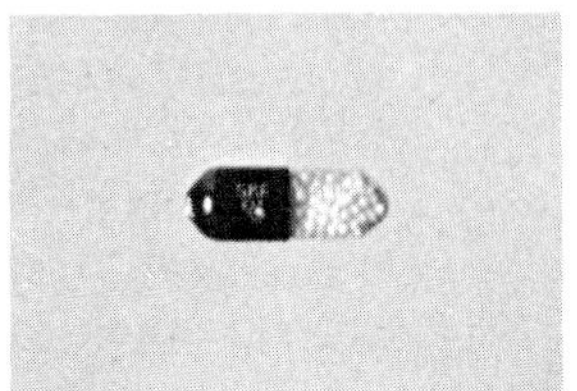

Amphetamines

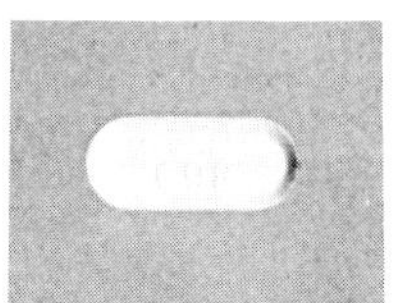

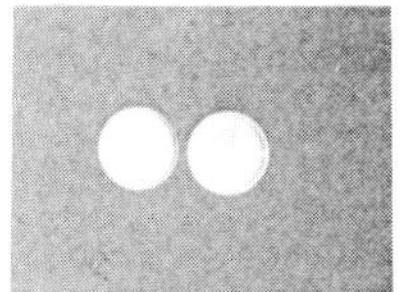

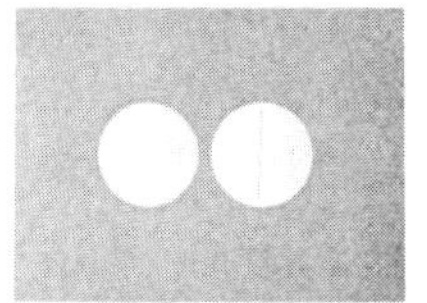

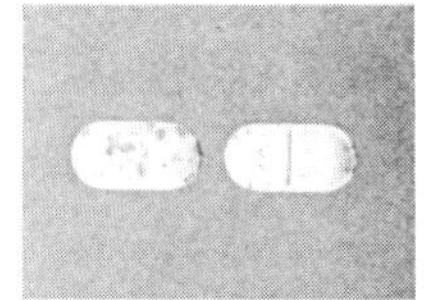

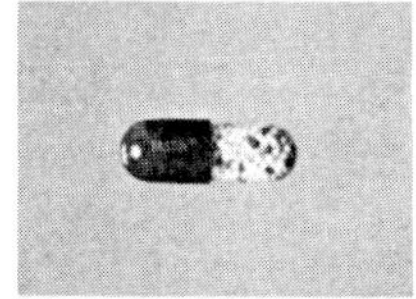

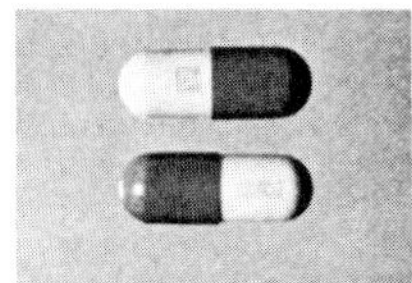

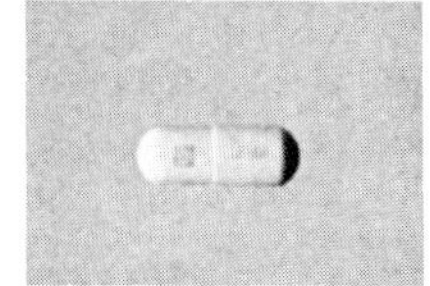

Other Stimulants

diet capsules. The moderate to large amounts of caffeine in most illicit amphetamines sometimes account for the bulk of the ingredients.

Cocaine

Cocaine is a central nervous system stimulant that has gained great popularity in a variety of drug forms. At first, cocaine was expensive; only the wealthy could afford it. Today, crack cocaine is used by every socioeconomic class, making it the scourge of humanity.

Brief History

1844—Conflicting reports that either Albert Nieman or Gaedecke isolated cocaine.

1878—W. H. Bentley espouses cocaine as a cure for morphine addiction.

1883—Aschenbrandt prescribed the use of cocaine to counteract battle fatigue of the Bavarian troops.

1883—Sigmund Freud wrote "Uber Coca" praising the medicinal effects of cocaine.

1887—Sigmund Freud recognized cocaine addiction and wrote a book retitled *Fear of and Craving for Cocaine.*

Cocaine is obtained from the leaves of *Erythroxylum coca,* a bush grown in parts of South America. Mountain Indians of Peru and Bolivia have chewed coca leaves as a social ritual for more than a thousand years.

The coca leaf was brought to Europe in the nineteenth century and became quite popular in certain circles. Sigmund Freud, the father of psychoanalysis, used cocaine extensively. In 1883 he recommended cocaine for treatment of morphine addiction, alcohol dependence, asthma, digestive disorders, and for the relief of depression and fatigue. Freud frequently recommended the drug for what was then called neurasthenia (i.e., nervous anxiety). Freud soon realized cocaine was addictive; in 1887 he wrote *Fear of and Craving for Cocaine* describing dependence on cocaine.

One of the most popular soft drinks of all time, Coca-Cola, originally contained extracts of the coca leaf. Coca was also present in wines such as Vin Mariana, a wine that was extremely popular with the pope and the royal families in Italy and other countries. Today, a little more than a 100 years after the cocaine problems of the 1880s, we have another cocaine problem caused by coca products that are far more addicting than those of the past.

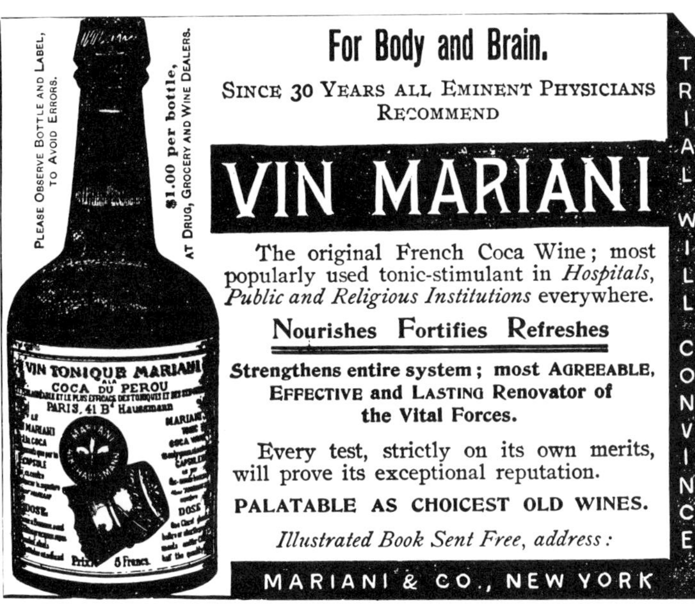

This late nineteenth century ad for Mariani wine, which contained cocaine, portrays the beverage as a panacea for all ills.

The Bettman Archive.

Street Names of Cocaine

Bernice, bernieds, big C, blow, bombita, bouncing powder, burese, C, charles, charlie, coke, cola, corrine, dream, dust, flake, fly, girl, gold dust, heaven, heaven dust, her, ice (not to be confused with the new form of methamphetamine), incentive, jay, joy powder, lady, lady snow, nose candy, nose powder, paradise, poison, powder, rock, schoolboy, snow, star dust, sugar, white, white lady, white powder, white stuff.

Routes of Administration

Cocaine can be inhaled, injected, or smoked. Cocaine hydrochloride is snorted or injected while crack cocaine is smoked. Table 3.3 shows how quickly all forms of cocaine reach a user's brain.

Freebase cocaine is another smokable form of cocaine. Heating up cocaine hydrochloride with a volatile solvent (usually ether) and a base (baby laxative), results in cocaine free of its hydrochloride base, with by-products of water and salt.

Cocaine HCl + ether + base + heat = Pure Cocaine + NaCl (salt) + H2O (water)

Because this cocaine is extremely pure, the volatile point, or the temperature at which cocaine burns, is raised. This allows freebase cocaine to be smoked without burning

Sigmund Freud—cocaine user in 1883–1884

it. Simply burning cocaine does not produce a high. Freebase cocaine smoke goes from the lungs to the brain in 6 seconds, resulting in an immediate and intense high. This high lasts only forty to fifty seconds and requires repeated doses, and making it extremely expensive to maintain a habit.

Crack cocaine is formed by combining cocaine with baking soda; this overrides the hydrochloride acid and allows the crack to be smoked. Crack is sold in small rocks at lower prices to lower economic populations.

Major Effects

The cocaine user experiences fifteen to thirty minutes of excitation and euphoria, tends to talk a lot, and feels energetic and self-confident. The effect of cocaine often gives the individual a supreme feeling of well-being, being in control, and enjoying activities that may previously have been mundane. At early stages of use, men report feeling a stimulation of sexuality. Cocaine is very short acting because it has an extremely short half-life; after the euphoria, psychological depression, nervousness, fatigue, and irritability set in.

Adverse Effects

With heavy regular use, depression and anxiety can be so severe that the user continues to snort, smoke, or inject cocaine every twenty minutes or so for several hours to avoid the onset of depression. This pattern may develop into binges—or twenty-four to forty-eight hours of cocaine use.

Another method to take the edge off cocaine is to inject heroin with cocaine (speedballing). This form of cocaine use

TABLE 3.3
Cocaine: Time to Affect the Brain

Snorting cocaine	6 minutes
Injecting cocaine	14 seconds
Smoking freebase cocaine	6 seconds

was implicated in the death of comedian and actor John Belushi. Addicts frequently turn to the sedative hypnotics (alcohol, tranquilizers, and barbiturates) to counteract the down side after using cocaine. This pattern of sedative hypnotic use may also cause a dependence on drugs in this classification.

Acute toxicity can occur from any method of cocaine use. In the past, cocaine was thought of as a rather benign drug. Today, we know that cocaine-related deaths are more common than once thought. Cases of sudden death from cocaine use are increasing. Large doses of cocaine may cause shallow breathing, fever, restlessness, anxiety, and confusion. Even small doses of cocaine can cause a slowing of the heart rate.

High doses also have an impact on the motor systems in the brain and spinal cord resulting in tremors and convulsive movements. Long-term chronic snorting of large amounts of cocaine can destroy tissue in the nose. Nausea, vomiting, and abdominal pains can occur. Death from cocaine overdose is usually due to convulsions, respiratory arrest, and/or the Casey Jones reaction, a condition during which the body acts like a runaway train exceeding its own metabolic limits.

People have done and seen some rather bizarre things under the influence of cocaine. Case studies in chapter 5 describe these in more detail.

Tolerance and Withdrawal

According to our behavioral definition of addiction, cocaine is the most addicting drug we know of today, especially freebase cocaine. Yet, a physical tolerance does not develop to cocaine. When cocaine is used, the dopamine neurotransmitters are blocked from reuptake stranding them in the synaptic clefts. This causes a cessation of stimulant response. However, this is not a classical tolerance reaction. This was one of the factors that led to the tragic miscalculation that cocaine

Celebrities and cocaine

was not an addicting drug. Its intense high and user's need to avoid the crash or depression makes cocaine highly addicting and contributes to the binge patterns of cocaine use.

Cocaine is one of the few chemicals (other than amphetamines and other stimulants) that exists outside of the body and stimulates catecholamine. Catecholamines are responsible for extraordinarily intense reactions to stressful situations (e.g., a father lifts a car to release his child pinned beneath it). The Casey Jones reaction previously mentioned is directly related to this catecholamine-enhancing property of cocaine. Once this reaction is set in motion, it usually results in death. Some people die from nontoxic doses of cocaine due to a phenomenon known as the kindling effect. The brain is primed or sensitized to the effect of cocaine, so that one additional dose may trigger firing or discharge leading to sudden death.

Cocaine Additives

Cocaine purchased on the illicit market is very seldom, if ever, pure by the time it reaches the consumer. As it makes its way from the original source down to the illicit market, the drug's purity is cut with various substances. These additives include mannitol (a mild baby laxative), lactose (milk sugar), or these psychoactive drugs: procaine (Novocain), lidocaine (xylocaine), benzocaine, tetracaine, and amphetamine. Some individuals have allergic reactions to these substances.

Cocaine Clinical Syndromes

Cocaine Euphoria

- Euphoria
- Affective liability
- Increased intellectual function
- Hyperalertness
- Hyperactivity
- Anorexia
- Insomnia
- Hypersexuality
- Proneness to violence

Cocaine Dysphoria

- Sadness
- Melancholia
- Apathy
- Inability to concentrate
- Painful delusions
- Anorexia
- Insomnia

Cocaine Schizophreniform Psychosis

- Anhedonia (inability to feel pleasure from what would have normally given pleasure)
- Disorientation
- Hallucinations
- Concern with minutia
- Stereotyped behavior
- Paranoid delusions (parasitosis)
- Insomnia
- Proneness to violence

Tobacco

Ironically, although tobacco is the last drug category discussed in this section, it is the most widely abused drug we know of today. Despite warnings regarding the health hazards, approximately one-fifth of adults in the United States continue to use tobacco products; tobacco use is the single leading cause of preventable death in this country (U.S. Surgeon General 1988). In comparing deaths related to alcohol and other drugs, smoking tobacco contributes to far more deaths.

Diseases Related to Smoking Tobacco

1. Heart Disease (coronary heart disease, increased artherosclerotic disease). Smoking elevates low-density lipoproteins (LDL or bad cholesterol), while reducing high-density lipoproteins (HDL or good cholesterol).
2. Peripheral vascular disease.
3. Cerebrovascular disease.
4. Cancer (lung cancer; cancer of the larynx, mouth, esophagus; contributing factor in urinary cancer, kidney cancer, and pancreatic cancer).
5. Chronic obstructive lung disease or colds (chronic bronchitis and emphysema).

Some alarming health consequences of tobacco products are

- more women die from lung cancer than breast cancer each year
- 20–25 percent of female smokers don't stop during pregnancy
- over three-fourths of smokers start during the developmental teenage years
- one out of every five high school seniors smoke cigarettes on a daily basis
- chewing tobacco (smokeless tobacco) is the leading cause of oral cancer
- approximately 75–80 percent of recovering alcoholics smoke cigarettes

In recent years we have seen a decrease in use of tobacco products by the general public. Yet the use of tobacco, especially by young people, makes them a significant population at risk for the development of smoking-related diseases.

Deaths from drug-related illnesses

From *Professional Counselor,* January/February 1990. Copyright © 1990 A & D Publications Corporation, Redmond, Washington.

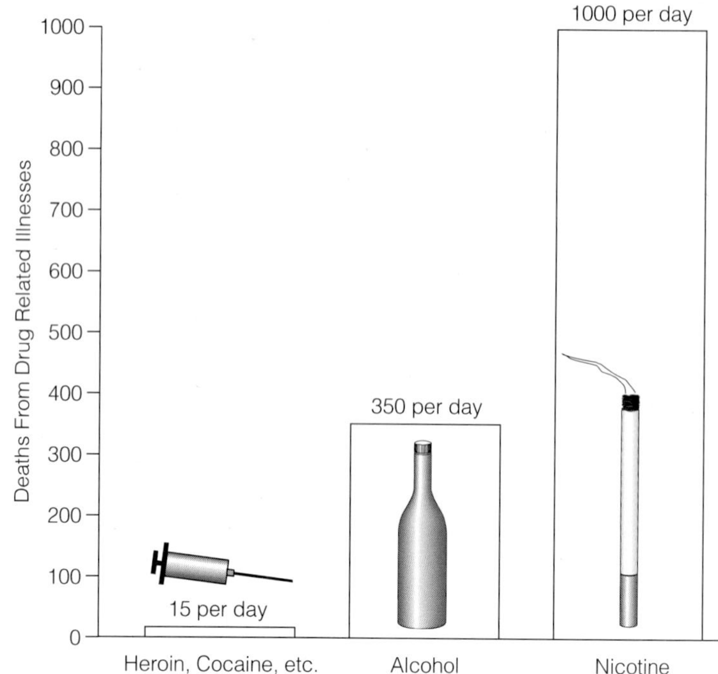

Deaths Related to Smoking Tobacco
Smoking and smoking-related diseases
• 360,000 to 390,000 deaths per year
• 1,000 preventable deaths per day
Fire and auto-related smoking fatalities
• 1,500 to 2,000 deaths per year
Smoking during pregnancy
• 18 percent of low birth weight babies, respiratory distress syndrome, and sudden infant death syndrome (SIDS)

Hallucinogens

The term *hallucinogen* is derived from the Latin word *hallucinari,* which means to dream or to wander in the mind. Other terms describing hallucinogens are *psychodelic,* which alters consciousness; *psychotomimetic,* which mimics psychosis; and *psychotogenic,* which produces psychosis.

DOONESBURY **by Garry Trudeau**

Hallucinogenic altered states of consciousness

Hallucinogens are capable of altering time and space perception; changing feelings of self-awareness and emotion; changing one's sense of body image; and increasing sensitivity to textures and shapes, sounds and taste. In addition, these drugs bring visions of luminescence, flashes of light, kaleidoscopic patterns, and landscapes. They can also induce hallucinations and feelings of enlightenment, spiritual or religious awakening.

In the past any substance whose function is to change the habitual way of perceiving and orienting one's self toward one's physical, psychological, and social environment was considered a hallucinogen. As a result, many drugs such as marijuana, PCP, and even cocaine, are inappropriately classified as hallucinogens because that is the category they seem to fit best.

In the 1960s, Timothy Leary advocated LSD as a means of "turning on, tuning in, and dropping out" of mainstream life-styles and thinking. Of the many natural and synthetic hallucinogens, LSD is the most potent by weight and the most thoroughly researched.

Mescaline is derived from the dried buttons or heads of the peyote cactus. Peyote buttons can be eaten or made into a tea. Psilocybin is found in a wide range of American and Mexican mushrooms.

Street Names

LSD

Acid, barrels, beast, Big D, blotter, blue acid, blue cheer, blue heaven, blue mist, brown dots, California sunshine, cap, chocolate chips, contact lens, cubes, cupcakes, D, deeda, domes, dots, electric Kool-Aid, flash, ghost, hawk, haze, L, lysergic, mellow yellows, microdots, orange cubes, paper acid,

Classification of Hallucinogens

- LSD-25 (lysergic acid diethylamide)
- Dimethyltryptamine (DMT)
- Psilocybin (mushrooms)
- Psilocin
- Bufotenine
- Harmine
- Mescaline (active part of peyote cactus)
- Diethytryptamine (DET)
- Dipropryltryptamine (DPT)
- Dimethoxymethamphetamine (DOM/STP)
- Methylenedioxyamphetamine (MDA)
- Belladonna alkaloids (atropine, scopoliamine, and stramonium are found in many medicines for asthma and stomach cramps)
- Nutmeg (myristicin)

peace, pearly gates, pellets, pink owsley, purple haze, sacrament, strawberries, strawberry fields, sugar, sugar cubes, sunshine, tabs, ticket twenty-five, wedges, white lightning, window pane, yellow

Mescaline

Beans, big chief, buttons, cactus, cactus buttons, mesc, mescal, moon topi

Peyote

Bad seed, big chief, buttons, cactus, P, peyotl, topi

Brief History

1000 B.C. or earlier—Religious and tribal use of hallucinogenic mushrooms.

700 B.C.—Hallucinogenic mandrake root was referred to by the Assyrians and mentioned in Genesis as a fertility substance.

A.D. 38—Datura was used by the early Incas and other Indians of South America.

Peyote cactus (mescaline) was used by Incas and later by American Indians.

1899—Oklahoma was the first state to outlaw the use of peyote.

April 16, 1943—Albert Hoffman, a chemist working at Sandoz Laboratories in Basel, Switzerland, discovered LSD-25.

1965—LSD Conference during which Sidney Cohen summarized the research on LSD use with psychiatric patients and other experiments.

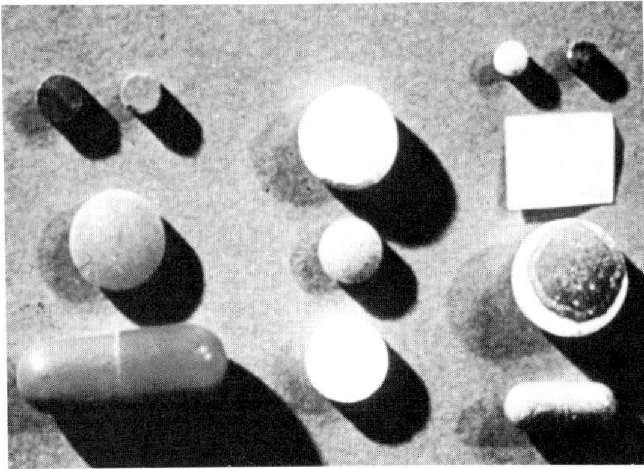

Hallucinogens

Psilocybe Mushroom

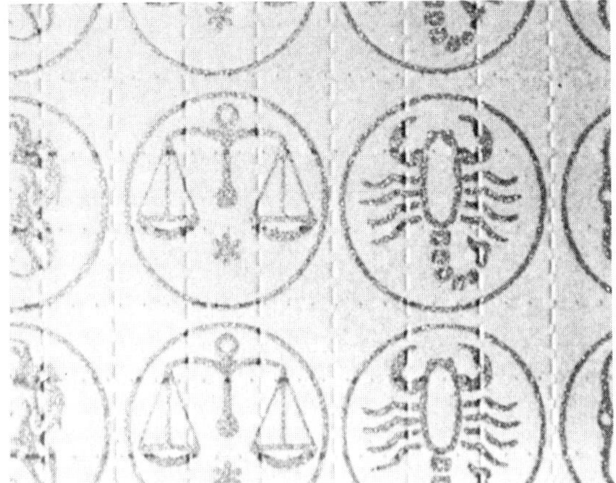

LSD Blotter Paper

Peyote Cactus

Phencyclidine (PCP)

Estimates of Use

In comparison to the use of hallucinogens in the late 1960s, today's use rate is smaller. But, contrary to media reports, that use has not all but died out. These drugs continue to be taken by millions of people in the United States each year. LSD is easily manufactured, and hallucinogenic mushrooms grow wild in many states, as do many plants with hallucinogenic or toxic-hallucinogenic properties (NIDA 1989).

Routes of Administration

Hallucinogens are usually ingested orally, but may be smoked, snorted, or injected. Because such small amounts are required at any one time (25 to 150 millionths of a gram), LSD is often impregnated in sugar pills, blotter paper, or small gelatin squares. The nasty taste of some hallucinogens requires mixing them with other substances to counteract their taste. Teas and broths are a common method of ingesting hallucinogens.

Major Effects

The effects of hallucinogens are influenced by the personality of the user, the expectations of use, the user's general experience with drugs, the mind set of the individual, and most important, the setting. The right group of trusting friends, a comfortable soothing environment (i.e., dim lights and soft music), and someone experienced with hallucinogens, is described as integral in developing a good hallucinogenic trip.

As a result of all these variables, users of hallucinogens report a wide range of reactions. Some individuals feel an insight and expanded consciousness, while others report discomfort and fear of losing control that is quite disturbing.

Generally, low to moderate doses of hallucinogens produce mood and perceptual alterations. LSD and other hallucinogens can produce profound effects on the user's thinking, self-awareness, and emotions. Hallucinogens distort time and space perception and induce hallucinations.

Adverse Effects

Hallucinogenic experiences can sometimes add to existing neuroses, or character disorders, and can produce transient waves of mild anxiety, paranoia, or severe panic. Flashbacks (recurrence of negative hallucinogenic experiences) usually occur within a year or less from the last use of hallucinogens. However, the incidence of flashbacks occurring is relatively small. Flashbacks can occur in individuals who have used hallucinogens excessively and in the occasional or first-time user.

Accidents are very common under the influence of hallucinogens. The high degree of suggestibility and perceptual distortions and hallucinations often lead to accidents. Such accidents include walking through a plate glass window;

The panther mushroom

jumping from a roof due to the coaxing of a friend (high degree of suggestibility); and accidental falls, drownings, and car accidents that occur under hallucinogens when individuals take unnecessary risks.

Tolerance and Dependence

Researchers have observed psychological dependence in long-term LSD users but have rarely reported dependence as a consequence of other hallucinogenic use.

Hallucinogenic trips can be of long duration compared to other drug use. Users tend to trip for from four to six hours to twelve to twenty-four hours. Following these trips, they are usually quite tired. This often necessitates periods of getting back to normal functioning before again using hallucinogens. Because of this pattern of occasional or intermittent use of hallucinogens, physical dependence is unlikely under most conditions. Tolerance has been shown to develop to some of the psychological and physiological effects of LSD. Quite frequently there is cross-tolerance to other hallucinogens. For example, an individual who has recently been taking LSD generally shows a reduced response to mescaline and psilocybin.

Cannabis Sativa

Cannabis refers to any product of the plant *Cannabis sativa*, which grows in most parts of the world. In North America, the most commonly used products derived from this plant are marijuana and hashish. Marijuana is the unprocessed, dried

Marijuana plant

leaves, flowers, seeds, and stems of the plant. Hashish is a more potent product processed from the resin of this herb.

Researchers have obtained more than 300 cannabis products (cannabinoids) from cannabis. They have isolated and synthesized the most active ingredient in marijuana. This product, tetrahydrocannabinol (THC), is the psychoactive compound found in the greatest amount in the plant; it is thought to produce most of the high.

Street Names

Marijuana—Old and New

Acapulco gold, ace, African black, aunt mary, baby, bale, bomb, boo, brick, broccoli, bush, Canadian black, charge, Colombian, doobie, dry high, fatty, fingers, flowers, gage, ganga, gauge, giggleweed, grass, green, grefa, greta, grifa, grillo, grunt, hay, hemp, herb, homegrown, Indian hay, Indian hemp, J, jane, jay smoke, joint, joy stick, juanita, kick sticks, kif, killer, killer weed, kilter, loco, mary, maryann, maryjane, mary warner, mary weaver, meserole (messerole), Mexican brown, Mexican green, Mexican locoweed, MJ, mooca, moota, mooters, mootie, mota, mother, mu, muggles, muta, number, Panama gold, Panama red, panatella, pin, pode, pot, ragweed, rainy day woman, red dirt, reefer, roach, root, sassafras, sinsemilla, smoke, snop, stick, sweet lucy, tea, Texas tea, twist, weed, wheat, yerba, Zacatecas purple

Hashish

Black hash, black Russian, blond hash, canned sativa, hash, Lebanese, mahjuema

Brief History

2737 B.C.—Earliest reference to marijuana by a Chinese treatise on pharmacology attributed to the Emperor Shen Nung.

Marijuana and hashish

Marijuana (illicit)

Hashish (illicit)

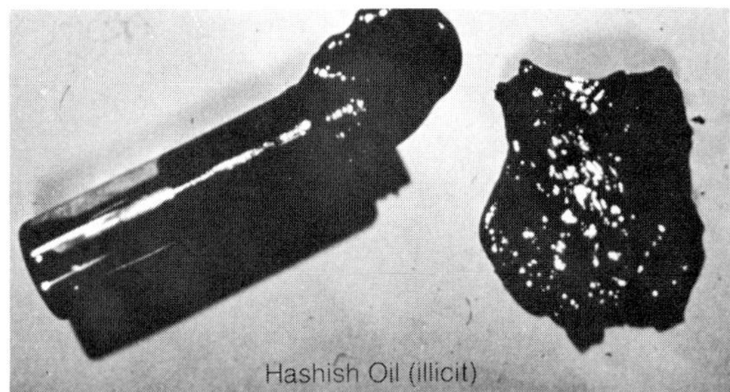
Hashish Oil (illicit)

650 B.C.—Use of cannabis mentioned in Persia and Assyria.
400 B.C.—Use of cannabis mentioned in Rome.
1545—First record of a marijuana plant in the New World when Spanish traders introduced marijuana to Chile.
1629—After the Civil War, marijuana as a major crop in North America.
1765—George Washington grew marijuana hemp, and is said to have experimented with the medicinal or intoxicating potency of the plants.
1804–1844—Jacques-Joseph Moreau of France used it as a psychotropic drug.
1937—Henry Anslinger, commissioner of the Bureau of Narcotics, campaigned on the dangers of marijuana.
October 1969—A Gallup poll estimated that 10 million Americans, half of them under twenty-one years of age, has smoked marijuana.

Estimates of Use

Marijuana is the most widely used of all illicit drugs. By various estimates 35–50 million Americans have tried this drug and between 12–18 million are regular users of two or more joints per week (NIDA 1989).

Medical Uses

Cannabis, primarily in the form of synthetic THC, has been under scientific investigation in recent years to ascertain its potential therapeutic uses. One approved therapeutic use is as an antiemetic (antivomiting) agent for the nausea and vomiting associated with chemotherapy treatment for cancer patients. It is also medically used to relieve the intraocular pressure accompanying glaucoma. Both these medical uses are the most well researched.

Other potential medical uses of marijuana researched thus far include: spasm relief, asthma relief, anxiety reduction, and relief of alcohol withdrawal symptoms. Studies in these areas have not been as prolific, nor as conclusive, as those regarding chemotherapy and glaucoma (Solomons and Neppve 1989).

Thirty-four states currently have statutes on the books allowing marijuana, typically in the form of THC, to be used in medical research and/or medical treatment as a part of a clinical investigation. The number of states that have actually implemented these procedures is much smaller.

The political and moral/ethical emotionality of our times may further hinder these investigations into the effectiveness of marijuana in medical research. For this reason, other synthetically produced cannabis derivatives are also under investigation.

Routes of Administration

Marijuana can be smoked in hand-rolled cigarettes or joints. Today's higher-potency marijuana is usually smoked in a pipe, most frequently a water pipe. This allows the most intense high with the least waste of the marijuana.

Generally hashish has a much higher THC content, though it may vary widely in potency. Hashish can be crumbled and rolled into a cigarette for smoking; often it is mixed with a lower-grade marijuana or tobacco. In this country, hashish is normally smoked in a water pipe.

Marijuana and hashish can also be eaten in cookies, brownies, and other food or made into a tea. In this form, the high lasts longer, since it is slowed down by the digestive processes.

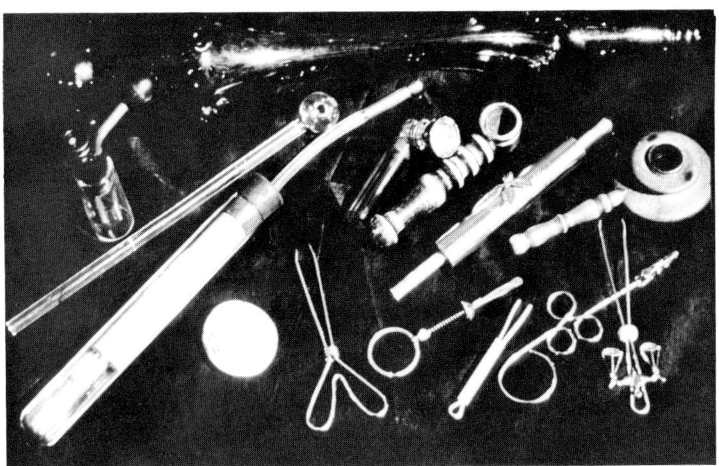

Cannabis paraphernalia

Cannabis resin is not water soluble, so the drug cannot be injected. The few who have tried using it this way usually experienced violent convulsions and unpleasantness.

Major Effects

The effects of cannabis depend on the potency of the drug, the method of use, the experience and expectations of the user regarding what will happen. For low-dose periodic use, the common effects of marijuana use are

- feelings of exhilaration, relaxation, giddiness
- minor increase in heart rate
- drowsiness, dry mouth and throat, bloodshot eyes
- impaired short-term memory
- altered states of time and space
- pupils dilate.

Increase in Potency of Marijuana

Some readers might remember hearing about types of marijuana such as Acapulco Gold, Maui Wowi, or Panama Red. Most of the potent marijuana in the 1960s was imported from these places. Today, homegrown marijuana is the staple of American pot smokers. The more than 22 million pot smokers in the United States prefer the high-potency sinsemilla grown in hidden caches throughout the United States. Humboldt County in California is an example of this homegrown cultivation. The California gold rush still goes on in Humboldt County in the form of marijuana crops despite increased eradication efforts.

In the 1960s, the THC content of marijuana was 1–2 percent in potency. Most users would smoke half a joint to get high. Two or three joints passed among friends could get everyone high. Today, the THC content of marijuana averages 6 percent. One hit is enough to keep an individual loaded. Today, hashish is 10 percent THC and hash oil is 20 percent THC.

This increase in the potency of marijuana means we are looking at a new drug with new problems. The research of the past with marijuana in the 1–2 percent THC level does not apply to marijuana used in the 1990s.

Subjective effects of cannabis intoxication have been reported in hundreds of different ways. Common reports include feelings of happiness, warmth, conviviality, camaraderie, and the ability to enjoy music and art better than when not stoned. Reactions to marijuana depend a great deal on the attitude of the user and the compatibility of the surroundings (set and setting). Cannabis is sometimes classified as a mild hallucinogen. With the increase in potency of marijuana, this classification may be warranted.

Adverse Effects

The long-term effects of chronic cannabis use are at the heart of the current medical debate on this drug. Strong psychological dependence does develop in many regular users of marijuana, as evidenced by a need for cannabis use every day to perform certain tasks, to relax and unwind, or to sleep. The individual's life begins to revolve around the use of marijuana as a primary activity. The user tends to use marijuana more frequently throughout the day and evening.

Withdrawal symptoms after steady use may include irritability, decreased appetite, restlessness, sleep disturbances, sweating, nausea, or diarrhea. Hangovers the next morning are not uncommon. However, unlike the alcohol hangover causing headaches and sensitive optic nerves, the cannabis hangover is more likely to be light-headedness characterized by the inability to gather thoughts. When the drug is ingested, the effect can linger on for an entire day, along with nausea, body aches, and other symptoms.

Despite the lack of classic withdrawal symptoms, some patterns of marijuana use fit the behavioral definition of addiction. Researchers have well established the fact that chronic marijuana use can cause physical dependence by identifying full-blown withdrawal symptoms in newborn babies of marijuana-dependent mothers. Treatment for the addiction to marijuana requires the support of an outpatient treatment counselor knowledgeable about drug/alcohol recovery and marijuana dependence. Marijuana Anonymous groups have also developed to meet the rising incidence of dependence on marijuana.

Anxiety and panic reactions are more common with chronic marijuana use. Many individuals who have used marijuana to self-medicate affective disorders such as depression or manic-depressive disorder can experience severe anxiety and panic reactions. Individuals experiencing psychologically negative reactions may require temporary hospitalization so they don't get out of control and hurt themselves or others.

Damage to the Respiratory System

The tars in cannabis smoke are 50 percent greater by weight than tobacco tars and 70 percent higher in cancer-producing substances. Considering that marijuana is deeply inhaled and the smoke is held in the lungs by the user, instead of passively inhaled as in cigarette smoking, the cancer causing risk is increased by marijuana smoking.

Long-term, heavy smoking of cannabis is associated with bronchial problems, sore throat, and chronic coughing. These conditions may be more severe in chronic hashish users. In addition, those who smoke tobacco as well as cannabis products have an added risk of bronchial problems and cancer.

Immune Systems

Recent studies suggest that cannabis, particularly when used regularly, tends to suppress the body's immune response and ability to combat infections (Cohen 1986). Marijuana temporarily arrests the maturation of developing t-cells that protect the body from colds and other bacterial infections. This increases the chances of illness due to either bacteria or viruses. The most prominent indication of this effect is the higher incidence of bronchial infections, coughing, bronchitis, and the possibility of pneumonia noted among chronic heavy marijuana users.

Reproductive System

Chronic use of cannabis also decreases sperm motility and serum testosterone in men and interferes with the menstrual cycle in women, thus affecting fertility. Most of these effects are reversed after marijuana use is discontinued. Marijuana is suspected to be harmful to the fetuses in pregnant women; research with rhesus monkeys has shown pregnancy problems such as still birth and spontaneous abortion. Reduced birth weight is also a characteristic of surviving fetuses.

Brain System

Considerable debate continues over the effects of cannabis on the brain. A certain percentage of users develop lethargy, apathy, and disorientation that persist long after chronic use has been discontinued. Fortunately, these effects appear to gradually wear off. Some researchers claim that long-term changes occur in some brain wave patterns; these claims are being investigated further.

Impairment of Maturation Process

Most researchers are in agreement that cannabis use, during the primary developmental years of eleven to fifteen in particular, interferes with physical and mental maturation processes and impedes emotional development. Research describes an amotivational syndrome with symptoms of apathy, lethargy, and a general lack of involvement and motivation in growth and developmental activities.

Marijuana and Driving

Cannabis intoxication and chronic marijuana use impairs short-term memory, alters the user's sense of time and space, and impairs overall coordination and motor functioning. The ability to track other vehicles is also impaired and is a major problem in driving a car. Tracking involves judging time, distance, and the speed of other cars. Skills like merging into traffic, making U-turns, and other driving tasks require tracking skills. Adding another drug such as alcohol only makes the situation worse.

Smoking marijuana also makes it very dangerous to operate machinery and other equipment, since perception and timing are off, and the drug may also produce fatigue and drowsiness.

Many persons insist that their driving performance is improved under the influence of marijuana. This is due to their increased sensitivity to enjoying driving, not to a realistic evaluation of driving ability.

A recent study of airplane pilots reported that after smoking marijuana, performance is impaired up to two to three days later, despite the pilots thinking that they did extremely well on simulated tests (Rohn 1989). Other problems include (1) true allergic reactions to cannabis for a small minority of users; (2) gastrointestinal disturbances and weight loss among a small percentage of heavy users; and (3) difficulty in medical control of some diabetic users.

Solvents and Inhalants

From time to time, the phenomenon of inhalant use is brought to public attention. In the 1960s we had an epidemic of glue sniffing. Nowadays, there is still a consistent use of various solvents, aerosols, and other gases that people inhale to get high. For young people, people of color, and minorities who do not have the money to buy drugs, inhalant use is more prevalent. And in certain locations, the problem is much more serious because of the number of young people who use inhalants to get high. Yet, this is hardly a modern-day phenomenon.

Brief History

Some inhalants and anesthetics such as nitrous oxide, ether, and chloroform were used recreationally in the nineteenth century, especially during times of liquor scarcity. This occurred in Europe, Great Britain, and North America, where ether inhalation parties were common among students and physicians.

In the 1960s, the inhalation of volatile substances such as plastic model glue, nail polish removers, and aerosol sprays occurred frequently among adolescents. A wave of anti-glue sniffing publicity at the time resulted in many local and state laws prohibiting minors from buying such substances. In spite of these laws, inhalant vapors and sprays continue to be used to this day, partially because of the widespread application of such products in household use and partially because of ineffective legislation and enforcement.

In the 1970s and 1980s, paint became the primary inhalant of abuse. Users sprayed cans of paint, preferrably gold and silver, into rags that they stuffed under their noses to inhale the fumes. These huffers (paint inhalers) were often inner-city Latinos and other young people of color. American Indian youth have an extremely high incidence of gasoline inhalant use.

Route of Administration

Inhalation is accomplished in any number of ways depending on the ingenuity of the user. Inhaling the fumes can be accomplished by placing the substances on a rag, placing or spraying the substance in a plastic bag, or in the case of some pressurized gases, filling up a balloon, then waiting for the frozen vapor to warm up (if necessary) before inhaling.

Absorption of gases and volatile liquids is efficient and rapid. Absorption into tissues begins with the nasal mucous membranes. The major absorption site is the lungs, where substances enter the bloodstream. From the lungs, substances are distributed directly to the brain and other organ systems. They also enter fatty tissue.

Classification of Inhalants

A wide variety of names apply to inhaled substances. Many liquids also contain alcohol and petroleum distillates.

- Naphtha
- Benzene
- Acetone
- Toluene
- Carbon tetrachloride
- Fluorocarbon propellants
- Nitrous oxide
- Amyl nitrite, butyl nitrite
- Anesthetic gases (e.g., ether, chloroform)
- Gasoline

Assessment of Huffers in Hawaii

In 1976, while I was in Hawaii teaching a class on drugs/alcohol for the National Institute on Drug Abuse, some local drug counselors described the widespread use of paint inhaling in Honolulu. The kids did a good job of removing all the signs of silver and gold paint around their mouths before coming into the recreational and treatment programs. Inadvertently these barefoot or sandal-clad kids forgot to remove the traces of silver and gold paint on their feet. A good counselor would check out the kids' feet to determine if they were huffing paint.

Available Forms

Glue, model cement, fingernail polish removers, various cosmetics, various cleaning solvents, gasoline, paint, paint thinners, lighter fluids, antifreeze, aerosol cans, and white-out correction fluids can all be inhaled.

For example, kids go into a food market, smash the bottom of whipped cream cans, and squirt the gas from the broken containers into the backs of their throats. This aerosol freon gives them a cheap high.

Major Effects

Users report a feeling of well-being, a reduction of inhibitions, and an elevated mood. In many respects the effects are similar to those produced by alcohol and other sedatives. Higher doses often produce laughing and giddiness, feelings of floating, dizziness, time and space distortions, and illusions (see Table 3.4). Some substances induce psychedelic effects. An inhalant's effects may last anywhere from five minutes to an hour, depending on the substance and the dose.

Many people do not understand why anyone would actively seek a high from inhalants. They forget how young children often twirl to feel the effect of dizziness. And how

TABLE 3.4
Signs and Symptoms of Inhalant Use

1. slurred speech
2. odor of the substance being used
3. mental disorientation or confusion
4. headaches, dizziness, and weakness
5. muscle spasms in the neck, chest, or lower extremities
6. euphoria, heightened, exaggerated feeling of well-being
7. loss of balance and ataxia (uncoordinated walk)
8. nystagmus (eye movement from side to side)

children, adolescents, and even adults are exhilarated by the rides at amusement parks, especially the rides that give them feelings of vertigo. These effects are altered states of consciousness that are reinforcing to many individuals. Such is the case with inhalant abusers. Other reasons for using inhalants include (1) recreation (fun, mood elevation, getting high); (2) peer group influence ("it was what everyone was doing"); (3) cost effectiveness (a quicker and cheaper high); and (4) easy availability.

Tolerance and Dependence

When use of volatile substances continues for a long time and becomes heavy, tolerance may develop. Physical dependence with withdrawal symptoms has also occurred among some chronic users. These withdrawal symptoms include hallucinations, headaches, chills, delirium tremens, and stomach cramps. Hangovers lasting several days have also occurred.

There is cross-tolerance between some solvents and central nervous system depressants. As an example, skid row alcoholics inhale hydrocarbon vapors from kerosene or spray paint when they run out of liquor. These solvents forestall withdrawal symptoms from the alcohol, especially delirium tremens.

Alcohol and barbiturates potentiate some of the adverse effects of certain solvents. Consequently, users risk unconsciousness or even heart failure if they add the effects of alcohol to the effects of volatile solvents.

Acute Adverse Effects

Acute use of solvents often brings on confusion, drunkenness, slurred speech, a feeling of numbness, runny nose, tears, headache, and muscular incoordination. Frequently there is nausea and vomiting. Due to impaired judgment from solvent use, users often feel confusion, panic, irritation, tension, hyperactivity, and physically aggressive.

In cases of high dosage, the general sedative-anesthetic effects take over resulting in drowsiness, stupor, respiratory depression, and unconsciousness. Extremely heavy use can inhibit breathing and bring on death.

Many of these substances are capable of sensitizing the heart to adrenaline. Since the early 1960s heart failure due to this effect has been suspected in hundreds of users. This has been referred to as Sudden Sniffing Death Syndrome (SSD).

Some deaths have been directly attributed to solvent use. Most of them are due to suffocation when the users faint from inhalation and their noses and mouths remain covered by the plastic bags or they suffocate in their own vomit. Additional acute adverse effects depend on the specific products and their chemical makeup.

Long-Term Effects

Some temporary abnormalities take place in liver and kidney function and bone marrow activity; gastritis, hepatitis, jaundice, blood abnormalities, and peptic ulcers also occur.

Chronic users have exhibited slow-healing ulcers around their mouths and noses. Other effects are loss of appetite, weight loss, and nutritional disorders. Brain damage also results from regular solvent use; most of the time this has been reversible (without permanent effect) once the use was stopped. Reports of chromosome damage and blood abnormalities as a result of solvent inhaling have not yet been conclusively proven and remain under study (Ashton 1990).

With so many different kinds of solvents and hydrocarbons with chemically different structures, it is impossible to predict the long-term effects of the inhalation of all possible substances. Recent information suggests that some substances, such as toluene, may actually be less harmful than previously believed. On the other hand, long-term use of other substances such as n-hexane, which is commonly found in some plastic cements, gasoline, various adhesives, and rubber cements may cause permanent damage to the muscles. Because spray paint, aerosols, glues, and other such substances often contain a half-dozen or more ingredients in combination, researchers have had a great deal of difficulty ascertaining the exact damage potential on humans (Ashton 1990).

Phencyclidine

Phencyclidine (PCP) is a drug that cannot be classified properly as a hallucinogen, a stimulant, or a depressant, causing us to list it in a separate drug category. Originally, PCP was developed in the 1950s as a sedative, general anesthetic, and analgesic. In clinical testing, it worked fine as a painkiller although subjects often developed visual disturbances, severe agitation, and other unpleasant side effects. These side effects caused its discontinued use with humans. Until 1978 phencyclidine was sold as a veterinary medication for immobilizing primates and other large animals. Its use as an illicit drug began in the mid-1960s.

Street Names

Angel dust, animal trank, aurora borealis, DOA, dust, elephant, hog, PCP, peace, peace pill, rocket fuel, supergrass, tic tac

Estimates of Use

The geographic patterns of PCP use are haphazard. It has long been popular on the West Coast and certain large cities; recently, the geographical pattern of use has become more widespread.

The majority of users are young, approximately twelve to eighteen years of age, though there is use by young children and adults. (PCP users inadvertantly exposed infants to PCP when they stored their drugs in empty milk bottles.) Few users have been involved for as long as ten years, probably due to negative effects resulting in discontinuance or a switch to another intoxicant (Thombs 1989).

Routes of Administration

PCP is a white crystalline powder, soluble in water. Most commonly smoked or ingested, occasionally it may be injected. When ingested as tablets or capsules, PCP commonly comes in various sizes and colors. When smoked, users sprinkle the drug over mint leaves, marijuana, tobacco, or other substances; or they spray or dip PCP liquid on to the substance to be smoked. One popular method is to dip cigarettes into liquid PCP. Given all these possibilities, this drug may appear as a drug or be disguised to look like any number of other substances.

Major Effects

With a moderate or low dose, PCP produces a state of euphoria lasting three to five hours when smoked, or five to eight hours when eaten. Reactions to the drug vary greatly; much depends on the personality of the user and the circumstances surrounding the use (set and setting). Users who have bought this drug thinking it was THC have sworn that the high was like a heavy marijuana intoxication. When PCP has been misrepresented as a hallucinogen, users report LSD experiences.

Users who believe they are getting PCP, however, seldom have these convictions.

The most common reactions from moderate to low doses are auditory, visual, time, and other sensory disturbances. The most consistent effect is deadening of the extremities. Due to the drug's anesthetic properties, users lose control of their muscles. Depending on the individual, the overall reaction may vary anywhere from hyperactivity to complete immobility. The drug, though not a true hallucinogen, may mimic hallucinogenic drugs in some ways. It has been described by one authority as a *delusionogen,* a term which may more accurately describe its effect on the user.

Intoxication by PCP produces an experience of tranquilization, euphoria, inebriation, dissociation, and usually tactile and auditory hallucinations. The most common effects are changes in body imagery, perceptual distortions, and feelings of apathy and estrangement. The experience often includes feelings of drowsiness, inability to verbalize, and feelings of nothingness or emptiness. Reports of difficulty in thinking, poor concentration, and preoccupation with death are frequent.

Adverse Effects

As with most other drugs, for some users occasional recreational or social use of small amounts of PCP does not cause undesirable side effects. However, this situation is likely to change when users take or smoke larger doses or smaller amounts consistently day after day. Users often smoke or ingest other drugs in addition to PCP causing many unusual reactions.

Accidents

With high doses of PCP, accidents are common. Because PCP produces a loss of feeling, users frequently report cuts, bruises, and torn muscles and ligaments. The dissociative effects of PCP may make users believe these injuries are happening to someone else at the time.

In the heyday of PCP use in southern California in the 1960s, high doses resulted in many drownings. In those drownings, the individuals under the influence of PCP became disoriented; once underwater, they did not know which way was up. Drownings also result when users are so anesthetized that they forget to breathe; friends who are also stoned may not realize what is taking place (Thombs 1989).

Violence

Higher or consistent doses of PCP have also led to incidents of violence. These vary widely but many are characterized by the user's inability to feel pain. The result is situations where the user feels extraordinary strength and immune to pain. Police have reported high-dose PCP users breaking out of steel handcuffs, failing to stop an attack even though shot several times, or bleeding to death because of an inability to feel the injury inflicted during an attack. Despite several hundred reports of incidents like these, in relation to the millions who use this drug, they are considered rare.

More common adverse reactions include

- paranoia
- severe agitation
- a severe withdrawn feeling, or isolated feeling
- bizarre delusions
- increases in heart rate, blood pressure
- sweating, salivation, and flushing of the skin (these increase according to the dose)
- nystagmus (jerky eye movements) and other reactions.

PCP is unsafe to use during pregnancy, though the exact potential for damage to the fetus is unknown. PCP may also interfere with the hormones governing normal growth and development in the adolescent user. The principal proven negative effects on youthful users, however, relate to a decreased learning capacity, difficulty in concentration, poor grades, and poor social adjustment.

Unpredictable episodes of panic may occur. Latent psychopathology may be unmasked or triggered by either acute doses or patterns of chronic use as evidenced in episodes of violence, paranoia, and so forth. With prolonged regular PCP use, the effects can linger on after the intoxication has worn off, necessitating therapy or rehabilitation. Flashbacks are also reported from prolonged PCP use. With very large doses, convulsions or coma may occur.

Several PCP deaths were due to the direct effects of the drug. Other deaths were attributed to PCP combined with other drugs, particularly central nervous system depressants. As mentioned earlier, deaths are more frequently due to accidental causes while under the influence.

Tolerance and Dependence

PCP does not appear to be physically addictive even though some tolerance does develop in regular users. When used orally, PCP is most often used only occasionally. When smoked, it is very often used more frequently, and can create a very stong psychological dependence. Few data substantiate a withdrawal syndrome with PCP, though the drug often produces aftereffects lasting many months after use is discontinued. One of these aftereffects is depression, which can last up to a year; if untreated, it can lead to relapse and suicide.

Athletes and Drugs

Individual athletes have been using drugs to enhance their performance since ancient times. The use of drugs by athletes is almost as old as the Olympic games themselves.

In the marathon event of the 1904 Olympic games in St. Louis, Missouri, the winning runner was American Thomas Hicks who was aided by a heady cocktail of brandy and strychnine (a stimulant at low doses, a poison at high doses). Today, the list banning psychomotor stimulant drugs in Olympic competition includes more than 50.

Caffeine

Comedian George Carlin once described coffee as "the low end of the speed spectrum." The International Olympic Committee found this joke contained a grain of truth. After high concentrations of caffeine were found in several competitors' urine during the 1976 Summer Olympic Games, studies were conducted to see if caffeine affected athletic performance.

Controlled studies involved both athletes and nonathletes using cycle ergometers. Results showed that the caffeine present in two and a half cups of coffee was sufficient to increase endurance as measured by maximal oxygen consumption when cycling to exhaustion. A further study involving five young athletes concluded that small doses of caffeine significantly increased the power of leg muscle contractions. The enhancement, however, was limited to endurance athletes. Caffeine does not significantly improve performance during maximal short-term bursts of exercise (Lombardo 1990).

Based on this information and other reports, the International Olympic Committee banned caffeine in amounts greater than 12 ug-ml. An average of four cups of coffee could produce this level.

Caffeine is also produced synthetically, used in some pain-killing preparations, and sold over the counter in diet preparations and caffeine tablets.

Adverse Effects of Caffeine

The adverse effects of caffeine are mainly dose related. Depending on the individual's sensitivity, symptoms may include headaches, tremors, nausea, and irregular heartbeat, especially in the 200 to 500 milligram dose range.

A particular effect that may have significance to athletes is the increase in urine output. This might not only increase the number of involuntary pit stops during an endurance event but also have potential implications for the athletes' hydration status.

Caffeinism is now a recognized entity. People have gone to emergency rooms complaining of heart palpitations, restlessness, anxiety, insomnia, and myriad other symptoms directly attributable to their high caffeine intake. People who consume significant amounts of coffee daily and then taper off too rapidly suffer from Caffeine Abstinence Syndrome. Withdrawal symptoms include headaches, drowsiness, lethargy, irritability, and depression.

Coffee and cycling

Chewing Tobacco

Epidemiologically, the percentage of smokers among athletes in the United States has declined along with the decreasing trend in the general population. Use of chewing tobacco, however, remains inordinately high among athletes. Part of this can certainly be ascribed to new marketing and promotion campaigns by the tobacco companies, as well as the almost mythic traditional relationship of "chawing" tobacco to the great American pastime of baseball. Ironically, the original baseball cards advertised tobacco. Long ago politicians recognized the health hazards and declared chewing and spitting tobacco illegal in most places—except the baseball park.

From 1978 to 1985, celebrity athletes promoted chewing tobacco. Free supply programs and heavy advertising at sporting events stimulated the sale of chewing tobacco. As a result, chewing tobacco saw a 55 percent rise in sales at a time when cigarette sales dropped off. In 1970, men fifty-five and older were the heaviest users of chewing tobacco. By 1985, males under the age of twenty displaced them. Smokeless tobacco, a marketing label for chewing tobacco, is used by kindergarten children in Arkansas and Alaska; in Texas reportedly up to one-third of varsity football and baseball players use smokeless tobacco (Lombardo 1985).

Many people have been misled into thinking that smokeless tobacco is a safe alternative to smoking. The Surgeon General's *Report on the Health Consequences of Smokeless Tobacco Use* concluded that smokeless tobacco is causally related to oral cancer and gum recession, that it can lead to dependence on nicotine, and that it is not a safe alternative to smoking cigarettes (U.S. Surgeon General).

America's favorite pastime: baseball. Yet players still chew tobacco.

Nonetheless, some athletes use nicotine products for its perceived stimulating effect before their events, while others paradoxically use the tobacco for its calming effect. Still others state they use nicotine for its effect on the satiety center (i.e., "I'll gain weight if I stop smoking"). Some just use tobacco products for personal rather than performance reasons.

Regarding the widely held misconception that smokeless tobacco enhances performance, it is critical to make known to anyone that nicotine does not heighten energy or strength. In reality, the user who smoked, chewed, or snorted nicotine is simply experiencing elevation in heart rate and blood pressure. The perceived relaxation is actually relief from the craving associated with nicotine withdrawal.

Clearly, young people will continue chewing smokeless tobacco unless professional athletes, old time coaches, and managers act as role models and point out the negative effects of all tobacco products.

Amphetamines

The first widespread abuse of drugs in professional sports occurred in the late 1960s and early 1970s when professional football players used amphetamines. Mandell (1972) reported this in a so-called Sunday Syndrome of amphetamine use to enhance performance. However, athletes in many other sports, notably those involved in endurance events, also have used amphetamines.

Amphetamines have an appetite suppression effect attractive to a variety of athletes for whom making and keeping a required weight is essential (e.g., jockeys, gymnasts, wrestlers, boxers, etc.). Numerous studies have attempted to document the effects of amphetamines on performance. Some looked at psychomotor tasks, others examined certain variables related to overall performance, and still others studied athletic performance (Derlet and Heischober 1990).

Smith and Belcher (1978) reported that approximately 75 percent of trained swimmers, weight lifters, and runners showed improvements in performance after administration of amphetamines. However, Karpovich (1982) found improvement in only three of twenty athletes, and one athlete actually performed more poorly. A review in 1981, using criteria based on knee-extension strength and running to exhaustion, showed that performance usually improved by only a small percentage. Yet, in highly competitive sports, even a 1 percent improvement can mean the difference between victory and defeat.

Most people also would probably agree that the alertness of the fatigued person whether an athlete, truck driver, student, or subject of an experiment, increases with the use of amphetamines. However, Chandler and Black concluded in 1980 that "amphetamines do not prevent fatigue but rather mask the effects of fatigue and interfere with the body's fatigue-alarm system which could lead to disastrous results, especially under extreme environmental conditions."

Adverse Effects of Amphetamines on Athletic Performance

Deaths caused by amphetamine use have involved cerebral vascular accidents (strokes) secondary to hemorrhages in the brain, acute heart failure with arrhythmias, and hyperthermia. The elevation of body temperature, if not fatal, can combine with heat exhaustion and circulatory collapse to cause heat stroke because amphetamines obscure the athlete's normally protective physiologic fatigue level.

By diminishing pain thresholds, amphetamines allow athletes to continue to compete despite injury, thus potentially causing more tissue damage to the injured areas. Finally, there is added potential of injury to others in contact sports because of the increase in aggressiveness caused by amphetamine use.

Steroids and Athletes

All of the previously described drugs used in sports and athletics can be labeled *ergogenic* because they are performance enhancing substances. By far, the most controversial ergogenic drug used by many athletes, especially young developing boys and girls, is steroids.

Brief History

Steroids were developed in the 1930s for the treatment of anemia and a variety of diseases that wasted away muscles. Physicians have also used steroids to treat cancer, burn victims, intestinal problems, asthma, and emaciation. After World War II, steroids restored body tissue to victims of starvation. The increased aggressiveness caused by steroid use was one of the benefits sought in the use of steroids by German soldiers in World War II.

In 1988, Canadian sprinter, Ben Johnson, lost the gold medals he won in the Olympic games because he tested positive for steroids. Today, steroid use is not only a problem with world-class Olympic athletes but also with teenagers. Steroid use has become the adolescent rage of the 1990s. Studies indicate that 6 to 10 percent of high school boys will use steroids by graduation, as will 1 percent of girls. Unfortunately, two-thirds of these young people will start to use steroids prior to the age of 16. Most young people who use steroids do so to enhance their performance in sports. Yet, a surprisingly large percentage (25 percent) use steroids for appearance. The skinny kid on the beach, who gets sand kicked in his face no longer chooses the old Charles Atlas weight training program to bulk up. Instead, steroid use with weight training and diet create the hulking bodies that young people desire. Beefing up and strengthening their bodies, gives these young people added self-confidence because they feel attractive (Hough 1990).

Steroids are illegal without a prescription. Federal officials estimate the illicit steroid market at $400 million.

Terminology

Androgenic steroids, which includes testosterone, function primarily to develop and maintain male sex characteristics. So-called **anabolic** steroids are synthetic derivatives of testosterone developed in an attempt to minimize testosterones' androgenic or masculinizing effects on the individual, while promoting protein synthesis and muscular growth.

Because none of these compounds is purely anabolic or purely androgenic in their effects, and since athletes usually stack, or use the steroids in combination, technically the more correct designation is "anabolic-androgenic steroids" (A-AS) rather than just anabolic steroids (AS).

Major Effects

Many of the early studies regarding the effectiveness of steroids produced conflicting results. More recent studies have clearly indicated significant increases in strength as a result of the steroid use. The American College of Sports Medicine in their position statement on steroids in 1989 concluded that "gains in strength can occur through a variety of mechanisms in the highly trained athlete who takes steroids."

Increases in lean body mass do occur in A-AS steroid use. In the past, this was thought to be the result of water retention. It is now clear that there is an actual increase in muscle tissue and enhancement of muscle contractility. In addition, some reports cite an increase in actual bone density. However, most of these changes do not increase strength unless their use is combined with high-intensity weight training and a properly balanced diet.

A-AS steroids also increase the ability to perform high-intensity training sessions. In part, this is due to increased protein metabolism as well as the inhibition of the metabolic (breaking down) effects of corticosteroids that are released in increased amounts whenever the body is stressed. The result is the body requires less recuperation time between intensive workouts to repair itself. However, most studies have also shown that aerobic capacity is not affected or improved at all with steroid use.

Adverse Effects

The problem with steroids is that they do not act exclusively on one muscle or tissue group. Therefore, they stimulate muscles and tissues making the individual at risk for other adverse effects. The body's homeostasis is disrupted with the use of steroids causing a variety of physical problems. "Heart disease will probably be the most widely noted side effect with anabolic steroid abuse. Blood pressure elevates significantly when an individual takes anabolic steroids due to the retained fluid and increased blood volume. . . . High Density Lipoproteins (HDL-C) that aid the body in removing cholesterol, and are important to cardiac longevity, are drastically reduced with the use of androgens" (American Osteopathic Academy of Sports Medicine 1989).

For adolescents, the drug can cause stunted growth, and premature closing of growth plates. Other problems resulting from steroid abuse by men may include:

- liver and kidney damage
- breast development
- acne, baldness
- cysts
- shrinking of the testicles and sterility
- reduced sex drive
- headaches, nausea, and dizziness

For females the drug can cause:

- infertility
- clitoral enlargement
- breast atrophy
- menstrual irregularities
- male pattern baldness and voice change

More and more evidence is accruing that the most significant effect of A-AS use may be psychiatric. Psychological reactions such as extreme aggressiveness, mood swings, depression, and delusions are reported in some individuals. Signs and symptoms similar to drug and alcohol dependence (i.e., loss of control; continued use despite known adverse consequences, tolerance, and withdrawal) suggest that both physical and psychological dependence can occur with A-AS use.

Other Drugs/Alcohol in Sports

The pressures of professional athletic competition and the accompanying life-style can create a situation where athletes seek both relief and enhancement of performance by using drugs and/or alcohol. Many high school, college, even professional athletes are ill prepared for these pressures.

The widespread use of cocaine, marijuana, alcohol, amphetamine, and other drugs in professional sports came to the attention of the general public in the drug scandals of the last three decades. This was an indicator of the high level of denial and enabling behavior by players, coaches and management. Today, teams are making more concerted efforts at education, assessment, and treatment. They have programs that help athletes develop the skills to deal with the pressures. However, drug/alcohol problems are still enabled and/or denied at many levels of athletic competition. Additional efforts are needed to resolve the issue of drug/alcohol abuse and addiction at all levels of athletic endeavor.

Summary

Drugs/alcohol are found everywhere in our society and every family is vulnerable to the problems associated with drugs/alcohol. The following terms are commonly used in the chemical dependency field:

physical dependence;
withdrawal;
psychological dependence;
metabolism, absorption, excretion;
routes of administration;
set and setting;
tolerance and cross tolerance;
synergism, antagonism; and
toxicity.

The behavioral definition of addiction includes compulsive use of a chemical, becoming obsessed with the drug, losing control or inability to stop using, and continued use despite known adverse consequences. A drug is a nonfood substance that affects the structure and function of the body. Drugs are classified as either nonpsychoactive or psychoactive.

Nonpsychoactive drugs are the substances that in normal doses do not directly affect the brain. Psychoactive drugs affect brain functions, mood and behavior, and are subdivided primarily on the basis of physiological and psychological effects.

The major psychoactive drug categories are

1. Narcotic analgesics—painkillers and designer drugs (Fentanyl)
2. Central nervous system depressants—sedative hypnotics (alcohol, tranquilizers, and barbiturates)
3. Central nervous system stimulants—amphetamine, cocaine, nicotine, and caffeine
4. Hallucinogens
5. Cannabis sativa—marijuana and hashish
6. Inhalants—volatile solvents
7. PCP

Each of these psychoactive drugs has specific major effects, hazards, withdrawal symptoms, and special problems.

Substances that athletes use to enhance athletic performance discussed in this chapter include caffeine, chewing tobacco, amphetamines, and steroids. The current problem of steroid use by athletes, especially young people, can be a major tragedy.

References

American Society of Addiction Medicine. *Review Course Syllabus.* New York: A.S.A.M., 1987.

Ashton, C. H. "Solvent Abuse, Little Progress After 20 Years." *British Medical Journal* 300, January 1990, 135–38.

Blum, Kenneth. *Handbook of Abusable Drugs.* New York: Gardner Press, 1984.

Brecher, Edward M. *Licit and Illicit Drugs.* Boston: Little, Brown, 1972.

Chandler, J. V. and S. N. Blair. "The Effect of Amphetamines on Selected Physiological Components Related to Athletic Success." *Medicine and Science in Sports and Exercise* 12 (Spring 1980).

Cohen, S. "Marijuana and Learning." *Drug and Alcohol Newsletter, Vista Hill Foundation* XI, no. 3, (April 1989).

Cohen, S. "Marijuana Research: Selected Recent Findings." *Drug and Alcohol Newsletter, Vista Hill Foundation* XV, no. 1 (January 1986).

Cohen, Sidney and Robert O'Brien. *Encyclopedia of Drug Abuse.* New York: Facts on File, 1984.

Derlet, R. and B. Heischober. "Methamphetamine, Stimulant of the 1990s." *Western Journal of Medicine,* December 1990, 153625–628.

Doosa, A. "Effects of Anabolic Steroids on Athletes." *Clinical Pharmacology* 6, September 1987.

Drug Use among American High School Students, College Students, and Other Young Adults. National Trends through 1988. Rockville, Md.: NIDA, 1989.

Estroff, T. and M. Gold. "Psychiatric Presentation of Marijuana Abuse." *Psychiatric Annals* 16, no. 4 (April 1986).

The Health Consequences of Smoking, Nicotine Addiction, A Report of the Surgeon General. Rockville, Md.: U.S. Department of Health and Human Services, 1988.

Hough, D. "Anabolic Steroids and Ergogenic Aids." *Academy of Familty Practice* 41, no. 4 (April 1988): 1157–64.

Johnson, N. Peter. "What'd He Say? Street Drug Terminology." *The Journal of the South Carolina Medication Association,* January 1990.

Karpovich, P. V. "Effect of Amphetamine Sulfate on Athletic Performance." *Journal of American Medical Association* 170 (1969).

Kleiber, Herbert. *Journal of Psychoactive Drugs* 14, no. 4 (October–December 1984).

Lombardo, J. "Stimulants and Athletic Performance, Amphetamine and Caffeine." *The Physician and Sports Medicine* 4, no. 11 (April 1990): 1157–64.

Mandell, A. J. "The Sunday Syndrome: A Unique Pattern of Amphetamine Abuse Indigenous to American Professional Football." *Clinical Toxicology* 15, no. 2 (1979).

National Household Survey on Drug Abuse Population Estimate 1988. Rockville, Md.: NIDA, 1989.

Rohr, V. "Withdrawal Sequelae to Cannabis Use." *The International Journal of the Addictions* 24, no. 7 (1989): 627–31.

Smith, David and Donald Wesson. *Treating Cocaine Dependence.* Center City, Minn: Hazeldon Foundation, 1988.

Smith, G. M. and H. G. Beecher. "Amphetamine Sulfate and Athletic Performance." *Journal of American Medical Association* 170, no. 5 (1959).

Solomons, K. and V. M. Neppve. "Review Article, Cannabis—Its Clinical Effects." *S.A.M.T.* 76, August 1989.

Tamura, M. "Japan: Stimulant Epidemics, Past and Present." *Bulletin on Narcotics* XLL, no. 1 and 2, 1989.

Tashkin, D. and H. Gung. "How the Lungs Are Affected by Marijuana Smoking." *The Journal of Respiratory Diseases,* November 1987.

Thombs, D. "A Review of P.C.P. Abuse, Trends and Perceptions." *Public Health Reports* 104, no. 4 (July/August 1989) 325–28.

Woods, James H., Jonathan Katz, and Gail Winger. "Use and Abuse of Benzodiazepines." *Journal of American Medical Association* 260, no. 23 (December 1988).

Family Dynamics: The Arena of Drug/Alcohol Problems

This chapter describes characteristics of family systems that make family members vulnerable to problems with drugs/alcohol. Imbalanced/ dysfunctional family interaction is the most critical feature making children at risk for drug/alcohol dependence and addiction. Within the family system patterns develop that make the individual more vulnerable to drugs/alcohol.

Parental imbalance is evidenced by rigid parenting, with either or both parents being emotionally and, perhaps, physically unavailable. Parental dysfunction often involves marital discord, drug/alcohol dependence, physical and emotional abuse, and sexual violation.

Imbalanced family systems are also characterized by inadequate boundary setting, and physical, sexual, and emotional abuse. The unresolved grief and impaired mourning related to these violations perpetuates feelings of loss, abandonment, shame, and rejection.

This chapter explores all of these issues as significant factors in passing on the disease of alcoholism and drug addiction to the next generation. Breaking through the denial and enabling behavior of an imbalanced family system is the difficult task in family counseling.

A major theme of this book is that families can make a difference by preventing, intervening, and seeking help for drug/alcohol problems.

Chapter Goals

1. Describe families as systems.
2. Describe the need for the entire alcoholic/addict family system to seek recovery.
3. Explain Satir's metaphor of the family as a mobile.
4. Identify some of the dysfunctional styles of communicating outlined by Virginia Satir.
5. Identify and describe some of the dysfunctional survival roles in the alcoholic/addict family system.
6. Identify the five stages of grieving and apply the stages of grieving to the alcoholic/addict family system.
7. Define enabling behavior, and give examples for each of the five types of enabling behavior.
8. Identify some issues involved in professional enabling.
9. Clarify the reasons for utilizing the term *imbalanced family systems* instead of dysfunctional family systems.
10. Define and describe parental imbalance/dysfunction.
11. Describe the rules, verbalizations, values, mottos, and communication patterns in rigid, ambiguous, distorted, and overextended family systems.
12. Cite historical examples of loss and trauma in the American family system and the alcoholic/addict family system.
13. Explain how impaired mourning is related to problems with drugs/alcohol.
14. Define such terms as *clear boundaries, enmeshed boundaries, disengaged boundaries, boundary inadequacy, ambiguous boundaries, overly rigid boundaries,* and *invasive boundaries.*
15. Define triangulation and describe its impact on the family system.
16. Describe the family life cycle in the alcoholic/addict family system.
17. Describe methods used to engage resistant family members into treatment, especially fathers of alcoholics/addicts.
18. Describe the difficulties in working with alcoholic/addict family systems and the application of noble ascriptions.
19. Identify the special characteristics necessary to be an effective drug/alcohol family counselor.

Family as Systems

Initially, one must look at the family as a system. Some key elements of family systems are that they all have rules, values, verbal and nonverbal methods of communicating, boundaries, roles, and patterns of interaction. Systems always seek some level of homeostasis, or balance. Alcoholism and drug dependency is a dysfunctional element in family life. The result is a disequilibrium or imbalance forcing family members to compensate and give up aspects of their own sense of self in an attempt to keep the family in balance. One could describe the alcoholic/addict family as a top-heavy top that tries to spin in a functional pattern, but instead swerves to one side and skids in a diagonal direction until it stops. The individuals in this system are all compensating in different yet similar ways. It's as if they were walking around with a heavy weight on one shoulder; they either have to lean to one side to walk properly or use all their energy to try to compensate and look like they are walking upright. Both positions require a great deal of energy. Family therapist Carl Whitaker (1978) has described the family as the source of all kinds of electrical energy, with positive and negative voltages.

The Need for the Family to Seek Recovery

Virginia Satir (1967), the famous family therapist, was the first to describe the family using the metaphor of a mobile: if the wires on one of the pieces of the mobile are twisted, the mobile would spin improperly. Instead of a delicately balanced mobile, each piece would get entangled and out of balance at the slightest breeze. A well-balanced mobile, or family system, could sway and flex with the strong gusts and heavy winds of life. The family with drug/alcohol problems is described as an imbalanced, or a dysfunctional family system. In a healthy family, the system is flexible and fluid, open (not rigid), predictable (not inconsistent), and balanced in meeting both the individual's and the family's needs.

Looking at the family as a system is imperative in addressing the problem of drug/alcohol dependence and addiction. For example, after showing improvement in treatment, frequently adolescent and young adult schizophrenic patients return to their families, and the signs of schizophrenia recur. What happened is that the same imbalanced patterns of family interaction caused the symptoms to return. This holds true for alcoholics/addicts unless families are also in recovery. If the family system does not change and the family members do not do their recovery work, the same

dysfunctional styles of communication and interaction make the addict/alcoholic at risk for drug/alcohol relapse or the development of some other dysfunctional behavior.

To effectively treat the alcoholic/addict, the rest of the family system also needs treatment. The dysfunctional aspect of the disease has affected all family members. The high drug/alcohol relapse rate is often attributable to the lack of recovery by the family members. Too frequently the alcoholic/addict is the focus of help, and the family members deny their own enabling and codependent behavior. The messages from the family are "Just fix the addict/alcoholic." "Just get him/her to stop using drugs/alcohol and then everything will be O.K."

Family members avoid being active in treatment because they resist looking at their own behavior; they fear getting in touch with painful feelings that may be overwhelming.

Another real fear is whether the family system can survive reexperiencing these feelings. They wonder "Has the family been hurt beyond repair?" "Will the family be able to work through the violations of the past?" These questions and others need to be addressed for the effective recovery of the alcoholic/addict and the family members.

The expression *dry drunk* refers to those individuals who stay sober and do not use drugs/alcohol. However, their overall personalities are very similar to when they were using drugs/alcohol. Essentially, they have chosen not to deal with the underlying issues that contributed to the negative aspects of their personalities. For some it is certainly enough that they are sober. Others who are still experiencing feelings of depression, fear, rage, and anxiety may decide to get help and address the problem.

A major portion of my private counseling practice is with recovering addicts/alcoholics who after one to five years of being sober, realize that they are still having problems, especially in interpersonal relationships. This is often described as the addicts' "second bottom." The first bottom is the realization that they can no longer continue to use drugs/alcohol. The second bottom is the realization that they are still not having fun, due to unresolved personality issues. They ask themselves the question, "Now that I am —— years sober, am I having fun yet?" The answer frequently is, "No, my life is more manageable but I'm still not feeling better."

The family of the addict/alcoholic also goes through a kind of dry drunk. The family may glow in the joy of the addict/alcoholic's initial sobriety. The family may now feel validated that they are indeed okay. From the viewpoint of their friends, neighbors, and community, "they did the right thing." There is no discounting that the family was courageous in struggling to get the addict/alcoholic into treatment. However, they must continue the struggle to develop a healthier family system. In many cases, the family returns to old dysfunctional patterns. It is fair to say that recovery from the disease of alcoholism and drug addiction is an ongoing process for the individual and the family.

Satir's Family Patterns of Communication

Virginia Satir, author of *Conjoint Family Therapy* (1967), *Peoplemaking* (1972), and *Helping Families to Change* (1976), emphasizes the feeling component of family patterns of communication. She describes a dysfunctional family as one that maintains rules that do not fit the reality of what is felt and believed.

Satir's work is monumental and popular. According to Satir, individuals with poor self-concepts see pots that are half empty. Individuals with the ability to differentiate (i.e., those with good self-concepts) see their pots as half full. The former group feels hopeless and negative, the latter group is positive and hopeful.

Satir identified the following dysfunctional styles as well as a functional style of communicating:

1. Placaters discount themselves. Their goal is frequently to avoid conflict and to avoid others' anger. Their communication patterns feature:
   a. Words that agree and avoid conflict: "Whatever you want is O.K." The placaters' worth is based on others accepting, not rejecting, what they say.
   b. Bodies that placate: "I am helpless." The placaters' worth is based on being physically available, even when that may not be consistent with what they feel.
   c. Feelings: "I am worthless." Placaters believe they have no choices but to be dependent in dysfunctional relationships because there is no way out, and they are not strong enough or worth the struggle.
2. Blamers elevate themselves by discounting others. Their goal is to avoid looking at themselves, their own issues, and their own responsibility. Others' feelings are often discounted. If others would only do it the right way—which is their way—then things would work out. Their communication patterns feature:
   a. Words that are critical, judgmental, shaming put-downs: "You never do anything right." "It's all your fault."
   b. Bodies that blame: "I am more powerful, more dominant."
   c. Feelings: "It is your fault that I am unhappy."
3. Intellectualizers discount their own feelings. Their goal is to place rigid emphasis on the cognitive to figure out problems, to deny the role feelings play in relationships and decisions, and to avoid the emotional impact of feelings. Intellectualizers are the brains, the computers, the cognitive persons who think, "If I can only understand this, I'll be okay."
   They often feel that if they can only find that missing piece of the puzzle, they will find the cause of their problems. They fail to integrate the key elements of the puzzle—their feelings—and

fail to realize that the puzzle may not be solvable, especially with their linear approach. Their communication patterns feature:

a. Words that are extremely logical: "That makes sense and is reasonable."
b. Bodies in control or shut down.
c. Feelings: "I am vulnerable and feel threatened when I get in touch with my feelings, especially feelings of vulnerability."

4. Distracters discount context. Their goal is to keep others and themselves away from painful feelings, to distract and avoid conflict. Distractors are the elusive, sometimes charming, magicians. They are difficult to hold accountable or responsible because they keep the focus elsewhere, not on themselves. Many addicts and alcoholics are masters of this style of communication and avoid or deny their problems with drugs and alcohol. Their communication patterns feature:

a. Words—confusing and irrelevant. They are unable to establish clarity, or to set specific goals.
b. Body—acting as if they are somewhere else when the content gets too specific and focused. They want to frustrate, discount, and escape from others.
c. Feelings: "Nobody cares. I am not happy."

According to Satir, **leveling** is the healthy state of communication. Words, body, and feelings are consistent with the message. The individual is congruent and acts in a congruent fashion.

Wegscheider-Cruse's Alcoholic/Addict Family System Survival Roles

Sharon Wegscheider-Cruse, a leader in the field of adult children of alcoholics (see chapter 6), popularized the concept of survival roles in the alcoholic/addict family system. These roles describe the coping mechanisms members use to survive in a dysfunctional alcoholic/addict family. They include the following:

Chief Enabler

The chief enabler assumes primary responsibility for the chemically dependent family member. The chief enabler shelters and protects, even denies, the dysfunctional aspects of a family member's drug/alcohol use.

The major enabling approaches are

1. avoiding and shielding
2. attempting to control
3. taking over responsibilities
4. rationalizing and accepting
5. cooperating and collaborating (Nelson 1988)

(We describe all of these methods of enabling later in this chapter.)

The chief enabler softens the consequences for the chemically dependent family member's lack of responsibility or enables that member to avoid the consequences of drug/alcohol use.

Family Hero

The family hero is the achiever, the responsible child, the good child, the model child. The family hero is often the firstborn who escapes the dysfunctional aspects of the alcohol/drug family through personal achievement. The family's sense of self-worth is often the conscious or unconscious responsibility of this family member. Unfortunately, the family hero achieves for the family and ignores personal feelings, values, and goals. The family hero in adulthood often experiences a depression or sense of loss due to the incongruency of internal feelings with external behaviors. The hero may be outwardly successful but feel like a charlatan, or empty inside. When this conflict is not dealt with, the family hero is vulnerable to drug/alcohol problems, and/or problems in interpersonal relationships.

Family Scapegoat

The primary function of the family scapegoat is to divert the family members away from the real issues in the family (e.g., marital discord, marital infidelity, or parental drug/alcohol problems) and the painful emotionality of these family issues. The family members can then blame the scapegoat for all of the family problems. The family scapegoat often exhibits acting out behavior in school and at home, antisocial behavior, and drug/alcohol abuse due to underlying feelings of anger and resentment.

Lost Child

The lost child's role is often the most tragic. This is the child whose primary function is to allow the dysfunctional family—especially the parents—to expend less energy. This child often identifies with the pain of their parents and other siblings and wants to decrease the family members' level of pain by

Case Study
The Lost Child
Michelle

Michelle was beginning her senior year in high school when her family began therapy. At that time her stepbrother, Jack, was heavily into drugs (marijuana, hallucinogens, speed, and cocaine) and alcohol. Her other sisters were extremely angry with Jack's attitude and behavior. Michelle was an A student, attractive, student body president, on the cross-country team, and very popular. She had a quiet, affable presence, and acted older than her seventeen years. She was the only one in the family to whom Jack related. During the course of treatment, it was very difficult for Michelle to express any feelings. Even in individual sessions she would deny feeling any pain or negative emotions.

Later that year Michelle was accepted to a college a few hours drive from home. During her first semester away at school, despite good study habits, she ended up dropping a course, and receiving C grades. Also, she didn't make any friends at school. Michelle was running on the college track team but was unmotivated and not running to her true potential. This was quite traumatic for Michelle because she was so popular and such a good student and athlete in high school. Fortunately, she called and set up an individual counseling appointment during her college break. For the first time, Michelle was in touch with her pain and grief. I believe that if she had not reached out for help, Michelle would have been another college student unable to cope with the pressures or to effectively deal with backlogged feelings that eventually might have caused her to take her own life.

not contributing to the problem, perhaps even taking on the family's pain. The family inadvertently reinforces this child for not having needs. The child denies feelings and needs, frequently disconnecting emotionally and even physically from the family. At some point, the child can no longer deny personal feelings and pain. Thus, lost children frequently get overwhelmed with emotions and are at risk for suicide.

Family Mascot

The primary function of the family mascot is to divert attention away from the family issues and family pain. The mascot uses humor, silliness, and even self-disparaging ineptness (making fun of oneself) as a way of diverting the family from its pain. Frequently, the mascot discounts a sense of self as the price to pay for calm in the family. As a result, the mascot may feel unworthy of love, unless able to alleviate someone's pain.

These are just a few family roles. The roles are stereotypic classifications for purposes of identifying some common role features in dysfunctional or imbalanced family systems. Please note that the roles are illustrations of dysfunctional patterns of family interaction and should not be used to pigeonhole someone into a static classification. Usually people maintain a variety of traits from each of the roles. Family roles may also change based on different family situations and adjustments in the family process.

Other important family therapists—Theodore Lidz, Lieman Wynne, James Framo, Ron Jackson, and Jay Haley emphasize a systems approach in their work with families. All of them emphasize changing dysfunctional patterns of family communication and interaction.

These family therapists have different styles, theories, and methods of working with families. Some see the entire family together in a counseling session. Others may see family members separately, or sometimes see the father and son, mother and daughter, or just the children. Family therapists even use a multigenerational approach that includes grandparents, or an expanded family approach of including other relatives. In summary, the key element of all of these approaches is looking at the family as a system, a system that is affected and changed by the actions and events in the lives of each of the family members.

Family Grieving of Drug/Alcohol Problems

Families have a wide range and variety of reactions to drug/alcohol problems. Yet, there are some common generalizable patterns to a family's response. The grieving model describes the stages that the family goes through: denial, anger, bargaining, depression, and acceptance.

Denial

Again, denial in the alcoholic/addict family system is pervasive; at various times, all family members maintain some form of denial. The underlying function of denial is to assuage the family members' feelings of embarrassment, humiliation, and shame, and their own feelings of frustration in trying to control the disease of alcoholism and/or drug addiction.

Frequently, family members feel a personal sense of guilt and inadequacy, a sense that they are somehow directly responsible for the addict/alcoholic developing the disease. This sense of guilt and inadequacy is often felt by the innocent children of addicts/alcoholics.

The major defense mechanisms of rationalization and minimization maintain the illusion that the family is normal, or just like other families. Family members who grew up in alcoholic/addict family systems have trouble recognizing what is normal or functional. They might have suspected something was different in their families but acted as if everything was all right (i.e., the normal family illusion).

Denial's Linkages to Society At the denial stage, family members rarely acknowledge that something is wrong, although they sense something might be different about their family. The spouse or family members may seek help in an indirect, nonspecific manner, such as talking to friends and/or relatives. Unfortunately, those friends and relatives often reinforce the denial. One such example is the following:

Denial Transaction: Between Mary and her Sister-in-Law, Maureen:

Mary: "The other night at the party, do you think Harry drank too much?"
Maureen: "Oh, that happens to everyone once in a while."
Mary: "You don't think he has a problem with alcohol, do you?"
Maureen: "No, of course not. He drinks like most of us in the family, and we certainly don't have a problem. You're overreacting."

In reality, Harry and Maureen grew up in alcoholic family systems and they both have drinking problems.

Anger

Anger is an effective defense to keep family members from talking about issues and feelings that might indicate an alcohol/drug problem in the family. Anger can be expressed as verbal, physical, emotional, and/or sexual threats, abuse, and/or violation. Anger can be actual or threatened rejection and abandonment. Addicts/alcoholics use anger to blame and shame other family members as inadequate and responsible for their predicament. In reality, the anger is a way for the addict/alcoholic to avoid feelings of shame, a way to control others in the family, and to deny responsibility for problems in the family system.

Once they were in recovery, many adolescent and adult patients/clients of mine admitted that causing a conflict or big fight was a way to get out of the house and use drugs/alcohol. Many clients rationalized that they were already in trouble with the family, so what was the difference if they got into more trouble?

An adolescent patient/client of mine, once described her alcoholic/addictive family system as "raging and rag-

Case Study

Anger in an Alcoholic Family System

John

John, a forty-three-year-old insurance salesman, described having a few drinks after work one day and then realizing he was late for an important dinner with his family. He rationalized that since he was already in trouble, what was the use in calling; he would just get yelled at.

Since he was already late and wanted to delay the pain of his wife's anger, he might as well continue drinking and be really late. Once he was drinking, the hours passed quickly. When the bar closed, John went home.

ging" (nagging). "Dad is the one who rages around the home, and mom attempts to control him by ragging at dad and everyone else. It is no wonder that I don't spend much time at home."

The combined effect is an unsafe, unpredictable family system with underlying feelings of confusion, fear, anxiety, shame, and sometimes immobilizing trauma.

This conflict between family members creates a climate of confusion and a lack of clarity as to what is an appropriate approach to the problem of drugs/alcohol. The result is often a trial-and-error approach. At first, family members try extreme control or rigid threats: "The next time you use drugs/alcohol, I will" (not let you in the house, confine you to your room for one month, get a divorce or separation). When this doesn't work, the next approach might be to let go, or to try and ignore the addictive behavior completely, as if the addict didn't exist. The resulting pattern of control-release is chaotic. This trial-and-error approach creates further anger, confusion, and feelings of hopelessness.

Anger's Linkages to Society At this stage, the family might go beyond relatives and friends and talk to a minister, priest, or rabbi, family physician, or school counselor. Some of these people may not be adequately trained in recognizing and assessing drug/alcohol problems, and the family members may be vague in disclosing the degree to which drugs/alcohol are used. At this stage, family members are still not quite sure they need help and are embarrassed in seeking help. They may start to get help, get frightened or be resistant to experiencing the pain associated with acknowledging the problem, and then back off from getting help.

Bargaining

The bargaining stage is usually preceded by a major crisis. The family can no longer deny or ignore the problem and cannot cover up the feelings of frustration and anger. The family is essentially saying "we have had enough of this, it's too chaotic." The family is still not ready to effect change in the system, instead the goal is to strike some arrangement or bargain. Being held hostage by the addict, the family is willing to pay ransom to have the addict stop bothering them with outrageous behavior. Unfortunately, the ransom often goes beyond what is reasonable or tolerable, and the family initially agrees to do almost anything to survive in this chaos.

Many of the bargains are financial or object related: "If you stop abusing drugs/alcohol, I'll buy you ________." "If you tolerate my drug/alcohol use, I'll give you economic security."

The underlying and false assumption of most bargains is that the addict can stop using. The assumption is that the addict can override the drive and allure of the drugs/alcohol for some reward. Unfortunately, the drive to use drugs/alcohol is stronger than the reward of the bargain, and willpower alone is not strong enough to overcome the drive to use drugs/alcohol.

Some of the bargains are far more subtle. Couples, families, and friends develop lives based on the bargain of maintaining addiction. Common bargains related to alcoholism and drug addiction are

Let's ignore the addict's behavior and it might just stop. The more you ignore the destructive behavior, the more intense and dramatic the situation becomes.

Let's separate or withdraw from the addict temporarily. Unless there is strong therapeutic and personal support, the addict feeds on the partner's or family members' weaknesses. The individual usually does not have the support to break the codependent dance of addiction (see chapter 6).

Avoid making a decision, maybe it will get better with time. It's very rare that a spontaneous recovery occurs from alcohol/drugs. In chapter 8 we discuss drug/alcohol intervention and "raising the addict's bottom" in an attempt to salvage and avoid further damage. Rarely does an addict decide on her own to get help. Sometimes it is so late that scary consequences are involved such as

Case Study

An Alcoholic Bargain

Linda and Tom

Linda, forty-two, had been to a number of therapists over a three to four year period, prior to being referred to me. Married for twelve years, she has two boys, ages five and eight. Her husband Tom, forty-five, was a practicing alcoholic since they had met and his drinking was maintained throughout the years of their marriage. During one counseling session, Tom agreed that he was alcoholic but was not willing to change. When asked what it would take for him to stop drinking, he thought for a minute. Then he said, "The only thing that would stop me from drinking would be to have my liver fall apart."

This was an honest response espoused by others similarly addicted to alcohol. Linda knew that Tom had numerous extramarital affairs throughout their marriage and he continued to seek women in the bars and restaurants that he frequented most evenings. The tragic, innocent victims of Tom's alcoholism were his two young sons.

When asked why she put up with this behavior, Linda replied: "What can I do? I'll lose my home and my life-style would change."

For Linda, and many other spouses, the fear of abandonment is symbolized in the physical home. Linda had grown up in an alcoholic family and she feared the feelings of abandonment that she would reexperience if she left the relationship.

After more than three years of individual counseling and Al-Anon meetings, Linda left the relationship. Both boys are in a program for children of alcoholics. Unfortunately, Tom is still drinking and is in another bargain relationship, this time with a woman who is also an alcoholic.

the threat of physical harm, criminal justice and legal problems, job and financial problems, or death.

Bargaining's Linkages to Society At the bargaining stage, family members might seek help from experts in the field because their bargains are not working and they need advice and direction. Even when family members are fortunate in finding a counselor who knows about drug/alcohol intervention and treatment, the family members may still not follow through. The attitude at this stage is still a form of bargaining. The therapeutic bargain is to fix the identified patient (the addict) so the bargainer can avoid feeling pain. In some situations, family members may even sabotage counseling to avoid the pain of looking at their roles in the dysfunction. In a distorted sense, the failure of the trained professional validates the failure of the family member: "If the counselor can't help ________, then I guess we didn't do such a bad job." Many families seeking counseling soon find out that addiction is a family disease and effective treatment involves the entire family.

Feeling Stage

At the feeling stage, family members can no longer deny, cover up with anger, or bargain their feelings away. Many feelings come to the surface and are easily accessed. Family members are crying at the slightest provocation, anxious to the point of being hypervigilant (checking things out obsessively), and in some cases feeling immobilized. These feelings are undeniable and force the family to seek help.

Acceptance Stage

At the acceptance stage, the family has recognized that they have a problem. They are ready to do the work necessary to heal and develop healthier ways of relating. Recognizing that all the family members are suffering, they have the courage to get help. At this stage the addict/alcoholic and the family members have begun to work on the problem. This is when treatment and recovery begin.

Enabling Behavior

In an attempt to avoid recognizing problems, the family enables the continued use of drugs/alcohol and other dysfunctional behaviors. Enabling is described as an unhealthy doing for, or killing with kindness. Parents may have good intentions in enabling their children. Their lack of insight into the dynamics of the enabling process, however, causes problems to continue and to get progressively worse.

"Protecting one's child is normal and appropriate, but overprotection can cause problems. Enablers overprotect and find it difficult to separate what their child needs from what their child wants. The price of overprotection is prolonging the dependency of immaturity and thereby aiding the progression of chemical dependency" (MacDonald 1984).

Enabling behavior has been defined as taking responsibility for someone else's lack of responsibility, or softening the consequences for someone's irresponsibility. Enablers are under the delusion that no one knows about the problems and they can continue to cover them up. The reality is that others are aware of the problems and are directly and indirectly letting the family know they need help. Only the family maintains this denial to the real dimensions of the problem.

Charles Nelson (1988) identified the following five styles of enabling behavior.

Avoiding and Shielding

Any behavior by a family member that covers up or prevents the user or the family member from experiencing the full impact of the harmful consequences of the drug use. Enabling behavior includes:

- Making up excuses to avoid social contact during drinking and drugging periods.
- Side-stepping or avoiding participation in discussions about drugs.
- Taking alcohol, sedatives, and/or other drugs to try and lower one's own anxiety or stress about a family member's problems with drugs.
- Not standing up for one's rights in fear of the family member going into a binge cycle of drug use.
- Cleaning up the family member's vomit after a drug/alcohol episode.
- Staying away from home as much as possible to get away from the situation.
- Shielding the addict from a crisis that could send her into therapy.
- Telling the alcoholic to leave until he quits drinking but then immediately going out and looking for that family member.
- Helping the addict keep up appearances or cover up around relatives, friends, neighbors, or her employer.

Attempting to Control

Any behavior by a family member that is performed with the intent to take personal control over the addict/alcoholic's use of the drug. Enabling behavior includes:

- Trying to buy things that might divert the addict from drug use (sports equipment, tools, car, house, etc.).
- Spending the night at a hotel or motel to get the user to quit.
- Spending the night at a friend's house to get the user to quit.
- Screaming, yelling, swearing, or crying in an attempt to get a family member to stop drinking or drugging.

Threatening to hurt oneself in an attempt to get a family member to quit.
Threatening physical violence to get the user to quit.
Checking or measuring the addict's drug stash to determine how much he has been using.
Encouraging the addict to do the drug at home to avoid more problems away from home.
Using or withholding sex as a way to control a partner's drug/alcohol use.
Throwing away, hiding, or destroying the family member's stash or paraphernalia.

Taking over Responsibilities

Any behavior by the family member designed to take over the user's personal responsibilities (i.e., finances, household chores, or employment). Enabling behavior includes:

Cleaning the family member's drug paraphernalia when left out.
Waking the alcoholic in time for work.
Reminding the user to eat at times.
Staying home from work to take care of the family member's problems resulting from drug use.
Preaching to the addict about her failures as a warning about the personal effects of the drug use.
Doing the family member's chores.
Waiting hand and foot on the family member.
Paying all the bills.
Taking a second job to cover the bills piling up after money was diverted to drugs.
Covering the addict/alcoholic's bad checks.

Rationalizing and Accepting

Any behavior by the family member that conveys a rationalization or acceptance of the addict/alcoholic's use of the drug. Enabling behavior includes:

Believing and/or communicating that the family member's episodes of drug use were only isolated instances and not patterns of use.
Believing and/or communicating that the use of the drugs was safe.
Believing and/or communicating that the family member's use of drugs increased that person's self-confidence.

Believing and/or communicating that the use of drugs helped the family member communicate better.

Believing and/or communicating that the use of drugs helped the addict to be happier or less depressed.

Believing and/or communicating that drugs gave more energy, endurance, coordination, or any other function aiding the family member's performance in physical activities.

Believing and/or communicating that use of drugs helped the addict to be more open.

Rationalizing and/or communicating that the drugs gave more alertness, creativity, clearer thinking, studying powers, or any other function aiding the addict's mental activities.

Cooperation and Collaborating

Any assistance or involvement by a family member in the buying, selling, adulterating, testing, preparing, or using the drug. Enabling behavior includes:

Helping the family member to take the drugs (e.g., injecting, pouring, etc.).

Helping the family member adulterate (cut) the drugs.

Allowing the addict to use one's house for drug adulteration purposes.

Helping the family member weigh or package drugs.

Helping the family member keep accounting records of drug sales.

Helping the addict chop, crush, or screen drugs.

Helping the family member to wash, clean, or purify drugs.

Making available to an addict any paraphernalia for taking or preparing drugs.

Loaning or giving money to the addict for drugs.

Supplying the family member with drugs.

These examples are quite specific and comprise a general guide to each type of enabling behavior. Such examples can help readers classify behavior that might be considered enabling.

Professional Enablers

Enabling behavior is not limited to family members. Many professionals (psychologists, counselors, doctors, clergy, and others) inadvertently, or sometimes consciously, enable the excessive use of drugs/alcohol. Professional enabling involves a number of dynamic factors:

1. Avoidance: Professionals may feel that "it's not my responsibility." They rationalize that talking about drug/alcohol problems is not in their treatment domain. For example, the physicians may justify that their domain is to focus on the physical aspects of alcohol or drugs, not psychological or personal habits of drinking/drugging. Realistically, professionals fear that if they bring up the issue of drug/alcohol abuse, client/patients might seek care somewhere else.
2. Attitude: Many professionals are not adequately trained in drug/alcohol assessment and treatment. Their own personal view and pattern of drug/alcohol use may cause them to have perceptual problems when it comes to drugs/alcohol.
3. Fear: Professionals take a risk by talking about problems with drugs/alcohol. Professionals who address or question someone's use of drugs/alcohol may fear alienating the client/patient.
4. Distancing: Some professionals have difficulty in expressing their concern, and prefer keeping a professional distance from their client/patients. They therefore avoid bringing up the issue of drug/alcohol use.

Professionals in the health care fields are important gatekeepers in directing clients/patients to appropriate drug/alcohol treatment. They can be supportive, positive resources for families experiencing the pain of drug/alcohol problems.

Imbalanced Family Systems

Imbalanced, Not Dysfunctional

Throughout the literature of the drug/alcohol and mental health fields—and even in this textbook—we frequently see the term *dysfunctional* describing families, systems, relationships, parenting, behavior, and individuals. The term *dysfunctional* is frequently a shame-based negative label, with a negative emotional tone. Labeling them as dysfunctional discourages families and individuals who are struggling with the problems of drug/alcohol dependence. Many people have been annoyed and discouraged at being told they were dysfunctional. It sounds hopeless. For example, what good does it do to tell a patient, relative, or friend, "You come from a shame-based dysfunctional family system." Or, "You have a codependent enabling, dysfunctional relationship with your spouse and children." This doesn't really help them and may even shame them, making them feel helpless and hopeless. Most people feel a sense of betrayal in even thinking about their families in such a derogatory manner.

Instead of using dysfunctional, replace it with the term *imbalanced*. For this is truly what we are looking at; an imbalance in the individual and family members' lives. Remember Satir's image of an out-of-balance mobile. It is so much more hopeful to seek treatment if one has the expectation of becoming balanced. It is a far more positive approach.

Imagine the difference in your reaction if you brought your car in for repairs and the mechanic said, "Your car is dysfunctional," rather than "Your car is out of balance." There is truly an emotional systems imbalance in the alcoholic/addict family. The term *imbalance* gives hope that there is a way to get help and better manage the system. The goal is to establish balance and order by addressing the problems in the family.

There are different kinds of imbalances in family systems. Drugs/alcohol serve a different function in each of these imbalanced systems. Next we describe rigid, ambiguous, overextended, and distorted family systems to better explain imbalanced family systems. In each family system, the drug of choice and its function is an illustration, not an empirically proven fact.

Rigid Family Systems

Rules—Strict interpretation of the rules with no exceptions; inflexibility with no extenuating circumstances. The rules keeper (usually father) is exempt from the rules.

Values—"There is only one way to do things and that is the right way—my way." Things are always black or white, right or wrong.

Motto—"Do it right, or else."

Communication—Linear, hierarchical. The father is usually dominant, powerful, and unapproachable. Mother softens the impact of father's harshness.

Drugs of choice—Alcohol and/or heroin, other sedative hypnotics, and narcotic analgesics.

Functions of drug—Suppress feelings, especially anger, and stay numb to the trauma in this family system.

Ambiguous Family System

Rules—We have rules but we don't enforce them, and we change them if someone is annoyed or inconvenienced.

Values—Forever changing, based on the situation.

Motto—"Keep peace at all costs, avoid conflict."

Communication—Mixed messages that are crazy making. "Do what you know we want, without us letting you know what it is we want."

Drugs of choice—Alcohol and/or heroin, marijuana, and hallucinogens.

Functions of drug—Suppress feelings of discomfort, kill pain, shut out reality, and/or distort reality.

Overextended Family System

Rules—Be productive, get busy, stay on the move.

Values—Look good, achieve, do it with willpower, feelings are for wimps.

Motto—"We can achieve anything we set our minds to." "The right stuff."

Communication—Feelings are not expressed or integrated; decisions are based on results and what will please the parents.

Drugs of choice—Cocaine, methamphetamine, and other stimulants, alcohol.

Functions of drug—Keep on working/doing even though feelings are not congruent with work or intimate relationships.

Distorted Family System

Rules—Don't let outsiders know we are crazy. Act like we are a normal family, just a bit eccentric.

Values—Maintain an illusion of normalcy, despite significant physical, emotional, and interpersonal problems of the family. Keep outsiders guessing about us.

Motto—"Aren't most families like ours?"

Communication—Mixed messages; parents and children are unavailable and have limited common perceptions of situations.

Drugs of choice—Alcohol, hallucinogens, marijuana, and inhalants.
Functions of drug—Distort reality that is already distorted to try and make sense, or no sense, of it.

Parental Imbalance

In her review of the literature, Karol L. Kumpfer (1987) identified various factors that contributed to parental imbalance. Often parents are dysfunctional as caregivers; sometimes they are overwhelmed by problems of their own. This prevents them from providing the kind of care, support, structure, and healthy encouragement that children require to effectively develop and grow. Kumpfer summarized these characteristics of parental imbalance:

1. Increased alcoholism, drug use, and nicotine dependence are characteristic of parents whose children have problems with drugs/alcohol.
2. Increased antisocial or sexually deviant behavior in parents.
3. Increased mental and emotional problems, such as depression, personality disorders, or narcissism.
4. Increased marital conflict.
5. Increased parental absenteeism due to separation, divorce, death.

Chemically dependent and/or imbalanced parents often

- lack knowledge and skills in parenting
- have unrealistic expectations and lack information on what is developmentally appropriate behavior at various ages
- are insensitive to the special needs of their children
- have decreased family management skills
- have inappropriate disciplining techniques and maintain inconsistent, rigid, or ambiguous boundaries
- have decreased positive responses and reinforcement of the children
- have decreased parental involvement and poor bonding or parent/child attachment.

Parents who are not aware of their own emotional and psychological issues, may deny the impact their anger, rage, and physical and emotional unavailability has on their children. Parents play an integral role in the development of their children. A positive caring relationship is essential for healthy development. The effective parent establishes bonding experiences that develop a positive regard for the child and reinforces a positive sense of self. When a parent loses this positive bonding with a child, the child's sense of loss and anger may never be assuaged. This loss is often found in alcoholic/addict family systems.

Ironically, children who grow up in an abstinent family system may also develop drug/alcohol dependence and addiction. People who become alienated from their abstinence backgrounds may use excessive drinking to express their frustration with early rigid familial, religious, and community teachings. Problem drinking or excessive drug use is symbolic of a rebellion or revolt against early family values that became overly rigid.

Loss and Trauma and the American Family

American families have experienced significant traumas over the last 200 or more years: wars, economic disasters, and social change have threatened the structure of the American family. The trauma of war dates back to the American Revolution with death; destruction; family separation; and financial, physical, and emotional hardships. The family system of those early years was shaped by a tremendous struggle for survival.

Strong families survived the trauma of the Civil War with brother killing brother. The world wars, the Korean War, and the Vietnam War have had everlasting effects on the American family system as will the Persian Gulf War. The absence of parents in the service and the deaths of sons and daughters continue to significantly affect our families.

The American family system has survived periodic recessions, the Great Depression, and the savings and loan debacle. Economic growth has meant the destruction of a previous core of the American culture, the American farm family. Despite our national wealth, we have lost the war on poverty; homeless families live the trauma of despair.

The American family system has also weathered social change. Civil rights and human rights issues still cause dissension in some families. As extended families become rare, families are getting smaller; many have latchkey kids and two breadwinners. Stereotypical family roles are slowly crumbling, yet the American family continues. More recently, the AIDS epidemic, drug/alcohol addiction, and child neglect and abuse are a few of the many issues in the consciousness of the American family.

This is both an extremely exciting and frightening time in our history. During roughly the last twenty years, we as a nation have just begun to recognize how these changes and events have affected our families. The fields of psychology and family systems help us to understand the effect wars, economic disasters, and social change have had from generation to generation. We must use this new awareness of family systems to break the cycle of family imbalance so that the American family survives and adapts to the challenges of the twenty-first century.

Impaired Mourning

Most children of alcoholics/addicts and children growing up in imbalanced families have suffered a significant loss or experienced significant trauma. "Parents of youthful drug abusers have often suffered profound emotional losses within their own families of origin" (Kaufman and Kaufman 1981). The losses experienced by the children in imbalanced families involve

- loss of parents via death, divorce, separation
- frequent moves and relocations make attachments to friends, community, and home difficult
- trauma, accidents, illness, and dramatic incidents of loss lead to feelings of distrust, immobilization, and fear
- rigid, imbalanced, or unstructured parenting, resulting in an environment that is unsafe and limits differentiation and interpersonal growth
- verbal, emotional, physical, and sexual violations, resulting in feelings of worthlessness, hopelessness, and being numb to feelings
- parents who are physically and emotionally unavailable, who disparage and neglect their children, creating unresolved feelings of rejection, shame, and abandonment.

"There is a higher percentage of parental loss due to death in the families of addicts. These deaths are often traumatic, untimely, and unexpected" (Stanton 1982). Impaired mourning is a result of never having worked through these issues of loss and trauma. The result is unresolved grief often denied by the individual and avoided (denied) by the family.

Impaired mourning leads to a special kind of sadness, melancholia. Melancholia, or reactive depression is a condition in which the individual's bonding or ties to the lost love object are never given up, and there is a failure to adequately differentiate from the love object (*Diagnostic and Statistical Manual* 1987). Therefore, there is difficulty in developing close, appropriate, and feeling relationships with one's spouse, children, and others. This inability to "transfer affections fully to new love objects (such as the spouse and children in the family of procreation), contributes to problems in the family, making its members vulnerable to drugs and alcohol" (Kaufman and Kaufman 1981).

Impaired mourning is the basic work of psychotherapy; depending on the kind of therapy, it is given different labels. In the drug/alcohol field, especially with adult children of alcoholics (see chapter 6), impaired mourning is called grief work, or working through family of origin issues.

Whatever the theoretical framework and psychodynamic approach, the same dynamic is there: (1) the loss has never been worked through; (2) the ties to the lost love object in the family of origin are maintained; and (3) the loss causes present-day difficulties in developing healthy relationships with others.

When people are unable to grieve these losses, they do not work through their conflict over the loss. This loss is then projected onto the present-day family and living situation. Others are then blamed for the painful feelings of unresolved grief. "Their unresolved grief survives intact and contaminates their families. . . . It creates the dull, deadened, negativistic, lifeless, loveless atmosphere so characteristic of drug-abusing families" (Kaufman and Kaufman 1981).

Unresolved mourning is a result of denial of feelings related to any loss: For instance, when the pet dog that was an emotional companion to the child is not buried or eulogized. When the family moves, the children's loss of friends is discounted as no problem—"You'll just make new friends," rather than talking about the feelings associated with relocation. The basic dynamic is that the parents are uncomfortable with their own and their children's feelings of loss. The emotional dynamic is to pat the child on the head, and say, "There, there, everything will be all right." In effect, this discounts what children are feeling, causing them not to value their feelings and to see their feelings as inappropriate to the situation.

Boundaries in Imbalanced Families

Minuchin (1974) defined three types of boundaries; clear boundaries are essential to balanced families. Enmeshed and disengaged boundaries are characteristic of imbalanced families.

Clear boundaries allow mutual respect and concern by allowing separateness for each member, yet maintaining closeness. Freedom and flexibility in these healthy relationships are developed by clear, direct, and understanding communication. Clear boundaries allow children to develop, grow, and differentiate from the family. Individuation can only be accomplished when clear boundaries are functioning within the family system.

Enmeshed boundaries are inflexible, unyielding, and leave no room for differences. Differentness or separateness is not tolerated; individuation is not a goal of enmeshed relationships. Families with enmeshed boundaries view differentness as disloyalty and as a threat to the rules of the system. The needs of the individual are subjugated to the needs of the parents or system. Satisfying the parents definition of unity and sameness is stressed. Individual boundaries are blurred and the individual is often absorbed or swallowed up by the system. Individuals discount their own feelings, needs, and desires; they feel smothered and numb. They often use alcohol/drugs to counteract these feelings and the underlying resentment and anger.

Disengaged boundaries are overly rigid, with little or no opportunity for communication. Individuals in families that maintain disengaged boundaries have little sense of belonging, often feeling isolated from one another. The family also isolates from community and society. The parents are emotionally unavailable to each other and to the children, or for that matter, anyone else.

Boundary Inadequacy

Boundary inadequacy has been defined as the inability to set consistent and appropriate boundaries in relationships. The three major forms of boundary inadequacy identified by Eli Coleman and Phillip Colgan (1986) are

> Ambiguous boundary inadequacy involves a pattern of double messages exchanged within the relationship. The double messages . . . create an atmosphere of tension wherein the recipient of the communication can never be sure what can be believed. The inability of the communicator to send clear messages lays the groundwork for the cycle of ambiguity to begin.
>
> Overly rigid boundary inadequacy is characterized by patterns of behavior wherein smooth and efficient functioning is a priority over being

> responsive and adaptable. Adherence to a preset code of behavior, regardless of intervening situational variables are maintained, wherein roles are played and rules strictly enforced.
>
> Invasive boundary inadequacy involves patterns of behavior wherein an imbalance of power is used to objectify people. . . . Other people become objects for the person to use in satisfying all needs (i.e., sexual and physical abuse).

Eli Coleman (1987) underscored the importance of setting appropriate boundaries for members of imbalanced families:

> Developing skills at boundary setting is an essential ingredient in the recovery from chemical dependency or codependency. For many it is learning to say "no" to someone's request for physical, sexual, or emotional intimacy. Through saying "no," the individual learns that he or she can have a personal boundary and have it respected. This leads to a clear sense of self-wants and self-desires and it develops a sense of power and control in interpersonal relationships. After learning to say "no," the individual can learn to say "yes," and not lose a sense of individuality.

Triangulation—Another Boundary Issue

Jay Haley, the noted family therapist, defined triangulation (*figure 4.1*) as at least two adults involved in an offspring's problem, where the parent-child dyad is pitted against a more peripheral parent, step-parent, or grandparent. The triangle may involve a parent's lover, an estranged parent, or some other relative.

The destructive nature of the triangle is that the parent-child dyad or alliance is established at the expense of the peripheral parent. Often the parent-child dyad creates a marital conflict. The parent is overly enmeshed in this alliance seeking the child's favor despite the reality of the situation.

Case Study

Triangulation

John and Mary

John and Mary have significant marital problems. John is the head of the fire department for the county in which they reside and escapes the conflicts at home by spending much of his time with the men at the various fire stations. The couple actively attend community events and act as if their marriage is perfect. Their adopted sixteen-year-old daughter Michelle knows the truth. Michelle frequently argues with her mom to the point of hysteria. Mary often gives Michelle reason to be angry by giving her ambiguous mixed messages (i.e., I want to be close to you, yet I don't trust you because you are stealing my husband who I can no longer hold in the marriage). Mary buys Michelle clothes and jewelry, but is emotionally cold and unavailable. Mary has no insight into the way she antagonizes Michelle. Michelle is very bright but acts out her frustration with her mom by ditching classes, stealing things from her dresser, and by being extremely flirtatious with boys. John and Michelle maintain an enmeshed dyadic alliance. John is frustrated with his wife's coldness, emotional and sexual unavailability, and her constant arguments with Michelle and nagging of him. Michelle makes sexual overtures to young men while with her father and makes other sexually inappropriate remarks. In effect, she was flirtatious with her father; they were acting out their unconscious desires to be intimate with each other. These unconscious conflicts put more pressure on Michelle and she began to use drugs/alcohol excessively and to have sex with numerous young men. At this point the family sought counseling, a process that involved unraveling this triangulation, and establishing clearer boundaries and lines of communication.

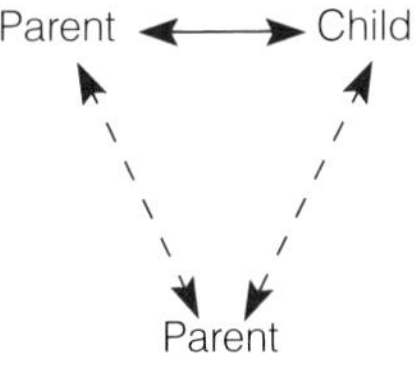

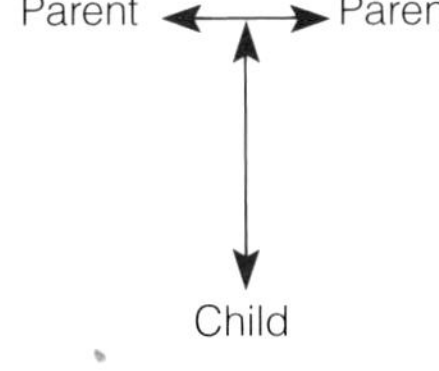

Figure 4.1
Triangulation

Imbalanced Life Cycles of Families

Jay Haley (1971) described the following major stages in the family life cycle:

1. relationships between families through unattached young adults
2. joining of families through marriage
3. family and the young child
4. family and the adolescent
5. launching of children
6. later life

As a result of the imbalance in alcoholic/addict family systems, developmental and interpersonal tasks are impaired at each stage of the family life cycle.

During the first two stages, the relationships between families are often filled with conflict and tension. Cooperation between families is difficult because the alcoholic/addict family system is trying to deny, minimize, and cover up the family secret of alcoholism/addiction. This results in the families' inability to develop trust and closeness.

Family and the Young Child

At the third stage, the family is either isolated or involved with other families that have similar problems with alcohol/drugs. The child is the innocent victim at this stage. The young child is often embarrassed by his parents' unpredictable behavior. As a result, the child frequently prefers playing at other children's homes and rarely invites other children to her home. Often, children from alcoholic/addict homes literally adopt their friends' parents. Becoming step-children, they spend a great deal of time with their friends' families.

Family and the Adolescent

The fourth stage is the time of most turmoil. Tumultuous even in the balanced family system, adolescence becomes even more dramatic in an imbalanced family system. The adolescent's exploration of a healthy personal identity is incongruent with the imbalanced unhealthy alcoholic/addict system. The conflict of holding allegiance to the family, imbalanced as they are, and exploring self through individuation and differentiation, creates tremendous guilt and anxiety for adolescents. If this conflict is unresolved, adolescents can either internalize their own frustration and anger and develop an imbalanced sense of self, or act out their anger in a demonstrative and destructive manner. The acting out behavior often includes problems with drugs/alcohol, sexual promiscuity, problems in school and with authority figures, and criminal justice problems. The internalized anger is sometimes more subtly manifested in the need for constant approval from peers, a poor self-concept, insecurity, or fears of abandonment and rejection.

Launching of Children

During the fifth stage, when the children are launched, the parents' alcohol and drug use usually intensifies. The empty-nest syndrome forces the parents to look at the dissatisfaction in their own marital system. The usual way to avoid the issues of marital imbalance is to increase the use of drugs/alcohol.

Of course, adult children of alcoholics/addicts are at risk for imbalanced relationships with their partners and for recapitulating the family of origin by developing imbalanced

Case Study
An Imbalanced Family System
Steve

At the age of eight, Steve was always with his friend Joe's family. He would have breakfast and dinner with them and spend most of his free hours playing with Joe and talking with Joe's parents. When Steve had problems, concerns, or conflicts, he would talk to Joe's parents, and not discuss the issues with his own family. Steve's actions illustrate that children with imbalanced families often adopt surrogate families to survive.

family systems as well. If there is no help, the result is the repetition of the same imbalanced system from generation to generation.

Later Years

In the sixth stage the issues intensify in an alcoholic/addict family system. Now consciously and/or unconsciously the adult recognizes the imbalanced patterns of relating during childhood. Adult children of alcoholics/addicts enter treatment, as they notice the imbalances in their own lives. Contacts with their parents in these later years may bring highly emotionally charged conflict to the forefront, making it difficult to have caring or effective relationships with their parents. If the parents are still using alcohol/drugs, this even further intensifies the difficulty in maintaining or developing better relationships. Working through the stages of grief and accepting the painful limitations of these imbalanced relationships is another developmental task for adult children. Healing may occur before the parents die. Perhaps the legacy of alcoholism/addiction will not be passed on to the next generation.

Family Resistance to Counseling

How do you get resistant family members to come and participate in counseling? Alcoholic/addict families are among the most difficult families to get into treatment, whether the setting is inpatient, residential, or outpatient treatment. Families often abdicate responsibility for the addicts/alcoholics' problems. It is too difficult for them to admit their feelings of embarrassment, shame, and personal feelings of inadequacy in trying to control family members' abuse of drugs/alcohol. P. Mason (1958) reported that of 1,000 eligible parents of alcoholics/addicts, only 30–40 would appear at monthly parent-staff meetings and almost none of these attended more than three times.

Not only are family members resistant to attending sessions but also the addicts/alcoholics themselves often sabotage family involvement. Addicts/alcoholics are often self-protective of their families, not wanting them to experience more pain. Addicts/alcoholics may even feel a sense of betrayal in assisting counselors to get the rest of the family involved. This would be disloyal to the rules of the imbalanced, enmeshed family system.

For many addicts/alcoholics, having their spouses or other family members involved in treatment might blow their cover. Addicts/alcoholics may have lied or deceived counselors in giving inaccurate or distorted information about their drug/alcohol use, family interactions, or other information. There is also fear that counselors would blame, criticize, or shame other family members; then these family members would get back at the addicts/alcoholics.

Fathers of Addicts/Alcoholics

The fathers of addicts/alcoholics are by far the most difficult family members to get into family sessions. A large percentage of these fathers have drug/alcohol problems themselves, and don't want this brought to the attention of the counselor (the same may hold true for mothers). The father is difficult to engage in the process of family therapy because he has generally been unavailable to the drug user and other family members. The father is often angry and defensive.

I have heard many a father say, "Since nobody ever listened to me or allowed me to follow through in what I thought would work in the first place, I am angry and don't want to get involved." The truth of the matter is that most fathers are frightened by the emotional content of counseling and profess not to believe in counseling. They see therapists as invading the family systems they tried to control. Fathers are also trying to avoid their own emotional pain and issues.

In an attempt to engage fathers in treatment, K. Labate (1975) recommends a kind of romancing of the father by acknowledging the positive intentions that the father possesses, and emphasizing that the father's participation in treatment is needed to make treatment successful. Labate suggests

1. reassuring the father that he is of importance
2. pointing out that changes depend on his participation
3. making the father aware that he has the power to sabotage treatment

4. noting that the father has choices, such as transferring to another counselor who might work with him individually
5. placing responsibility for change squarely on the father's shoulders
6. getting the father to consider realigning his priorities (e.g., choosing his family's happiness over acquisition of more material goods)

Lebate's strategies can be used on any family member of the addict/alcoholic—the spouse, brothers, sisters, or other family members who may have the same resistance to family treatment.

Noble Ascriptions to Counteract Defensiveness

"Anyone working with addicts' families for the first time is impressed with the tremendous defensiveness that most of them show. It sometimes seems as if they are just waiting for the therapist to cast even a minor aspersion so they can protest or perhaps abort therapy prematurely" (Stanton 1982). In approaching addicts/alcoholics and family members in treatment, it is essential that the counselor's style be nonpejorative, nonjudgmental, sensitive to the patient's issues of shame, and in no way blaming. Duncan Stanton suggested that the treatment be put in the context that each family member's intentions were and are indeed noble, and that there is a good reason or adaptive function for even the most destructive behavior. For example, anger, frustration, and generally attacking behavior can be relabeled as "a concern that is painful to tolerate," rather than, "You are really angry for no reason," or "There he goes again, using anger to hurt and control us." Destructive enabling behavior can be nobly ascribed as "It is difficult to see your child in pain. Pain that you would prefer that the child not go through."

"Simply defining problems as interactional or familial stumbling blocks serves to have them viewed as shared, rather than loading the blame entirely on one or two members—'we're all in this together' " (Stanton 1982). This approach does not abandon the therapist's role in challenging thoughts, beliefs, and behaviors that might hinder the family from becoming more functional. Instead, the counselor expresses perspectives and viewpoints in a human, caring, and nonshaming manner facilitating trust in the therapeutic alliance. The ascribing of noble intentions or characteristics takes the shame out of the therapeutic work. Shame that would inevitably cause one or more family members to sabotage treatment.

Characteristics of Effective Drug/Alcohol Family Counselors

As you can tell by now, conducting drug/alcohol treatment with families is a difficult task. The need for specialized training in this field is essential. B. Berg and N. Rosenblum (1977) found that the success of drug/alcohol family therapists in recruiting and engaging family members into treatment directly correlates with their amount of training in family therapy.

Stanton (1982) outlined the following basic characteristics required for therapists working with families experiencing drug/alcohol problems: (1) a high energy level as the recruitment process can be demanding in time and effort; (2) enthusiasm for the work is essential; (3) persistence and ability to tolerate rebukes by family members; and (4) flexibility and lack of rigidity. All are essential for success.

Summary

To understand the family's role in drug/alcohol problems, one must put families in the framework of a system. All family systems have rules, values, verbal and non verbal communications, boundaries, and roles and patterns of interaction.

Virginia Satir described dysfunctional styles of communicating as illustrated in the placater, the blamer, the computer, and the distractor. For Satir leveling is the healthy state of communication. Sharon-Wegscheider Cruse defined several alcoholic/addict family system survival roles—the chief enabler, family hero, the family scapegoat, the lost child, the family mascot.

Enabling is an unhealthy doing for in an attempt to deny problems with drugs/alcohol. This is done by either taking responsibility for someone else's lack of responsibility, or softening the consequences for someone's irresponsibility. Charles Nelson's categories of enabling behavior include (1) avoiding and shielding; (2) attempting to control; (3) taking over responsibilities; (4) rationalizing and accepting; and (5) cooperation and collaboration. Nelson has provided examples of these different types of enabling responses by family members. To effectively treat the addict/alcoholic, the rest of the family system also needs counseling to address their own enabling behavior and the systemic problems within the family.

The family system that has not effectively dealt with issues of loss, trauma, shame, and separation (abandonment) develops unresolved grief, feelings of melancholia and depression. These unresolved feelings often lead to dysfunctional/imbalanced behavior such as drinking and drugging.

Imbalanced families often have difficulty in setting appropriate boundaries. Boundary inadequacy is defined as the inability to set consistent and appropriate boundaries in relationships, as evidenced by ambiguous, overly rigid and invasive boundaries. Triangulation is another form of boundary inadequacy where the parent-child alliance is established at the expense of the peripheral parent. Frequently, these problems in boundary setting lead to physical and sexual violations and emotional and psychological abuse. This is especially true in alcoholic/addict family systems.

References

Ackerman, Nathan. *The Psychodynamics of Family Life: Diagnosis and Treatment of Family Relationships.* New York: Basic Books, 1958.

———. *Treating the Troubled Family.* New York: Basic Books, 1966.

Berg, P. and Rosenblum, N. "Fathers in Family Therapy: A Survey of Family Therapists." *Journal of Marriage and Family Counseling* 3 (1977): 85–91.

Bowen, Murray. *Family Therapy in Clinical Practice.* Northvale, N.J.: Aronson, Jason, 1978.

Coleman, Eli. *Chemical Dependency and Intimacy Dysfunction.* New York: Haworth Press, 1987.

Coleman, Eli and Phillip Colgan. "Boundary Inadequacy in Drug Dependent Families." *Journal of Psychoactive Drugs* 18 (1986) 21–30.

Colgan, Phillip. "Assessment of Boundary Inadequacy in Chemically Dependent Individuals and Families." *Journal of Chemical Dependency Treatment* 1, no. 1 (1987).

Cousins, Norman. *Anatomy of an Illness, as Perceived by the Patient, Reflections on Healing and Regeneration.* New York: W. W. Norton, 1980.

Diagnostic and Statistical Manual III-R, 3d ed. Washington, D.C.: American Psychological Association, 1987.

Haley, Jay. *Changing Families: A Family Therapy Reader.* New York: Grune and Stratton, 1971.

———. *Problem-Solving Therapy: New Strategies for Effective Family Therapy.* New York: Harper & Row, 1981.

Kaufman, Edward, and Pauline N. Kaufman. *Family Therapy of Drug and Alcohol Abuse.* New York: Gardner Press, 1981.

Kumpfer, Karol. "Special Populations: Etiology and Prevention of Vulnerability to Chemical Dependency in Children of Substance Abusers." In *Youth at High Risk for Substance Abuse,* eds. B. S. Brown and A. R. Mills. NIDA Monograph, DHHS Pub. No. (ADM) 87-1537, 1987.

In *Youth at High Risk for Substance Abuse,* eds. B. S. Brown and A. R. Mills. NIDA Monograph, DHHS Pub. No. (ADM) 87-1537, 1987.

Labate, K. "Pathogenic role rigidity in fathers: Some observations." *Journal of Marriage and Family Counseling* 1 (1975): 69–79.

MacDonald, Donald Ian. *Drugs, Drinking and Adolescents.* Chicago: Year Book Medical Publishers, 1984.

Mason, P. "Mother of the Addict." *Psychiatric Quarterly Supplement,* 32 (1958): 189–99.

Minuchin, Salvador. *Families and Family Therapy.* Cambridge, Mass.: Harvard University Press, 1974.

Nelson, Charles. "The Style of Enabling Behavior." In *Treating Cocaine Dependency,* ed. David E. Smith and Donald Wesson. Center City, Minn.: Hazelden Foundation, 1988.

Satir, Virginia. *Conjoint Family Therapy.* Palo Alto, Calif.: Science and Behavior Books, 1967.

———. *Peoplemaking.* Palo Alto, Calif.: Science and Behavior Books, 1972.

Satir, Virginia, James Stachowiak, and Harvey A. Taschman. *Helping Families to Change.* Northvale, N.J.: Aronson, Jason, 1976.

Satir, Virginia and Michele Baldwin. *Satir—Step by Step—A Guide to Creating Change in Families.* Northvale, N.J.: Aronson, Jason, 1983.

Stanton, Duncan M. and Thomas C. Todd, and associates. *Family Therapy of Drug Abuse.* New York: Guilford Press, 1982.

Wegscheider-Cruse, Sharon. *Another Chance, Hope and Health for the Alcoholic Family.* Palo Alto, Calif.: Science Behavior Books, 1981.

Whitaker, Carl and Augustus Y. Napier. *The Family Crucible.* New York: Harper & Row, 1978.

Feelings of Shame, Abandonment, and Rejection in Imbalanced Family Systems

This chapter focuses on the issues of shame and abandonment in alcoholic/addict families. The imbalanced family system causes feelings of excessive shame, abandonment, and rejection. Too frequently peers, authority figures, and even religious and educational institutions instill these same feelings. The feelings of shame and abandonment may not be avoided in life, and at an appropriate level may instill adaptation and growth. Problems develop when unbalanced parenting and trauma of sexual violation, physical and emotional abuse occur. When parents do not meet the child's needs for security, consistency, safety, encouragement and nurturance, so necessary to thrive in life, the child is negatively affected. One of the outcomes of excessive shame, abandonment, and rejection is the development of drug and alcohol problems.

Chapter Goals

1. Define *shame* and explain its role and function in the addict/alcoholic and dysfunctional family system.
2. Explain how the family, peers, and institutions such as schools and churches can be shaming.
3. Describe the impact of shame on feelings.
4. Explain the role shame plays in the developmental tasks of sexual identity and sexual intimacy.
5. Identify Masterson's diagnostic criteria of abandonment depression.
6. Describe how childhood experiences of abandonment and rejection can cause problems in adulthood.
7. Explain and describe rejection sensitivity, difficulty in making decisions or choices, distorted thinking, and difficulty in adaptation.
8. Identify common insights about the characteristics of addicts/alcoholics and their feelings of shame, abandonment, and depression, as shown in the case studies.

Shame

Shame is a powerful and all-consuming feeling in the alcoholic/addict family system. Understanding the role shame plays in this family system is essential to develop effective treatment, intervention, and prevention approaches to drugs/alcohol.

Shame is a deep-rooted feeling, often a result of traumatic childhood experiences that are excessively shaming. Parental imbalance and parenting dysfunction are at the core of these feelings of shame. The disease of alcoholism and drug addiction is perpetuated in the next generation by this shame-based family dysfunction. Admitting that one is having problems with drugs/alcohol often involves shame-based feelings of personal inadequacy and failure. Denial is the major defense mechanism used to avoid these feelings of shame.

Merle Fossum and Marilyn Mason (1986) defined shame as "the self looking in on itself and finding the self lacking or flawed." Individuals may feel exposed, vulnerable, and fearful that others know they are feeling inherently bad and inadequate. Shame is more powerful than simple embarrassment, which is a temporary situation with little long-term impact. In shame, people feel that they will never recover from the negative way others see them.

Shame is a feeling that has an integral role in the individual's development. "Shame is a basic, natural human emotion, which in moderation is adaptive, healthy, and absolutely essential for development. We could not elminate shame even if we wanted to. It's inbred in the species" (Kaufman 1989).

The origins of shame might go back to the beginning of time, back to the Garden of Eden. Adam and Eve eating the apple of knowledge may be a metaphor for the original feeling of shame. Until that costly error in judgment, Adam and Eve had not experienced shame. They were innocent children, frolicking in paradise. This shameful experience caused paradise as they knew it to change. From that day forward, the snake has represented the shadow or dark side of humanity; it crawls on its belly, reminding us of the shameful nature of their act.

Sigmund Freud used the word *guilt* to describe feelings of shame. Erik Erickson, in his description of the human life cycle, outlined two developmental stages that focused on guilt and shame: autonomy versus doubt and shame, and initiative versus guilt. Countless stories throughout the Bible, mythology, literature, and history deal with the concept of

© John Callahan, represented by Levin Represents.

© 1986 Doug Marlette.

Characteristics of Shameful Experiences

1. Unexpected exposure; being judged on a vulnerable aspect of oneself.
2. Feeling as if there is a loss of choice.
3. Feeling out of place, flawed, defective, or inadequate.
4. A threat to the core of one's identity.
5. Mistrust in ability to perceive things properly; unsure of self in making decisions or relating to people.
6. Trust of self and others is jeopardized; boundaries are distorted; and physical, emotional, and/or sexual violations may occur.
7. Difficulty in assessing what is reality.
8. Feeling helpless, powerless, and trapped with no way out. (Fossum and Mason 1986)

shame. Two examples of shame themes in early American literature are Nathaniel Hawthorne's *The Scarlet Letter* and Stephen Crane's *The Red Badge of Courage.* Hester Prynne, in *The Scarlet Letter,* proudly wears the shame-based A of adultery and ignores condemnation of her pregnancy out of wedlock. In *The Red Badge of Courage,* Henry Fleming, a young soldier during the Civil War, struggles with the shame-based issue of cowardice.

Shame is also imbedded in the rituals of many cultures. The Japanese ritual of hara-kiri is a result of loss of respect, shame, and disgrace. Excommunication and expulsion from societies is a cultural or community form of shame. Taboos, moral values, and even religious customs can be shame based.

Shame is a fascinating topic because it affects us all in some way. Most individuals can overcome feelings of shame and grow as a result of it, getting on with their lives. However, some individuals have been shamed dramatically and frequently, especially during early developmental years, and are unable to overcome it. These individuals are at risk for alcoholism and drug dependence or developing relationships with addicts/alcoholics. Too much shame creates trauma which leads to feelings of hopelessness and helplessness.

Early Shame in the Family

I suspect that unborn fetuses can pick up feelings of shame. This means the mother who has an unwanted pregnancy communicates this to the developing fetus. Perhaps one day we will be able to measure how these negative messages are communicated across the placental barrier.

At birth and early infancy, children may pick up negative feelings of shame. Infants' feelings focus on comfort versus discomfort. A mother's (and/or father's) negative feelings about an infant may result in resentments toward the child for demanding comfort. The parents may not meet the child's basic needs to be fed, nurtured, and protected.

Shame and Imbalanced Family Systems

As outlined in chapter 4, the messages in imbalanced, and addict/alcoholic family systems are usually shaming. Parental imbalance results in shame-based styles of communication and family interaction. These messages take a tremendous toll on the self-concepts of children growing up in these family systems.

Growing up in an alcoholic/addict family creates a foundation of shame. Additional feelings of shame are perpetrated by peers, the school system, other institutions, and other authority figures in the child's life. These shame-based messages are internalized by children. The result is a vicious pattern of feelings and behavior that perpetuate the feelings of shame.

Individuals from shame-based family systems often feel that (1) there is no hope for change; (2) shame is inescapable and inevitable; (3) shame is exterior based, not an internal process; and (4) they are bad, no good, flawed, or worthless as individuals (Fossum and Mason 1986).

For these individuals, feelings of shame can include verbalizations such as,

> No matter what I do, it's never going to be good enough. So why try? Each time I try, I fail anyway. The result is always negative.
>
> I must try so much harder than others. It's so much easier for others. So I must be inferior and inadequate.
>
> You have to be perfect to be OK.
>
> Look at __________ . Now if I could only be like them.
>
> It's never going to get any better. No matter how hard I try.
>
> If only others would feel good. Then I would be happy.

Shame, the School System, and Other Institutions

Unfortunately and unwittingly, the school system is also a source of shame. Most school systems have as their mission the well-being and development of educated and healthy young people. However, some teachers and educational systems maintain teaching methods that are shaming. These shame-based teaching methods include experiences of being humiliated or singled out as somehow bad or inferior in front of peers. Other punishments include sitting in the corner, wearing dunce hats, or writing 1,000 times "I will not _____ in class." Taking oral examinations in front of the class, doing oral reading, receiving verbal and physical abuse, and suffering due to emotional insensitivity have all increased students' shame quotas. In the past, rigid, parochial methods that required punishment kept students on task. The result was children who were obedient because they were so afraid of being shamed. These shame-based methods in the school system perpetuated and reinforced for some children what they had already experienced and felt in their own families: that they were, indeed, no good.

Other institutions can also be shaming. Unfortunately, many rigid religious systems are shame-based and insensitive to members' feelings. Communities and regions can be shaming of outsiders, or things they don't understand or are threatened by such as homosexuality, AIDS, or homelessness. Racial and religious prejudice is another form of shame. Oppression of the wishes and good intentions of citizens is the shame of dictatorial governments. Apartheid and other civil rights and human rights violations all cause feelings of shame. The Holocaust and concentration camps are graphic examples of shame that strips away aspects of human identity and dignity.

Individuals who can work through feelings of shame are able to recognize, feel, and implement behaviors demonstrating that

1. There is hope and there are choices they can make.
2. Everyone makes mistakes and errors in judgment.
3. They can make amends and recover from those mistakes.
4. Their shame will feel better with the passage of time.
5. Others don't define who they are, that is an internal process.
6. They are human, humans make mistakes; they are not in total control of their lives.

7. Most important, they are worthwhile (Fossum and Mason 1986).

The twelve steps of Alcoholics Anonymous and other self-help support groups reflect these life-affirming traits. As discussed in this text, AA and other support groups are effective because they are not shame-based and counteract feelings of shame.

Shame and Feelings

Shame-based messages that are internalized have a major impact on feelings. When shame is attached to normal everyday feelings, it tends to escalate those feelings. For example, when an internalized shame-based message is attached to normal everyday feelings of frustration or anger, it tends to escalate that feeling to rage (anger + shame = rage). The person feeling shame then directs this rage toward others, blaming and holding them responsible for feelings of anger and frustration. The rage violates others, pushes them away, and creates more of a feeling of isolation, loneliness, and hopelessness with no way out. This out-of-control emotional freight train picks up speed from all the remembrances of shame experienced in the family of origin. For some, the way to slow down this runaway emotional pain is to self-medicate with drugs/alcohol. Unfortunately, this temporary solution may even speed up the emotional turmoil or cause it to be repeated over and over. When people do not deal with feelings of shame, this pattern continues. The next time, even less anger and shame are needed for escalation to rage.

Affect-Shame Binds

anger	+	shame	=	rage
anxiety	+	shame	=	panic
fear	+	shame	=	terror
sadness	+	shame	=	depression
depression	+	shame	=	despair
despair	+	shame	=	suicidal thoughts
suicidal thoughts	+	shame	=	suicide attempt
hurt	+	shame	=	pain
pain	+	shame	=	trauma (deep or chronic pain)
trauma	+	shame	=	phobia
phobia	+	shame	=	loss of reality
unavailability	+	shame	=	lack of trust of others
lack of trust of others	+	shame	=	paranoia
paranoia	+	shame	=	loss of reality

Shame and Human Sexuality

One of the largest domains of shame is human sexuality, as evidenced by our society's problems in establishing intimate and caring relationships. We look at three areas in particular: adolescent sexual identity, sexual violation, and drugs and sex.

Adolescent Sexual Identity

The developmental task of exploring and defining one's sexual identity is probably the most difficult task of adolescence. Shame-based messages by parents, schools, institutions, and peers may be devastating to adolescents and delay the development of a secure sense of sexual identity. Some of the shame-based messages include:

> You are bad if you ____________________ .
> (masturbate, are feeling sexual, are aroused, etc.)
> Having sexual feelings before marriage is unnatural.
> Sex is dirty.
> That's all that men want. Men are bad and evil.
> Women use sex to manipulate you to get what they want.
> Don't watch television, it promotes sexual arousal.
> In our family, we don't talk about sex with others.

Sexual Violation

Sexual violations are common in alcoholic/addict and imbalanced family systems. Children often feel responsible for sexual violation, as if they caused the violation (e.g., I must be responsible for this sexual feeling in others because I am so cute, attractive, shy, or outgoing.). Usually, the violation is not talked about or is enabled by the mother or, in some cases, the father. When told of the violation, the parent often denies that it happened or that it is possible and rationalizes the action: "Your uncle is that way with everyone. Try to stay away from him." Such parents fail to adequately protect children from future violations. When the behavior is acknowledged by children, usually no one in the family seeks therapeutic help for the victim and/or the perpetrator. Families deny sexual violations for fear of exposing the inappropriate and violating behavior and to avoid familial shame. Instead of families getting help, they maintain denial and scapegoat the victims by not acknowledging the violations or their pain. They take no or limited action to prevent future violations to the victims or to someone else.

Drugs, Sex, and Shame

Cocaine, marijuana, alcohol, methaqualone, and other drugs are often described as sex drugs, or aphrodisiacs. At early stages, drugs/alcohol do reduce inhibitions. This confuses people who define them as aphrodisiacs. In reality, all drugs impair performance, especially at middle and later stages of use.

Under the influence of drugs/alcohol individuals also experience impaired judgment and may take part in sexual activities in which they would not normally engage if they were sober. The shame of these sexual experiences can be devastating. So, they use drugs/alcohol to blot out these feelings of shame. This can become a vicious negative addictive cycle. This cycle involves drug/alcohol use, followed by sexual activity, and feelings of shame. More drug/alcohol use follows (to numb the feelings of shame), succeeded by sexual activity, and more shame and feelings of loss of control.

Abandonment Depression

James Masterson (1976), in his work with borderline personality disordered individuals, coined the term *abandonment depression*. He identified abandonment depression as an affective disorder with six key elements:

1. homicidal rage
2. suicidal depression
3. panic
4. feelings of hopelessness and helplessness
5. emptiness and void
6. guilt

Masterson, described the individual suffering from abandonment depression as "a hollow eggshell with the insides removed." All the good stuff—the nutrients, the seed, the juices of life—has been removed, rotted, or destroyed.

Separation Stress

Masterson believes that a significant separation stress precipitates abandonment depression. It is also likely that this separation occurred early in life between eighteen and twenty-four months of age. He describes three elements that may produce separation stress, making the child unable to successfully individuate or become a separate being.

1. Nature: "Possible genetic or constitutional deficiencies such as inability to tolerate separation anxiety or to synthesize positive and negative affects as well as such conditions as attention deficit disorders and developmental disharmonies."

Childhood Experiences of Abandonment and Rejection

- Lack of physical and emotional availability of parents.
- Negative blaming, verbal and nonverbal behavior or attacks.
- Mixed messages (double-binds) saying one thing and meaning something else.
- Unreasonably high expectations or standards; or ambiguous unclear expectations of behavior, performance, and affect.
- Lack of warmth, sensitivity, security, safety, or high regard for feelings, situations, and conflicts.
- Discounting of child's sense of self or physical and psychological boundaries.
- Disparaging, blaming, and generally rejecting attitude about the child's difficulty with developmental tasks.
- Disregard, ridicule, blaming, teasing, or other verbal and nonverbal behavior that is either rejecting or shaming.
- Threatening to abandon or leave a child in a joking or real manner.
- Negative and rejecting statements, actions, and comments about something that is of minor or major importance to the child.

2. Nurture: "Maternal libidinal unavailability for the child's move toward separation-individuation or self-activation (i.e., the mother is unable or has difficulty in identifying, acknowledging, and supporting the child's emerging self-activation, experimentation, and exploration). The reasons for maternal libidinal unavailability may be many—death, divorce, physical or emotional illness, etc."
3. Fate: "Any accident of fate that impairs the child's ability to separate and/or individuate. On the separation side, events such as death or divorce can prevent the mother from being emotionally available. On the individuation side, events can impair or prevent the child from practicing his emerging individuation. For example, the child may be sickly or in a restricted environment.

Interpersonal Relationships

Individuals suffering from abandonment depression express complaints having to do with intimacy. They are unable to emotionally enter into healthy relationships and are unable to differentiate their needs from others' needs. They experience difficulty in identifying and communicating feelings, or accepting feelings and communication from others. There is either a fusing of others into self, or a fission causing them to emotionally break away from others.

Masterson described persons suffering from abandonment depression as experiencing difficulty in establishing intimacy in relationships due to a limited capacity for spontaneity, empathy, and sensitivity. These persons have difficulty in making an emotional commitment to a relationship. Such individuals experience twin fears—the fear of losing (abandonment) that leads to clinging behavior and the fear of being engulfed (smothered) that leads to feelings of depersonalization, shutting down, distortion of reality, and desensitization (numbing or shutting down, disconnecting from the body).

At first, using alcohol and drugs to facilitate feeling in interpersonal relationships may seem effective; however, as time goes on this becomes dysfunctional and destructive. Persons feeling pain also use drugs/alcohol to alleviate the core feeling of abandonment.

Another option those suffering feelings of abandonment may choose is to enter into dysfunctional and/or alcoholic/addict relationships, or relationships with individuals emotionally and physically unavailable.

The *Diagnostic and Statistical Manual III–R* (1987) lists diagnostic criteria for borderline personality disorder that include the following descriptive criteria. These often result from early childhood experiences of abandonment.

1. impulsivity or unpredictability in at least two areas that are potentially self-damaging
2. a pattern of unstable and intense interpersonal relationships
3. inappropriate, intense anger, or lack of control of anger
4. identity disturbances manifested by uncertainty about several issues relating to identity, such as self-image, gender identity, long-term goals or career choice, friendship patterns, values, and loyalties
5. affective instability
6. intolerance of being alone
7. physically self-damaging acts
8. chronic feelings of emptiness or boredom

Case Study
Rejection Sensitivity
Frank

A colleague, old friend, and workshop training partner of mine tells a story of his fear of rejection. Growing up in an imbalanced, alcoholic family system, Frank learned how to defend against shame by being likable, and by avoiding conflict. He figured that if everyone liked him and he avoided conflict, he would not be subject to rejection, attack, or shame. Unfortunately, his likable quality put him in a real dilemma back in the third grade.

As Frank tells the story, his classmates really liked him and nominated him for third grade class president. Normally, he would be just likable enough, but not too popular because that would bring the unwanted attention he feared. That year there were no outstanding choices for class president, and his likable, nonaggressive style became the qualities that the class wanted in its president. His classmates reacted to the nomination with genuine acceptance and encouragement. Frank felt this put him in a lose-lose position. Frank thought that if he ran and lost, he would experience tremendous feelings of rejection and shame. If he ran and won, he would disappoint his classmates by being an inadequate class president, unable to meet the responsibilities of the office. Ultimately, this would lead to the same feelings of rejection and shame. Either way, Frank felt he would be rejected and shamed. His only choice was to reject the nomination for office. He did this rather adroitly by taking the nomination as an opportunity to lend his support to another more popular classmate. "Thanks for the nomination," he said, "but my support goes to Larry. He would make a far more capable class president than me, and he was the one I had intended to nominate." Unfortunately, Frank missed out on the opportunity to grow from experiencing what it is like to run for office and perhaps the opportunity to be class president.

Additional Characteristics of Shame and Abandonment

Rejection Sensitivity

Feelings of shame and abandonment can make individuals extremely sensitive to rejection, so much so that they choose not to try to grow and develop. Persons suffering from rejection sensitivity avoid situations that may be potentially shaming for fear of the situation triggering feelings of abandonment or rejection. Healthy individuals can tolerate shame, rejection, or abandonment and respond adaptively to these feelings by making the necessary adjustments and healthy choices in their lives.

Fear and Difficulty Making Decisions or Choices

Feelings of rejection, abandonment, and shame result in a variety of fears. Some of these fears are so traumatic that individuals cannot choose to change extremely uncomfortable situations. The fears of failure that may activate or trigger feelings of rejection, abandonment, and shame are so great that individuals choose to maintain self-effacing, even violating situations, instead of choosing healthy, growth-oriented paths.

Case Study

Difficulty in Making Decisions

Norman

Norman, twenty-nine, is an adult child of an alcoholic. He grew up in an extremely abusive and physically violating dysfunctional family system. Norman described his earliest childhood memories at ages two to three as the fights between his parents. On one occasion in an alcoholic rage Norman's dad shoved his mom's head through the front window of their living room. Another time, his mom hid his dad's car keys in the garbage because his dad was drunk. They both struggled with the garbage and she severely cut her hand on the jagged edge of a coffee can. Later, two tall police officers came to quiet them down during another domestic dispute. These were just a few of his memories.

His parents' fighting had a far-reaching impact on Norman and the other children in the family. The fear of abandonment, shame, and rejection caused Norman to act out during his childhood in many destructive ways. He did not achieve at school, despite being very bright and capable.

One day in individual counseling, Norman talked about a trip he took to Reno, Nevada. This trip was a metaphor for his fear of making a career change. After watching for some time at the roulette table with his wife and a friend, he decided to place his bet. Norman placed a two dollar bet on the red, and a two dollar bet on the black. He surmised that this was a secure bet. He smiled to himself smugly as the roulette wheel spun and the ball bounded around from number to number. When it landed on a red number, the croupier just pushed his two dollars from the black spot to the red spot, and Norman collected his bet. Despite the odd looks from the croupier, and his friend's efforts to explain why this was a stupid bet, Norman continued to play two dollars on black and two dollars on red simultaneously. After several spins, he stopped betting. He felt entertained and justified that he had played roulette. I didn't hesitate to point out to Norman that the numbers zero and double zero on the roulette wheel are green. If either of those numbers had come up, he would have lost both bets.

This was analogous to what Norman was doing in his conflict about his career. He was betting on his current job for security, but not actively putting himself on the line to find a more fulfilling job. The longer he waited to take action, the more time he was wasting. And, the more likely it was that zero or double zero would come up, either in the form of losing his current job due to his dissatisfaction projected to the work setting or not being able to motivate himself to find a better job because he was suffering from feelings of rejection, shame, and abandonment.

Even with this therapeutic insight, Norman waited several months to take any direct action. After a great deal of work, he eventually landed a new job in the field that he really wanted. That job didn't work out but it lead to another job. After two years of struggle, Norman found himself in a career position that was consistent with his feelings of entitlement and accomplishment; his job affirmed his skills and capabilities.

The fear of success can also bring fears that once some level of success is attained, it will fall apart and return the individual to previous feelings of failure and rejection. People then sabotage the gains in anticipation of deeper feelings of shame, rejection, and abandonment. What is missing is individuals believing in themselves, their own self-worth, and their emerging talents, skills, and capabilities.

Poor Frustration Tolerance

When goals are blocked, even temporarily, persons who feel abandoned and rejected cannot tolerate this frustration. Such individuals believe there are no alternative choices or solutions to their blocked goals. Poor impulse control and self-destructive thinking may cause people to shoot themselves in the foot or self-sabotage the progress they have made.

Other Reactions and Defenses

Common reactions and defenses to avoid feelings of abandonment and rejection include being overly defensive, extremely critical, or judgmental; showing rage or distorted thinking; and masking of true feelings and emotions. People in pain deny the real issues and feelings by being overly defensive and critical of others. These persons view the world as being similar to the depriving, rejecting, and abandoning mothers and fathers they knew while growing up. Their distorted thinking tells them that the world will respond to them in the same way.

Inability to Adapt

Developmental psychologist Jean Piaget (1980) did extensive work in studying the development of children. In Piaget's quest to clarify human intelligence, he came to regard the ability to successfully adapt to a changing world, as the key element in intelligence. The two key components of adaptation are the ability to successfully and appropriately assimilate and accommodate information into an understanding of the world. Individuals suffering from the trauma of abandonment, rejection, and shame have difficulty in adapting to life's changes.

Addiction Case Studies

The following case studies highlight both the impact of shame, abandonment, and rejection on the addict/alcoholic and specific features of chemical dependency. Names, details, and the circumstances of these cases have been changed to maintain anonymity.

A variety of alcoholics have stuffed their feelings of shame, abandonment, and rejection. Some seem so resistant to change; others stop drinking alcohol but maintain an existential despair about life. Many times the most frustrating and well-defended clients/patients are the ones who provide the most hope, joy, and support for others in recovery. The secret is hanging in there with them. These clients are the miracles and the models for others who feel hopeless. They are the ones who others have given up on and who have been told they couldn't make it. Eventually, others recognize these clients/patients as having that special quality of recovery that they would like to have.

Inhibited Alcoholic

It is fairly easy to spot the extroverted alcoholic/addict, the person who is extremely outgoing, boisterous, and demonstrative when using alcohol/drugs. One of my clients described them as chemical clowns when under the influence of alcohol.

The alcoholics/addicts who often go unnoticed are those who isolate themselves when they drink/drug or who drink alcohol/or use drugs to be able to deal with extreme self-consciousness in most interpersonal and social situations. Without alcohol/drugs, they are passive, nonassertive, inhibited, and extremely fearful of shame, rejection, and abandonment.

Often, these persons were overprotected by a parent and not given the developmental skills or opportunities to develop social interpersonal skills. These individuals use alcohol as the primary means to feel better about themselves in interpersonal and social situations.

Chemical clown

High-Functioning Addict/Alcoholic

Some individuals appear to function effectively even though they are alcoholic. As a group, the high-functioning alcoholics are often the most difficult to work with because they tend not to identify themselves as alcoholics. They are convinced that they are not alcoholics because they believe they do not act, look, or function like alcoholics.

Physically Strong Addicts/Alcoholics

Some addicts/alcoholics are extremely tolerant to the hangovers related to excessive drug/alcohol use. Perhaps, this is a physical curse; our bodies' normal reaction to the toxicity of drugs/alcohol is physical pain and withdrawal symptoms. These addicts/alcoholics' physiological systems work in such a way that hangovers are not very severe. These individuals have no significant physical feedback that drinking/drugging is bad for them.

Case Study
A High-Functioning Alcoholic
George

George, fifty-nine, works for a major corporation as an engineer and has never missed any work as a result of alcoholism. George drinks on a regular basis in the evenings, often in isolation. He rarely gets drunk in public settings, except on special occasions or holidays, where he blends in with others who are drunk. He has weekend binges of drinking excessively, usually followed by periods when he cuts back to one or two beers a night, instead of his Smirnoff's vodka each evening.

George considers himself a connoisseur of fine wines and liqueurs. For George, alcohol plays a major role in enjoying the finer things in life. He has difficulty going out for dinner without enjoying a fine bottle of wine with a fish or steak dinner, or a mug of beer with pizza.

This might sound like normal drinking behavior. Many people enjoy alcohol, drink at parties, drink with dinner, or drink after work. For George and alcoholics like him, it is difficult identifying the third element in our definition of addiction—continued use despite negative consequences. George doesn't miss any work as a result of drinking alcohol, he can reduce his alcohol consumption for periods of time and suffers few observable physical problems as a result of alcohol use. He also seems to have a high tolerance to the hangovers from excessive alcohol consumption. The reality is that George is using alcohol to cover up deep feelings of despair, loss, depression, and a fear of being ill and alone.

Unwilling to look at these painful issues, George prefers the pleasure of alcohol to escape his pain. When these issues come to the surface, George cries spontaneously with uncontrollable deep sobs symptomatic of his deep feelings of depression. George quickly covers up these feelings and returns to work vigorously. At this stage, he quits counseling and tries some new endeavor to distract him from his issues. After some time, the feelings come back and he repeats the cycle of heavy alcohol use followed by a period of cutting back with no real goal of dealing with the issues of recovery. George suffers from a dual disorder: he has problems with alcohol and an underlying mood cycling disorder (see chapter 9).

Case Study
Physically Strong Addict
Kim

Kim, thirty-one, was an addict/alcoholic able to outdrink and outdrug the best of her friends, male and female. Surprisingly, she was thin, tall, blond, and attractive with beautiful delicate features. Not only was she physically able to tolerate drugs/alcohol with no significant hangover but despite thin arms, she was also one of the best arm wrestlers in the state.

Her normal weekend behavior was to drink and drug at a local bar. Due to her good looks, she was frequently approached by men at the bar. Often these men had drank beyond their capabilities and could be quite obnoxious. To stop their advances and obnoxious behavior, Kim would challenge them to arm wrestling matches. The stakes of the arm wrestling match were simple: if she lost, she would buy him a drink; if he lost, he would buy drinks for the house. Suffice it to say, she was extremely popular at the bar.

Human Bar Press Response

Animal studies with cocaine have revealed some interesting results that are not observed with any other drugs, including alcohol. Cocaine is such a reinforcing drug that when put in a Y-maze and given a choice of cocaine or a receptive female, rats choose the cocaine. Monkeys, who abhor electric shock, go across an electric grid that gives them significant shocks to get to cocaine. Rats can be taught to press a bar for cocaine rewards. Some animals press the bar hundreds or thousands of times to get cocaine; with other rewards the animals lose interest. Cocaine is the only drug we know of today that animals use until they die when given unlimited access. In experiments with unlimited access to alcohol, the animals usually stop at certain points before attaining toxic or lethal dose levels.

While I was conducting the Annual Institute on Drugs/Alcohol Conference at UCLA with a colleague of mine, Michael Leeds, we went out for dinner one evening in Westwood, California. That night Michael pointed out a human bar press example. Across from our restaurant we could clearly see the instant teller (ATM) at a bank on Westwood Boulevard. A few minutes before midnight, numerous UCLA students were lining up getting cash out of their accounts. The students went from the ATM directly to the back of the line. Apparently they had withdrawn their limit for one day; once it was past midnight they could withdraw their limit for a new day. As the shops in Westwood are closed that late at night, we concluded the only plausible reason for this behavior was that these students ran out of money on a cocaine run and needed more money to continue using cocaine. So we saw human subjects bar-pressing the ATM, trying to get as much money as possible, to get more cocaine.

Case Study

Cocaine Freebasing

Bobo

Bobo came to me for assessment and referral for addiction to freebase cocaine. He was thirty-one years old and looked twenty years older due to his obesity and sunken eyes. His name really described the way he looked. He acted quite defensive and paranoid, talking most of the session about drug enforcement agents wanting to bust him for cocaine dealing. He talked about drug agents searching him on a cruise that he took to Mexico. To this day I don't know what to believe about him but I certainly suspected that Bobo was dealing cocaine and chose to get into an inpatient treatment program because the drug agents were a little too close for comfort.

Bobo had big black sores on his face and forearms. These were the result of freebasing cocaine. Frequently, freebase addicts experience recurrent itching sensations causing them to scratch at their skin. Sometimes addicts feel as if snakes or bugs are crawling on their skin. A colleague, Ronald K. Siegal, asked one of his cocaine freebase patients to bring in these bugs. Using a tweezer the client removed thick patches of skin from his arms and placed them in a bottle for Dr. Siegal to analyze.

Bobo reported severe depression and fatigue; he wanted to get into treatment. Immediately I referred him to an inpatient drug/alcohol treatment program with a strong medical component.

Bobo's medical complications cleared up after two weeks in the hospital-based drug/alcohol treatment program. He was active in his recovery program and participated in all groups. He seemed well-liked by others in recovery. Who wouldn't like this man who was so big and physically powerful? One day when I was visiting the treatment facility, I saw Bobo and almost didn't recognize him, he looked so good.

Unfortunately, only two weeks after leaving treatment Bobo was back doing freebase cocaine. A few weeks later he died of a complication from cocaine freebasing.

Other cases are certainly as dramatic when people are involved with cocaine, especially injecting cocaine or freebasing cocaine. Whenever cocaine is around, there are usually guns, paranoia, dealing, drug enforcement agents, police, crime, and violence. People get into almost paranoid-schizophrenic states where they imagine holographs in their backyards, people hiding in closets, or people out to get them. Cocaine addicts in paranoid states have been known to exhibit quite bizarre behavior. One patient of mine climbed on the roof of his home, suspecting that the police were coming at any time.

Case Study

Let's Bury the Cocaine

Cocaine Addicts

Cocaine is so addicting that these negative consequences often do not deter continued use. In one situation, three men who were using and dealing cocaine decided that the situation was getting out of control. They lived in a large mansion with high walls and a sophisticated security system. Late one evening, because things were getting out of hand, they dug a six-foot-deep hole in their backyard and stored all their cocaine in this hole. They covered it up and put an extremely heavy cement statue on top. By only 3 A.M., the allure of the cocaine had gotten to them. Flashlights and shovels in hand, they were busy digging up their stash.

Case Study

High-Functioning Cocaine Addict/Alcoholic

Ralph

Ralph, thirty-seven, is a high-functioning addict/alcoholic. When his cocaine use became a problem, he actually signed himself into outpatient treatment through an employee assistance program at work. He did extremely well in the intensive outpatient treatment program, which involved both individual and group counseling. Ralph stopped using cocaine completely. When told that he must also stop using alcohol and attend regular Alcoholics Anonymous or Narcotic Anonymous meetings, Ralph resisted. He candidly admitted tht he felt the issue was his cocaine use, not his alcohol use. He admitted that he was a cocaine addict but believed that he was not an alcoholic because he never drank alcoholically.

As the normal pressures and stress of work, family, and marital life intensified, Ralph periodically got drunk to fall asleep. After this pattern persisted for a while, he cut back his alcohol consumption and exercised on a regular basis. Ralph enjoyed the diversion of long-distance running and was in remarkable shape considering his use of alcohol. Running also allowed him to get out of the house and release the pressure from work. Ralph maintained this cycle of control and then release for over a year. Meanwhile, he still attended counseling sessions although not heeding the warning by the counselor about the potential for relapse to cocaine.

During the following six-month cycle, Ralph returned to cocaine use. A pattern of cocaine binges then occurred for six months before Ralph concluded that alcohol often led to these binges. Today, Ralph is abstinent from alcohol/drugs and is active in a spiritually-based AA-oriented self-help group.

Case Study

The Ideal Coupling

Alcohol and Cocaine

Alice was thirty-five and Gary was twenty-nine when they first met. He was struggling to be a movie producer and she was working as the office manager in an off-Broadway theater. They were opposites in many ways.

Gary grew up in the shadow of his father's accomplishments as a major Hollywood movie producer. His family was Jewish, wealthy, and had no history of problems with drugs/alcohol. Alice grew up on the east side of New York. Her father was an alcoholic, and her mother was dependent on Valium and pain medication. She grew up in a rigid, abusive family system, with strong Catholic indoctrination.

Gary began smoking marijuana at age thirteen and used hallucinogens throughout the early 1970s. Despite his drug use, he was bright enough to graduate high school and was accepted to a college film program that he failed to complete. Gary was talented and bright. His underlying shyness stemmed from a fear of rejection and a fear of failure. He would vacillate between grandiosity and hopelessness.

Alice began drinking alcohol at the age of ten and had adverse reactions when she tried marijuana. Her drug of choice was alcohol. An extremely rebellious child, Alice had a tough time in Catholic school and barely graduated. Alice was bright, aggressive, and resourceful. Despite their different backgrounds both Gary and Alice had fathers who were emotionally unavailable, and smothering mothers who were enmeshed and needy of their affection.

The differences between Alice and Gary initially made them a good team. Gary was working on a film project in New York City when they first met. She was the perfect partner, someone who could encourage him when he was feeling insecure or down. He was the sensitive partner who represented everything that Alice didn't have when she was growing up. Alice was also able to bridge the relationship with Gary's father, which enabled Gary to get support and contacts for film projects and allowed Alice to access the powerful father figure that she never had growing up. Things were going well as Alice and Gary struggled in New York City. They enjoyed their friends, the life-style, and the exposure to the inner workings of the city.

Unfortunately, New York City also represented Alice's shame-based childhood; contact with her mother triggered sad memories. As a result, Alice pressured Gary to move back to Los Angeles where the major studios were and where his father's contacts could move his career faster.

Once in Los Angeles, other things moved faster, but not Gary's career. Alice quickly moved into the fast-lane life-style. Her flirtations and attention to others made Gary extremely jealous and angry. Before too long, Alice was again drinking heavily, and Gary's attempts to have her cut back only escalated further conflicts. At the same time, Gary was again smoking marijuana heavily. A short time later, he was snorting cocaine and eventually smoking freebase cocaine. Periodically, they swore off alcohol and cocaine. However, in a few days they would have an argument and return to using. The conflicts between Gary and his family created feelings of shame and rage. Initially, Alice was close with his family but when she began drinking and hanging out, she was snubbed by them. This brought back her feelings of rejection, shame, and feeling lesser than everyone else.

Next, they taught each other about their drugs of choice, and soon they both were using alcohol and cocaine on an addictive level. With her entrepreneurial aggressiveness, Alice began dealing cocaine to support their habit, and Gary scammed his parents for additional money to keep them in cocaine, alcohol, and the fast-lane life-style. They continued to abuse cocaine and alcohol; after a twenty-four to thirty-six hour cocaine binge, they drank alcohol to counteract the depressive crash of the cocaine. Many times they drank alcohol excessively, which lead to cocaine use. Most of these binges were followed by two to five days of sleep, excessive food binges, and a generally reclusive existence. Once a partnership of different backgrounds, now their partnership was based on alcohol and cocaine addiction.

My contact with them began when Alice was trying to get sober and struggling to get Gary into treatment. Alice finally got out of this dysfunctional codependent relationship based on alcohol and cocaine. She entered an inpatient drug/alcohol treatment program. Two years later, Alice told me that she was the director of marketing for a drug/alcohol treatment program. She had not been in contact with Gary but suspected that he was doing drugs/alcohol with a new girlfriend and going through the same addictive cycle.

Case Study
PCP Use
Petra

A shy, sixteen-year-old girl, Petra had recently moved with her family from Texas to Van Nuys, California. She had some difficulty adjusting to California and making friends. One day a girlfriend invited her to go with two guys for a car ride; they all smoked some PCP in the car. She didn't know the girlfriend very well and had just met the two boys. The three of them decided to scare Petra and told her there was a snake in the car. Under the influence of PCP, she became frightened by their joking, even though she thought they were kidding. She was also hurt and upset with her girlfriend for going along with the joke. The truth was that they really did have a live snake in the car—a large harmless, green garter snake one of the boys had caught. When the snake was let loose in the car, Petra jumped out and was hit by an oncoming car. She was not injured, just bruised and in shock. After six months of counseling, she began to overcome the trauma of the incident and to start to trust others again. This rather unique bizarre situation illustrates the potential psychological harm PCP can cause.

Case Study
Crack Cocaine Use
Janet

Janet was a unique and special woman. When she was smoking crack cocaine, she described herself as being able to get money out of the cracks in the sidewalk. She was a master at manipulation and plied her trade as well as a crack addict could.

Janet was thirty-eight when I met her in a program for cocaine addicts. She had been struggling with staying sober when she entered the counseling group. She would be sober for four to six weeks and then slip up. She was a welcome addition to the group because she was extremely glib, black, and street smart. When Janet began talking, everyone listened. Her inflections and speech pattern were extremely engaging. Once she began, a continuous barrage of common sense and wisdom lasting for fifteen to twenty mintues issued from her lips. Her recovery throughout the next year was remarkable. She attended Narcotics Anonymous meetings on the same street where she once sold her body for crack cocaine. With tremendous strength, she walked past the places in which she had used drugs without responding to the triggers of drug cravings. Although crack was easily available, she walked right down the street and into the Narcotics Anonymous meeting.

Janet had not finished high school but was extremely bright. When she was very young, her alcoholic father left the family. Her mother was a proud woman who worked as a housekeeper while she raised five children. Through her relationship with men in her early years, Janet was introduced to alcohol, drugs, and then crack cocaine. She became dependent on her relationships with men. Every time she would try to stop prostituting and using drugs/alcohol, she would be drawn back to the drugs by the man she was involved with at the time.

During her first three months in the program, Janet continued this pattern of trying to get straight and then lapsing back to the drugs and the man in her life. As soon as she began to understand codependent relationships, she began to make progress. It also helped that her man was arrested and jailed for ten months. During this time, Janet was one of those amazing recovery stories. She chaired a Narcotics Anonymous meeting, went back to school, and got her high school diploma. After maintaining sobriety for one year, Janet was encouraged by her friends and support group to apply for a job in a drug/alcohol treatment center. Her recovery, her dynamic style, and her ability to reach others got her the job. Janet still is active in recovery and is an effective model for young people in the inner city.

Case Study
Polydrug Abuse
David

My therapeutic work with David continued for over two years. We focused on the trauma he experienced growing up in an imbalanced alcoholic family system and his experiences on the road, especially his incarceration in two psychiatric hospitals. To David's credit, he survived those ordeals and is now living a productive life at the age of thirty-five. His story is not unique, many have experienced the same kind of childhood trauma.

David came from an alcoholic family system. He adored his mother, who was extremely attractive and a wonderful singer. She was talented, playful, and creative—when she wasn't drinking. When she drank alcohol, she seemed to forget that he was even there, as if he were invisible. David hoped and dreamed that her boyfriend, Ben Grayson who owned a large restaurant, would marry his mother. David's dad left David and his mom, when he was seven years old. Grayson let David and his mom live in the quarters behind the restaurant. She was the hostess and spent long days and long nights working in the restaurant. Often she drank with the patrons, and gradually her drinking got worse. Her beauty was marred by physical illnesses, complicated by the alcohol and a two- to three-pack-a-day cigarette habit. As the years went on, any hope David had for a stable family life was dimmed by his mother's continued use of alcohol and cigarettes.

Although he was a bright child, school was just a place for David to meet other kids, have fun, and smoke marijuana. Drugs, alcohol, and fights were a big part of his adolescent development. The lack of parental availability and supervision and his mother's alcoholism resulted in David becoming a street-smart, self-reliant kid.

As the years went on, the situation at home became more intolerable. When David reached puberty, he became more aware of his mom's sexual escapades with a variety of men. The trauma of those years led David to set off for New York City from Phoenix, Arizona.

In the late 1950s—the beginning of the hippie movement—drugs and alcohol were David's constant companions during his journey from Phoenix to New York City. On the road he slept where he could—in parks, alleys, storefronts, or fields. He frequently smoked marijuana and drank alcohol while traveling. Due to his friendly, affable style, David was befriended many times. David was so likable that many people invited him to stay and shared their marijuana, acid, speed, peyote, mushrooms, food, and shelter. David truly got by and high with a little help from his friends. Unfortunately, not all of his experiences on the road were positive. He was beaten on numerous occasions, raped, threatened at knifepoint, and frequently found himself in other life-threatening situations.

As time went on, David got deeper and deeper into drugs and the hippie subculture. His use of drugs was so intense that he would spend hours under the influence talking about existential issues. David's affable style had a charismatic quality, especially when he was under the influence of drugs. He soon became a cult leader. David was an avid accomplished musician. He played guitar, talked music, and entertained others with his stories of his travels. At this stage, his stories began to become fabrication, yet David believed they were real. When he was under the influence of drugs, he would threaten violence with an ominous look that communicated a kind of homicidal rage. David began having paranoid and delusional thinking. One day, he decided to leave New York City. He went to Idlewild Airport (now John F. Kennedy Airport), under the delusion that the Beatles had sent him an airplane ticket. He was to fly to London to consult with them on the lyrics and music for their next album. When he told the security police this, he was arrested and escorted to the locked ward of a psychiatric hospital. David was under the influence of a hallucinogen at the time, delusional, paranoid, without any known residence or means of support. He looked bizarre, acted unstable, and was argumentative and aggressive with the police.

Case Study
Continued
David

Once at the psychiatric hospital, David was maintained on antipsychotic medication, diagnosed as paranoid schizophrenic, and spent six weeks in a stupor that he described as a *One Flew Over the Cuckoo's Nest* experience. After the six weeks David received a one-way ticket back to Phoenix. A few days later, David again ran away, this time to the Haight-Ashbury District of San Francisco. David fondly recalled the early days in the Haight as the true beginning of the peace and love movement. To this day he is proud to have been one of the people there when it all began. David described the next few months as the only time in his sixteen plus years that he felt loved and accepted, and had a family. Unfortunately, his use of drugs/alcohol escalated, and he had another psychotic break with reality. Again, he was hospitalized in a locked psychiatric ward. Fortunately, as the drugs cleared, a young psychiatrist realized that David was presenting paranoid-schizophrenic behavior that was drug induced. This was a critical point because David was beginning to believe that he was truly crazy. The psychiatrist effectively counseled David and helped him realize that the drugs/alcohol and his traumatic life situation were the main problems; he was not clinically crazy.

The next twenty years continued to be difficult years for David. He continued to experience additional traumas, with the death of a young child, a divorce, and in the early 1980s addiction to cocaine. By the grace of God and his own survival skills, David got into recovery for drugs/alcohol. He and his second wife supported one another through those early years of recovery. David is now sober from all drugs/alcohol, still in a healthy relationship with his second wife, and effectively parenting two healthy and functioning children (James is fifteen, and Kristin is six). David and his wife have worked on their adult child of alcoholics issues, and continue to work on their issues while maintaining recovery from drugs/alcohol.

Summary

Shame is a powerful concept that affects us all in some way throughout our lives. Most individuals can survive and adapt to shameful feelings and experiences. In alcoholic and imbalanced family systems, however, shame has a dramatic impact on family members.

This chapter defines shame as "the self looking in on itself and finding itself lacking, or flawed." Shame in the alcoholic/addict and imbalanced family system is often inescapable, creating feelings of hopelessness and helplessness. The shame-based individual then continues this vicious negative self-cycle duplicating life situations and interpersonal situations that are shameful, one of them being the shame of alcoholism and drug addiction.

This chapter summarizes how shame is induced by imbalanced parenting, unhealthy family systems, peers, and some schools and religious institutions. Shame is also explored in the context of human sexuality, which can be the most damaging arena of shame.

When shame attaches to normal feelings, the feelings get exaggerated or exacerbated. For example:

anger + shame = rage
anxiety + shame = panic
depression + shame = despair.

Another damaging feeling often experienced in the alcoholic/addict and imbalanced family is abandonment. James Masterson's definition of abandonment depression has six basic elements: homicidal rage, suicidal depression, panic, hopelessness and helplessness, emptiness and void, and guilt.

Other characteristics that result from shame, abandonment, and rejection include rejection sensitivity, difficulty making effective decisions and choices, poor frustration tolerance, and poor impulse control.

References

Diagnostic and Statistical Manual III-R, 3d ed. Washington, D.C.: American Psychological Association, 1987.

Fossum, Merle A. and Marilyn J. Mason. *Facing Shame: Families in Recovery.* New York: W. W. Norton, 1986.

Kaufman, Gershen. Interview in *Focus Magazine,* June–July 1989.

Masterson, James. *Psychotherapy of the Borderline Adult—A Developmental Approach.* New York: Brunner/Mazel, 1976.

Piaget, Jean. *Adaptation Intelligence: Organic Selection and Phenocopy.* Chicago: University of Chicago Press, 1980.

Adult Children of Alcoholics: Our Emerging Awareness

This chapter focuses on adult children of alcoholics (ACAs), a significant, emerging issue in the fields of drug/alcohol treatment and clinical/counseling psychology. More than 28 million Americans have at least one alcoholic parent and it is estimated that an equal number have at least one parent with a drug problem. Children growing up in addict/alcoholic family systems experience traumas that result in specific adult behavioral characteristics and developmental disabilities. They often exhibit symptoms that can be compared to post-traumatic stress disorder, codependent personality disorder, and atypical depression. Adult children have trouble establishing effective boundaries in relationships and are often either overseparated or overattached in partner relationships. Recovery for adult children involves dealing with unresolved grief of childhood and working through the feelings of shame, abandonment and rejection. By gaining an understanding of the impact of alcoholic family system on children, perhaps we can better address the needs of the next generation.

Chapter Goals

1. Describe the factors that contributed to the emerging awareness of adult children of alcoholics (ACA) issues.
2. List several behavioral characteristics of ACAs.
3. Compare growing up in an alcoholic family system to post-traumatic stress disorder (PTSD) and describe the five major symptoms of PTSD.
4. Identify the scope of the ACA problem including an estimate of how many people are affected.
5. Describe the behaviors and communication patterns of parents and children in an alcoholic family system.
6. Describe the kinds of denial that children in an alcoholic system maintain and some behavioral characteristics that identify children of alcoholics.
7. Give some examples of how ACAs deny feelings and shut down emotions.
8. Describe the factors that produce damage in the lives of children of alcoholics.
9. Define and describe codependent personality disorder, the disengaged ACA, and the ACA suffering from atypical depression.
10. Explain the role feelings play in making decisions and the model of ACAs as suffering from an emotional learning disability.
11. Define boundary inadequacy and describe the thoughts, feelings, and behaviors of overseparated and overattached individuals.
12. Describe some common features and characteristics of couples engaging in codependent dances.
13. Explain the dysfunctional beliefs that ACAs maintain in developing intimate relationships.
14. Describe methods that help ACAs develop awareness of feelings.
15. Discuss the rationale for doing grief work with ACAs and highlight reasons for this work being done by trained and experienced professional counselors.
16. Describe the application of affirmations and second order change in ACA recovery.
17. Describe the issues involved in ACAs developing more effective, balanced, interpersonal relationships.
18. Identify the eleven curative factors of group psychotherapy and their application for ACA therapy groups.

The Adult Children of Alcoholics Movement

In the 1980s one of the most significant drug/alcohol issues brought to the attention of the general public was the awareness of the characteristics of adult children of alcoholics. Children who grew up in alcoholic families are now adults, hence the term *adult children of alcoholics* (ACA). These adults report difficulties in establishing effective, intimate interpersonal relationships.

The talent and dedication of people such as Timmen Cermak, Claudia Black, Stephanie Brown, Rockelle Lerner, Sharon Wegscheider-Cruse, Robert Ackerman, and Lori Dwinell, has created an emerging awareness of the trauma of growing up in an alcoholic family system. Because of this new awareness, our society has not only recognized but is also dealing with the dysfunctional aspects of alcoholism on the family members.

In 1979, a *Newsweek* article about adult children of alcoholics reported the early work of Stephanie Brown and Claudia Black, who both described and labeled the characteristics of ACAs. Brown (1988) describes the reaction after the *Newsweek* article as "a prairie fire of interest." The proliferation of articles, materials, books, general information, workshops, and speakers on ACA issues has been dramatic from 1979 to the present. Adult children of alcoholics were finally recognized as a treatment population that had generally been ignored for years. This explosion of interest was in direct proportion to the neglect and oversight that occurred as professionals focused myopically on the alcoholics while ignoring the children who grew in alcoholic families. W. Bosma appropriately described children of alcoholics in 1972 as **victims in a hidden tragedy.** In 1983, the National Association for Children of Alcoholics (NACOA) was formed. Timmen Cermak, one of the founders, was its first president. Numerous planning meetings established NACOA as a central organizing force in disseminating information, providing direction, and developing resources for adult children of alcoholics. NACOA organized national conferences to provide a forum for the dissemination of ACA treatment information for both professionals and the lay public.

Scope of the Problem

NACOA developed some basic facts about children of alcoholics in its charter statement. Some of those facts are

- An estimated 28 million Americans have at least one alcoholic parent.

- More than half of all alcoholics have an alcoholic parent.
- Children of alcoholics are at the highest risk of developing alcoholism themselves or marrying someone who is alcoholic.
- In up to 90 percent of child abuse cases, alcohol is a significant factor.
- Children of alcoholics are frequently victims of incest, child neglect, and other forms of violence and exploitation.

The popularity of the ACA movement also brought with it some concerns for overgeneralization and a lack of clinical foundation. Appropriately, this point is made by one of the pioneers of the movement. "Like many social movements, the sudden recognition, widespread interest, and emotional intensity have been powerful and helpful for many children and adults. However, there continues to be a lack of a solid clinical research and theoretical foundation on which to base important decisions for intervention, education, prevention, and treatment" (Brown 1988).

Characteristics of Adult Children of Alcoholics

Some of the behavioral characteristics ACAs experience are

1. a fear of losing control
2. all-or-none, black or white thinking
3. fear of experiencing feelings
4. overdeveloped sense of responsibility or irresponsibility
5. difficulty with intimacy and with asking for what is wanted or needed
6. flashbacks of childhood, yet many memory gaps
7. feeling little, or like a child, when under stress
8. unreasonable loyalty
9. addiction to excitement
10. difficulty relaxing
11. feelings of guilt, abandonment, and/or depression
12. tendency to confuse love with self-pity
13. a backlog of shock and grief
14. compulsive behaviors
15. living in a world of denial
16. guessing at what is normal
17. a tendency toward physical symptoms (e.g., headaches, gastrointestinal problems, etc.)

ACAs and Post-Traumatic Stress Disorder

Cermak has stated that growing up in an alcoholic family system is analagous to the post-traumatic stress disorder (PTSD) of war veterans or survivors of the Holocaust because the same coping mechanisms are utilized. The soldier who helplessly watches as a buddy is shot and killed shuts down his own emotions to survive the trauma, which can later be reexperienced in a safe environment. This same reaction of shutting down emotionally occurs in the children of alcoholics. After these children become adults, they reexperience feelings of childhood traumas and suffer chronic symptoms of acute anxiety, depression, sleep disturbances, and nightmares, and an inability to work or function effectively at daily activities.

The following major symptoms of PTSD are similar to symptoms experienced by ACAs:

1. Reexperiencing the trauma, as evidenced by
   a. nightmares
   b. recurrent obsessive thoughts
   c. sudden reemergence of survival behavior in the face of events that resemble the original trauma
   d. emotional overload
2. Psychic numbing, as evidenced by
   a. a sense of depersonalization
   b. not fitting into one's surroundings
   c. a feeling of emotional anesthesia
   d. constriction of emotions, especially in situations demanding intimacy, tenderness, or sexuality
   e. having no feelings during times of stress
   f. suddenly experiencing a wall between the self and the feelings
   g. being confused instead of having feelings
   h. having a lump in the throat instead of allowing feelings to emerge; or pressure and tightness in the jaw, shoulders, or other parts of the body
   i. feeling that emotions will be overwhelming if one gets in touch with them
3. Hypervigilance, as evidenced by
   a. inability to relax
   b. frequent startle responses
   c. chronic anxiety
   d. panic attacks
4. Survivor guilt, as evidenced by
   a. chronic depression
   b. a sourceless sense of guilt
5. Intensification of symptoms by exposure to events that resemble the original trauma

Case Study

ACA and Post-Traumatic Stress Disorder

Joe was a client who had experienced both the trauma of growing up in an alcoholic family system and post-traumatic stress as a result of military service in Vietnam. Joe was referred to me by a colleague, who was counseling Joe's twelve-year-old daughter.

Joe came home drunk one evening, went to his daughter's bedroom to kiss her good night, and began crying and talking about how unhappy he was. Although there was no sexual violation, the daughter was extremely upset by her father's behavior. She was frightened and concerned about his drinking and his deep emotional sadness.

Joe was one of those patients for whom I initially had very little hope; he turned out to be a case that reinforced my belief in the inherent goodness in people. Joe was twenty-five minutes late for his first counseling session. Joe insisted that his lateness was due to a business appointment and wondered why I was so concerned with time. He believed that his only problem was his business. He said "If I could only get out from under the financial pressure, everything would be back to normal." Joe agreed to come back for counseling to help with stress management although he felt that his daughter needed assistance, not him.

Gradually, I was able to establish a therapeutic bond with Joe. Once I got to know him, I soon realized that he had the heart of a puppy dog and he had suffered significant disappointments and trauma in his life.

Joe's alcoholic father, who was well-read and extremely bright, owned his own business. His dad spent most of his time drinking at the office and the local bar while discussing many topics with his customers and friends; he was well-versed in politics, philosophy, religion, physics, even psychology. Although he was a friendly and entertaining drunk with his friends, he was emotionally unpredictable at home. At times Joe's dad was maudlin about his childhood and his father's death when he was eight. At other times he would rage around the house screaming resentments for his need to work so hard to support his wife and the children. Once Joe was so angry with his father that he took a baseball bat and was going to smash him in the face.

Sometimes Joe felt sorry for his father and put him to bed after a drinking binge; when things got to be overwhelming, Joe would just run out of the house. On those evenings, Joe frequently went down to the school and threw rocks at the classroom windows. This and similar aggressive behavior kept him in trouble throughout his childhood. Joe was extremely bright and despite his aggressive behavior, pulled good grades in high school. Because he spent more time drinking than studying in college, in 1968 his military deferment was revoked.

In the service, Joe was put through training for military intelligence and could have avoided Vietnam if his alcoholism and aggressive anger hadn't gotten him into trouble with his top sergeant. In Vietnam, Joe's major job was to fly to battle zones after conflicts and get a body count for Vietnamese and American soldiers.

Joe felt sadness for the Vietnamese children; he described them stealing and cheating and manipulating the GIs to survive. It reminded him of his own childhood anger and aggressive behavior. In counseling sessions, Joe initially denied the emotional trauma of his experiences in Vietnam. He insisted that he had it good compared to others. Joe suffered from this traumatic exposure as well as from survivor's guilt. He experienced all the traditional signs of post-traumatic stress: sleep disorders and nightmares, night sweats, inability to concentrate, hypertension, disorientation, and explosive temper. All of these symptoms were complicated by his alcoholism.

After a year and a half of individual counseling, followed by group counseling with other ACAs, Joe was able to maintain sobriety, grieve the loss of his father, and also grieve his experiences in Vietnam. After some time in counseling, Joe and some other group members visited the Vietnam War Memorial in Washington, D.C. This was an important event in his painful journey to recovery.

Child growing up in an alcoholic family

Childhood in an Alcoholic Home

Children in alcoholic families learn to distrust their own observations (what they see and hear), and feelings (what they sense), and feel powerless to change the family system. They cannot speak out and they cannot trust their feelings because the rules in an alcoholic family system are "don't talk, don't feel, and don't trust." Because these children distrust their own observations and feelings, they must wonder or guess at what is normal. At a time when most functional families are providing structure, discipline, and natural consequences for their children's behavior, alcoholic families provide control, rigidity, fear, irresponsibility, immaturity, and most importantly, **unpredictability.** Children in alcoholic families try to control the behavior of the alcoholic parent and the codependent spouse by becoming super-responsible and trying to do everything correctly to obtain the parent's approval. They soon find out that despite their best efforts to be perfect, the parent always finds fault with something. While desperately trying to predict or control the behavior of their parents, children do not realize that alcoholism and drug addiction is a disease that results in unpredictable behavior.

Identifying Children of Alcoholics

Robert Ackerman (1978) described the various behavioral characteristics that identify children of alcoholics. These criteria include

- being superachievers, perfectionists, or exhibiting efforts that go far beyond the reasonable criteria of the task
- exhibiting an inordinate need to control their environment, and therefore becoming anxious with the slightest threat to their security (e.g., a teacher who unknowingly comments on homework not done, or an unusually low grade may provoke emotional upset)
- displaying social disengagement from or excessive attention to the peer group (isolated loner, acting out, or class clown)
- exhibiting signs of physical neglect (untidy, soiled clothing, poor hygiene) and/or physical abuse (bruises, cuts, etc.)
- being unable to concentrate and sometimes showing marked variations in academic performance, especially when parents are in a binge pattern of alcohol use or in codependent conflict

ACAs Deny Feelings

The alcoholic family swears an allegiance to the family secret of alcoholism. Family members dedicate themselves to denying that dad and/or mom is out of control. The children hope that perhaps their family secret will change and continually explore ways to make it change. Sometimes this becomes an almost magical quest by the children to find that special way of being or ritualistic behavior that can make dad and/or mom change. Children give up their own sense of self in their search for the key that will change their parents' dysfunctional behavior.

Alan Flock tells this story illustrating how children's feelings are discounted: When the alcoholic dad falls down drunk and spends the night on the front lawn, still in his work clothes, does the child really believe mom's explanation? "You know your Dad loves astronomy, he came home late last night, laid down to gaze at the stars, and since he was tired from working late, he just fell asleep gazing at the constellations."

Children must maintain the **illusion of normalcy,** the illusion that their families are normal. The child defensively maintains the belief that this is what other families go through.

Howard Clinebell (1968) reported that the following factors produce damage in the lives of children of alcoholics:

1. *Role reversal:* Children may undertake parental duties because the parent is unable to be responsible or because the parent forces responsibilities on the children. The alcoholic may be treated as a child and, in return, act helpless. In incestuous families, the daughter and mother often switch roles.
2. *Unpredictability:* An inconsistent and unpredictable relationship with the alcoholic emotionally deprives the children.
3. *Unavailability:* The nonalcoholic, inadequate parent is struggling with major problems; because this parent's own needs are unmet, he or she is unable to attend to the needs of the children.
4. *Social isolation:* The damaging factor is the social isolation of the family, as protection from further pain and suffering, due to embarrassment.

Even periods of parental sobriety have negative effects on the children in alcoholic families. This is primarily due to the inconsistency and shattered hope that this time it will be different. The alcoholic father "inspires the natural love of his offspring, who build there from an ideal father image of omnipotence and loving kindness. This disillusionment of the drunken episode is shattering to the frail superego structure of the child who is subjected to alternating experiences of exalted hopes and blighting disappointments" (Newell 1950).

The Perspective of the ACA

M. Cork (1969) interviewed 115 children living in alcoholic families in an attempt to understand the child's perspective. Cork found that the child reacted to the alcoholic family system in a number of common ways.

The children in alcoholic families

1. would not go to a friend's house because they would not dare reciprocate and invite friends to their homes due to the unpredictability and embarrassing behaviors of their parents.
2. were angry at everybody.

Problems of Alcoholic Families Affecting More than One Person

Marital

- marital instability and fighting
- prolonged separation
- divorce
- death of a spouse
- physical abuse of a spouse

Parental

- inadequate parenting
- lack of structure
- inconsistencies
- emotional neglect of children
- inability or unwillingness to perform parental duties

Cross-Boundaries—Parent and Child Relationships

- physical and sexual abuse of children
- parentification of children (child becomes the parent)
- role reversal
- family conflict
- isolation of family from society
- isolation of individual family member within the family
- incongruent communication (mixed messages)
- lack of trust between family members
- family secrets

Source: Lawson, Peterson, and Lawson 1983

3. were preoccupied at school with worry about what would happen when they returned home.
4. envied their friends who seemed to have fun with their families.
5. felt alone when they were only children.
6. felt neglected when both parents were drinking.
7. felt they had to be parent-like, especially if the mother was drinking.
8. worried about each parent's loneliness if the parents were separated. They wished for their parents to reunite even if their home was calmer during the separation. The children seemed to feel an even deeper loss if the alcoholic parents moved out of the house.
9. were unable to separate and individuate from their parents as adolescents. It was difficult to break away from somebody with whom they had no ties. One child poignantly said, "I want to be somebody, but I feel like nobody."

TABLE 6.1
Problems of Children in Alcoholic Families

Physical neglect or abuse	Acting-out behaviors	Emotional reaction to alcoholism and chaotic family life	Social and interpersonal difficulties
serious illness accidents	involvement with police and courts aggression alcohol and other drug abuse	suicidal tendencies depression repressed emotions lack of self-confidence lack of life direction fear of abandonment afraid of future	family relationship problems peer problems adjustment problems feeling different from norm embarrassment overresponsible feeling unloved and unable to trust

Source: Lawson, Peterson, and Lawson 1983

10. excused the alcoholic of his or her behavior and often condemned the nonalcoholics for being hostile and angry. Children could deduce from this that love and caring would come from alcoholics. Research unfortunately indicates that many ACAs do marry alcoholics to try out their hypothesis.
11. experienced multiple separations and reunions of their parents and learned not to depend on any consistent state.
12. continued to have problems even when the alcoholic stopped drinking. See table 6.1 for a list of these problems.

ACAs Define Self through Others

ACAs define their sense of identity by the impressions others have of them. ACAs have a strong, often imbalanced, need for affirmation from others that they are indeed worthwhile. They approach their world from the outside in versus the inside out stance of self-confident people.

Even though many of my ACA patients have been extremely successful in their professional lives, they still feel inadequate and don't trust their talents, skills, and accomplishments. Many feel that they are charlatans and will be exposed as inadequate persons. They fear that at any time their professional abilities may all be taken away from them. Then they will relive their ultimate fear of being all alone, helpless, abandoned, and rejected; the fears they felt growing up will be played out again. Successful careers and stylish and attractive life-styles camouflage their poor sense of self, and they are surprised when others don't see through their disguises.

Codependency

Timmen Cermak quotes the metaphor of Charles Alexander (1985), that codependency is "like being a lifeguard on a crowded beach, knowing that you cannot swim, and not telling anyone for fear of a panic." This is the sense of desperation that ACAs feel as they guess at what is normal.

Cermak, himself an adult child of an alcoholic, has defined codependency in diagnostic terms in the hope that codependency would be recognized as a psychiatric disorder. These diagnostic criteria for codependent personality disorder are

ACA lifeguard who doesn't know how to swim

- Continual investment of self-esteem in the ability to influence or control feelings and behaviors in the self and others in the face of obvious adverse consequences
- Assumption of responsibility for meeting others' needs to the exclusion of acknowledging one's own needs
- Anxiety and boundary distortions in situations of intimacy and separation
- Enmeshment in relationships with personality-disordered, drug-dependent, and impulse-disordered individuals
- Maintaining a primary relationship with an active substance abuser for at least two years without seeking outside support, and/or exhibiting three or more of the following characteristics:
  - —constriction of emotions with or without dramatic outbursts
  - —depression
  - —hypervigilance
  - —compulsions
  - —anxiety
  - —excessive reliance on denial
  - —substance abuse
  - —recurrent physical or sexual abuse
  - —stress-related medical illnesses

An individual who has all five criteria of codependency would then be diagnosed as having a codependent personality disorder. A personality disorder affects all aspects of one's life because pervasive personality traits become inflexible and maladaptive. The result is significant subjective distress and social and occupational impairment. Treatment for codependent personality disorder often involves extensive education, counseling, therapeutic interventions, and sometimes medication to deal with major anxiety and depression.

If you find yourself identifying with some of the diagnostic criteria for codependent personality disorder but not all of them, you probably would be described as having some codependent traits, not a full-blown disorder. If these codependent traits result in significant difficulties in establishing effective, caring, and intimate relationships, they probably need to be investigated.

The Disengaged ACA

Growing up in alcoholic families with parents who are unavailable, children often develop patterns of interpersonal disengagement. ACAs may maintain this pattern of disengagement in most interpersonal relationships. Cermak describes disengaged ACAs as having the following behaviors:

1. hard driving, workaholic; always preoccupied by projects and things that have to be done; rarely satisfied with accomplishments; in denial of feelings, relationships take a back seat
2. defensive, fearful of closeness to others; plays cards close to the vest; unable to deal honestly on an emotional level; longing for relationships; chronic anger
3. overwhelmed by feelings, buffeted by emotional storms; desperately trying to get other people to behave properly; often unable to work effectively.

Disengaged ACAs exhibit behaviors that on the surface make them seem self-sufficient and self-actualized; in actuality, they are depressed and suffering from deep emotional pain.

Atypical Depression

Another diagnostic category recently associated with ACAs and others who grew up in imbalanced family systems is atypical depression. Atypical depression is an impairment in interpersonal and social skills due to an extreme sensitivity to rejection. Because these individuals are highly sensitive, they overreact, thinking others' remarks, opinions, and/or actions are personal attacks. Many individuals suffering from atypical depression report this sensitivity began in early childhood and have histories of physical, emotional, and/or sexual violation.

ACAs in Relationships

Boundary Inadequacy

Boundary inadequacy is the inability to set consistent and appropriate boundaries. The result is vascillating or ambiguous boundaries, overly rigid boundaries, and invasive boundaries. As a result, ACAs have difficulty in relationships; often they choose an alcoholic, addict, or a generally dysfunctional partner, or develop codependent relationships. If one were to ask persons with strong codependent traits and difficulties in setting appropriate boundaries to choose persons they were interested in from 100 people—90 of whom are fairly functional and stable—their choices would probably come from the 10 dysfunctional people.

For ACAs, boundaries are often distorted in interpersonal relationships; sometimes they are excessively involved (overattachment) or excessively detached (overseparation).

Overattachment and Overseparation

In their work on chemical dependency and intimacy dysfunction, Eli Coleman and Philip Colgan (1987) have focused on overattachment and overseparation in men who grew up in alcoholic families. They identified thoughts, feelings, and behaviors common to both the overseparated and overattached individuals. Table 6.2 lists these thoughts, feelings, and behaviors.

The thoughts of the overattached and overseparated sound like common lyrics to country western songs. These codependent lyrics include: "You should be grateful." "I want so little." "You don't care." "What am I doing wrong?" "I'm nobody without you." Many people identify strongly with either the overseparated or the overattached column in table 6.2; others cross over, having both overattached and overseparated characteristics. Overseparated individuals tend to develop relationships with overattached individuals, and vice versa. Frequently, ACAs duplicate the kind of relationship their codependent parents had. Not only does the disease of alcoholism and drug addiction progress from generation to generation but also the patterns of inadequate boundary setting and codependent relationships.

Codependent Dances

The most traditional codependent dance is between alcoholics/addicts and their codependent partners. Alcoholics/addicts and their partners are both codependent; alcoholics/

TABLE 6.2
Overseparation and Overattachment

Overseparation	Overattachment
Thoughts	
You're not good enough.	I'm not good enough.
They want so much.	I want so little.
They give so little.	I give so much.
I'm ambivalent.	You don't care.
If only they would . . .	What am I doing wrong?
I am a rock.	I'm nobody without you.
You should be grateful.	I'm so unappreciated.
Feelings	
Fear, smothering	Fear, abandonment
Self-controlled	Out of control
Indifferent	Needy, burdened
Unsafe with others	Unsafe alone
Trapped	Shut out
Numb	Desperate
Behaviors	
Self-protective	Self-sacrificing
Controls others	Pleases others
Acts to guard feelings	Acts contrary to feelings
Denies	Explains
Compulsively independent	Compulsively dependent

From Eli Coleman and Philip Colgan, "Chemical Dependency and Intimacy Dysfunction" in *Journal of Chemical Dependency*, Vol. 1, No. 1, 1987.

addicts need partners who enable them to continue to use drugs/alcohol and not suffer the full impact of their addiction. Their partners need alcoholics/addicts to avoid their own fears of abandonment and depression. Both of them fear feelings of loneliness, isolation, anxiety, and depression.

The fear of abandonment and rejection is so strong for ACAs that they choose not to develop an individual sense of self. This neglect of one's self while preoccupied or obsessed with changing the partner is codependency. The codependent dances these couples perform have some common features: (1) shame-based styles of communicating and interacting; (2) a denial by at least one partner of dysfunctional and/or codependent behavior; (3) a relationship of bargaining, not an intimate partnership; and (4) a shame-based litany of the past. Each partner holds on to unresolved conflicts and continues to use them to shame the other.

Recovery of Adult Children of Alcoholics

An ACA's prognosis for treatment is directly related to the severity of the parental alcoholism and the levels of abuse, violation, and trauma experienced while growing up in the alcoholic/addict family system. The onset of the alcoholism is also a factor in the ACA's recovery. The earlier the alcoholism in the family, and the younger the child when exposed to direct or indirect consequences of the parents' alcoholism, the more extensive the damage, and therefore the deeper the wounds. Impact at early ages can have dramatic developmental consequences (Brown 1988).

The following poem describes a common problem of adults who grew up in imbalanced family systems. In these families, boundaries are inadequately defined, creating boundary inadequacy in adulthood.

Healing My Child
Michael Bales (1990)

I hurt, the love I feel
for my mother betrays me.
The mistaken identity of being made a husband
when I was only a child, distorts
my experience of motherhood.

I hurt, the love I feel
for my father betrays me.
The mistaken identity of being made a rival
when I was only a child, distorts
my experience of fatherhood.

I hurt, the love I feel
for my lover betrays me.
The mistaken identity of being made a man
when I was only a child, distorts
my experience of manhood.

I hurt, the love I feel
for my soulmate betrays me.
The mistaken identity of being made a god
when I was only a child, distorts
my experience of adulthood.

I hurt, the love I feel
for myself betrays me.
The mistaken identity of being made mature
when I was only a child, distorts my experience of
childhood.

Inherited Family Belief Systems

A major recovery issue at the heart of all ACAs' problems is their core belief system. The "process of recovery involves challenging the deepest core beliefs about others and the self that were constructed to preserve core attachments" (Brown 1988). As discussed earlier in this chapter, these core beliefs serve to deny the ACAs feelings and maintain the illusion of their parents' normalcy. ACAs avoid exploring these holes in their belief systems for fear that their swiss cheese system might fall apart. When ACAs can acknowledge how the belief systems acquired from their parents have prevented them from attaining what they want, recovery can begin.

In *Struggle for Intimacy,* Janet Geringer Woititz (1985) devotes an entire chapter to some of the misconceptions, or inappropriate beliefs, that ACAs have when it comes to establishing intimate relationships. Table 6.3 lists these misconceptions.

Overview of ACA Recovery

Once ACAs are aware that their belief systems are not serving them, and preventing, blocking, or sabotaging the development of effective relationships, the next step is to develop a more reality-based belief system.

The first step in developing this reality-based belief system is to recognize the dysfunction and trauma of the past and unlock the feelings denied by this dysfunctional belief system.

A trusting therapeutic alliance with a counselor/therapist allows ACAs to feel the loss, grief, and trauma of the past. This difficult process involves (1) giving up the old defense mechanisms and dysfunctional beliefs; (2) feeling; (3) and choosing to honor and integrate those feelings in a new more functional belief system.

Eventually ACAs loosen their defensive controls and develop the ability to respond to different situations and circumstances with flexibility. ACAs can now establish effective boundaries in relationships, stop engaging in dysfunctional behavior and relationships, and establish a core belief system that allows for effective choicemaking and change.

Powerlessness in the Alcoholic Family System

Just as alcoholics/addicts must first admit they were powerless over drugs/alcohol, so must ACAs admit that as children they were powerless to change the alcoholic family system. They were innocent children whose feelings were ignored while living in unhealthy imbalanced situations. Recognizing that as children they were not responsible for their parents' disease of alcoholism frees ACAs to honor their own feelings.

TABLE 6.3
ACA's Dysfunctional Belief versus Reality

Dysfunctional Belief	Reality
If I am involved with you, I will lose me.	Healthy relationships enhance the self and do not absorb it.
If you really knew me, you wouldn't care about me.	You probably aren't as good an actor or actress as you think you are. Your beloved probably already knows you and cares about you anyway.
If you find out that I am not perfect, you will abandon me.	Nobody is perfect, and perfection does not exist.
We are as one.	You are you, and I am me, and then there is us.
Being vulnerable always has negative results.	Being vulnerable sometimes has negative results and sometimes has positive results, but it is the only route to intimacy.
We will never argue or criticize each other.	Couples argue from time to time and are critical of each other's behavior.
Anything that goes wrong is my fault. I am a terrible person.	Some things that go wrong are your fault. Some things are not. Terrible things happen, but you are not terrible.
To be lovable, I must be happy all the time.	Sometimes people are happy and sometimes they are not.
We will trust each other totally, automatically, and all at once.	Trust builds slowly.
We will do everything together, we will be as one.	Couples spend time together, alone, and with friends.
You will instinctively anticipate my every need, wish, and desire.	If needs, desires, and wishes are not clearly communicated, it is unlikely they will be fulfilled.
If I am not in complete control at all times, there will be anarchy.	One is in charge of one's life and takes control of situations as needed, by conscious decision and agreement. There are also times to share control, and times to give up control.
If we really love each other, we will stay together forever.	People stay together and people separate for many reasons. You can love someone and still terminate a relationship.
My partner will never take me for granted and always be supportive and noncritical.	Things do not always go smoothly, but you always have a right to your feelings.

Source: Janet Geringer Woititz, *Struggle for Intimacy.* Copyright © 1985 Health Communications, Inc., Deerfield, Florida.

Feeling Awareness

For ACAs who have spent a major portion of their lives denying feelings, the most difficult task of recovery is recognizing and integrating feelings in making decisions, resolving conflicts, and in developing interpersonal relationships.

Jerry, a patient of mine who is a recovering alcoholic and an ACA, quizzically and candidly commented, "Feelings, I am not quite sure what you mean when you ask 'What do I feel?' I don't know what you mean or want from me. When you ask me if I feel sad, or I sound angry, I don't recognize that I am experiencing those feelings until you mention it."

Human emotions are an essential part of the human equation.

Many ACAs have similar reactions. Unaware of what they feel, they are equally inexperienced in recognizing what others feel. This makes it difficult to effectively communicate with others—especially family members—and to establish sensitive, caring, and intimate relationships.

Identifying Feelings for ACAs

Jael Greenleaf, an ACA counselor in Los Angeles, describes ACAs as having an emotional learning disability. ACAs have learned not to trust their feelings; thus they make decisions based on what they think is appropriate, without integrating what they feel. Feelings are what make us, or define us as being human. The famous television series "Star Trek" gave us Mr. Spock, the cognitive logical unemotional alien, and in the later version of the series, DATA, a robot with extensive computer capabilities. DATA was often fascinated and marveled at human feelings and emotions and tried to understand them. Mr. Spock does not understand human emotions that may override the logic of a decision. The captain of the *Enterprise* reminds Spock and DATA that human emotions are essential and part of the human equation in approaching life.

By being sensitive to what we feel, we can begin to understand our feelings (affective self) and integrate them with what we know (cognitive self). When our affective self is congruent with our cognitive self, the application (whatever action we take) is often more successful. Decisions become easier to make when feelings are balanced with the cognitive side, and there is an interplay of these two sides of our self. Our decisions become more fulfilling, our goals more attainable, and our relationships more effective, when we integrate our feelings. The struggle for the ACA begins with identifying, understanding, and integrating feelings.

A good technique to help ACAs access their feelings is journaling, or writing a feeling diary. Often a counselor asks the ACA to buy a special notebook and keep it nearby—in the car, at work, and at home. Whenever the ACA is aware of an emotional reaction, thought, or feeling, he or she writes about it in the journal. By writing rather than thinking, ACAs soon find that they are accessing feelings that they may not have been aware of previously.

Another method of feeling awareness involves ACAs verbalizing and communicating what they feel directly to others. One method would be using the statement: "I feel ______________, when I ____________." For example:

> "I feel upset when I notice you haven't taken the garbage out, after you said you would."
>
> "I feel confused, and both sad and angry, when I didn't get a present for Valentine's Day."
>
> "Right now, I am not feeling close and caring toward you. I do not want to have sex. I am still feeling hurt by the fight we had earlier today. I would prefer talking about it tomorrow when our emotions are not running so deep."

Therapists help ACAs identify and explore a wide variety of feelings (shame, rejection, abandonment, loss, loneliness, isolation, and grief) that were experienced growing up in an alcoholic family system. ACA therapists use various treatment methods to access feelings including guided imagery, gestalt exercises, art therapy, role plays, workbooks, and books and articles on ACA issues (bibliotherapy).

ACA Grief Work

As previously described, ACAs experienced loss, violation, and trauma growing up in imbalanced alcoholic family systems. Frequently there was not an opportunity to mourn the loss. Mourning is a process of allowing feelings of loss to come to the surface, be felt, and grieved.

The analogy would be the improper healing of a cut. In the ACA's case, an emotionally damaging cut or violation of self has occurred. The cut has healed over but was not cleaned out first; the dirt (leftover unresolved issues and feelings) was not removed. The result is a numbing pain that was tolerated and denied for years and thought to be quite normal. Grief work involves going back and cleaning out this wound by gently and sensitively removing the dirt. By avoiding the feelings and pain accompanying proper healing of this infected wound, individuals are unable to function to a fuller potential. Once their wounds are cleaned, true healing allows ACAs to make more effective choices.

Grief work requires the help of a professional therapist trained and experienced in ACA recovery. The counselor/therapist must be sensitive to the patient's ego-strength, general level of functioning, underlying psychiatric issues, and support system. Attempting to do ACA grief work without an experienced professional may cause unnecessary emotional harm by going too deep, too quickly into traumatic issues of the past. A professional trained and experienced in ACA recovery recognizes the pace and depth of the work to be done and shows appropriate judgment in helping patients through this work.

Choice Making

Changing old dysfunctional patterns is possible only if individuals feel they have choices. Discouraging voices of doom and gloom need to be quieted for recovery efforts to be implemented. Self-pity, victim roles, and the poor-me syndrome prevent ACAs from even entertaining a choice to change. The old familial belief system whispers in the ACA's ear: "Change is not possible. So why even try? You'll just waste time and energy and fail anyway, just as you always have in the past."

Changes involve integration and congruency with feelings, and choosing not to respond in dysfunctional codependent ways. There is the acknowledgment that change is difficult, takes time, may involve pain, and requires support. Sometimes small changes and positive choices can establish the foundation for more significant growth-related choices later. As the Rolling Stones' lyric goes, "You can't always get what you want, but if you try sometime, you may get what you need."

Choosing Effective Interpersonal Relationships

A variety of therapeutic issues must be explored before the ACA can improve interpersonal relationships. Some of the cognitive and affective therapeutic themes are

- family of origin issues (beliefs, roles, rules, and thinking about relationships)
- sense of self, or self-concept and interpersonal interaction, choosing relationships, and maintaining dysfunctional imbalanced relationships
- boundary setting and decision making in interpersonal situations
- self-sabotaging or destructive behavior, poor impulse control, poor anger and frustration tolerance, and an inability to set and maintain healthy long-range goals.

Second Order Change

Second order change is a cognitive-behavioral technique to change the way one traditionally responds to situations and interpersonal interactions. Many interactions are often mechanical, automatic, even rhetorical in nature. These are first order interactions. Individuals can choose to respond differently to the first order cues in communication and interaction. This new response or new order of interaction is second order change. The following examples illustrate a very common first order interaction and one possible second order change. The meta message, or the underlying true feeling message, is in parentheses.

First Order—Phone Call from Mom

Mom: Why haven't you called? (Shame on you for not caring about your mom. You probably don't like me. I know I'm just a bother now that I am old.)

Adult child: Well Mom, I have been very busy with my new job and everything. (Please give me a break, Mom. I'm not in the mood for shame right now. I feel overwhelmed considering the new job, and other adjustments I am going through. I don't need this right now.)

Mom: Well, I guess your job is more important than your mother. (Double shame on you for not making your mother number one in your life.)

Adult child: Mom, it's not that my job is more important than you. I just didn't get around to calling because I've been so busy at work. (Let me explain. Please, please, understand.)

Mom: You haven't asked me how my back is. (More shame. I don't care about your silly job. I want you to be more concerned with my ailments.)

Adult child: Now Mom, that isn't fair. You didn't even give me a chance to ask you how you were. (I'm beginning to get angry and lose patience with you. Here we go again. I can't even talk with you without getting angry. Self-shame.)

Mom: Now don't get so upset, dear. (Watch it. This is your powerful supermom, able to abandon and hurt you with the slightest provocation.)

Adult child. (Change in tone) How are you feeling mom? I have been worried about you. (I don't want to fight or be abandoned. I'll just give her what she wants. I'm feeling like a helpless child again.)

Mom: Well, you know those doctors want me to come in for some more tests. But I don't think they know what they are talking about. I just don't have any way to get into the hospital with my back hurting the way it does. (I am helpless. I want you to come home and be with me and take care of me. If you don't, I'll just punish you by suffering.)

Adult child: Mom, can't you get Aunt Joanie to take you in for the tests? (I am worried. I can't come. Maybe I can fix it for you by getting you some help.)

Mom: Oh dear, don't worry about me, I'll be all right. (Worry about me. Shame on you for not coming right away. You ungrateful daughter, I'll just suffer alone.)

This dialogue need not be carried out in this first order manner. The anger, resentments, and shame do not have to be responded to in this traditional codependent dance. The following second order change occurs after the adult child has done some therapeutic work on the underlying issue of her mom not wanting to let go of her daughter, for fear of having to work on her (mom's) own issues of loneliness and abandonment.

Second Order Change

Mom: Why haven't you called? (Shame on you for not caring about your mom.)

Adult child: Mom, boy I've been wondering about you. How are you doing? (I'm not going to respond to the shaming question. I'll change the focus to you and your reason for calling.)

Mom: Well, I'm surprised that you asked. Most of the time you're too busy with your job to even call me.

(I'll try some more shaming to see if I can get you angry, because I am angry that your job comes before your dear old mom.)

Adult child: Mom, it's unfortunate that I had to move out of town for this job promotion. I know it's hard on you. By the way, how is Aunt Joanie? (I had to take care of myself. I recognize that you feel abandoned and would prefer that I stay at home, but we all have to let go sometime. Why can't you understand like Aunt Joanie?)

Mom: She's fine. But you know my back has been killing me. The doctors want me to come to the hospital for some more tests, but I hurt too much, and I don't know how I can get there. (Poor me, won't you please come home and help me?)

Adult child: I know your back has been a problem for quite some time now. It would be nice to find out what the problem is. (I'd like to see you get in for the tests but I can't help you get to the hospital. If you want some results, you'll have to figure out transportation.)

Mom: So would I. But I need someone to help me, and Aunt Joanie doesn't drive. (Please, won't you come back home and help?)

Adult child: Well, there are other ways for you to get a ride to the hospital. I hope you can figure out a way. (I'm not coming, just for this. There are other solutions to the problem and you are capable of figuring it out.)

Mom: Well, I just don't know if I can do it myself. (Poor me. Shame on you for not helping your poor old mom.)

Adult child: Well mom, I'm sure you'll be able to figure it out. You were always pretty resourceful when we were growing up. I love you. I'll talk to you soon. (You must take care of this yourself. You were very capable raising three children practically on your own considering Dad's alcoholism. I'm not jumping in to help. I still love and admire you. I am ending this conversation and not giving you an opportunity to feel sorry for yourself.)

You can see the difference in the second order change. The ACA avoided the shame-based messages and did not get emotionally hooked by displaying anger, rage, or lack of emotional control. Instead, in the second order model the ACA focuses on the real issues, and stays balanced and in emotional control while maintaining appropriate boundaries.

Changing Interactions with Family

Robert Ackerman, a noted author, speaker, and counselor specializing in ACA work, tells a story that illustrates the difficulty in changing interactions with family: After working with Ackerman for a few months, one of his patients felt she had made enough progress to share her new therapeutic awareness with her family.

She was going home for Christmas (an emotional time for most families, especially alcoholic families), and wanted to talk to her parents about her new insights. Ackerman suggested that she think about what her goal was in sharing her insights. Essentially ignoring his advice, on returning home she told her parents all about her childhood pain resulting from growing up in an alcoholic family and described how this had affected her relationships with men. Initially, her parents were actively listening and seemed to understand. However, the next few days the family returned to the traditional dysfunctional arguments, escalated emotions, and shame-based communications of the past. The daughter had to spend the next few days at an old friend's home to survive the rest of the holiday.

At her next therapy appointment the patient expressed surprise that her parents could engage her in the old dysfunctional dances. She asked, "Why were they still able to push all of my buttons?" Dr. Ackerman, in the wisdom of his years of experience, matter-of-factly said: "They installed the buttons."

The same struggle goes on for most ACAs who interact with their families. Some of these families have members still actively using alcohol/drugs, or maintaining dysfunctional behavior. It might be necessary for ACAs to let their parents know how they feel about their continued use of alcohol/drugs. In some situations, with the help of their therapists patients have decided to send a letter to their parents who are still using drugs/alcohol. The goal of the letter is to assist ACAs in healing and accepting their parents' disease. It is a way for ACAs to get in touch with their feelings about their parents continued use of drugs/alcohol. Patients decide for themselves whether the letter is appropriate for the goal they have in mind, and whether they want to send the letter.

Case Study

Letter to Parents from a Recovering Alcoholic and ACA About the Parents' Alcoholism

Dear Mom and Dad,

It's hard to write a letter like this, so I guess I'll just get right to the point. I'm writing because I'm concerned that you both continue to drink a lot despite the fact that you have both been in ill health recently. And I'm sure that you, Dad, have been warned more than once by doctors that to continue to drink threatens your health.

I've wanted to talk to you both about your drinking for years, but so far I have never been able to break the silence and tell you how truly worried I am about it. Believe me, the whole family is concerned, and I have discussed your continued drinking with my brothers and sisters.

Their attitude is basically that "it's their problem, and it's up to them to do something about it." This is certainly true; only you can make a decision to stop drinking. But I feel very strongly that I must tell you both, with love and compassion, how concerned I am, and how much it hurts me to see you continue to damage yourselves through drinking.

I am sure that in your hearts you know that you have a problem, for I have seen you both struggle with it; seen your efforts to control what and when you drink; seen your efforts to cut back. I know I rejoiced during that period when you sobered up entirely for a few months, and you found renewed health and happiness together.

I am also sure you are both aware that the stakes are high; that you are endangering your health as you mix alcohol and various prescription medication, and that drinking can only worsen your struggles with heart disease, diabetes, and the effects of aging.

You know what you have to do. It's so simple, and yet I know from experience how hard it can be. You both so desperately need to stop drinking now, throw out all the booze in the house (even the supply reserved for guests), and get some help staying sober, for you have proven by slipping back into drinking that you cannot do it by yourselves.

I suspect getting help will be the hardest part; it certainly was for me. But it's really the most necessary part of getting better and infinitely better than struggling alone.

Getting help could mean any of the following: Telling Dr. Green that you know you have a problem with alcohol and are tired of struggling with it; that you want to get some counseling or get into a treatment program. Calling AA and attending a meeting together; the nearest AA meeting is right down the street on Maple Rd. Calling the local drug/alcohol helpline and getting a referral to a counselor, social worker, or therapist experienced in working with alcoholics who want to recover.

This letter is not meant to blame or shame or accuse you; it is merely a plea for you to help yourselves for your own sakes, and for the sake of our family. It is an effort to tell the truth about the problem that our whole family has struggled with for so many years.

The truth hurts sometimes. The truth is that all of us have begun to insulate ourselves from your drinking, to control the time and length of our visits, to arrange sober holidays in our own homes, as my sister did this Christmas. We have all shied away from confronting you because it is so painful to see you both caught in this awful disease.

I hope that this letter has not made you angry or resentful. If it has, so be it; but I want you to know that I love you both, and that I want to help you, if there is any way in the world that I can. If you want to talk about this letter, please call me; if not, if it makes you too upset or uncomfortable, we need never discuss it.

Ultimately, there may be an element of selfishness in this letter; because, in the end, I want to be able to look into my heart and say "I tried to help. I told them the truth and encouraged them to get help and save their own lives." For me, it's an important step in dealing with my past and working on my own sobriety.

Please, for your own sake and the sake of us all, share this letter with each other, and talk about it openly together. I pray that you both will find the strength to quit drinking and get some help together.

Your loving son,

Many ACAs must ultimately let go and accept that their parents may never choose to stop using alcohol/drugs. Each ACA continues to struggle with personal recovery issues in an ongoing process of self-discovery, supported by others in recovery. At times it is a process of two steps forward, and one step backward, but the process and progress continues.

Group Psychotherapy

Group psychotherapy is the next step once ACAs have worked through some of the previously described core issues. Group psychotherapy is a dynamic process in which each group member gets feedback from other group members. Members share their perceptions, feelings, and insights into each other's behavior.

Irvin D. Yalom (1975) describes the following eleven curative factors that make group psychotherapy such an effective process:

Curative Factors

1. *Instilling hope:* ACA group members see firsthand the growth of other group members. Continued contact with other group members who have improved while doing their work in the group gives ACAs hope for their own recovery and confidence in the group process.
2. *Sharing universality:* ACAs realize that they are not alone and that others share common problems. Group therapy reveals that ACA characteristics are universal to those who grew up in alcoholic/addict family systems, as well as imbalanced family systems. ACAs no longer suffer in social or interpersonal isolation. There is the opportunity for affirmation by other group members, who understand them and identify with the issues they have in common.
3. *Imparting information:* Group therapy provides information, education, and training on ACA issues including family systems, alcoholism/addiction, codependency, and boundary setting in relationships. Both the therapist and other group members offer suggestions, advice, or direct guidance about life problems.
4. *Fostering altruism:* Altruism is the act of giving to others and caring about others' life situations. The group is a place for support, reassurance, encouragement, insight, and sharing, all of which help both the giver and the receiver to grow.
5. *Recapitulating the primary family group:* Recapitulation offers an opportunity for the group to act as a functional family with positive

corrective capabilities. Early familial conflicts can be acted out or recapitulated. With the help of the group, ACAs can resolve these conflicts in a functional manner, rather than the previously dysfunctional and rigid manner of the family of origin.

6. *Developing socializing techniques:* Socializing is an obvious curative factor of group therapy. ACAs can explore maladaptive social behavior through honest and caring feedback from group members. Alternative social choices and techniques can be developed with the feedback of the group. ACAs are particularly vulnerable to choosing dysfunctional relationships and maintaining codependent interactions in relationships. The group can alert ACAs who try to return to codependent ways of interaction and dysfunctional choice making.
7. *Imitating behavior:* By seeing the reactions and behaviors of others, ACAs have numerous new models of behavior.
8. *Sharing interpersonal learning:* The group is a social microcosm of the real world. ACAs tend to duplicate the way they approach the real interpersonal world in their therapy group. Insights into ACAs' interpersonal behavior and corrective emotional strategies can be explored in the safe environment of the group setting.
9. *Developing group cohesiveness:* The bonding that occurs in therapy groups results in a cohesiveness understanding that makes the group a safe place to go with stressful problems, interpersonal conflicts, difficult decisions, and other issues. The group develops a functional interpersonal cohesiveness allowing members to pull for and struggle with the difficult issues in their lives.
10. *Sharing catharsis:* Group is a place where ACAs feel safe in expressing emotional feelings not safely expressed in other settings. Fears, insecurities, destructive thoughts, suicidal ideation, rage, shame, and other emotions are safe to express in the group.
11. *Exploring existential factors:* The group helps its members explore meaning in their lives. Issues of attachment in relationships, congruency in work efforts, and spirituality are all safe for each group member to explore and develop. In other words, the functional therapy group explores the human condition.

Case Study
Interpersonal Relationships
Naomi

Naomi was a very attractive, young, and active director of marketing for a major retail clothing manufacturer. She grew up in an alcoholic family and compensated by being extremely successful in all endeavors. She described her mom's sense of self as being directly related to all of Naomi's accomplishments. Unfortunately, Naomi approached interpersonal relationships outside of the family in the same manner and tended to attract friends who mirrored her accomplishments back to her. In group therapy, Naomi began to use this same interpersonal dynamic of trying to control others so they reflected a positive mirror image of her success back to her. Initially, she was worried that the group would ask her to leave when they began to see her self-centeredness. Instead the group was able to make her aware of her imbalanced need for affirmation. The group gave her permission to explore her issues and be herself, while not having to look good all the time. In fact, they enjoyed the Naomi who wasn't always on and saw this aspect of her personality as more relaxed, fun loving, vulnerable, available, present, and worth getting to know.

In summary, group therapy is a dynamic process that has a tremendous potential for ACA recovery, especially after ACAs have spent time exploring their issues in individual counseling.

Additional Help for ACAs

Educational presentations, seminars, classes, workshops, and conferences are available emphasizing both educational and therapeutic work for adult children of alcoholics. Therapists and counselors are being educated and trained to work more effectively with adult children. Individual and group counseling is available conducted by counselors who specialize in codependency and issues related to growing up in an alcoholic and/or imbalanced family system. The therapeutic work for ACAs requires supportive relationships that help individuals establish appropriate boundaries and healthy relationships. This goal requires the support of friends and the utilization of self-help support groups such as Al-Anon, Adult Children of Alcoholics, and Codependency Anonymous.

The emerging awareness of adult children of alcoholics has had widespread implications for the fields of drug and alcohol recovery. Similar education, self-help, and treatment has been expanded to other childhood traumas such as incest and physical, sexual, and emotional abuse.

Summary

Children who grew up in alcoholic families experienced the trauma of abuse and violation, inconsistent and imbalanced parenting, boundary inadequacy, shame, abandonment and rejection. As adults, these ACAs have poor self-concepts and difficulty in establishing effective and intimate interpersonal relationships.

According to the National Association for Children of Alcoholics (NACOA), an estimated 28 million Americans have at least one alcoholic parent. Some of the characteristics of adult-children of alcoholics are a fear of losing control or experiencing feelings; thinking in black or white terms; difficulty with intimacy and with asking for what is wanted or needed; difficulty relaxing; feelings of guilt, abandonment, and/or depression; compulsive behaviors; and guessing at what is normal.

The characteristics most often identified with by ACAs is guessing at what is normal. The ACA learns to shut down feelings to survive growing up in the alcoholic home. Therefore, ACA symptoms are similar to post-traumatic stress disorder in which once buried traumas resurface later in life.

Four factors that produce damage in the lives of children of alcoholics are (1) role reversal—the child being the parent; (2) inconsistent and unpredictable parenting leading to emotional deprivation of the child; (3) parents emotionally unable to attend to the needs of the child; (4) and social isolation of the family.

ACAs define themselves based on others' opinions of them and therefore tend to develop codependent relationships.

Codependency is "continual investment of self-esteem in the ability to influence/control feelings and behaviors in self and others in the face of obvious adverse consequences." Another way of defining it is "like being a lifeguard on a crowded beach, knowing that you cannot swim, and not telling anyone for fear of a panic."

Partners in codependent dances have (1) shame-based styles of communication and interaction; (2) developed bargaining, not an intimate partnership; (3) denial by at least one partner of dysfunction or codependent behavior; and (4) a shame-based litany of unresolved conflicts that each partner holds on to and continues to use to shame each other. The escalated conflicts prevent the couple from establishing a safe, feeling, and intimate relationship, where they can resolve conflicts. As a result, the relationship becomes a bargain instead of intimate.

The prognosis for ACA recovery is directly related to the severity of the parental alcoholism and the levels of abuse, violation, and trauma experienced while growing up in the alcoholic/addict family system.

The first step, much like the first step of alcohol/drug recovery, is to admit powerlessness in trying to control others, and the powerlessness felt as innocent children growing up in alcoholic family systems.

The second step, counseling, usually involves helping ACAs to identify what they feel and to honor those feelings. The therapeutic work entails working through issues of unresolved grief and responding in a growth-producing way to present-day family and interpersonal interactions.

The third step, group counseling, has proven to be a dynamic and effective modality. In a caring and supportive therapeutic setting, the group can provide new insight, direction, and encouragement for further growth.

References

Ackerman, Robert J. *Children of Alcoholics: A Guidebook for Educators, Therapists, and Parents.* Holmes Beach, Fla.: Learning Public, 1978.

Black, Claudia. *It Will Never Happen to Me.* Denver, Colo.: M.A.C. Publications, 1982.

Bosma, W. "Children of Alcoholics: A Hidden Tragedy." *Maryland State Medical Journal* 21 (1972): 34–36.

Brown, Stephanie. *Treating Adult Children of Alcoholics, A Developmental Perspective.* N.Y.: John Wiley, 1988.

Cermak, Timmen. "Children of Alcoholics and the Case for a New Diagnostic Category of Co-dependency. *Alcohol, Health and Research World* 8 (1984): 38–42.

Clinebell, Howard J., Jr. *Understanding and Counseling the Alcoholic through Religion and Psychology.* Nashville, Tenn.: Abingdon Press, 1985.

Coleman, Eli and Philip Colgan. "Chemical Dependency and Intimacy Dysfunction." *Journal of Chemical Dependency Treatment* no. 1 (1987): 75–91.

Cork, M. *The Forgotten Children.* Toronto: Addiction Research Foundation, 1969.

Lawson, G., James S. Peterson, and Ann Lawson. *Alcoholism and the Family: A Guide to Treatment and Prevention.* Rockville, Md.: Aspen Publications, 1983.

Newell, "Alcoholism and the Father Image." *Quarterly Journal of Studies on Alcoholism* 11 (1950): 92–95.

Woititz, Janet Geringer. *Struggle for Intimacy.* Pompano Beach, Fla.: Health Communications, 1985.

Yalom, Irvin D. *The Theory and Practice of Group Psychotherapy.* N.Y.: Basic Books, 1975.

CHAPTER

7

Prevention of Drug/ Alcohol Problems

Drug/alcohol prevention has often been a misunderstood and neglected aspect in addressing the American drug problem. This chapter provides a foundation so that readers can apply prevention efforts at home, in school systems, and in the community. Prevention efforts have shifted from promoting scare tactics to emphasizing the worth of people and the affective skills needed to avoid a destructive pattern of drug/alcohol dependence. Specific prevention skills include goal setting, decision making, and conflict resolution. The goals of the prevention curricula described in this chapter are to develop active, involved, empowered, and capable young people. The last section of the chapter lists alternative activities as a prevention strategy and includes a worksheet to help readers further identify their own alternative activities.

Chapter Goals

1. Identify the problems associated with drug/alcohol use by young people.
2. Describe the ineffectiveness of early prevention approaches, including scare tactics, converting programs, and drug specific information.
3. Define primary prevention and the three basic themes of primary prevention that are outcomes of the Delphi II Prevention Planning Conferences.
4. List some of the skills emphasized in the 1980s prevention programs.
5. Define and describe aspects of an effective prevention approach.
6. Describe the role of credibility in prevention programs and list issues that hurt credibility.
7. Define primary, secondary, and tertiary prevention.
8. List the competencies and coping skills emphasized in school-based prevention programs.
9. Describe the basic tenets of teaching problem solving, goal setting, developing capabilities, decision making, and empowerment.
10. Identify the special issues in developing prevention programs for people of color.
11. Identify the specific problems and needs in prevention efforts with elders.
12. Describe the function and role of alternative activities in prevention.
13. Describe the characteristics of alternative activities that make them more successful as prevention tools.
14. Identify the level of experience, corresponding motive, and possible alternatives to drugs/alcohol use.
15. Outline the domain of prevention efforts relating to families.

Early Prevention Approaches

For years society has searched for easy solutions to prevent drug dependence and addiction. Initially, frightening movies and horror stories of drug abuse failed to make young people too scared to use drugs. Early prevention efforts to deter potential drug use focused primarily on supplying:

- information on the dangers of specific drugs
- warnings of physical, social, and psychological harm
- punishments for sale, use, and possession

As described in the introduction of this textbook, these scare tactics proved to be an ineffective prevention strategy. Much of the information was invalid, exaggerated, and overgeneralized, causing young people to question the credibility of the program.

Similar programs were developed and labeled by drug educator Walter M. Mathews (1975) as **converting programs.** These programs attempted to dissuade young people from using drugs by:

1. Directing: Teacher tells students what they must believe, value, and do.
2. Preaching: Similar to directing, with an added appeal to the students' duty to a vague external authority.
3. Convincing: Teachers appealed to logic where lecturing was the method used.
4. Scaring: Teachers emphasized the dangers of drug use.

Additional converting approaches emphasized admonishment, indoctrination, persuasion, distortion, and fear.

Adolescence is a time of questioning and self-exploration. The information provided in these approaches was not geared to the sensitivity of young people; it insulted their individuality and ability to make decisions. Adults in authority told them what to do rather than talking with them. These propaganda approaches did not emphasize communication and open discussion.

The failure of these approaches led to a new prevention strategy of providing factual information about drugs, or **drug specific approaches.** These approaches emphasized the drug and its pharmacological properties and assumed young people would make responsible decisions about drug use if they knew the negative effects. Inadvertently, these drug specific approaches heightened curiosity and caused the opposite attitude of alleviating fears of drugs. Many students acquired the knowledge to better attain desired levels of intoxication.

As a result of the failure of scare tactics and drug specific approaches, the government's Special Action Office on Drug Abuse Prevention (SAODAP) declared a six-month moratorium in 1973 on all prevention materials development, prevention program implementation, and prevention activities. The moratorium allowed further review of research and determined that because scare tactics and drug specific information did not significantly deter drug use, they were ineffective. In 1974, Robert DuPont, then the director of the National Institute on Drug Abuse (NIDA), surveyed drug education programs and concluded that the educators and students believed that the majority of school-based drug education programs were ineffective and should be abolished. In a review of research on school-based drug education programs, Michael Goodstadt (1975) concluded that "There is an almost total lack of evidence indicating beneficial effects of drug education, very few educational programs have been evaluated and almost none have shown any significant improvement in anything other than levels of knowledge; attitudes and drug use have generally remained the same."

In 1974, the prevention branch of the National Institute of Drug Abuse initiated a nationwide, fourteen-month planning process to develop a national strategy for primary prevention. This planning process involved over 400 prevention specialists in a series of nine planning conferences. In 1975, the institute published the resulting recommendations in *Toward a National Strategy for Primary Drug Abuse Prevention.* The report defined primary drug abuse prevention as "A constructive process designed to promote personal and social growth of the individual to full human potential and thereby inhibit or reduce physical, mental, emotional, or social impairment which results in or from the abuse of chemical substances."

The report established three basic themes for primary prevention: (1) Primary prevention must be understood as the development and reinforcement of positive behaviors. (2) Primary prevention programs must be responsive in both design and operation to the needs of those they are intended to serve or support. (3) Primary prevention should, wherever possible, employ collaborative efforts to utilize the already available capacities and resources of existing human service institutions.

The result of SAODAP's moratorium and prevention planning meetings was a major shift in focus from drugs to an emphasis on the young people, and from pharmacological effects to an emphasis on developing healthy children.

In 1977, NIDA and other agencies developed an interagency report entitled *Recommendations for Future Federal Activities in Drug Abuse Prevention.* The three major goals for prevention activities outlined in that report were

1. Reducing the percentage of frequent use of the three gateway drugs (tobacco, alcohol, and marijuana) by 15 percent among eight to twenty year olds.
2. Reducing the destructive behavior associated with alcohol and other drug abuse by 20 percent among fourteen to twenty year olds, as evidenced by a reduction in overdose deaths, emergency room visits, drug arrests, and other drug/alcohol related incidents.
3. Retraining attitudes concerning the use of psychoactive substances, especially the gateway drugs, by maintaining current levels of awareness regarding the addictive nature of heroin and alcohol and raising awareness of the addictive nature of tobacco by 50 percent.

In the 1980s, the new preventive strategy shifted from drugs to people, emphasizing

- educational information
- coping skills
- personal competence
- decision making
- refusal skills
- alternative activities

The goal of these programs was to develop capable young people able to make responsible decisions about drugs/alcohol. The focus changed to understanding the impact of drugs on individuals rather than the pharmacological properties of drugs/alcohol. The affective aspect focused on the individual's needs, feelings, and emotions about drugs/alcohol.

These new prevention programs develop the following skills:

- clarifying personal values and ethics
- improving self-concept

- learning effective decision making
- understanding and listening to each other's viewpoints
- communicating about drugs/alcohol with peers, parents, and others
- being involved in social and interpersonal activities
- dealing effectively with feelings of anger, depression, and anxiety
- having the ability to relax, play, and enjoy daily activities
- developing and exploring ways to alter one's sense of consciousness through alternative activities

Scope of Prevention

Agencies originally focused on prevention in secondary schools for adolescents twelve to seventeen years of age. It became apparent quickly that in many cases it was already too late to provide preventive education to adolescents. This group required more intervention, skill building, and treatment-related approaches.

As a result, drug and alcohol curricula and primary prevention activities shifted to kindergarten through the sixth grade. Agencies also developed secondary and tertiary prevention approaches for grades seven to twelve. They defined prevention in three basic categories:

Primary prevention assumes that the individual has never tried drugs or alcohol and enforces a no-use norm by building positive self-esteem, developing good coping and refusal skills, and providing information on drugs and alcohol.

Secondary prevention assumes that the individual is in the early stages of use but does not regularly use drugs. Secondary prevention/intervention strategies try to stop drug use by providing drug information, developing decision-making and refusal skills, improving family communication, and may also include individual counseling.

Tertiary prevention assumes that the individual is regularly using drugs but has not become a habitual user. Tertiary prevention/intervention includes counseling, drug education, and family therapy. There is a very fine line between the tertiary level of prevention and intervention and treatment services.

Developing Effective Prevention Approaches

Effective prevention involves imparting information through communication. Any prevention effort that provides only one aspect (either information without communication, or communication without information) is usually ineffective.

Effective prevention = Information + communication

The information must be accurate and be presented in an unbiased fashion by distinguishing between opinion and fact and identifying sources. The prevention educator must be

- a good listener and a person who understands
- credible
- respectful
- interesting
- flexible yet structured
- a sensitive and powerful role model

The communication process must be functional and effective in establishing a climate of trust and openness, yet being appropriate to the audience.

Establish Credibility

Credibility is a basic premise for the effectiveness of any drug prevention program. "The perceived source of the information must be seen as both credible or expert and trustworthy by those to whom the information is given" (Nowlis 1975).

Credibility is sacrificed when we separate drugs from alcohol. Alcohol is a drug. Setting up a double standard by excluding alcoholism from our war on drugs hurts credibility with young people. The same holds true when we deemphasize adults' use of drugs and alcohol and develop programs that focus only on children without including the parents.

Credibility is also impaired when our messages are not consistent with the values, attitudes, styles of life, patterns of drug/alcohol use, attitudes toward authority, and overall self-esteem of the target group. There must be sensitivity to cultural differences, community values, religious, and multicultural biases.

Drug/alcohol prevention staff should be able to facilitate the attainment of the goals and objectives of the program; most important, they must believe and live the program. The staff should be knowledgeable, have expertise in the field, and be composed of individuals easily respected and assimilated by the community.

Address Community Needs

Drug/alcohol prevention should also address itself to the needs of the community and interface with community leaders, agencies, and the people. Edward M. Brecher (1972) states

> Stop viewing the drug problem as primarily a national problem to be solved on a national scale. In fact, as workers in the drug scene confirm, the drug problem is a collection of local problems. The predominant drugs differ from place to place and from time to time. Effective solutions to problems also vary; a plan that works now for New York City may not be applicable to upstate New York and vice versa. With respect to education, . . . the need for local wisdom and local control is particularly pressing. Warning children against drugs readily available to them is a risky business at best, requiring careful, truthful, unsensational approaches.

Include Youth

A prevention program must take into account the consumer of that program. To develop prevention programs in a vacuum, or from a strictly theoretical base, does not take into account the most important variable, the needs of youth.

Use a Long-Term Approach

Prevention is a long-term strategy. Longitudinal studies over five to ten years are necessary to really determine the effects of prevention. Unfortunately, most prevention programs have short-term funding that limits many prevention evaluation projects. Currently, we focus on the short-range perspective of drug enforcement and interdiction without the balance of a comprehensive prevention strategy to deal with the demand side of drugs/alcohol with youth. Our true hope is the prevention and family approaches with the three to ten year olds. Our hope is with the next generation who may break this cycle of problems with dependence and addiction to drugs/alcohol.

In summary, an effective drug/alcohol prevention strategy should

Emphasize cognitive and affective skills that help young people accept responsibility and motivate them to make wise decisions about drugs and alcohol.

Focus on people, not pharmacology, emphasizing educational information, coping skills, personal competence, decision making, refusal skills, and alternative activities.

Develop prevention programs that provide information plus communication, establish credibility, and meet community needs.

Take into account the needs of youth and develop prevention approaches cooperatively with young people.

Develop primary efforts (those who have never used drugs/alcohol); secondary efforts (those in early stages of drug/alcohol use), and tertiary prevention efforts (those in regular stages of drug/alcohol use).

Develop longitudinal commitment to long-term prevention efforts.

School-Based Prevention Programs

The Jean Rhodes and Leonard Jason model emphasizes the development of attachments, competence, and coping skills as preventing risk for substance abuse. The more stress the child experienced, without appropriate and strong bonding to parents, attachment to drug-free role models, access to models with a strong sense of self, plus poor coping skills and resources, the higher the risk of substance abuse.

Based on Albee's social stress model, Rhodes and Jason illustrate two potential tracts or pathways that drug use may take.

Abuse Tract

If attachments, coping skills, and resources are not available early, initiation to drug/alcohol use can allay stress during early childhood. If functional coping mechanisms, attachments, and resources are still not available during adolescence, drug/alcohol use may proceed to heavy use. When this same pattern continues into adulthood, drug/alcohol abuse occurs.

Coping Tract

Low stress combined with good attachments, coping skills, and resources lead to abstinence during childhood, abstinence or limited experimentation during adolescence, with reduced risk of problems with drugs/alcohol in adulthood.

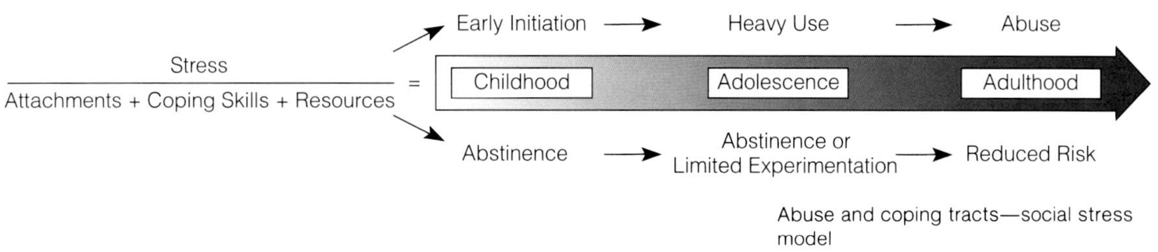

Abuse and coping tracts—social stress model

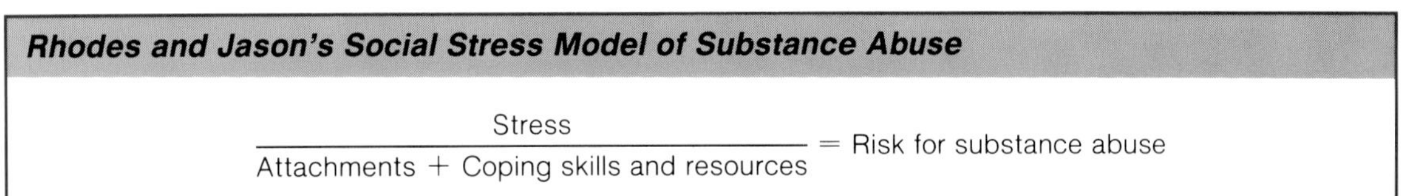

School-Based Prevention Curricula

In 1983, "Drug Abuse Prevention Research," a U.S. Department of Health and Human Services monograph, outlined four dimensions of prevention:

1. Course content centers on mental health, drug information, human development, nutrition, ethics, and chemical safety. These courses usually fit into regular social studies, language arts, science, and other subject area curricula.
2. Courses values clarification, problem-solving and decision-making skills, communication skills such as reflection and confrontation, alternative means for meeting needs, group process skills, role playing and dramatization.
3. Courses include competencies in human development, interpersonal relationships, personal autonomy, self-esteem, identity, decision-making skills, personal accountability, and accurate attributions of causality.
4. Courses also include general knowledge, conceptual frameworks, implicit assumptions and perspectives that define and describe the way each individual perceives the meaning of self, the nature of the world external to self, and interrelatedness of things.

The following school-based prevention programs reveal typical competencies and coping skills emphasized in such programs. Prevention programs are not limited to drug/alcohol prevention; many health issues are included in school-based prevention programs.

Here's Looking at You—Kindergarten through Senior High School

One of the most widely used school-based curriculums, *Here's Looking at You* was originally published in 1975. With significant revisions in 1978, 1982, and 1985, it is one of the most highly tested and developmentally sound curricula in the prevention field.

Program goals for students include developing

- self-concepts to realize they are unique and special persons who are continually growing and changing and who are capable of directing their growth
- decision-making skills for making responsible choices
- coping skills so they can cope responsibly with stressful situations

CLASP (Counseling Leadership Against Smoking Pressure) Project

One of the major efforts of prevention has been the reduction and elimination of cigarette smoking by young people. A variety of successful programs have been developed; one of the most successful is CLASP. The key element of this project is the utilization of peers as leaders. Peer leaders promote and develop group strategies for coping with peer pressure.

Other antismoking program methods focus on dealing with social pressure, the use of personalized role models and peer opinion leaders, and group commitment to nonsmoking. All of these programs are implemented by the seventh grade.

Cognitive-Behavioral Skill Training

Schinke and Gilchirst (1984), who have done extensive research in the area of pregnancy prevention, developed a cognitive-behavioral model that systematically teaches skills necessary to enjoy positive lives and to avoid unnecessary risks. Their junior and senior high school model emphasizes

- social coping skills necessary to handle current problems
- anticipating and preventing future problems and conflicts
- skills in mental health awareness
- issues of health, social, economic, and physical well-being
- strategies to enhance skills such as decision making, problem solving, and interpersonal communication in a variety of social situations

Cognitive Interpersonal Skills Training

Spivak and Shure (1982) developed a program similar to Schinke and Gilchirst's for kindergarten to first grade. The method utilizes games designed to increase cognitive skills, followed by training in alternative responses to interpersonal problem solving. The concepts taught in this model are

- alternative solutions to problems
- developing sensitivity to interpersonal problems
- understanding means-ends relationships

Life Skills Training

The methods used in the *Life Skills Program* are instruction, modeling, rehearsal, and role playing. Botvins's (1985) program has five major skill areas:

- enhancing self-esteem by developing goal-setting skills, behavioral change techniques, and increasing positive self-statements
- resisting persuasive appeals by first identifying persuasive appeals and formulating counter arguments
- coping with anxiety by relaxation training and mental rehearsal
- developing verbal and nonverbal communication skills
- developing a variety of other social skills, such as initiating social interactions, social communication skills, complimenting, and assertiveness skills

Law Related Education

Developed by the Center for Action Research, *Law Related Education* deals with the criminal-justice system. Its goal is to deter the antisocial behavior of young people by increasing their conceptual and practical understanding of the law and legal processes. The program's target populations are kindergarten through sixth grade, and sixth to twelfth grade. The goals of the program are

- to improve citizenship skills
- enhance ability to work with the legal system
- to promote favorable attitudes toward law enforcement and the justice system

Skills for Adolescence

As part of the program, students set goals for healthy living. The students also develop projects offering their service to others in the community. This program for grades six through eight focuses on:

- entering the teen years
- building self-confidence
- learning about emotions
- improving peer relationships
- strengthening family relationships
- developing critical thinking skills

Skills for Living

A high school program, *Skills for living* emphasizes self-discipline, responsibility, good judgment, and the ability to interact with others. The curriculum focuses on

- building self-concept
- dealing with emotions
- building constructive relationships
- preparing for family life
- building trust and commitment
- successful parenting
- understanding financial management
- goal setting and life planning
- developing a personal perspective

Prevention for At-Risk Students

The prevention programs are usually targeted for the general school population rather than the high-risk students who have already exhibited problem behaviors in and outside of school.

Clinicians and researchers have identified a variety of factors as predictive of later drug/alcohol abuse by young people. Antisocial behaviors and aggressiveness can predict, as early as the first grade, early drug/alcohol initiation and later substance abuse. Family imbalance, parental problems with alcohol/drugs, and parental dysfunction are also predictive of children having problems with drugs/alcohol.

At-risk youth require a more intensive and modified prevention program than students with no real social and interpersonal problems, who are supported by fairly functional family systems.

Often teachers and parents cooperatively identify at-risk youth appropriate for the program. Sometimes, key school personnel—teachers, coaches, dean of students, school nurse, counselor, psychologist—develop a team approach with parents in identifying students at-risk for drug/alcohol problems.

Interpersonal Problem Solving

One school-based program for at-risk youth is *Interpersonal Problem Solving*. The program's major focus is on effective problem solving and developing effective interpersonal skills. Program topics include

- how to deal with authority figures
- developing empathy
- standing up for one's rights
- skills to resist peer pressure
- skills to improve behavior in school
- how to get along better with family members

Lessons in Prevention Skills

A model lesson for goal setting would include lessons on (1) setting of goals; (2) ranking of priorities; (3) making decisions in relation to the goals; (4) persevering in face of difficult situations; and (5) maintaining effort (motivation) until goals are attained or modified.

Other prevention lessons involve developing capabilities. I had the good fortune fifteen years ago to work with Stephen Glenn at the National Drug Abuse Center in Washington, D.C. Today, Glenn lectures throughout the United States on the family prevention theme of developing capable people. His model for developing capable children includes:

1. identification with viable role models
2. identification with and responsibility for family process
3. faith in personal resources to solve problems
4. adequate development of intrapersonal skills (responsibility)
5. adequate development of interpersonal skills (communication)
6. well-developed situation skills (demand skills)
7. adequately developed judgment skills (application)

During my codependency workshops I define capability as the ability to

- resolve conflict
- make effective choices
- deal effectively with criticism
- persevere through times of crisis
- effectively communicate
- deal with competition (rivalry) and competence

- establish credibility and integrity in our approach to people and life in general
- express concern and empathy for others
- be creative

Prevention Skills in Decision Making

Many prevention lessons focus on effective decision making. After students improve their decision-making skills, they can identify what they feel about an issue. Then they can make a decision taking into account their feelings, rather than ignoring feelings that signal a potentially destructive decision. The decision-making model teaches individuals to

1. explore personal values, feelings, and goals related to a decision
2. gather information on the subject of the decision (e.g., factual written resources: consumer reports, opinions of others in the field or who have made similar decisions successfully, opinions of others who are valued and supportive)
3. review alternatives and consequences
4. evaluate resources, responsibilities, and support necessary
5. make a decision
6. reevaluate the decision and explore feelings about the decision
7. make necessary adjustments

Passive to Proactive

Another core theme in prevention programs is teaching young people to stop being passive and start being active or **proactive.** Drugs/alcohol use is a passive activity. Being proactive involves taking initiative, anticipating potential problems, and taking charge in dealing with issues. No matter what an event is (even negative events), students have the freedom to choose their responses to it. Taking action and responsibility leads to awareness, which in turn, allows them to choose to change. Their ability to adapt to situations and circumstances of life is an essential ingredient of survival and fulfillment.

Empowerment

Another term often used in prevention programs is *empowerment.* Many prevention programs emphasize the empowering of the individual. The basic goal of prevention is to empower individuals and prevent the destructive choice of drug/alcohol dependence and addiction. Empowerment is a feeling that is developed by being able to

- say "no" when that is what one feels and wants
- establish the core aspects of a sense of self
- be aware of what one feels, and integrate and communicate those feelings to others in establishing goals and making decisions
- establish and set boundaries, especially in interpersonal and intimate relationships
- establish integrity in relationships and a healthy, nondestructive, nonsabotaging approach to life

People of Color and Prevention Programs

There are a variety of factors that make people of color or minorities at risk for drug/alcohol problems. Minorities as a group have more unemployment, less prestigious occupations, and live in poverty and lower socioeconomic conditions. Thus, they experience more feelings of frustration, anger, resentment, and powerlessness. Inadequate education, housing, income, and other factors create additional stress and pressure that may lead to problems with drugs/alcohol. problems with drugs/alcohol.

For people of color prevention must go beyond the approaches previously described. One of the biggest problems facing people of color is the crack epidemic in the inner cities, and the increase in young cocaine and heroin addicts giving birth to cocaine and heroin-addicted babies.

Prevention for people of color and minorities must be community based. Residents must conceptualize the problem and jointly develop appropriate strategies.

Community-based prevention programs also must emphasize a systemic strategy to uproot factors in the system that oppress people of color, such as prejudice and racism, and to implement training in methods of accessing the system.

Elders and Prevention

Our elders make up another arena of prevention that is often forgotten or ignored. The rolelessness experienced by some elders leads to feelings of loneliness, boredom, frustration, rejection, abandonment, anxiety, fear, and depression. When elders complain about these feelings, sometimes the response is to prescribe more medication.

Prevention efforts with elders frequently involve training and education projects to assist them to keep accurate records of their medications, or to develop methods to have someone monitor their medication. Elders need to be approached with individuality and dignity. They need to be empowered to develop their own advocacy. Pharmacists, physicians, and other health providers must act in cooperation and be sensitive to each individual case. Drug dosages and regimens must meet individual needs and be sensitive to the elders' ability to maintain treatment plans.

Stewart and Cluff (1972) found that the rate of elder noncompliance with medication directions ranges from 20 to 80 percent. J. P. Doyle and B. M. Hamm (1976), found that 72 percent of the elders in Florida reported that they did not discuss medications given by one doctor while being treated by another physician simultaneously.

Monitoring and educating the elder population is a necessary prevention strategy. Advocacy for alternatives to medication are also essential, as well as the expansion of senior services. The more active and involved the life-styles of elders, the healthier the later years of their lives. Prevention with elders also involves proactive approaches to healthy activities that promote physical movement (health permitting), interpersonal interaction, and a sense of value and worth. In the years to come, a majority of the population will be elders. Prevention programs and services need to be further developed now to meet the needs of this ever-expanding population.

Prevention and College Students

During their first year of college, most students dramatically increase alcohol/drug use. The newly acquired freedom of being away at college allows students more opportunities to use drugs/alcohol. The anxiety of adjustment to college and living away from home can result in escalated drug/alcohol use. The functions of drugs/alcohol on college campuses are many—to party, to stay up late and study, to explore a personal sense of self and identity, to facilitate social and interpersonal relationships, and so forth. See Table 7.1 for more about the role of drugs/alcohol on campus.

Alternative Prevention Activities

In chapter 1, we mentioned the primary function of drugs/alcohol is serving our natural innate drive to alter our sense of consciousness. Ronald Siegal describes altering one's consciousness as the fourth drive, after hunger, thirst, and sex. The primary goal of alternative activities is to teach people that they are capable of altering their consciousness in a meaningful, longer-lasting, life-enhancing and satisfying way that is incompatible with drug/alcohol use.

TABLE 7.1
College Students' Alcoholism and Chemical Dependency

55 percent of undergraduates have driven after drinking.
41 percent have driven knowing they had too much to drink.
20 percent of undergraduates have come to class after drinking.
25 percent have missed classes because of hangovers.
22 percent of seniors believe that at one time they had drinking problems.
64 percent of fraternity and sorority house undergraduates drink in a moderately heavy to heavy manner.
45 percent are sexually active after drinking or drug use when they might not otherwise be. More than 20 percent engaged in unprotected intercourse while under the influence of drugs.

From Timothy Ravinius, "Alcoholism/Chemical Dependency and College Students" in *Journal of Chemical Dependency*, 1988. Copyright © 1988 Haworth Press, Binghamton, New York. Reprinted by permission.

The 1970s saw a strong movement toward alternative activity programs for young people. The programs usually involved wilderness activities requiring teamwork, challenge, and risk that developed feelings of competence, skill, and self-worth. Unfortunately, the first thing some young people wanted to do was to intensify the high of the alternative activity by "doing some drugs in this beautiful wilderness experience." Today, alternative experiences include education and training on the drug/alcohol recovery process. Many adolescent and adult inpatient and residential drug/alcohol treatment programs are including alternative activity program elements as a natural part of their recovery program.

Qualities of Successful Alternative Activities

Alan Cohen (1972), a strong advocate of alternative activities, defines alternatives as pursuits that are valued and truly preferred by individuals and seen as incompatible with drugs. Cohen emphasizes that alternatives are not just a substitution for drugs; they are an integrated and valued part of the person's life.

Alternative Is Actively Pursued by the Individual

Cohen felt that for the alternative to be successful, the process of searching for the alternative is a potent alternative in itself. Individuals are encouraged to find alternative activities they can develop, persevere through to mastery, and enjoy. The process of being able to choose ways to get high naturally through one's own interests is truly empowering. It follows that alternatives are more effective if they call for activity, assertion of will or will power, and effort and commitment. Alternatives are less successful if individuals are passive recipients of the activity. This is consistent with the function

Hang gliding is an alternative activity.

of drug dependence and alcoholism as a rather passive activity. All addicts/alcoholics have to do is sit back and passively wait for the drug/alcohol to take effect.

Cohen illustrates this in the example of listening to music: "Passively listening to music is not necessarily a promising alternative to drugs, since one could be passively stoned at the time. Training in active listening and deep study of music is more likely to be frustrating to drug use since the clarity of one's senses and cognition become important in successful completion of the task."

Acceptable, Attractive, and Attainable Alternatives

Alternatives must be acceptable and attractive. Any alternative we offer must be realistic, attainable, and meaningful. Alternatives must also assist people in finding self-understanding and improve self-image and personal awareness. Dohner outlined the following characteristics for positive alternatives:

1. They must contribute to the individual's identity and independence.
2. They must offer active participation and involvement.
3. They must offer a chance for commitment.
4. They must provide a feeling of identification with some larger body of experience.
5. Some of the alternatives must be in the realm of the noncognitive and the intuitive.

Alternative Mentors and Role Models

Another essential feature of alternatives is a successful role model or mentor: someone who can guide, facilitate, and encourage the successful attainment of the alternative skill. This person could be a positive parent model, a coach, a teacher, a peer, or anyone who understands and respects the boundaries in the development of the alternative skill.

Alternatives Integrate Self-Concepts

Alternative activities are effective as preventive tools if they enhance the development of skills associated with improving one's sense of self. Table 7.2 lists Alan Cohen's categories for various alternative activities based on personal attributes and attraction.

TABLE 7.2
Motives for, and Alternatives to, the Use of Drugs

Level of Experience	Corresponding Motives	Alternatives to Drugs
Physical	Desire for physical satisfaction, physical relaxation, relief from sickness, desire for more energy, maintenance of physical dependency	Athletics, dance, exercise, hiking, diet, health training, carpentry, or outdoor work
Sensory	Desire to stimulate sight, sound, touch, taste; need for sensual-sexual stimulation; desire to magnify the brain's sensoriums	Sensory awareness training; sky diving; experiencing sensory beauty of nature (lovemaking, swimming, running, mountaineering); *skiing, surfing, massage
Emotional	Relief from psychological pain, attempt to solve personal perplexities, relief from bad mood, escape from anxiety, desire for emotional insight, liberation of feeling, emotional relaxation	Competent individual counseling, well-run group therapy, instruction in psychology of personal development (sensitivity training); *self-help meetings, *emotional support system
Interpersonal	To gain peer acceptance, to break through interpersonal barriers, to communicate especially nonverbally, defiance of authority figures, cement two-person relationships, relaxation of interpersonal inhibition, solve interpersonal hangups	Expertly managed sensitivity and encounter groups, well-run group therapy, instruction in social customs, confidence training, social-interpersonal counseling, emphasis on assisting others in distress via education, marriage; *participating in organizations and community activities within personal interests
Social (including sociocultural and environmental	To promote social change; to find identifiable subcultures to tune out intolerable environmental conditions	Social service; community action in positive social change; helping the poor, aged, infirm, young; tutoring handicapped; improving the environment; *Peace Corps work with the homeless, hungry, impoverished, and oppressed

TABLE 7.2
Continued

Level of Experience	Corresponding Motives	Alternatives to Drugs
Political	To promote political change; identify with antiestablishment subgroup to change drug legislation out of desperation with the sociopolitical order; to gain wealth or affluence of power	Political service; political action, nonpartisan projects such as ecological lobbying, fieldwork with politicians, and public officials
Intellectual	To escape mental boredom; out of intellectual curiosity to solve cognitive problems; to gain new understanding in the world of ideas; to study better; to research one's own awareness for science	Intellectual excitement through reading, discussion; creative games and puzzles; self-hypnosis; training in concentration; synectics-training in intellectual breakthroughs; memory training; *attending seminars, workshops, and conferences; joining study or discussion groups; work with computers; writing a book or article
Creative-aesthetic	To improve creativity in the arts, to enhance enjoyment of art already produced, to enjoy imaginative mental productions	Nongraded instruction in producing and/or appreciating art, music, drama, crafts, handiwork, cooking, sewing, gardening, writing, singing
Philosophical	To discover meaningful values, to grasp the nature of the universe, to find meaning in life, to help establish personal identity, to organize a belief structure	Discussions, seminars, courses in the meaning of life; study of ethics, morality, the nature of reality; relevant philosophical literature; guided exploration of value systems
Spiritual, mystical	To transcend orthodox religion, to develop spiritual insights, to reach higher levels of consciousness, to have divine visions, to communicate with God, to augment yogic practices, to get a spiritual shortcut, to attain enlightenment, to attain spiritual powers	Exposure to nonchemical methods of spiritual development; study of world religions, introduction to applied mysticism, meditation, yogic techniques; *attending churches with recovery orientation; all activities that enhance spiritual awareness (nature, human connectedness, and activities that deal with existential despair)
Miscellaneous	Adventure, risk, drama, kicks, unexpressed motives; prodrug general attitudes	Outward Bound survival training; combinations of preceding alternatives; pronaturalness attitudes; brainwave training; meaningful employment

From Allan Y. Cohen, "The Journey Beyond Trips: Alternative to Drugs" in David E. Smith and Dr. George R. Gay, Eds., *It's So Good, Don't Even Try it Once.* Copyright © 1972 Prentice-Hall, Inc., Englewood Cliffs, New Jersey. The author's additions are indicated by asterisks.

Use the alternatives worksheet to list your motives and preferred alternatives to drug/alcohol use. Also identify the steps and resources necessary to implement each alternative.

Alternatives Worksheet

Level of Experience	Corresponding Motives	Steps and Resources to Implement Alternatives to Drugs/Alcohol
Physical	______	______
Sensory	______	______
Emotional	______	______
Interpersonal	______	______
Social	______	______
Political	______	______
Intellectual	______	______
Creative-aesthetic	______	______
Philosophical	______	______
Spiritual, Mystical	______	______
Miscellaneous	______	______

Figure 7.1

A conceptual model for preventive approaches to alcohol and drug abuse

Sacramento, California: Attorney General John Van De Kamp's Commission on the Prevention of Drug and Alcohol Abuse, 1986.

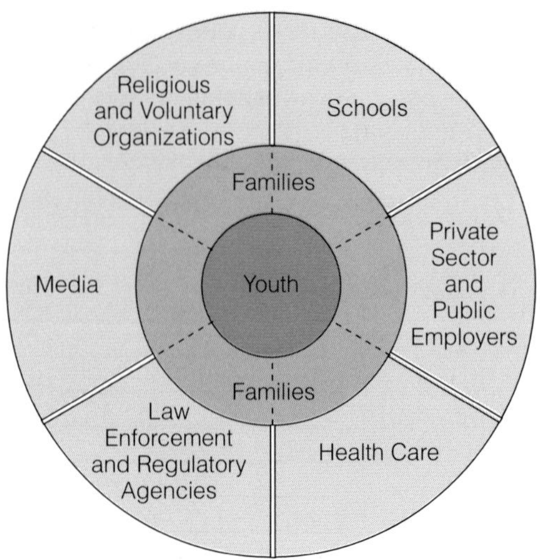

The Ultimate Domain of Prevention—The Family

Unfortunately, prevention activities take place almost exclusively in school systems. We expect the school systems to prevent this epidemic of drug/alcohol use. The reality is that the families are the real first line defense against drug/alcohol use by young people (see *figure 7.1*).

Schools, religious and voluntary organizations, the media, the private sector, law enforcement and health care are the secondary line of defense against drug and alcohol abuse by young people. Families can make a real difference. Secondary approaches have little effect if the home and family environment is not involved and supportive of prevention efforts.

In conducting drug/alcohol educational and skill activities for parents over the last fifteen years, I have found that the parents who don't need the information and are already effective parents are the ones that come to each and every event. The parents who need help are either in denial, too embarrassed, or too out of control to attend. Until we develop programs that can get these parents to participate, we are fighting an uphill battle.

Summary

The early prevention approaches focused primarily on supplying information on the dangers of specific drugs; warnings of physical, social and psychological harm; and punishment for sale, use, and possession. These scare tactics were ineffective, as were other converting programs that tried to direct, preach, or convince young people not to use drugs. The information in these early prevention approaches was often invalid, exaggerated, and overgeneralized, causing young people to question the credibility of the prevention efforts.

The next prevention effort focused on drug specific information in the hope that young people would make wise decisions about drugs. Unfortunately these approaches heightened curiosity and alleviated fears, leading to an increase in drug experimentation, rather than the intended decrease.

In the 1980s, the thrust of new prevention strategies shifted from drugs to people, emphasizing educational information, coping skills, personal competence, decision making, refusal skills, and alternative activities. Today credibility is a basic premise for the effectiveness of any drug prevention program. Effective prevention must also include youth, be sensitive to community needs, as well as make a longitudinal commitment to long-term prevention efforts. Examples of effective school-based curricula give readers a better understanding of the content and skills emphasized in effective programs.

These curricula develop skills such as

1. goal setting, problem solving, conflict resolution;
2. developing capabilities and dealing with authority figures;
3. developing proactive versus passive involvement and empowerment.

Special programs are also necessary for prevention efforts for at-risk students, people of color, college students, and elders.

The chapter closes with a description of the development of successful alternative activities in prevention, including an alternative worksheet to help readers explore their own alternative interests.

The concluding emphasis, consistent with previous chapters, is that the family is the primary domain of prevention. For prevention to be successful, the family must be involved in all prevention efforts.

References

Brecher, Edward M. *Licit and Illicit Drugs.* Boston: Little, Brown 1972.

Cohen, A. Y. "Alternatives to Drug Abuse: Steps toward Prevention." Rockville, Md.: National Institute on Drug Abuse, 1972.

Doyle, J. P. and B. M. Hamm. *Medication Use and Misuse Study among Older Persons.* The Cathedral Foundation of Jacksonville, Inc. Jacksonville, Fla.: 1976.

"Drug Abuse Prevention," Research Monograph No. 33. Washington, D.C.: Department of Health and Human Services, 1983.

Glenn, Stephen. *Raising Self-Reliant Children in a Self-Indulgent World.* Rockland, Ca.: Prima Publishing, 1990.

Goodstadt, Michael. "Evaluating Drug Prevention Programs." In *Balancing Head and Heart: Sensible Ideas for the Prevention of Drug and Alcohol Abuse,* edited by E. Schaps, A. Y. Cohen, H. S. Resnick, et al. Lafayette, Calif.: Prevention Materials Institute Press, 1975.

Julien, Robert M. *A Primer on Drug Action.* San Francisco: W. H. Freeman & Co., 1981.

Mathews, Walter M. "A Critique of Traditional Drug Education Programs." *Journal of Drug Education* 5, no. 1 (1975): 57–64.

National Institute on Drug Abuse. *Toward a National Strategy for Primary Drug Abuse Prevention,* Final Report, Delphi II, 1975.

National Institute on Drug Abuse. *Recommendations for Future Federal Activities in Drug Abuse Prevention.* Rockville, Md.: U.S. Department of Health, 1977.

Ravinius, Timothy. *Alcoholism /Chemical Dependency and College Students.* New York: Haworth Press, 1988.

Rhodes, Jean E. and Leonard A. Jason. *Preventing Substance Abuse among Children and Adolescents.* New York: Pergamon Press, 1988.

Schinke, S. P. and L. D. Gilchrist. "Primary Prevention of Tobacco Smoking." *Journal of School Health* 53 (1983): 416–19.

Spivak, G. and M. Shuve. *The Social Adjustment of Young Children.* San Francisco: Jossey Bass, 1979.

Stewart, R. B. and L. E. Cluff. "A Review of Medication Errors and Compliance in Ambulatory Patients." *Clinical Pharmacology and Therapeutics* 13 (1972): 463–68.

Drug/Alcohol Intervention

A drug/alcohol intervention is a caring, nonjudgmental, behavior-specific effort by the family to get an addict/alcoholic into treatment. Intervention is also of tremendous benefit to the family because it creates an awareness of the actual dimensions and progressive nature of alcoholism/drug addiction. Intervention empowers family members to change their codependent, enabling behavior. Many people are under the misconception that addicts/alcoholics must hit bottom before they stop using drugs/alcohol. An intervention can raise that bottom, break through denial, and prevent continued destructive behavior by the addict/alcoholic as well as enabling behavior by family members. A drug/alcohol intervention is a key approach in solving the problems of drug/alcohol dependence and addiction.

Chapter Goals

1. Define intervention and identify the primary and secondary goals of intervention.
2. Explain why intervention is effective for the family.
3. Outline and describe the four basic stages of a formal intervention.
4. Describe the kinds of information to be elicited at the assessment stage of the intervention.
5. Describe the need for the development of caring, behavior-specific communication during the intervention, and the avoidance of generalized and blaming statements.
6. Outline the script format and the tasks of the preintervention phase of the intervention.
7. Describe the key elements in the actual intervention.
8. Explain the bottom-line script in the intervention.

What About People Who Choose Not to Get Help for Drug/ Alcohol Problems?

On a hot summer day in 1984, I attended the Olympic Games in Los Angeles. Like most spectators that day, I tried to find a shady area on the lawn outside the stadium while awaiting the afternoon field events. While we watched Carl Lewis qualify for the long jump, a quiet, unsettling nervousness ran through the crowd in anticipation of the finish of the first women's marathon in Olympic history. The wide screen monitor at one end of the stadium broke the boredom and heat by showing little Joan Benoit with a significant lead in the marathon. The men's 800-meter qualifying race drew our interest, distracting us from the heat of the afternoon.

The slow methodical repertoire of the shot-putters was in full progress when the wide video screen came alive with Joan Benoit in great shape maintaining a significant lead. The crowd began to buzz with excitement. The shot-putters were caught by surprise as the more than 40,000 people in the coliseum began to applaud Benoit. The ensuing thirty to forty minutes were like a New Year's Eve party as the crowd counted down the minutes until Benoit entered the stadium for the final two laps of her twenty-six-mile ordeal. We were all standing watching both the video screen and the western entrance to the coliseum. Finally the moment came: The crowd exploded in cheers as Benoit entered and began her last two laps around the track. As she circled the track, each section of the stadium stood, cheering and waving little American flags. It was truly a wave of human emotion and pride affirming her accomplishment: The first women's Olympic marathon winner was an American. This was the crowd's hope and for some their only reason for attending the Olympics this day.

A few minutes later, I became aware of another struggle. A Swedish runner whose name I don't recall was approximately the sixth runner to enter the stadium. Benoit had already finished the race, and the crowd was still alive with energy. Its focus soon shifted to the Swedish runner, who on entering the track was swaggering. She took two steps forward, then two steps sideways, then another step forward. Clearly, she had hit the wall and was suffering from oxygen deprivation. As she advanced on the track, each section of the crowd rose and cheered her on. The human wave was in slow but full motion as the section where I was sitting stood up and cheered her on. I was also caught up in the frenzy of the moment. As she began her second and last lap around the track a medical team, dressed in their whites, ran alongside her. The thought struck me: What if we were all cheering and encouraging her to her death? The woman was clearly suffering. Yet we applauded her to continue on despite the possibility of bodily harm. Fortunately, she did finish the race without any permanent physical damage. A physician in attendance told me that within a few hours her vital signs and physical functioning were back to normal. However, what if she had not been that fortunate?

This raises some important questions: Should there have been a medical intervention to assess her condition? In the heat of the race do runners have a proper frame of physical and mental reference to decide if they are capable of continuing? Do we have a responsibility to intervene when someone is in danger of harming themselves?

This brief scenario from the 1984 Olympics illustrates one situation in which we might intervene. Other sports, on recreational to professional levels, also illustrate situations when there may be a need for intervention. Boxing, football, weightlifting, even team sports such as soccer, basketball, and baseball may require interventions to safeguard players. The use of protective equipment, rules that lower the risk of serious and/or permanent injury, and other advances minimize unnecessary harm to athletes. Yet, some athletes choose to disregard their own health to enhance performance. As pointed out in chapter 3, they use steroids, painkillers, stimulants, and drugs to attain a competitive edge. Advances in sports medicine are being applied as an intervention and preventive approach to injuries, in an attempt to stop serious long-term damage. Another situation where we might intervene is when individuals have drug/alcohol problems and may harm themselves or others.

Intervention

Intervention Services

The concept of drug/alcohol intervention began in the 1960s, when Vernon Johnson—at that time a pastor—felt frustrated when he was unable to help spouses of alcoholics. Deciding to abandon the traditional approach of waiting until the alcoholic/addict hit bottom, Johnson tried a new strategy that he later called intervention.

Intervene is defined by *Webster's Ninth New Collegiate Dictionary* as "to occur, fall or come between points of time or events."* Drug/alcohol intervention is a process that

*By permission. From *Webster's Ninth New Collegiate Dictionary* © 1990 by Merriam-Webster, Inc., publisher of the Merriam-Webster® dictionaries.

prevents, alters, or interrupts the progression of the disease. Drug/alcohol intervention is a process of getting involved or stepping into a situation in an attempt to interrupt the disease and to get the individual into drug/alcohol treatment. Persons who intervene choose to talk about the issue of drug/alcohol dependence that is destructive to the individuals, their families, and friends. Due to the addict/alcoholic's strong denial system, a trained interventionist with an expertise in drug/alcohol treatment must lead or facilitate the intervention.

Drug/alcohol intervention services are offered by most drug/alcohol inpatient and residential treatment centers. Trained drug/alcohol counselors also specialize in conducting interventions. The choice of the interventionist is a critical element in determining the success of an intervention. Local, state, and national drug/alcohol helplines are excellent referral sources for finding trained and experienced interventionists.

Intervention Approaches

There are a variety of approaches to the drug/alcohol intervention, including formal and informal drug/alcohol interventions, in which each interventionist has his/her own style of conducting the intervention. The principles described in this chapter form a basic framework within which most interventionists work.

Professional Intervention Assistance

The information in this section provides a basic understanding of the development of a successful drug/alcohol intervention. Whatever the format or style, conducting an intervention without professional guidance is often doomed to failure, no matter how powerful the individual. Untrained, grandstanding individuals who coerce someone into drug/alcohol treatment often cause further resistance by the individual needing help. Do not use this information to try to conduct an intervention on your own; consult a professional interventionist for help.

Intervention Is a Caring Response

The most important aspect of an intervention is that it is a caring effort designed to interrupt the disease of alcoholism and drug addiction. Individuals involved in an intervention can only be effective if they maintain a caring behavior-specific approach and support each other within the basic guidelines of their intervention group.

Goals of Intervention

The primary goal in developing an intervention is to get the addicted person to recognize that he or she has a drug/alcohol problem and to get that person into appropriate drug/alcohol treatment. Usually the treatment is a minimum twenty-eight day inpatient or residential program.

Secondary goals of the intervention are to:

1. Provide an opportunity for those who care about the alcoholic/addict to express concern about the impact the alcoholic/addict's dysfunctional behavior has had on them.
2. Provide information on drug/alcohol addiction and family patterns of interaction such as enabling behavior to the significant others (parents, spouses, family members, employers, and peers).
3. Promote the development of a healthy family system and to provide resource information for family members to continue working on their issues.

Family Interventions

Regardless of whether the addict/alcoholic decides to get help and go to treatment, family members go on with their recovery. The family has begun a process of change. The growth that the family experiences in developing an intervention can empower them to continue to be true to their feelings and to their own individual recovery whether or not the addict/alcoholic decides to seek treatment. Via the intervention process, the family learns about the disease of drug/alcohol addiction. The family recognizes their own enabling behavior and the role they play in the dynamics of the disease. The intervention may be the first time in a long time that the family has interacted together by functionally discussing their feelings. It may be the first time they have candidly discussed the impact the alcoholic/addict's drug/alcohol use has had on each of them.

Candidates for Intervention

Using a formal intervention process on adolescents, or young adults, who are developmentally still at the adolescent stage, is ineffective. Adolescents usually feel violated by the process of intervention. Because they are still exploring their own issues of identity and boundaries, they feel that it is unfair for family members to be planning an intervention without their knowledge. Adolescents fail to recognize or acknowledge that all previous direct efforts have not been effective in getting them to listen and understand the true dimensions of their problems.

Interventions are far more effective in getting individuals into treatment, when addicts recognize that their behavior has been a problem. The addict who still values and respects members of the intervention group is the best candidate. In some situations, addicts have alienated so many people that only job-related people are left. This relationship with an employer or business associates might be the integral element that makes some addicts good candidates for intervention.

Stages of the Intervention

The four basic stages of an intervention are assessment, preintervention, intervention, and postintervention. The rest of this chapter describes these stages with many examples and a case study.

Assessment

Families consider a drug/alcohol intervention because a family member recognizes that the family needs to do something about the person with the drug/alcohol problem. Likely, people have approached the addict about getting help on numerous occasions. Despite their efforts, the addict still chooses not to recognize the problem or get help.

A family member begins the intervention process by contacting a professional who conducts interventions. The interventionist schedules an appointment with family members to assess the drug/alcohol problem and to determine if an intervention is appropriate.

An experienced interventionist is trained to assess drug/alcohol problems. In the initial assessment sessions several family members, friends, colleagues, and even the employer describe what they know about the alcohol/drug use of the person being assessed for the intervention. Individuals seeking to intervene on a family member with a drug/alcohol problem are often at a late stage of frustration with the addict/alcoholic's dysfunctional and destructive behavior. Many look at the intervention as a last-ditch alternative. Despite the family's urgency to conduct an intervention, the interventionist conducts a proper assessment to determine if the person really does have a drug/alcohol problem.

The key element of the assessment is eliciting **behavior-specific information** and avoiding hearsay and or

Case Study

Intervention without Proper Assessment

J. R.

J. R., an aspiring vice-president in a developing company, contacted an interventionist and requested an intervention for another vice-president in the same company. The family of the person with the supposed alcohol problem believed that Roger had been drinking regularly but were not sure that he had an alcohol problem. Insisting that his coworker's drinking was a problem, J. R. was unable to come up with any behavior-specific examples of increased alcohol use. Despite the limited information and secondhand generalizations, the interventionist decided to go ahead with the intervention. The result was disasterous. Roger did not have an alcohol problem and quickly identified sabotage by his colleague who desired his sales territory. Needless to say, Roger was justified in proceeding with litigation against the interventionist for not conducting a proper assessment.

This story illustrates the pivotal importance of making an accurate assessment of the drug/alcohol problem before proceeding with the intervention. This is a very rare situation. In most situations, it is very clear that there is an alcohol/drug problem and that an intervention is justified.

generalized information. The interventionist needs specific times, dates, and firsthand knowledge of the actual level of consumption of drugs and alcohol. Some assessment questions are "What makes you think the individual has a problem with drugs/alcohol?" "What have been the consequences of this individual's drug/alcohol use?" The interventionist asks family members to explain or clarify the:

- Frequency of use, amounts used (dose and routes of administration), set and setting of use
- Patterns of use—binges, periods of nonuse, cycle of use
- History of negative consequences—overdoses, medical complications, physical and emotional harm
- Periods of abstinence, if any, and methods utilized
- Any medical conditions that effect drug/alcohol use
- Use of coffee, cigarettes, medications, and other addictions
- Difficulties with the criminal justice system
- Financial problems and interpersonal problems

Family members at the assessment sessions are asked to describe specifically what they know about the addict's use of drugs and alcohol and resulting dysfunctional and destructive behavior. The assessment clarifies the dimensions of the problem with drugs/alcohol. The family, and others present, usually recognize, confirm, and validate their own worst fears—the individual has a drug/alcohol problem.

Another extremely important aspect of the assessment is to determine whether the person you are going to intervene on is able to listen and understand. Someone who is going to physically attack, verbally explode, or rage at others at the intervention is not appropriate for an intervention. During the assessment stage, interventionists often ask the family members and others present, "How does the person you are planning to intervene on deal with anger?" "What do you think his/her reaction is going to be to the intervention?" These questions should elicit responses that determine if the individual is violent, and if there have been some physical violations in the past. Sometimes individuals can be paranoid and/or delusional, especially if they have been using cocaine, crack, or free base. Obviously you do not want to do an intervention if there is a high risk that the individual will be violent, or unable to listen and understand. An alternative utilized by a colleague who conducts interventions regularly with difficult addicts/alcoholics was to videotape the intervention and give it to the addict. This situation involved a violent cocaine addict who carried his gun to the actual intervention.

Some people have a negative reaction to the concept of a drug/alcohol intervention. They believe that it is an invasion, or violation, of the individual and his/her right to use drugs/alcohol. For the intervention to be effective, it must be planned without the knowledge of the person being intervened on. Some individuals have difficulty with this behind the scenes aspect. Once the interventionist has assessed that an intervention is warranted, members of the intervention group must decide whether they are comfortable in proceeding with the intervention.

Preintervention

The preintervention stage consists of all the sessions necessary to prepare for the actual intervention to take place. The ingredients essential for a successful intervention include: (1) commitment and participation of meaningful and significant others (family members, friends, relatives, peers, and children); (2) a proper assessment by the interventionist; and (3) specific nonjudgmental information about the individual's drug and alcohol behavior.

In preparation for the intervention, preintervention sessions develop a cohesive group of significant others. A group that has the combined goal of getting the addict/alcoholic into appropriate treatment.

The interventionist begins developing this group by educating group members, giving them information about the dynamics of drug/alcohol addiction. The education emphasizes the progressive nature of the disease of alcoholism/drug addiction that effects the entire family.

The group then develop their scripts and role play the intervention. Role playing allows the group to anticipate the reactions of the person they are going to intervene on. The group can then redevelop their intervention to make it more effective.

Behavior-Specific Communication

The addict/alcoholic is a master in distracting the intervention group from the goals of the intervention. When each family member communicates generalizations and judgments, the addict/alcoholic picks at their statements and distracts the group, thus weakening their ability to get the addict/alcoholic to commit to treatment. Therefore, the members of the intervention group must develop and communicate behavior-specific examples of the addict/alcoholic's dysfunctional and self-destructive behavior.

The following examples illustrate generalized statements followed by the addict/alcoholic's distracting statements. The appropriate behavior-specific statement follows each set of generalized and distracting responses.

Example 1

Generalized and Blaming: "Boy, you were really wasted at the party picnic and got violent. You were drunk and loaded on cocaine."

Addict/Alcoholic Distracting Statements: "What do you mean wasted! You were drinking just as much as I was. Weren't you? Boy are you hypocritical. You use cocaine."

Behavior Specific: "John I'm here because I care about you. On Saturday, July 4, 1991, at the company picnic, I saw you drink five beers from 1 to 3 P.M., then snort six lines of cocaine, which was followed by two more beers. You sat down in the outfield during the softball game and fell asleep. When I came over to wake you up, you threw a punch at me, right in front of the head of our company. You left the field. I found you a half hour later, with a six pack in the back of your car. Two of the cans of beer were already empty. I am worried about you. I'm afraid you are going to lose your job. You've been like a brother to me. I pray that you will get help. I know it's the drugs and alcohol."

Example 2

Generalized and Blaming: "You are an awful husband and father. You are always using drugs and drinking too much. Last month you were drinking and snorting cocaine all night. You scared the kids to death that night by yelling so loud at them, like a mad man."

Addict/Alcoholic distracting statement: "You think you are such a great mother? I remember the time you. . . ."

Behavior Specific: "John, I'm your wife and I'm here because I care about you. On Friday night, November 3, I went to the church meeting. When I came home at 10:15 P.M. I smelled alcohol on your breath and clothes. There was an empty gram bottle of cocaine on the kitchen table, and three lines of cocaine still on the mirror. There were twelve empty beer cans on the living room floor and the kids were hiding in their closet upstairs. When I came into their room they ran to me, shaking and out of control. That night I had to sleep with them because they were so frightened. The next day they told me you threw beer cans at them and told them you would kill them if they didn't stop bothering you. I love you John, I know it's the drugs and alcohol. I would like all of us to get help."

Each person involved in the intervention uses the following script format to avoid generalized, blaming statements:

Script Format

"I'm here because I care about you. You are my __________ I **care** about you."

"I saw __________" (describe the behavior-specific incidents that occurred)

"I feel ________" (whatever they may feel . . . embarrassed, hurt, frightened, worried, ashamed)
"I know it's the drugs." (or the alcohol, or the cocaine)
"I want you (us) to get help."

Script Example

"John, I'm here because **I care** about you. We've been friends a very long time. During Christmas, **I saw** you snort half a gram of cocaine. In the next hour you drank four beers. **I felt** embarrassed when you were trying to kiss your niece. **I felt** ashamed. **I saw** the hurt on your wife's face. I **know it's the cocaine. I know it's the alcohol. I want you to get help."**

Note: Some interventionists prefer, "I want you to get help." Others prefer "I want us to get help" because everyone in the family is going to get help to stop enabling the addict/alcoholic's use of drugs/alcohol.

During the preintervention, the intervention group identifies:

1. when the intervention will take place
2. where the intervention will take place; usually a neutral setting such as the interventionist's office is best
3. who will bring the person to the intervention
4. their scripts, role plays the intervention, and determines the most effective way of communicating their message
5. in which order each member will talk during the intervention
6. who is going to ask for a commitment to listen from the person being intervened on
7. arrangements have been made with the drug/alcohol treatment program; insurance and other details have been completed; a bed is reserved at the treatment center starting on the day of the intervention
8. all contingencies so the individual can go directly to the treatment program; bags have been packed and are in the car; a family member drives the addict directly to the treatment program.

Every detail is planned, even the seating arrangement. The actual intervention session will start and flow as planned. The family will be prepared to continue their own recovery regardless of the addict's decision. The session will not escalate into an uncontrollable situation. The family will approach the intervention as a process rather than a static event. Bear in mind, that if the preintervention sessions have gone well, the interventionist is available to help the family members during the intervention, but most often he/she plays a minimal facilitating role.

Intervention

Each intervention is different and unique. However, they all have the same common elements for success such as a nonjudgmental tone and behavior-specific caring responses by family and friends. The following is an example of an intervention:

Audrey is an attractive, energetic thirty-three year old. She owns a very successful travel agency. She is the single parent of two children: Andy is twelve years old and Bridget is seven years old. Audrey is dynamic, aggressive, and also—the most critical feature—alcoholic.

Audrey's sister Mary, thirty-nine, was concerned enough to seek intervention for her sister. Both sisters grew up in an alcoholic family system. Their father died of alcoholism when Mary was sixteen and Audrey was nine years old. Those involved with the intervention are

Mary—Audrey's older sister
Ann—a very successful businesswoman, Audrey and Mary's mother
Roger—Mary's son, Audrey's nephew, a twenty-year-old student at the University of Washington
Andy—Audrey's twelve-year-old son.

Mary brought Audrey to the interventionist's office under the pretense that they have been having some family counseling sessions for her son Roger. She said they wanted Audrey to participate in one session. All the family members are present at the office waiting for Audrey and Mary to arrive.

Mary: Audrey, this is Dr. Fields. (Shakes hands.) Just sit right here. Audrey, we are all here because we care about you. We are concerned about you and the children. We would like to be able to talk to you about our concerns. We would each like to say some things. We need your commitment to listen to us and not to respond, until we are finished. You will have an opportunity to respond then. Will you promise to first listen to us and not talk until we are finished?

Audrey: But, I thought we were here for Roger . . .
Mary: We are here for you, Roger, and all the family members.
Audrey: Yeah, but you didn't let me know what this was about.
Mary: Audrey, we wanted you to come. Will you just hear us out? Then you can have your chance.
Audrey: I, I . . . don't . . . yeah, I guess so. OK, I'll listen to what you have to say.

(Establishing ground rules allows each family member to talk without being distracted by the addict's ambiguous arguments. Having the addict agree to listen and not talk back is an essential ingredient for the intervention to be successful. Even though Audrey has been deceived in getting her to the intervention, she knows or suspects what the meeting is about. She is curious and even challenging the group to try to affect her.)

Roger: Thank you. You've been like a big sister to me, even though you are my aunt. You have provided a lot of opportunities to me. You've taken me on vacations and introduced me to all sorts of people, activities, and even jobs that I never would have had access to. I care about you a great deal. You've been a tremendous influence and I am very proud of you. I am here because I love you.

Lately, however, I find that I'm not so proud of you anymore. I'm worried about you. I am worried about Andy. I'm worried about Bridget. At your birthday party on January 7, you came home smelling of alcohol. You had three margaritas within an hour. I saw you in the kitchen, downing two doubles, as if they were water. You stumbled out of the kitchen and fell and cut your lip.
Audrey: That was my birthday party. Don't you understand?
Roger: You promised you would listen.
After you cut yourself, when Andy, Bridget, and I came into the kitchen to help, you screamed and yelled at us to get away.

Andy was so frightened he hid in his room and Bridget couldn't stop crying. They said they were so frightened that you were going to hit them again.

This isn't the first time this has happened. The same thing happened when we went down to Mexico. You had four drinks at the airport bar and four drinks on the flight. I was so embarrassed when you were flirting with the man next to you. The kids were embarrassed when you were kissing him and when you yelled at me for interfering. When we got to our hotel, the first thing you did was to order more booze.

In February, I was at the travel agency and you went into the bathroom. You invited me in and you had some lines of cocaine that you offered me. I saw you do ten lines of cocaine, and then come out and act as if everything was OK. You made six trips to the bathroom in the hour that I was there.

Audrey: I didn't do that much. As if you are so innocent!

Roger: You promised that you would listen and not interrupt. I was with you the night you got arrested for driving under the influence of alcohol. The kids were frightened sitting in the back seat.

Despite my arguing with you, you insisted on driving. I was so frightened that we all would be killed. I went along because I felt guilty that you would kill yourself and the kids. I tried to take the keys away from you, but you wouldn't let me. I was so angry with your boyfriend, Al, for insisting that you were OK, when you couldn't even walk straight. I was so angry with you when the police arrested you in front of your children. But I was more upset with myself for allowing myself to get drawn into the whole situation.

Audrey, despite all of this I love you and the children and I want you to get help.

Audrey: What kind of help?

Roger: (No response, head tilted down to ground, feeling emotionally spent.)

Ann: Audrey, you were a beautiful child, I gave birth to you. I love you a great deal. You were always so fun loving, energetic, and interested in so many things.

We went shopping the other day, last Wednesday, and you had four beers at lunch, after you said you would cut back. You told me that you were just wired. You were agitated, nervous, jittery.

Audrey, I'm frightened for you. When we came home from the travel agency last Friday, you smelled of alcohol. You were driving erratically. I was afraid we would get pulled over and you'd be arrested again. When I told you that you were in no condition to drive, you yelled at me to stop nagging.

Audrey: You, you're always telling me what to do. You're always bothering me. You're always involved in my life, telling me how to parent my kids.

Mom: That day, I saw you drink three beers before we left the agency.

Audrey: You guys are in this together. I don't even know why I'm here.

Roger: You said you'd listen.

Audrey: How can I listen to you if you keep on getting together? How could you guys get together behind my back to do this?

Mom: We're here because we care about you. We love you. I know it's the drugs. I know it's the alcohol. I want us to get some help.

Mary: We've grown up together. We've always been close. I love you. I care about you. On February 3, we went out to Morgan's restaurant. You drank five margaritas within an hour and a half. You were snorting cocaine in the bathroom. You left the restaurant with two men who you didn't know. I am really frightened for you. The next day you called me and told me you had a problem with alcohol and wanted help. Two days later, on Sunday, when I asked you about getting help, you said that you were doing much better and were getting your act together.

It was only a week later, that Friday night, when you were back at Morgan's. I saw you drink three doubles in an hour. You insisted that I stay. It was too hard to stay and watch you order another drink. I'm afraid that you are hurting yourself. I worry about you. I want my younger sister back. I want you to get help.

Andy: (Tears rolling from his eyes) Mommy, I am afraid when you drink and use drugs that you will hurt me. I am afraid that you will hurt Bridget. I want you to go get help. Will you?

Audrey: (Hugs Andy) Yes, I'll get help. I love you and don't want you to be frightened.

Mary: We have reserved a bed at the treatment center and Roger will drive you there.

Audrey: You mean you want me to go right now?

Mary: Yes.

Audrey: But what about the appointments at the agency?

Mary: I've arranged for Natalie to come in and manage the agency while you are gone.

Audrey: But what about the meeting with the accountant on Thursday?

Mom: I can cover the meeting since I know all about the new bookkeeping system.

Audrey: What about clothes?

Mary: I packed some of your things in a suitcase. Anything else you want I can get to you tomorrow.

Audrey: Can the children come and visit?

Mary: After the first week, there are regular family visits and a family counseling program. We chose this program because it specializes in providing counseling for young children.

Audrey: I guess you thought of everything . . .

(In reality, the family did think of everything. Any potential form of denial was anticipated, so that Audrey and her family could get the help they needed.)

What if Audrey Decides not to Go into Treatment?

In the event that Audrey did not agree to go into treatment, the family had prepared another bottom-line script. The purpose of the bottom-line script is to let the addict know that if she refuses to go into treatment, the family is not going to continue to enable her drug/alcohol use, as they have in the past. In implementing the bottom-line script, family members have to be willing to follow through with their bottom lines. Otherwise there is no point in stating them. For example, if Audrey refused to go into treatment, the bottom-line stage of the intervention would follow.

Roger: Audrey, I care about you. You've been a person that I greatly admire. I love you a great deal. I'm frightened about the drugs and alcohol. I'm fearful that you'll hurt yourself or the kids. If you don't go into treatment, I can no longer come over to the house. I won't see you until you get help. It's too difficult for me to see you killing yourself.

Ann: Audrey, I love you. You are a wonderful, caring mother. I see you teaching the kids to read and doing wonderful, creative things with them. You'll always be my daughter. If you don't get help I'm going to have my lawyer start the process of declaring you unfit. It hurts me to do this, but I can't enable the children to be abused the way they are. I know it's the drugs and alcohol, and I want us to get help. (Ann cries)

Mary: We've been more than sisters. We've been best friends. If you don't get help, I'll help Mom to get the children in a safe environment and away from the alcohol and drugs. I'm afraid for the children and their future. Please get help.

The bottom-line script is only implemented if the individual refuses to get treatment. If the individual still refuses treatment after the bottom line, the intervention is over, and the family members implement the bottom line.

Postintervention

The trauma and emotion of the intervention affects all of the family members and friends involved in the intervention. Immediately after a successful intervention families are often relieved and hopeful. However, the road to family recovery has just begun. The family should get together with the interventionist within a month, and prior to the end of the thirty-day inpatient program attended by the person who was intervened on. This gives the family an opportunity to reflect on their original commitment to the intervention, their own enabling behavior, and to reiterate their commitment to recovery.

Summary

Drug/alcohol intervention is a "process that prevents, alters, or interrupts the progression of the disease of alcohol/drug addiction." An intervention is usually conducted if the individual is assessed as having alcohol/drug dependence or addiction.

For the intervention to be successful, it must be a caring response that is nonjudgmental and behavior specific.

The four stages of intervention are assessment, preintervention, the actual intervention, and postintervention.

Individuals and families should not conduct an intervention without the assistance of a professional interventionist.

The primary goal of the intervention is to get addicted persons to recognize their problems with drugs/alcohol and to have them agree to get into drug/alcohol treatment. Presently, most people are appropriate for inpatient drug/alcohol treatment.

Secondary goals of the intervention are to (1) provide an opportunity for those who care about the alcoholic/addict to express their concern for the impact the addict's behavior has on himself/herself and others around them; (2) educate the family as to the dimensions and patterns of drug/alcohol addiction and imbalanced family systems; and (3) encourage and promote boundary setting by the family, friends, and others for the development of a healthier family system.

References

Johnson, Vernon E. Intervention: How to Help Someone Who Doesn't Want Help. Minneapolis, Minn.: Johnson Institute Books, 1986.

CHAPTER 9

Double Trouble: Dual Disorder*

Only within the last five to ten years have counselors in the chemical dependency treatment fields recognized that many of their patients have underlying psychiatric problems/disorders. Many of these patients found it quite difficult to maintain sobriety because of their coexisting psychiatric illness. Despite active involvement in treatment and follow-up care, such patients continue to experience depression, anxiety, or other psychological problems and symptoms. At the same time, counselors in the mental health field are recognizing that alcohol/drug problems complicate management of psychiatric disorders. It is not enough to provide psychological treatments (counseling and psychotherapy) and biological treatments (medication) without first understanding what role a patient's drug/alcohol use may play in aggravating psychological symptoms. The concept of dual disorders—drug/alcohol problems and coexisting psychiatric problems—is more widely accepted today. Dual disorder education and training for professionals in both fields is very necessary to improve treatment in the 1990s.

*Russell Vandenbelt, M.D., wrote this chapter with my assistance.

Chapter Goals

1. Define the term *dual disorders* and cite some prevalance rates for dual disorders.
2. Clarify the diagnostic issues in identifying chemical dependency as a primary or secondary disorder.
3. Describe the vegetative signs of depression (affective disorders).
4. Describe the differences between major depression, dysthymic disorder, atypical depression, organic depression, and mood cycling disorders.
5. Describe some treatment approaches for affective disorders.
6. Identify some common problems, based on the chapter case studies, in treating a dual disorder of depression and chemical dependency.
7. Identify the several different types of diagnosable anxiety disorders and some common symptoms.
8. Explain how anxiety disorder symptoms may mimic drug/alcohol withdrawal symptoms.
9. Describe some common treatment strategies for anxiety disorders.
10. Identify some common problems, based on the chapter case studies, in treating a dual disorder of anxiety disorder and chemical dependency.
11. Define and describe some common features of personality disorders, especially the antisocial and borderline personality disorder.
12. Describe some common problems with a psychotic patient who also is chemically dependent.

Introduction

The term *dual disorder* refers to the condition of having both a psychiatric diagnosis and a chemical dependency diagnosis. Increasingly, clinicians are encountering patients who have signs and symptoms of both. The symptoms produced by psychiatric disorders and chemical dependencies can overlap. The concept of dual disorders reminds us of this overlap in symptoms and underscores the need to make an accurate diagnosis so that appropriate treatment can be provided.

Until recently, counselors in the mental health and chemical dependency fields have taken a somewhat provincial outlook. Each has accused the other of minimizing the importance of their own perspective. In many ways the situation has become like the story of the blind men asked to describe an elephant. Each described it according to the body part they could touch but without regard to the remaining, unseen portions of the beast. Recent years have witnessed the emergence of a greater understanding and acceptance of the dual disorders concept. Increasingly, members of both fields are educating themselves about each other's areas of specialty.

The evolution of the dual disorders concept has paralleled our expanded understanding of the biological nature of both alcoholism and certain mental disorders. The traditional psychoanalytic model of psychotherapy and psychiatry held that mental illnesses were the result of disturbances in development and interpersonal relationships. Recent research suggests that the causes of mental illness such as schizophrenia, depression, anxiety disorders, and mood swing disorders are substantially, if not primarily, biological in nature.

Genetic research of families with a history of alcoholism has supported the biological nature of alcoholism. The most recent research has begun to identify specific genes or gene pools and may soon lead to the identification of the specific biological component in alcoholism.

There is a higher rate of alcoholism and other drug abuse in the families of patients with anxiety or mood disorders and vice versa. Quite possibly the genetic traits that predispose one to depression or anxiety or chemical dependency may be quite similar.

Clinically, we think of patients as existing on a continuum between purely psychiatric disorders at one end and purely chemical dependency problems on the other. Most patients lie somewhere between the extremes. An evaluation would take into account the relative position on the continuum. Today, it is rare to find a patient who has purely one condition, either psychiatric or chemical dependency. Many psychiatric patients are affected by drugs/alcohol, and many patients with drug/alcohol problems have psychiatric symptoms.

> A study of inpatients at the Colorado Psychiatric Hospital in the early seventies proclaimed that . . . 40 percent of the adult inpatients had evidence of recent substance abuse demonstrated by urine and blood tests on admission, and the substance abuse was seen to be a major precipitant of the need for hospitalization.
>
> It is common to see prevalence rates of substance abuse ranging between 20 and 50 percent of any psychiatric population. A recent report of a commission of mental health providers in New York State estimated that of the 75,000 individuals hospitalized in New York each year for psychiatric conditions, close to 40,000 admissions "involve persons with dual disabilities or a serious psychiatric illness and an alcohol and/or drug abuse condition."
>
> *(Bauer 1987)*

A more recent community-based survey of 20,291 people found that 53 percent of drug abusers and 39 percent of alcohol abusers have at least one mental illness, and 29 percent of the mentally ill in the survey abuse either alcohol or drugs (Regier 1990).

Psychiatric Diagnostic Categories

The following sections describe major psychiatric diagnostic categories and how drugs/alcohol influence and mimic particular symptoms. As you read each case study, pay attention to the history given, diagnosis, and the formulation of the treatment plan.

Mood Disorders

Mood disorders is a diagnostic category for various affective or feeling disorders such as depression, dysthymia, cyclothymia, and others.

There is a significant overlap between symptoms seen in mood disorders and in various chemical dependencies. Abuse or addiction can mimic or exacerbate any of the symptoms seen in patients with primary mood disorders.

Certainly everyone experiences symptoms of depression from time to time. When symptoms become severe and persistent, however, diagnosis of a mood disorder could be warranted. As researchers employed various systems of classifying depression over the years, they have increasingly recognized the different types and subtypes of depression. What differentiates various types from one another is their **severity, duration, frequency, and precipitating factors.**

Regardless of what causes depression initially, once it has been present for long enough it locks in and takes on a life of its own. This is another way of saying the brain changes physiologically in response to internal or external events that have persisted for a sufficient time. After the physiological changes have taken place, a number of biological or physical signs of depression emerge. These vegetative signs include disturbances in the basic biological functions that the brain regulates. Vegetative signs of depression include:

- disrupted sleep patterns
- difficulty with appetite and weight regulation
- decreased cognitive functioning (including problems with concentration, memory, and problem solving)
- decreased libido or sex drive
- lack of motivation, decreased energy
- difficulty experiencing pleasure

Denial and Depression

The psychological aspects of depression bring with it feelings of shame. Many individuals are extremely frightened to be labeled depressed, manic-depressive (bipolar disorder) or labeled with other mood-cycling disorders. The denial of these feeling disorders is often self-medicated with the use of drugs/alcohol, in an attempt to avoid the shame. Despite the fact that a majority of those individuals suffering from affective disorders can be helped, only one in three depressed individuals seeks help. It is estimated that over 10 million people suffer from depressive illness, and 2 million people suffer from bipolar disorder. Serious depressions are "whole body" disorders affecting body, feelings, thoughts, and behaviors (U.S. Department of Health and Human Services 1987). Most people view themselves as weak and inferior in not being able to have the will power to overcome depressive feelings. This is much like the denial of the disease of alcoholism and drug addiction. In fact, depressive disorder is a disease much like drug/alcohol addiction in that it has a known etiology, gets progressively worse over time, and has significant negative consequences if untreated.

Depressive Disorders and Suicide

One can clearly understand why depressive disorders may lead to suicidal ideation and suicide. The combination of depression and alcohol/drug use places patients at an even higher risk for suicide. Self-destructive acts that otherwise might be contemplated and dismissed are frequently acted on impulsively by those who are intoxicated and disinhibited. In earlier chapters we described alcoholism and drug addiction as a kind of death wish. Disaster might also occur when a depressed, forgetful patient is drinking and inadvertently takes an overdose of antidepressant medication. The antidepressants, especially the tricyclic antidepressants, are lethal when mixed with alcohol.

The vicious psychological pattern of affect (feelings) plus shame can also contribute to suicidal ideation and actions.

For example,

depressive feelings + shame = feelings of despair

Shame is exemplified as "I shouldn't feel depressed, I'm weak to have these feelings. I feel unable to control my feelings and there must be something inferior about me."

This cycle continues to the next stage of

feelings of despair + shame = suicidal ideation

The shame takes the form of thoughts such as "I'm not worthy. There is no hope, things won't change, I don't have any choices. Things are so painful, and never change, they only get worse. There is nothing to get any pleasure or joy from life."

The next and often fatal stage is

suicidal ideation + shame = suicide

It is no wonder that initial or normal feelings of sadness, or melancholia from unresolved trauma from childhood is avoided and not grieved. The individual suffering from depressive illness is fearful that any negative experience will start this cycle of depression to self-destruction in motion. As a result, feelings of sadness and emotional pain are often self-medicated with drugs/alcohol. One can see the importance of supportive counseling for depressed patients in addition to the appropriate use of antidepressant medication.

Categories of Mood Disorders

Major Depression

This is a common depressive syndrome and may occur as a single episode or as repeated episodes over the years. This diagnosis generally connotes a severe depressive episode with fairly clear onset and accompanying vegetative signs.

Episodes of major depression typically last from six to twelve months and then clear sometimes even without treatment. However, an episode can last significantly longer. Episodes of depression that are longer in duration require adequate and careful attentiveness and sensitivity to potential suicide attempts (see *figure 9.1*).

Dysthymic Disorder

Dysthymic disorder is a mood disorder of longer term, but a lower-grade depression. Patients with dysthymic disorder frequently comment that they have never felt completely happy or that if they do achieve a period of feeling well, it is relatively short-lived. Anxiety symptoms, headaches, and muscle tension are frequent in addition to symptoms of depression (see *figure 9.2*). Patients with dysthymic disorder come to assume that their own baseline mood is normal; they are frequently surprised that they actually do experience improvement with treatment. Only 25 percent of patients with major depression receive adequate diagnosis and treatment. It is very likely that the percentage is even lower for dysthymic disorder given the less intense and less notable degree of symptoms.

Atypical Depression

Atypical depression describes a condition that is not common as the symptoms and duration of symptoms are different than those of major depression or dysthymic disorder.

Atypical depression is frequently the diagnosis for many adult children of alcoholics. Typically a patient with atypical depression experiences intense and sudden depressions in response to interpersonal loss or threatened interpersonal loss. We may, in fact, be talking about the same condition as that described by James Masterson as abandonment depression.

Atypical depressions are common in patients who may also have severe personality disturbances such as borderline personality disorder. Psychodynamically, a sudden severe depression in response to feelings of loss, rejection, and/or abandonment may be related to a childhood loss so traumatic that it triggers this depression when feelings of loss are activated in present-day situations. This early childhood trauma of loss and abandonment is the usual family history of most borderline personality disordered patients.

Figure 9.1

Diagnostic criteria of major depressive disorder

A. At least five of the following symptoms have been present during the same two-week period and represent a change from previous functioning; at least one of the symptoms is either (1) depressed mood, or (2) loss of interest or pleasure. (Do not include symptoms that are clearly due to a physical condition, mood-incongruent delusions or hallucinations, incoherence, or marked loosening of associations.)

1. depressed mood (or can be irritable mood in children and adolescents) most of the day, nearly every day, as indicated either by subjective account or observation by others
2. markedly diminished interest or pleasure in all, or almost all, activities most of the day, nearly every day (as indicated either by subjective account or observation by others of apathy most of the time)
3. significant weight loss or weight gain when not dieting (e.g., more than 5% of body weight in a month), or decrease or increase in appetite nearly every day (in children, consider failure to make expected weight gains)
4. insomnia or hypersomnia nearly every day
5. psychomotor agitation or retardation nearly every day (observable by others, not merely subjective feelings of restlessness or being slowed down)
6. fatigue or loss of energy nearly every day
7. feelings of worthlessness or excessive or inappropriate guilt (which may be delusional) nearly every day (not merely self-reproach or guilt about being sick)
8. diminished ability to think or concentrate, or indecisiveness, nearly every day (either by subjective account or as observed by others)
9. recurrent thoughts of death (not just fear of dying), recurrent suicidal ideation without a specific plan, or a suicide attempt or a specific plan for committing suicide

B. 1. It cannot be established that an organic factor initiated and maintained the disturbance
2. The disturbance is not a normal reaction to the death of a loved one (uncomplicated bereavement)

Note: Morbid preoccupation with worthlessness, suicidal ideation, marked functional impairment or psychomotor retardation, or prolonged duration suggest bereavement complicated by major depression.

C. At no time during the disturbance have there been delusions or hallucinations for as long as two weeks in the absence of prominent mood symptoms (i.e., before the mood symptoms developed or after they have remitted).

D. Not superimposed on schizophrenia, schizophreniform disorder, delusional disorder, or psychotic disorder NOS.

Figure 9.2

Diagnostic criteria for dysthymic disorder

A. Depressed mood (or can be irritable mood in children and adolescents) for most of the day, more days than not, as indicated either by subjective account or observation by others, for at least two years (one year for children and adolescents).

B. Presence, while depressed, of at least two of the following:

1. poor appetite or overeating
2. insomnia or hypersomnia
3. low energy or fatigue
4. low self-esteem
5. poor concentration or difficulty making decisions
6. feelings of hopelessness

C. During a two-year period (one-year for children and adolescents) of the disturbance, never without the symptoms in A for more than two months at a time.

D. No evidence of an unequivocal major depressive episode during the first two years (one year for children and adolescents) of the disturbance.

Note: There may have been a previous major depressive episode, provided there was a full remission (no significant signs or symptoms for six months) before development of the dysthymia. In addition, after these two years (one year in children or adolescents) of dysthymia, there may be superimposed episodes of major depression, in which case both diagnoses are given.

E. Has never had a manic episode or an unequivocal Hypomanic Episode.

F. Not superimposed on a chronic psychotic disorder, such as Schizophrenia or delusional disorder.

G. It cannot be established that an organic factor initiated and maintained the disturbance, e.g., prolonged administration of an antihypertensive medication.

Atypical depression is also different because these patients may not report a loss of appetite and insomnia, but instead an increase in appetite and sleep. Perhaps, this is also indicative of the frequent problems in body image, binge patterns of eating, and other eating disorders that are very common in borderline personality disorders and adult children of alcoholics. Patients with atypical depression may increase drug/alcohol use in a similar manner.

Organic Depression

Depression may also occur as a result of organic factors such as brain tumors, head injuries, nutritional deficiencies, physical illness, or drug use. Many chemically dependent patients have nutritional deficiencies as a result of decreased intake, malabsorption, and poor eating habits. Alcohol is especially high in calories with poor nutritional value. Other drugs disrupt the appetite (e.g., cocaine reduces appetite), and create problems in nutrition and obtaining a balanced diet. After initial recovery from drug/alcohol use, depression may continue for a while due to nutritional causes. However, once a normal diet and vitamin therapy have been reimplemented, organic (nutritional) depression should improve.

Head injuries are fairly common especially in end stage alcoholics and may contribute to cognitive deficits, as well as mood disturbances. Pancreatic cancer is also more common in the alcoholic population and can look identical to major depression clinically.

Prolonged use of opiates, benzodiazepines, alcohol, sedative hypnotics, and especially stimulant drugs can produce depression. Users of cocaine and amphetamine typically experience a crash at the end of a binge pattern of cocaine use. This occurs because of the depletion of the neurotransmitter chemicals that the stimulant drug causes to be released in greater than normal quantities.

Mood-Cycling Disorders

The mood-cycling disorders contain not only symptoms of depression but also of a high or manic state. The most commonly known reference to these disorders is bipolar disorder. The first bipolar disorder described and understood was the classic manic-depressive illness.

Manic-depressive illness consists of repeated depressive episodes over the years; these episodes are typically briefer than those in major depression. In addition, a manic-depressive has less frequent but equally intense highs or manic episodes. During the high or manic phase of the disorder, behaviors include

- euphoria
- irritability
- racing thoughts
- decreased need for sleep
- excessive spending
- grandiosity
- pressured speech
- an increased preoccupation with sexuality, religious, and/or philosophical themes

A manic episode may also include delusional beliefs and disorganization of thinking. Highs need not always involve euphoria and many patients simply become much more irritable, bizarre, and erratic in their behavior.

A variety of bipolar disorders have somewhat different patterns. Some patients experience recurrent depressive episodes with smaller and less intense manic episodes (hypomania) in between. During a hypomanic episode, a patient might typically experience all of the preceding symptoms except for the psychotic symptoms such as disorganization of thinking, delusional material, and bizarre behavior.

Patients with bipolar disorder are typically plagued by mood instability; they may experience mood swings as frequently as daily. Patients who have significant mood swings, more than four times per year, are said to have a rapid cycling bipolar disorder. A growing accumulation of evidence suggests that some of these rapid cycling bipolar disorders may actually be a variation of epilepsy. Some of these patients may respond favorably to medication that had previously been used only for epilepsy.

Mood-Cycling Disorder and Drugs/Alcohol

The frequency of the cycling and the amplitude of the highs and lows are aggravated by drug/alcohol use. A relatively low-grade mood-cycling pattern may become much more aggravated with the use of drugs/alcohol and the symptoms may be more clinically apparent.

Patients who otherwise have no psychotic symptoms, such as delusions, hallucinations, or disorganization of thinking, and have a mood-cycling disorder may develop psychotic symptoms given the extra push from drug/alcohol use. (This is especially apparent with cocaine, amphetamines, hallucinogens, and even marijuana use.) Again, this stresses the importance of taking a thorough drug/alcohol history with each patient.

Treatment of Affective Disorders

The primary treatment for affective disorders involves antidepressants for the conditions involving depression (see *figure 9.3*). Dysthymic disorders typically respond to lower doses of antidepressant medication than the other depression subtypes.

The MAO inhibitors are the older group of antidepressants and require dietary and medication restrictions. While they are particularly effective for atypical depression, they have generally been superceded by the heterocyclic antidepressants.

The natural element lithium is primarily used in the treatment of bipolar disorders. While lithium remains the mainstay of treatment for bipolar disorders, some patients

Case Study
Dysthymic Disorder
Duane

Duane is a thirty-nine-year-old married male who completed inpatient treatment for alcoholism and cocaine dependence nearly three years ago. Since then he has maintained sobriety, while regularly attending his aftercare counseling sessions, and cocaine and alcoholics anonymous meetings. He has also been involved in individual and group counseling to deal with the effects of growing up in an alcoholic and emotionally abusive family system. Despite these efforts he continues to experience symptoms of low energy, periods of irritability, and an inability to have fun without a great deal of effort. His therapist referred him for a psychiatric evaluation.

Most notable in Duane's past history is that earlier he was abstinent from alcohol and drugs for approximately four to five months. During this time he experienced the same depressive symptoms. Besides alcoholism, his family history includes several relatives with depression. A recent physical exam was unremarkable.

Discussion

Duane is a patient with a dysthymic disorder underlying his chemical dependency. His symptoms do not clear up after substantial periods of abstinence from drugs/alcohol. Although many patients with dysthymic disorder do respond to psychotherapy techniques, many would benefit from trying antidepressant medication. Typically, such medication could be expected to improve Duane's baseline mood with simultaneous improvement in energy level, mood stability, and ability to experience pleasure.

Antidepressants
- Imipramine (Tofranil, Presamine)
- Doxepin (Sinequan, Apapin, Sinequan)
- Desipramine (Norpramin, Pertrofrone)
- Amitriptyline (Elavil)
- Nortriptyline (Pamelor, Aventyl)
- Protriptyline (Vivactil)
- Chlomipramine (Anafranil)
- Fluoxetine (Prozac)
- Trazodone (Desyrel)
- Maprotiline (Ludiomil)
- Amoxapine (Asendin)
- Bupropion (Wellbutrin)
- Tranylcypromine (Parnate)
- Phenelzine (Nardil)

Antianxiety
- Diazepam (Valium)
- Chlordiazepoxide (Librium)
- Chorazepate dipotassium (Tranxene)
- Lorazepam (Ativan)
- Oxazepam (Serax)
- Alprazolam (Xanax)
- Clonazepam (Clonopin)
- Buspirone (BuSpar)
- Hydroxyzine (Vistaril, Atarax)

Antipsychotic
- Haloperidol (Haldol)
- Chlorpromazine (Thorazine)
- Fluphenazine hydrochloride (Prolixin)
- Trifluoperazine (Stelazine)
- Perphenazine (Trilafon)
- Thioridazine (Mellaril)
- Thiothixene (Navane)

Mood Cycling
- Lithium
- Carbamazepine (Tegretol)
- Valproic acid (Depakote)
- Clonazepam (Clonopin)

Not all medications in each group are listed.

Figure 9.3
Generic and (proprietary) names of psychiatric medications

Case Study
Major Depression and Addiction
Elaine

Elaine is a fifty-three-year-old divorced woman with two previous psychiatric hospitalizations for severe depression. These were treated successfully with antidepressant medication. She returned to her psychiatrist after a ten-year absence due to progressively worsening depression for two months. Further questioning reveals that she had experienced anxiety symptoms last year and her gynecologist had prescribed diazepam (Valium). She took the medication in low doses as prescribed until sustaining a neck injury in an automobile accident five months ago. At that time the doctor prescribed narcotic pain medication. Initially she took the pain medication as prescribed but later took the medication in increasing doses. She found that her pain and anxiety symptoms were manageable with the higher doses and she simultaneously increased her daily dose of Valium taking a moderate to heavy dose at night to help her overcome her physical discomfort and to improve sleep. Her escalating use of the medication surprises her since she has never used similar drugs in the past and has avoided alcohol and street drugs because of religious beliefs. She is troubled by a growing preoccupation with suicide and fears that she may commit suicide like her mother and maternal grandmother did. A physical exam by her internist later in the day revealed slightly elevated blood pressure, sweaty palms, and slightly dilated pupils.

Discussion

Elaine is a patient with a history of major depression episodes and a superimposed addiction to prescription drugs. Similar to many patients, anxiety symptoms predated the onset of depression symptoms. These were fairly well controlled with a low dose of the diazepam until she sustained an injury and developed chronic pain. Increase in use of pain medication and diazepam then followed and she rapidly developed a high tolerance to the medication. She is now experiencing mild withdrawal symptoms (sweaty palms, elevated blood pressure, and dilated pupils), and is also in the midst of a depression. She needs to be withdrawn from the narcotic and benzodiazepine medication. This might be accomplished as an outpatient, but her thoughts of suicide complicate the picture. It would be more prudent to hospitalize her for detoxification. Many patients experience irritability and agitation during withdrawal; these symptoms might make her more likely to act on her suicidal thoughts. Given her strong family history of depression (suicide by mother and grandmother) and her previous personal history of depression, it is likely that she will need treatment with an antidepressant. It might be best to wait for a few days until her physical symptoms of withdrawal subside before adding another medication to her system. She will benefit from an out-patient chemical dependency treatment program following inpatient detoxification.

cannot tolerate lithium or do not respond to it. Alternatives to lithium include carbamzepine (Tegretol) and Valproic acid (Depakote).

Clonopin is another agent used in mood-cycling disorders but because it is a benzodiazepine, it is generally avoided in chemically dependent patients.

Anxiety Disorders

Anxiety is a symptom that everyone experiences in everyday life. It has been variously described as nervousness, butterflies in one's stomach, apprehension, vague fear, or the jitters.

Case Study
Depression and Withdrawal Symptoms
Evan

Evan is a twenty-seven-year-old male who is receiving inpatient treatment for his cocaine dependency. He was referred for a psychiatric evaluation because of his current severe depression symptoms. He had been freebasing cocaine for two to three months prior to admission to the treatment unit three days ago. Now he is feeling severely depressed and experiencing cocaine cravings.

Evan has no history of depression and no family history of psychiatric disorders. During childhood he experienced hyperactivity and had mild learning disabilities. He notes that since beginning drug use in his mid-teens he has preferred stimulant drugs because they "calm me down." He has received inpatient treatment for cocaine dependence once previously and had two years of complete abstinence before relapsing several months ago. During his clean time he experienced no mood difficulties but continued to feel somewhat hyper.

Discussion

Evan is a patient who experiences severe depression as part of cocaine withdrawal. There is no reason to suspect an underlying problem with depression given his personal and family history. He would benefit from a short course of treatment with desipramine, an antidepressant that is particularly effective for treating acute depression and cocaine cravings during cocaine withdrawal. Such treatment typically lasts for two to four weeks.

His history suggests a childhood hyperactivity disorder (attention deficit hyperactivity disorder, ADHD) that has extended into early adulthood. Many patients with this type of history do gravitate toward stimulant drugs that produce a paradoxical calming effect much like Ritalin, which is commonly used for treating ADHD.

Evan could also benefit from individual and group counseling on relapse prevention strategies. Perhaps his relapse could have been avoided if he had established better support from self-help participation, a sponsor, and a program that kept him from relapse situations. At twenty-seven-years of age, Evan could also benefit from the support of counseling to assist him in assessing his developmental skills such as career, self-concept, and interpersonal relationships that may have been jeopardized by his cocaine use.

Anxiety need not be a disabling experience. In fact, anxiety motivates us to be more productive. The consummate actor, Sir Alec Guinness, suffered from stage fright. Once asked if he had butterflies before each performance, he said, "Yes, but they fly in formation, now." This shows that people can learn to cope or adjust to general nervousness and anxiety under pressure to perform. However, when anxiety becomes more persistent or there are severe symptoms, it can become extremely disabling and is an anxiety disorder. Diagnosable anxiety disorders include

- generalized anxiety disorder
- panic disorder
- post-traumatic distress disorder
- obsessive compulsive disorder
- social and other phobias.

Case Study
Bipolar Disorder
Gustav

Gustav is a forty-five-year-old salesman with a history of binge drinking and erratic job performance. He goes on two- to three-week binges every spring and uses alcohol only socially at other times. He feels remorseful about these binges. In the weeks preceding a binge he typically is quite productive, energetic, and successful in making sales. Gus comments that his springtime burst in earnings helps to compensate for his lackluster winter performance, when he typically feels lethargic and moody. In the past, he has used cocaine intermittently during winter months to help brighten his mood. His finances have not allowed him to do cocaine in recent years. His occupational history is notable for multiple sales jobs across the country. He has made a number of impulsive springtime moves to pursue hot job possibilities. He does not find this unusual because his father, uncle, and brother have all had similar histories. Closer questioning reveals that during the springtime bursts of increased sales activity he has less need for sleep, a feeling of euphoria and an increased philosophical preoccupation. Coworkers have commented on his high energy level and rapid speech. He has no history of previous psychiatric treatment.

Discussion

Gustav's history reveals a patient with a bipolar disorder who binge drinks when he is high. There is a seasonal component to his mood swings, as he experiences manic symptoms in the springtime and symptoms of depression in the winter. Notably he has a family history of similar mood swings and a personal history of minimal drug or alcohol use when he is not high. He is a good candidate for treatment with a mood-cycling agent such as lithium and would benefit from counseling on how to manage his impulses to drink. He should use available resources for support such as AA.

Given the nature of anxiety disorders, it is not surprising that patients use drugs/alcohol to alleviate symptoms associated with anxiety disorders. Estimates of those suffering from anxiety disorders who use drugs/alcohol have varied from less than 10 percent to more than 35 percent. Many patients who experience anxiety have symptoms such as nervousness, insomnia and other sleep disturbances, tremulousness, restlessness, and hyperarousal.

These patients commonly alleviate such symptoms with sedating drugs such as alcohol, cannabis, narcotic pain medication, and sedative hypnotics. Most of these drugs are readily obtained through licit and illicit channels. Persistent use of these drugs can produce dependence and addiction. This would create a vicious cycle of psychiatric symptoms, drug use, followed by a return of psychiatric symptoms sometimes with more intense manifestations, followed by a return to drug use. This truly becomes a dual disorder pattern of combined psychiatric problems and drug/alcohol problems.

TABLE 9.1
Shared Symptoms: Anxiety and Drug/Alcohol Withdrawal

Increased pulse (heart rate)
Increased respiratory rate
Sweating
Tremors
Nausea
Muscle weakness
Increased startle response
Insomnia
Irritability
Shaky feeling

Persistent use of drugs/alcohol to reduce anxiety can produce anxiety symptoms during acute withdrawal (see table 9.1). Alcohol and other drug withdrawals have many of the same symptoms as panic attacks. For example, alcohol withdrawal causes increased heart rate, rapid breathing, weakness, tremulousness, sweating, nausea, and an exaggerated startle response. Diazepam (Valium) withdrawal causes irritability, insomnia, muscle cramping, nightmares, panic attacks or even hallucinations one to three weeks after discontinuation of use.

Many patients experience the onset of panic attacks following use of marijuana or cocaine. These drugs apparently trigger panic attacks and can set off a chain of such attacks over the course of weeks, months, or even years. The acute effect of other stimulant drugs such as cocaine, amphetamines, MDA, or even caffeine (especially highly caffeinated espresso), can aggravate or mimic anxiety symptoms. Cocaine, in particular, is an unpredictable drug; the same dose that produces a euphoric effect one time may cause anxiety symptoms at another time. Cocaine can produce rapid irregular heartbeat, racing thoughts, fear, seizures, or even cardiac arrest.

Treatment of Anxiety Disorders

In the past, treatment of anxiety disorders commonly involved sedative-hypnotic drugs. Physicians frequently prescribed barbiturates (such as Seconal) and meprobamate (Miltown) in the late 1950s and early 1960s. Because these drugs had a high abuse or addiction potential, they were generally abandoned in favor of the benzodiazepine group in the 1960s and 1970s. Valium (diazepam) was the most famous and widely used member of this drug group. Even though the benzodiazepines were originally touted as being nonaddicting, in fact they lead to dependence in a large number of patients. Interestingly, recent studies have substantiated that the benzodiazepines are nonaddicting in 95 percent of the population provided that certain dosage guidelines are followed. However, this only holds true for those individuals who do not have a personal or family history of problems with drugs/alcohol. Those individuals with a personal history or strong familial history of chemical dependency are at greatest risk for developing addiction to benzodiazepines. Accordingly, patients with any history of problems with alcohol/drugs should avoid this group of medications. Alcohol and the benzodiazepines are cross-tolerant, meaning that one cannot be substituted for the other for ongoing treatment in a chemically dependent patient as the second drug will likely be as addicting as the first.

Physicians often use other treatment alternatives in the chemically dependent population. Antidepressant medications have a substantial degree of anti-anxiety effect, often at doses lower than those needed to treat depression. Both the older MAO inhibitors and newer heterocyclic antidepressants are effective. They are nonaddicting; they produce no high when abused and are chemically dissimilar to addicting drugs. Despite a historical resistance to using antidepressants in the recovering community, there seems to be more acceptance now as the benefits are acknowledged by recovering addicts/alcoholics.

Other alternative help with anxiety includes buspirone and hydroxyzine. Buspirone (BuSpar) is chemically similar to antidepressants, yet it is purely an anti-anxiety agent. Similar to antidepressants, buspirone usually takes two to three weeks before its full effect is achieved; it has no addiction or abuse potential. Hydroxyzine is a drug used in a number of arenas of medicine. Hydroxyzine has antihistamine, antinausea, and anti-anxiety effects, as well as an ability to potentiate (add power to) the effect of pain medications. Used in low doses, hydroxyzine can be quite effective for anxiety symptoms (see *figure 9.4*).

Patients who use an anti-anxiety drug are usually undergoing counseling or psychotherapy. Anti-anxiety drugs are ideal for short- or intermediate-term therapy. The medication helps reduce the severity of anxiety symptoms while the patient learns other coping techniques and stress reduction strategies.

Figure 9.4

Diagnostic criteria for generalized anxiety disorder

A. Unrealistic or excessive anxiety and worry (apprehensive expectation) about two or more life circumstances, e.g., worry about possible misfortune to one's child (who is in no danger) and worry about finances (for no good reason), for a period of six months or longer, during which the person has been bothered more days than not by these concerns. In children and adolescents, this may take the form of anxiety and worry about academic, athletic, and social performance.

B. If another Axis I disorder is present, the focus of the anxiety and worry in A is unrelated to it, e.g., the anxiety or worry is not about having a panic attack (as in panic disorder), being embarrassed in public (as in Social Phobia), being contaminated (as in obsessive compulsive disorder), or gaining weight (as in anorexia nervosa).

C. The disturbance does not occur only during the course of a mood disorder or a psychotic disorder.

D. At least 6 of the following 18 symptoms are often present when anxious (do not include symptoms present only during panic attacks):

Motor tension

1. trembling, twitching, or feeling shaky
2. muscle tension, aches, or soreness
3. restlessness
4. easy fatigability

Autonomic hyperactivity

5. shortness of breath or smothering sensations
6. palpitations or accelerated heart rate (tachycardia)
7. sweating, or cold clammy hands
8. dry mouth
9. dizziness or lightheadedness
10. nausea, diarrhea, or other abdominal distress
11. flushes (hot flashes) or chills
12. frequent urination
13. trouble swallowing or "lump in throat"

Vigilance and scanning

14. feeling keyed up or on edge
15. exaggerated startle response
16. difficulty concentrating or "mind going blank" because of anxiety
17. trouble falling or staying asleep
18. irritability

E. It cannot be established that an organic factor initiated and maintained the disturbance, e.g., hyperthyroidism, caffeine intoxication.

Case Study
Anxiety Symptoms
Anthony

Anthony is a forty-three-year-old married male who complained to his family doctor about heartburn, headaches, nervousness, and restless sleep. He requested some nerve pills like his mother used when she became anxious. He cited increasing job stress and marital conflict as contributors to his current situation. Further questioning revealed a number of nervous relatives and one or two with depression. Although Anthony has no family history of alcoholism or chemical dependency, he has increased his alcohol intake recently. For the past four to five months he has been drinking two to three glasses of wine or beer per night. He felt this allowed him to take the edge off and helped him get to sleep.

Notably his difficulties with restless sleep and awakening at 3:00 to 4:00 A.M. have also recently worsened. When asked further about stressors in his life, he admits that his recent job promotion has resulted in longer work hours. His school-age children are having academic difficulties and his relationship with his wife is faltering. A review of his medical records reveals that Anthony has always been in good health and that previous questions regarding alcohol and drug use have revealed only a social drinking pattern. A routine physical exam and routine laboratory studies revealed no abnormalities other than a slightly enlarged liver.

Discussion

Anthony is an example of a patient with anxiety symptoms arising out of situational stressors and aggravated by the use of alcohol. His family history is notable for persons with anxiety and depression symptoms which may indicate that he has a predisposition to develop anxiety symptoms. The physical problems he is encountering are attributable to his recent increase in alcohol consumption. Stomach irritation is quite common in alcohol abuse, as is insomnia.

The marital distress he is experiencing may well be fueled by increased irritability produced by repeated short-term alcohol withdrawal episodes. Given his insomnia, he experiences some alcohol withdrawal symptoms early in the mornings as the effect of the previous evening's alcohol use wears off. He has no previous history of alcohol or drug abuse or family history of problems with alcohol.

Recommendations

The first recommendation is to discontinue drinking, as this has perpetuated his symptoms. Second, Anthony is certainly a candidate for at least short-term counseling or psychotherapy to help him manage the stressors in his life. He may even be a candidate for couples counseling depending on the nature, extent, and severity of his marital discord.

His children are having academic difficulties and this is often a reliable indicator of family dysfunction. This may indicate family dysfunction due to depression, anxiety, or drug/alcohol problems of the parents. The third recommendation is that the children's learning problems be assessed.

Medication

Anthony might be a candidate for short-term use of buspirone or hydroxzine, to minimize the intensity of his anxiety symptoms, while he works through the therapeutic issues in counseling. A longer-term agent such as an antidepressant might also be considered, especially a more sedating antidepressant he can use at night to combat insomnia.

Benzodiazepines would not be the ideal choice for him given his recent abuse of alcohol. One might consider use of a low-dose benzodiazepine for a short time if there were medical contraindications to the agents noted earlier, or if they were ineffective.

Additional note: His physician suspects that Anthony may not be telling all. He may be discounting the actual frequency of alcohol use, or not revealing his use of drugs. Despite not having a family history of drug or alcohol problems, Anthony may have a drug/alcohol problem. The fact that his children are experiencing difficulties in school may also indicate problems with his wife or both parents. Further assessment of the cause of the children's learning problems is an important part of the treatment recommendation.

Case Study

Panic Disorder

Barbara

Barbara is a thirty-eight-year-old divorced woman who complained of heart problems to a cardiologist referred by her family physician. While a routine physical examination, EKG, and family history had revealed no evidence of cardiac disease, Barbara was quite concerned about the sudden sense of impending doom she was experiencing. Other symptoms included difficulty in breathing, light-headedness, nausea, sweating, and the sense that "my heart is going to jump out of my chest." Barbara has progressively become more afraid to travel to places far from medical care. She also reports feeling apprehensive in crowded places that might be inaccessible to ambulances. She comments, "I memorized the number 911."

Her history of drug use includes regular use of marijuana and alcohol during late adolescence and her early twenties. Thereafter, she lost interest in drugs and alcohol use and reverted to a pattern of occasional social drinking, about one to two drinks per week. She noted trying cocaine for the first time about two weeks before the onset of her first heart problem. A treadmill test and repeat EKG reveal no abnormalities. However, as she has become persistently more anxious, she has increased her consumption of alcohol.

Further questioning revealed that her panic episodes have become progressively more frequent since their onset a few months ago and that they typically last for ten to fifteen minutes. They occasionally awaken her and disrupt her sleep. Most recently, she has been anxious and worried about having these attacks.

Discussion

Barbara is a patient with a panic disorder that began shortly after the use of cocaine (see *figure 9.5*). This case study illustrates the importance of a thorough drug/alcohol history in assessment and treatment planning. She is experiencing progressively more frequent and more severe panic attacks and has developed anticipatory anxiety as well. She fears places and situations in which she might have a panic attack. This results in her progressively restricting her social activities. Should this phobia of these situations and places continue, she may develop agoraphobia, the fear of going out at all. Notably she went to her family physician first and was referred to a cardiologist for symptoms identified as physical. This is a common mode of presentation for patients with a panic disorder.

Medication

Like many patients who are anxious, Barbara has used alcohol to self-medicate some of the anxiety symptoms. Her previous history of alcohol and drug use made her more susceptible to become addicted to a high potency benzodiazepine like Xanax or Clonopin. Physicians frequently use these in the treatment of panic disorders; they are clearly problematic in a patient with a history of drug abuse or drug dependency problems. Xanax, a short-acting agent, is ideally suited for use in infrequent panic attacks. Clonopin is a longer-acting agent more suited for longer-term management in patients without chemical dependency problems who cannot tolerate antidepressant medication, or for whom it is ineffective. The recommended medication would be an antidepressant that provides an excellent antipanic effect.

Recommendation

Barbara would probably benefit from psychotherapy to treat her panic attacks. Cognitive behavioral techniques have been especially effective in addressing the situations and stimuli that increase feelings of panic, as well as management of symptoms once a feeling of panic is experienced.

In psychotherapy she may want to explore the impact of the divorce on her life and feelings of loss of control. Additional investigation of her early childhood and family of origin might indicate childhood trauma that has influenced her adult reaction to issues of stress, abandonment, and rejection.

Figure 9.5

Diagnostic criteria for panic disorder

A. At some time during the disturbance, one or more panic attacks (discrete periods of intense fear or discomfort) have occurred that were (1) unexpected, i.e., did not occur immediately before or on exposure to a situation that almost always caused anxiety, and (2) not triggered by situations in which the person was the focus of others' attention.

B. Either four attacks, as defined in criterion A, have occurred within a four-week period, or one or more attacks have been followed by a period of at least a month of persistent fear of having another attack.

C. At least four of the following symptoms developed during at least one of the attacks:

1. shortness of breath (dyspnea) or smothering sensations
2. dizziness, unsteady feelings, or faintness
3. palpitations or accelerated heart rate (tachycardia)
4. trembling or shaking
5. sweating
6. choking
7. nausea or abdominal distress
8. depersonalization or derealization
9. numbness or tingling sensations (paresthesias)
10. flushes (hot flashes) or chills
11. chest pain or discomfort
12. fear of dying
13. fear of going crazy or of doing something uncontrolled

Note: Attacks involving four or more symptoms are panic attacks; attacks involving fewer than four symptoms are limited symptom attacks.

D. During at least some of the attacks, at least four of the C symptoms developed suddenly and increased in intensity within ten minutes of the beginning of the first C symptom noticed in the attack.

E. It cannot be established that an organic factor initiated and maintained the disturbance, e.g., amphetamine or caffeine intoxication, hyperthyroidism.

Note: Mitral valve prolapse may be an associated condition, but does not preclude a diagnosis of panic disorder.

Some patients do have long-standing anxiety difficulties that persist despite psychotherapeutic techniques. In such patients longer-term use of a nonaddicting medication may be appropriate. Nonetheless, physicians should periodically attempt to taper the medication and not assume that the patient needs medication indefinitely.

As coping skills improve, patients may be able to explore the source of trauma experienced in their families of origin and gradually grieve the pain of that trauma. Slowly,

Case Study

Alcoholism

Charlie

Charlie is a fifty-three-year-old married engineer at a local aerospace company. He has a long-standing, but progressively worsening, history of irritability, nervousness, and difficulty sleeping. Charlie is under the care of Dr. Greenhorn, a physician just out of his internal medicine residency. Dr. Greenhorn has assumed the practice of Charlie's previous physician and golfing buddy, Dr. Barleycorn.

Dr. Greenhorn reviews the previous medical record and notes difficulties with stomach irritation and ulcers, elevated triglyceride and cholesterol levels, and persistent complaints of decreased libido or sex drive. Charlie requests some of the sleeping pills that Dr. Barleycorn prescribed. Further questioning reveals a history of regular heavy drinking that began when Charlie and Dr. Barleycorn were fraternity brothers. This heavy drinking behavior persisted over the years. Charlie typically drinks three to four mixed drinks or glasses of beer per weeknight and six to seven drinks per night on the weekends. He can recall going two to three days without alcohol during a church retreat several years ago. At that time he recalled feeling very shaky and irritable. Physical examination reveals a moderately enlarged liver and laboratory studies reveal elevated liver enzyme levels and mild anemia.

Discussion

Charlie is a classical example of a patient whose primary diagnosis is chemical dependency (alcoholism). The irritability and insomnia are a direct result of the alcohol and repeated episodes of the beginning phases of alcohol withdrawal. Maintenance drinkers can avoid withdrawal symptoms by frequent repeated administration of the drug in question or a cross-tolerant drug such as sedative-hypnotic sleeping pills.

Like many other patients with similar backgrounds, Charlie's problems with alcohol have long been overlooked or ignored. His relationship with Dr. Barleycorn is unique and points to the difficulty physicians may have in assessing their patients adequately because of their personal relationships with patients and their own drinking habits.

Recommendation

Treatment for Charlie should include abstinence from alcohol and cross-tolerant medications. Given his long-standing history of alcohol use, he will likely be referred to an alcohol treatment program. He will need help to gain better insight into how his drinking has affected his life.

Realistically, sleep disturbances and irritability may persist for even a few months and could be treated symptomatically with a nonaddicting sleeping agent, or even with a low-dose antidepressant.

anxiety symptoms become more manageable as individuals understand their associations to root feelings of loss of control. A combination of medication, counseling for coping skills, and psychotherapy for the trauma of childhood experiences, can be a successful treatment strategy that gives patients a sense of control to effectively manage the anxiety disorder.

Figure 9.6
Personality disorders

To qualify for a personality disorder diagnosis, an individual's traits and behaviors must be longstanding and must cause significant impairment in social or occupational functioning or subjective distress. The 11 DSM III-R personality disorders are

Cluster A	Cluster B	Cluster C
Paranoid	Antisocial	Avoidant
Schizoid	Borderline	Dependent
Schizotypal	Histrionic	Obsessive-Compulsive
	Narcissistic	Passive-Aggressive

Diagnostic and Statistical Manual - III-R (DSM-III-R)

Personality Disorders

In describing an individual's personality, we may think of traits that describe the individual's way of behaving, experiencing life, and interaction in interpersonal relationships. Most personality traits have both adaptive and maladaptive qualities or features. For example, being very logical and organized may have adaptive value in certain occupations but may limit one's capacity to be experiential and emotionally expressive, especially in interpersonal situations. Likewise, a highly creative, artistic, and emotional individual might not be ideally suited to a situation or occupation requiring logical, politically sensitive, and decisive action. We all have a mix of various personality traits that define us as individuals. When personality traits are persistently maladaptive and lead to chronic difficulty in interpersonal, occupational, and social functioning, there is a personality disorder. Currently, the *Psychiatric Diagnostic and Statistical Manual* recognizes eleven personality disorders. Some of the criteria for each of these personality disorders may overlap somewhat (see *figure 9.6*).

Difficulty Managing Emotions

Certainly one common precipitant of drug and alcohol abuse is difficulty managing one's emotions. We might expect that persons with personality disorders have significantly more difficulty managing their emotions and abuse drugs/alcohol more regularly. This is certainly quite clear with borderline and antisocial personality disorders, if not to some degree with all of the personality disorders. In fact, substance abuse is incorporated into the diagnostic criteria of both the borderline and the antisocial personality disorders. Interestingly, borderline and antisocial personality disorders have genetic relationships to each other and to alcohol dependence.

Antisocial Personality Disorder

Patients with antisocial personality disorder lack empathy for others and feel no genuine sense of guilt or remorse for violations against others' rights or property. Such individuals have a remarkably self-centered view of the world and have a low frustration tolerance. They typically have great difficulty delaying gratification. They are often impulsive and defy authority. The great majority of patients meeting criteria for this diagnosis are male and many of them had learning disabilities or attention deficit symptoms as children. Drug and alcohol abuse typically began during early adolescence and rapidly progressed. The pattern of heavy use then typically occurs in the early to mid twenties, and is maintained into the thirties and forties.

Treatment of antisocial personality disorder itself is remarkably unsuccessful. Yet treatment of antisocial addicts has been more successful, especially through the twelve step recovery network of AA, NA, and other self-help meetings. The twelve steps of AA and NA give antisocial addicts a foundation of principles by which to guide their lives. Group therapy with stronger peer pressure and support has also been beneficial with antisocial addicts.

Borderline Personality Disorder

Patients with borderline personality disorder have a marked instability of mood and often form intense interpersonal attachments. They typically feel abandoned and rejected during instances of real or perceived interpersonal loss. Many borderline patients engage in repeated self-destructive or suicidal acts during episodes of intense depression and despair. Theoretical explanations of the origin of this personality disorder range from developmental to biochemical explanations. In all probability, the condition is a result of both nature and nurture (i.e., inadequate bonding and parenting during early years and a genetic predisposition). Most clinicians agree that borderline patients have a great deal of difficulty regulating their degree of attachment to others. They want the closeness and trust that intimacy brings but fear the dependency, vulnerability, and possible rejection that may occur. Not surprisingly, these patients have a high incidence of chemical dependency as they attempt to blunt the intensity of their emotions by using drugs/alcohol. They are especially prone to becoming dependent on addicting prescription drugs such as benzodiazepines. Their impulsivity, frequent thoughts of suicide, and substance abuse make them especially at risk when prescribed psychiatric medication. Many psychiatric medications are lethal when taken in amounts only five to ten times the usual dosage, especially if the individual is already toxic with alcohol or drugs.

Abstinence from drugs/alcohol is essential in treating borderline patients as their already fragile mood stability is quite sensitive to drugs/alcohol. Such patients generally need psychotherapy. When medication management is indicated, doctors commonly prescribe antidepressant or mood-cycling agents although low dose antipsychotic medication is also fairly commonly prescribed. Which medication the patient receives depends on the clinical symptoms that are most troublesome.

Psychotic Illnesses

The term *psychotic* refers to a number of severe psychiatric symptoms. The most notable of which includes hallucinations, delusions, or disorganization of thinking. Such symptoms can occur in a number of psychiatric diagnoses. At one point such symptoms were thought to inevitably point to a diagnosis of schizophrenia, but this condition is just one of many that can occur. A complete discussion of the psychoses and their management is beyond the scope of this chapter. Nonetheless, several general principles discussed in previous sections of this chapter apply to these diagnoses:

1. It is difficult to diagnose a psychotic illness during active drug use, since various intoxication or withdrawal states can produce literally any psychotic symptoms from paranoia to hallucinations to irrational behavior.
2. It is quite uncommon to find a patient with a pure psychotic disorder because most patients have had some involvement with drugs/alcohol.
3. Management of psychotic illnesses, like other psychiatric syndromes, is greatly complicated by any concurrent use of alcohol or drugs.
4. Community mental health centers and other treatment providers have ongoing difficulty maintaining patients in any treatment protocol while patients take drugs.
5. Patients typically discontinue medication when they relapse, thus further aggravating the underlying clinical condition.
6. As is the case with anxiety and mood disorders, many patients may be maintained without medication when they are sober and many patients are misdiagnosed because of their drug/alcohol use.

Summary

In this chapter we have discussed the significant overlap in symptoms between chemical dependency and many psychiatric conditions. Because use and abuse of addicting drugs can aggravate symptoms of an underlying psychiatric condition, treatment needs to be based on a thorough evaluation of the entire clinical picture.

The case studies in this chapter have illustrated typical clinical scenarios and highlighted the principles used in evaluating and treating dual disorder patients. The case studies placed a particular emphasis on dual disorders involving anxiety disorders and mood (affective) disorders. As we learn more about the biological underpinnings of psychiatric disorders and chemical dependencies, our ability to diagnose and treat these conditions will improve. Recent developments have seen the identification of a biochemical basis for the high that various drugs produce. This may lead to a future development of agents that may block or alter the effect of these drugs.

Our ability to become more specific in treatment of certain conditions will also improve as we understand more of the specific biochemistry involved. One example is the recent emergence of fluoxetine (Prozac) as a drug that specifically affects serotonin activity in the brain and not other neurotransmitters. Serotonin has been implicated in the pathophysiology of obsessive-compulsive disorder, eating disorders, certain subtypes of depression and alcoholism. Some patients who received only marginal benefit from other drugs are now able to attain a greater degree of clinical improvement with this serotonin specific agent. Undoubtedly, in the future other specific agents will emerge to improve our ability to treat a variety of conditions.

The task and challenge to those in the mental health and chemical dependency fields will be to keep abreast of developments in each field that enhance diagnosis and treatment. With advancements in biotechnology and genetic mapping, we may ultimately be able to develop practical, clinical diagnostic tests for psychiatric disorders and chemical dependencies.

References

American Psychological Association. *Psychiatric Diagnostic and Statistical Manual III-R.* Washington, D.C.: American Psychological Association, 1987.

Bauer, Anne. "Dual Diagnosis Patients: The State of the Problem." The Information Exchange (TIEUNES), A Quarterly Bulletin. Published by the Information Exchange on Young Adult Chronic Patients, Inc. Vol. 9, no. 3 (July 1987): 1-4, 8.

Masterson, James. *Psychotherapy of the Borderline Adult—A Developmental Approach.* New York: Brunner/Mazel, 1976.

Regier, Darrel A., et al. "Commorbidity of Mental Disorders with Alcohol and Other Drug Abuse: Results from the Epidemiologic Catchment Area (ECA) Study." *Journal of American Medical Association* 264, no. 19 (November 1990): 2511–18.

U.S. Department of Health and Human Services. "Helpful Facts about Depressive Illnesses." Pamphlet by DIART (Depression Awareness, Recognition, and Treatment), NIMH, Rockville, Md.

Treatment and Relapse Prevention of Drug/ Alcohol Addiction

This chapter gives a balanced overview of drug/alcohol treatment while placing major emphasis on relapse prevention. Sobriety and abstinence from drugs/alcohol is an ongoing process. Recovery is a life-long process involving not only addicts/alcoholics but also their entire family systems.

Chapter Goals

1. Identify the key elements of Alcoholics Anonymous (AA) and its advantages in drug/alcohol recovery. Also identify some problems people have with self-help meetings.
2. List some other self-help meetings in addition to AA.
3. Clarify the inappropriate application of psychoanalysis during early drug/alcohol recovery.
4. Describe appropriate treatment for early, middle, and later stages of drug/alcohol recovery.
5. Identify behavioral, cognitive, emotional, and relational symptoms in each stage of drug/alcohol recovery using Rawson's model.
6. Describe the four basic drug/alcohol treatment modalities of the 1970s.
7. Identify the factors that contributed to disinterest in the four treatment modalities in the late 1970s.
8. Describe the development of the insurance-reimbursed twenty-eight to thirty-day inpatient alcohol treatment program.
9. Clarify the impact the cocaine epidemic had on drug/alcohol treatment modalities.
10. Identify the problems and methods in engaging the addict/alcoholic into treatment.
11. Outline the various drug/alcohol treatment modalities.
12. Discuss the problems and issues involved in controlled drinking as a treatment goal.
13. Explain the importance of relapse prevention as part of the drug/alcohol recovery cycle.
14. Clarify the differences between a relapse-prone and recovery-prone orientation by the recovering addict/alcoholic.
15. Identify the three stages in changing a habit according to Marlatt.
16. Identify and explain the factors that make the recovering addict/alcoholic prone to relapse.
17. Define cravings and identify the relapse prevention approach to cravings.
18. Give some examples of triggers that cause craving for drugs/alcohol.
19. Describe how alcohol can induce a drug relapse.
20. Explain the key elements to deal with in relapse prevention.
21. Identify the advantages and drawbacks of structure in drug/alcohol recovery.
22. Identify the key elements in a good drug/alcohol recovery plan.

Self-Help Meetings

It's appropriate to start this chapter on treatment with the most widely utilized approach for recovery from alcoholism and drug addiction—self-help groups.

Alcoholics Anonymous

Alcoholics Anonymous (AA) was founded in the early 1930s by Bill W., a stockbroker, and Bob S., a surgeon. Both of these men found that willpower alone was not enough to keep them from using alcohol. After admitting to each other their common disease and shared frustration with alcohol recovery, they discovered that they could help one another to remain sober through mutual support. They soon discovered that others had the same experiences in struggling with recovery from alcoholism, and the movement was begun. Small groups of alcoholics met on a regular basis to share their experience, strength, hope, and support for one another. In 1938, the basic principles of AA were first outlined as the now famous Twelve Steps.

Regardless of one's biases, Alcoholics Anonymous has been the most successful program of recovery to date. There are AA meetings every day in almost every city and town in the United States. Throughout other parts of the world, more than ninety countries have AA meetings. The fellowship crosses all religious and racial barriers; the only requirement for membership is a desire to stop drinking. In July 1990, more than 45,000 people from the United States and other countries attended the AA national convention in Seattle, Washington.

> "There are no dues or fees for A.A. membership; they are self-supporting through their own contributions. A.A. is not allied with any sect, denomination, politics, organization, or institution; does not wish to engage in any controversy; neither endorses nor opposes any causes. Our primary purpose is to stay sober and help other alcoholics to achieve sobriety" (Alcoholics Anonymous 1978).

Advantages of AA as a Recovery Model

Lawson, Peterson, and Lawson (1983) identified the following key factors that contribute to the success of AA as a recovery model:

1. Mutual sharing by members provides solutions to alcohol-related problems and helps alleviate guilt by showing members that others have acted irrationally also.

The Twelve Steps

1. We admitted we were powerless over alcohol—that our lives had become unmanageable.
2. Came to believe that a Power greater than ourselves could restore us to sanity.
3. Made a decision to turn our will and our lives over to the care of God as we understood Him.
4. Made a searching and fearless moral inventory of ourselves.
5. Admitted to God, to ourselves, and to another human being the exact nature of our wrongs.
6. Were entirely ready to have God remove all these defects of character.
7. Humbly asked Him to remove our shortcomings.
8. Made a list of all persons we had harmed and became willing to make amends to them.
9. Made direct amends to such people wherever possible, except when to do so would injure them or others.
10. Continued to take personal inventory and when we were wrong, promptly admitted to it.
11. Sought through prayer and meditation to improve our conscious contact with God as we understand Him, praying only for knowledge of His will for us and the power to carry that out.
12. Having had a spiritual awakening as the result of these steps, we tried to carry this mesage to alcoholics and practice these principles in all our affairs.

2. Provision of a regular support group of individuals working toward the goal of abstinence.
3. Frequent and regular meetings to help members structure their time.
4. Availability of AA as an adjunct to other treatments such as counseling and psychotherapy.
5. Absence of membership fees and nondiscrimination by race, sex, or socioeconomic status.
6. Establishment of comprehensive goals covering the emotional, behavioral, and spiritual life of the members.

A number of studies have found favorable treatment outcomes from participation in AA (Armor et al. 1978; Bateman and Peterson 1971; Browne-Mayers et al. 1973; Kish and Herman 1971 and others). In 1965, a study by Robson, Paulus, and Clarke found that 71 percent of regular AA attendees improved and 57 percent improved from attending no more than ten meetings.

Despite these figures, treatment programs that are exclusively AA-oriented without the incorporation of other treatment methods and modalities have been less effective. Costello and associates (1976) found that the effectiveness of intermediate care was doubled (18–36 percent) when the unit converted from an exclusively AA-oriented model to a program with many treatment methods, AA being one of them.

Problems with AA and Other Self-Help Groups

Many individuals are resistant to attending self-help groups for a variety of reasons:

1. Difficulty with the concept of a higher power, or references to God
2. Lack of tolerance by self-help members, at times, to:
   a. use medication for affective or feeling disorders and other psychological conditions
   b. help understand that there are different types of alcoholism
   c. reject treatment (therapy and other treatment modalities)
3. People are uncomfortable in group settings and are concerned with the group maintaining strict confidentiality
4. The disruptive influence of some people (especially court-referred) who don't have a true desire to be sober.

Despite these drawbacks, which can be overcome, AA and other self-help meetings have been a positive and extremely beneficial source of inspiration and hope for millions of recovering alcoholics/addicts.

Application of Self-Help for Other Problems

Other self-help groups have adapted the AA twelve-step model for a variety of problems. These groups include:

NA—Narcotics Anonymous
CA—Cocaine Anonymous
MA—Marijuana Anonymous
Al-Anon—for family members of alcoholics

Narcanon—for family members of drug addicts
Alateen and Alatot—for teenagers and youngsters of alcoholics
ACA—for Adult Children of Alcoholics
FA—Families Anonymous
OA—Overeaters Anonymous
CODA—Co-Dependents Anonymous

There are self-help meetings for survivors of incest and sexual abuse; meetings for those addicted to gambling or compulsive sexuality; meetings to help those having problems with spending and those grieving the loss of a child. There are even self-help groups for people suffering from similar physical, psychological, and emotional conditions. In California, while working in a community mental health center, I ran across a group for people suffering from manic-depressive disorders. The group appropriately called itself the "Ups and Downs Group". Whatever the condition, the self-help model is being applied as a successful treatment modality, especially when it is integrated with a variety of other treatment modalities. Drug/alcohol self-help meetings are the most widely used modality for recovery from alcoholism and drug addiction.

Role of the Psychiatric Model in Alcohol/Drug Treatment

In developing a perspective on alcohol/drug treatment, it is helpful to understand what treatment is inappropriate and why it is. Not long ago psychoanalytically trained therapists maintained that they could cure alcoholics/addicts. Psychoanalysts tended to approach drug/alcohol users with the fixed, often rigid perception that all addicts had personality and/or affective disorders such as narcissism, depression, manic-depression, borderline, and others. The psychoanalysts then tried to treat alcoholics/addicts by personality reorganization, and lumped all of the disorders together. The psychoanalysts attempted to show the addicts that the etiology of their drinking/drugging, was due to personality disorders. "Analysts had unreal expectations of their patients, such as that they could give up their drug use immediately while in therapy, come in at fixed times, fit into the fifty-minute sessions, and adhere to the requirements of therapy" (Brill 1981).

Probing into feelings so early in recovery often caused addicts/alcoholics to reexperience traumatic emotional issues that they were not emotionally ready or capable of dealing

"Basically what I hear you saying, Mr. Smith, is 'Help!' "

with. As a result, addicts/alcoholics did what they had done before when feeling emotionally vulnerable—went back to using drugs/alcohol.

Unfortunately, this treatment still continues today, as professionals try to validate their theoretical models, without insight into when and how it is appropriate to deal with underlying issues and feelings. These psychoanalytical issues are best dealt with when addicts/alcoholics have maintained a significant period of sobriety (usually one to five years), have a strong support system, have the ego strength to tolerate the feelings, and have the insight and motivation to work on these issues. This happens during stage three of drug/alcohol treatment as table 10.1 shows.

TABLE 10.1
Stages of Drug/Alcohol Treatment

Stage of Treatment	Patient Status	Treatment
1	"I can't drink." (need for external control)	Alcohol detoxification, directive psychotherapy, AA, Al-Anon, family therapy, Antabuse.
2	"I won't drink." (internalized control)	Directive psychotherapy, supportive psychotherapy, AA, consider discontinuing Antabuse.
3	"I don't have to drink." (conflict resolution)	Psychoanalytically oriented psychotherapy.

Recovering Alcoholics/Addicts

The abstinence model of recovery adheres to the concept that addicts/alcoholics are never cured, because they are only one joint, fix, pill, or drink away from a full-blown return to addiction. That is why alcoholics/addicts refer to themselves as recovering rather than recovered. There is no cure for alcoholism/addiction.

Stages of Drug/Alcohol Recovery

Richard Rawson and associates (1988) outlined five basic stages of cocaine recovery that also apply to drug/alcohol recovery. The time periods vary from individual to individual and vary based on the kinds of drugs/alcohol used. The stages are

0–15 days—Withdrawal
16–45 days—Honeymoon
46–120 days—The Wall
121–180 days—Adjustment
181 + days—Resolution

Withdrawal Stage

Most of the physical aspects of withdrawal clear up after three to seven days. Emotional feelings of anxiety, fatigue, pain, and depression persist throughout the first fifteen days. Patients require education and direction during this withdrawal phase. Frequently, once patients go through the initial physical withdrawal, they want to leave treatment to avoid the emotional issues. (See table 10.2.)

TABLE 10.2
Withdrawal Stage (0–15 Days)

Behavioral Symptoms	Cognitive Symptoms	Emotional Symptoms	Relationships
Increased need for sleep Behavioral inconsistency Impulsive, erratic behavior Anergia (lack of energy)	Difficulty concentrating Cravings for drugs/alcohol Short-term memory disruption	Depression Anxiety Self-doubt Shame	Hostility Confusion Maladaptive coping responses (inappropriate actions and behavior) Fear

From Rawson, Richard A., Obert, Jeanne L., McCann, Michael J., Smith, Donald P., and Ling, Walter, "Neurobiological Treatment for Cocaine Dependency," in *Journal of Psychoactive Drugs,* 1990, 22, 159–171. Reprinted by permission.

Honeymoon Stage

The honeymoon stage is the opposite of the withdrawal stage. The neophyte to recovery has gone through the difficult withdrawal stage and now feels energetic, confident, and optimistic. Cravings for drugs/alcohol are usually reduced and moods improve. This may lead clients to believe that recovery is easier than they thought it would be. Unwittingly they begin to stray from those elements of their recovery program that helped them stay sober. Their behavior becomes more unstructured, inconsistent, and at times frenetic. They may go through a manic cycle, doing many things and overextending themselves. These behaviors then disupt their recovery from drugs/alcohol. This is the time when patients are most at risk to return to alcohol use, marijuana use, or other drug use. They may convince themselves that they had a problem with a particular drug, not that they are at risk with all drugs/alcohol. (See table 10.3.)

The Wall Stage

After forty-five days of sobriety, the largest percentage of relapses to drugs/alcohol occur. Personal and interpersonal issues are emotionally experienced more fully during this stage. Relapse vulnerability increases as patients start feeling these emotional issues and begin to further sort out some of the problems in their lives and in their relationships. Patients often get discouraged and may verbalize that they "feel this will go on indefinitely." Patients may lose hope, strength, and motivation to continue in their process of recovery. This is a time when the supportive elements of their recovery

TABLE 10.3
Honeymoon Stage (16–45 Days)

Behavioral	Cognitive	Emotional	Relationships
High energy (perhaps manic) Poorly directed behavior Excessive work and/or play Return to alcohol, marijuana, or other drug use	Inability to prioritize Abbreviated tension span Inability to recognize relapse potential	Optimism Overconfidence Feelings of being cured	Denial of addiction disorder Desire for things to return to normal Conflict between spouse or partner, family, and treatment

From Rawson, Richard A., Obert, Jeanne L., McCann, Michael J., Smith, Donald P., and Ling, Walter, "Neurobiological Treatment for Cocaine Dependency," in *Journal of Psychoactive Drugs,* 1990, 22, 159–171. Reprinted by permission.

TABLE 10.4
The Wall Stage (46–120 Days)

Behavioral	Cognitive	Emotional	Relationships
Sluggishness, anergia (lack of energy) Sexual disinterest/dysfunction Insomnia Discontinuation of treatment, recreational, exercise, diet, and/or occupationally appropriate behaviors Resumption of alcohol, marijuana, and/or other drug use	Cognitive rehearsal of relapse, thinking, planning, or playing over the idea of relapse Euphoric recall, remembering the feelings and good times of drug/alcohol use Increased frequency of drug/alcohol thoughts, dreams, and cravings Denying or rationalizing emotional feelings and reactions Difficulty concentrating	Depression Anxiety Fatigue Boredom Anhedonia (inability to feel pleasure with things that normally give pleasure) Irritability	Mutual blaming Irritability Devaluation of progress Threatened separation or expulsion from home

From Rawson, Richard A., Obert, Jeanne L., McCann, Michael J., Smith, Donald P., and Ling, Walter, "Neurobiological Treatment for Cocaine Dependency," in *Journal of Psychoactive Drugs,* 1990, 22, 159–171. Reprinted by permission.

program need to be strengthened, even though patients may attempt to alienate those who can help. Group counseling can be especially helpful at this stage. Others in the group who have gone through this difficult stage can share their struggle and ultimate success and lend support. (See table 10.4.)

TABLE 10.5
Adjustment Stage (121–180 Days)

Behavioral	Cognitive	Emotional	Relationships
Return to activities that may have been inappropriate and had relapse potential in early stages Return to normal behavior	Reduced frequency of drug/alcohol thoughts, dreams, and cravings	Reduced depression, anxiety, irritability Continued boredom Loneliness	Emergence of long-term relationship problems Resistance to assistance with relationship problems

From Rawson, Richard A., Obert, Jeanne L., McCann, Michael J., Smith, Donald P., and Ling, Walter, "Neurobiological Treatment for Cocaine Dependency," in *Journal of Psychoactive Drugs,* 1990, 22, 159–171. Reprinted by permission.

TABLE 10.6
Resolution Stage (181 + days)

Behavioral	Cognitive	Emotional	Relationship
Emergence of other excessive behavior patterns: gambling, sex, work, eating, alcohol use	Questioning the need for long-term monitoring and support	Emergence of psychodynamic material Boredom with abstinence	Conflict between recovery principles and relationship needs

From Rawson, Richard A., Obert, Jeanne L., McCann, Michael J., Smith, Donald P., and Ling, Walter, "Neurobiological Treatment for Cocaine Dependency," in *Journal of Psychoactive Drugs,* 1990, 22, 159–171. Reprinted by permission.

Adjustment Stage

The achievement of working through the intense feelings of The Wall stage gives patients new hope and energy for recovery. Patients begin to accept that this is a lifelong struggle. The achievement of being sober for 120 or more days affirms the addicts' ability to be sober for a long time. This is the longest time that most patients have ever been sober. (See table 10.5.)

Resolution Stage

Completion of an intensive six-month program signals a shift from learning new skills to monitor for relapse signs, maintaining a balanced life-style, and developing new areas of interest. Some clients may need individual psychotherapy or relationship work. (See table 10.6.)

After Resolution Stage

After the resolution stage, the individual may need to do more in-depth counseling on family of origin and family systems issues. Issues of underlying affective disorders and other psychiatric disorders may also be more fully explored during this stage.

Effective Treatment

The factor most predictive of drug/alcohol treament success is the counselor's attitude about treatment. When counselors truly believe that they can help patients, and have the necessary insight and training, treatment tends to be more successful. The same holds true for treatment programs.

Drug Addiction Treatment, 1970–1980

The four basic kinds of treatment that had federal, state, and local government support in the 1970s were

1. therapeutic communities
2. outpatient methadone clinics
3. outpatient drug-free programs
4. university-affiliated clinical research centers

Therapeutic Communities

In 1958, Synanon was established as a model for most therapeutic communities, and the approach was expanded to other programs including Day Top Village, Phoenix House, and Odyssey House in New York, and Delancey Street and The Family in California.

By 1978, a national organization, Therapeutic Communities of America, was organizing and unifying the goals of more than 300 therapeutic communities.

These communities were essentially residential programs, where addicts/alcoholics lived together in a family atmosphere that promoted

- addicts helping addicts to recovery in a structured life-style
- confrontational and group therapies
- adherence to the principles of AA and the twelve steps
- honesty, drug abstinence, self-reliance, and personal responsibility through example.

Methadone Treatment

The monumental methadone treatment work of Dole and Nyswander (1965) became a treatment model that spread throughout the United States. In 1980, forty-eight out of fifty states had methadone treatment programs.

Dole and Nyswander believed that heroin addiction was a metabolic disease and that a single administration of a narcotic could change a person's metabolism. Therefore, multiple administrations of the narcotic would have even more potency in changing the person's nervous system. Dole and Nyswander searched for a medication that would replace the metabolic need and craving for opiates (heroin). They found methadone, a long-acting orally administered drug that eliminates the craving for heroin and other opioids. By successfully reducing the need for heroin, methadone reduces the antisocial, crime-related behavior of many addicts.
cial, crime-related behavior of many addicts.

Methadone treatment involved detoxification and maintenance. **Detoxification** helped patients to gradually reduce their dependence on opiates by giving them decreasing doses of methadone over twenty-one days. After detoxification, the individual was then drug free.

Maintenance essentially helped addicts to develop a productive nondrug-using life-style. In effect, methadone replaced the devastating addiction to heroin and other opiates. Methadone does not affect the pleasure centers as do opiates, and addicts do not experience highs. The craving for heroin is stopped with the rather benign dependence on methadone. There is still some controversy with methadone maintenance because addicts are still dependent on another drug—methadone.

The treatment methods in both methadone detoxification and methadone maintenance include individual and group education, counseling sessions, self-help twelve-step recovery, and rehabilitative services.

Outpatient Programs

A variety of outpatient treatment clinics existed in the 1970s and 1980s including medically supervised programs and storefront centers. Medically supervised programs provided crisis-oriented medical services for drug/alcohol detoxification and overdose. At storefront drop-in/crisis counseling centers, treatment was unstructured, often focusing on crisis intervention, legal and criminal justice counseling, medical care and/or health-related services, welfare and social services, employment, and family and interpersonal problems. The outpatient clinics served as a community-based entry point into the health care system for drug users in low-income communities.

University Research Centers

The drug revolution of the 1960s saw some significant changes. Drug use was no longer confined to inner-city, lower socioeconomic groups. When drugs began affecting the campus population, government spending increased for drug/alcohol research and treatment. During this same period, the government foresaw that large numbers of soldiers returning from Vietnam would need treatment for heroin addiction.

As a result, university-based research treatment centers opened, and many affiliated with the Veterans Administration. These centers tested new pharmacological aids. They evaluated medications such as naltrexone, propoxyphene, levo-alpha-acetylmethadol (LAAM), and clonidine, for treatment of opiate craving and addiction.

Disinterest in Drug/Alcohol Treatment

In the late 1970s public interest in therapeutic communities, methadone treatment, outpatient programs, and university research centers seemed to wane. A variety of factors caused this loss of interest. First, the anticipated epidemic of heroin addicts returning from Vietnam was not realized. Many returning soldiers withdrew from heroin on the long boat and plane ride back home. For many of these young men, heroin use was inconsistent with their life-styles back home. Others did not have the connections at home to maintain their addiction to heroin. Most discontinued opiate use without significant involvement in the treatment system.

Second, a dramatic reduction took place in the use of hallucinogens, sedative-hypnotics, and amphetamines. The primary nonopiate drugs used by the white population shifted primarily to marijuana and cocaine. At the time, the treatment community and general public thought marijuana and cocaine had a low risk for dependency. Most experts were still referring to marijuana and cocaine as psychologically dependency producing rather than addicting. That mistake caused one of the major drug problems of the 1980s.

Third, the confrontive strategies of some therapeutic communities got out of control. Many therapeutic communities were exposed as dysfunctional systems much like the addicts/alcoholics' dysfunctional families of origin. Fourth, there was also opposition and public disenchantment with methadone maintenance on the principle that rather than recovering, heroin addicts were addicted to a new drug—methadone.

Fifth, the efficacy and success of drop-in counseling centers was questioned. The criminal justice system was often in conflict with these centers because clients were shielded or protected from criminal prosecution. Funding misappropriation and failure to adequately document client charts created tremendous conflict between centers and various government funding sources.

> Due to these developments, public interest in drug addiction problems decreased by the late 1970s. Although a treatment network had been established and some promising new treatments were in development, there appeared to be a societal loss of interest in drug addiction treatment. The one drug problem that obviously was going to persist was heroin. However, heroin was predominately a lower-income, inner-city, minority problem. Since middle-class Americans did not appear to be significantly at risk from heroin problems, there was to be a loss of commitment to continued funding for new treatments. Funding levels in many of the programs dropped, resulting in a reduction in treatment slots and a reduction in ancillary services for the remaining slots. Research funding decreased and many of the clinical strategies developed during the 1970s were put on the back burner. As the 1980s began, the drug treatment system appeared to have lost momentum (Rawson 1990).

Alcohol Treatment, 1970–1980

Private commercial, inpatient and residential twenty-eight to thirty-day treatment programs were rapidly expanding during the 1970s. Their tremendous financial success caused these programs to become a major standard of alcohol treatment. The twenty-eight to thirty-day length of stay was developed as a standard not as a result of empirical study, but instead as the negotiated arrangement between the hospital-based inpatient providers and the insurance companies. These inpatient programs were also successful because they were modeled after AA twelve-step principles and integrated AA self-help meetings as part of the program.

When Betty Ford entered an alcohol treatment facility, public disclosure of her alcoholism did much to bring this kind of treatment into public view and acceptance (Ford 1984). "Her forthright discussion of her alcoholism and addiction and subsequent sponsorship of the Betty Ford Treatment Center provided a turning point in the alcoholism field'' (Rawson 1990).

Changes in the 1980s

Cocaine Epidemic

The explosive emergence of cocaine addiction in the 1980s challenged the drug/alcohol treatment system to develop new treatment strategies. In 1984, Mark Gold described cocaine as a major public health concern. What experts thought was a rather benign, psychologically dependency producing drug became known as the most addicting drug to date.

Animal studies, human studies, and clinical human reports, all validate cocaine as the most highly addicting drug. Thus, warnings to not just try it even once are not scare tactics but frightening reality. The late Sidney Cohen, the most prolific writer in the drug field, predicted in the early 1980s that ''if cocaine were readily available and inexpensive, this would create the biggest drug epidemic we had ever known.'' His prediction has come true with crack cocaine.

In the early 1980s, there were no treatment programs for cocaine addiction. This new addict population, however, soon found treatment at inpatient alcohol treatment facilities. Facility directors responded to the need by developing cocaine treatment programs. Financial reward motivated these inpatient facilities that saw a tremendous treatment population developing. Their television commercials added taglines stating ''We treat cocaine addiction, too.'' The constant flow of sports figures, celebrities, and other public figures further created an attractive notoriety for these treatment programs.

The cocaine epidemic was even further catapulted into the public consciousness with the development of freebase cocaine. In the mid-1980s crack cocaine use made cocaine available to all socioeconomic levels. Crack cocaine was marketed to new populations: those who could not afford cocaine in the inner city and young people. ''Smokable cocaine, preprocessed in ready-to-smoke dosage units flooded major American cities from 1985 to today. Use of the drug in this form produced addiction very rapidly, and the availability of the drug in lower-cost dosage units made cocaine available to lower-income users. This combination produced a fire storm of addiction among lower income, minority, inner-city residents'' (Rawson 1990).

Risk of AIDS

Exacerbating our crack cocaine epidemic is the AIDS crisis. The fact that the AIDS virus can be spread by high-risk sexual practices and the sharing of needles used to inject drugs has identified intravenous drug users as high risk for the spread of the HIV virus.

Future Treatment Trends

Some research has indicated that intensive outpatient drug/alcohol treatment is as effective as inpatient treatment. Ritson (1968) found no significant difference in effectiveness between inpatient and outpatient alcoholism treatment programs and questioned the routine hospitalization of alcoholics.

Due to the high cost of inpatient treatment, the trend in the 1990s may be outpatient treatment. Instead of the expensive, traditional hospital-based twenty-eight-day inpatient drug/alcohol treatment program, the alternative is intensive outpatient programs for 30–180 days. This is a more appropriate recovery period because it allows support during the time when the recovering addict/alcoholic is most vulnerable to relapse. It also minimizes the costly aspects of inpatient hospitalization.

Engaging Alcoholics/Addicts in Treatment

"Since the addictive alcoholic patient is fundamentally hostile, his behavior is unconsciously designed to arouse negative feelings and to invite retaliation. Hostility and retaliation must be constantly guarded against by all treatment personnel" (Chafetz 1970). Many mental health counselors are uncomfortable working with addicts/alcoholics because of the hostility and resistance of drug/alcohol patients in complying with treatment. The addict/alcoholic's grandiosity and denial of reality causes them to always be just one step away from terminating treatment and to rationalize away the need for change. "The pervasive hopelessness that some clients feel regarding themselves and their lives is apt to be projected into the treatment process and the counseling relationship, so that the client feels, 'This is useless; it isn't going to get me anywhere' " (Marks, Daroff, and Granick 1987).

Breaking through denial and the evasive tactics of addicts/alcoholics and their families requires a special kind of counselor. Duncan Stanton described that counselor as needing to be energetic to engage clients/patients and their families into treatment.

Addicts and alcoholics are constantly testing counselors by pushing boundaries and testing to see if counselors know what they are talking about. Denial is the defense mechanism of addiction; addicts/alcoholics wonder if counselors are strong enough to break through their denial system.

Due to shameful feelings about self, addicts/alcoholics naturally seek or provoke rejection, hostility, anger, frustration, and even rage. Addicts/alcoholics test the counselor, as they do everyone in their own family systems. If counselors become provoked, addicts/alcoholics can play familiar "bad child at odds with authority" roles.

To effectively engage addicts/alcoholics and their families in treatment, counselors must exhibit a combination of both patience and boundary setting. Counselors need to be powerful yet sensitive, while recognizing both the need for limit setting and the inner vulnerability and sensitivities of the patients. Counselors must establish control of the therapeutic process, while being flexible to the patients' weak ego strength and sensitivity to shame.

Group treatment, group counseling, and self-help groups are effective treatment modalities because addicts/alcoholics can be confronted in a caring way by other addicts/alcoholics. Each person in the group observes other group members doing better. The struggles of each group member can be a tremendous source of encouragement, strength, hope, and support.

Drug/Alcohol Treatment Modalities

A treatment **modality** is a kind of classification of treatment such as twenty-eight-day inpatient or six-month intensive outpatient treatment. A modality is not to be confused with a treatment method (i.e., journaling your feelings, writing down your dreams, exercising on a regular basis, or methods to control anger). Each treatment modality utilizes a variety of treatment methods.

The treatment of drug/alcohol dependence and addiction utilizes a variety of treatment modalities. Each patient's personality is different and unique as is the function of drugs/alcohol in each person's life; therefore, they require different treatment approaches. A good drug/alcohol assessment can determine which treatment modality is best for each individual. The assumption that only one modality works and that each individual needs to be squeezed to fit into that modality is reminiscent of H. L. Mencken's statement that the solution to any problem that is simple is usually wrong.

This section describes some treatment modalities and the features of each. The modalities are arranged on a continuum from the least to most intensive treatment.

No Treatment

Those in the helping professions are justifiably eager to provide help. However, one needs to realize that some people do not need drug/alcohol treatment. Sometimes people may overreact to the use of alcohol and drugs, when in reality the use does not jeopardize the person's well-being and ability to function within the normal range of behavior. An overly zealous counselor may not conduct a thorough assessment and label a person as addict/alcoholic, or having a problem, when he/she does not. Perhaps providing information and outpatient counseling for the issues causing concern about the use of drugs or alcohol would be more appropriate than a program of drug/alcohol treatment.

Rarely does someone who doesn't have a problem seek help for a drug/alcohol problem but it does occur. If no treatment is recommended communicate this fact supportively, so the client does not feel neglected or discounted.

Education and Information

The general public is often misinformed when it comes to drugs/alcohol. Parents, children, family members, and users of drugs/alcohol have misconceptions and perceptual and informational problems in understanding alcoholism and drug addiction.

This text contains the kind of information that most people need in understanding drug/alcohol use, dependence, and addiction. For example, information on imbalanced family systems is invaluable in understanding alcoholism/addiction and the role family members may inadvertently play in the development of the disease.

Twenty-Four-Hour Helplines

The decision to get help for drug/alcohol problems is often spontaneous. When people wait until the next day, they often change their minds about getting help. The twenty-four-hour helpline is an invaluable service in getting persons to appropriate treatment. A combination of supervised, trained volunteers and paid professionals staff crisis lines. Most major cities and even smaller towns and cities have helplines. The helplines provide a variety of referral services—alcohol/drug treatment, adult children of alcoholics services, family therapy, support group referrals, or information about drug/alcohol detoxification. There are also hotlines and community services for other related crises: suicide prevention, child abuse, domestic violence, and others.

Crisis Intervention

Crisis intervention includes those agencies and professionals who provide physical, psychological, and interpersonal crisis care and counseling. Crisis intervention includes a wide range of services: the emergency room physician dealing with drug/alcohol overdose, the police officer calming alcohol/drug-related domestic violence, and the counselor working with the family in crisis. The crisis intervention modality is a short-term treatment with specific goals or outcomes. Once those goals are attained, the client is referred to the appropriate next step.

Drop-In Counseling Services

Drop-in counseling usually takes place in community-based drug/alcohol or mental health treatment centers. To better serve multiethnic groups, these centers have not adopted the traditional psychotherapy or clinical model of fifty-minute counseling sessions. The community-related slant of these programs is to establish a safe and appropriate place to get help with a variety of problems other than drugs/alcohol (e.g., health, welfare, housing, food stamps, employment, and community activities). "Some characteristics of programs offering these services are long hours, an extremely relaxed nonquestioning atmosphere, an environment conducive to 'hanging out', and as little distinction as possible between staff and clients (dress, manner, etc.). The assumption, of course, is that a relaxed atmosphere and flexibility of services will encourage clients to use the program" (Pittel 1975).

Despite a decrease in drop-in counseling centers as a treatment modality, a number of programs have drop-in counseling as a treatment method. Recreational centers where kids play sports and games, are often designed to provide opportunities for informal counseling.

Many school and community-based treatment programs have youth outreach workers who hang out in the community or school setting with kids and young adults. I remember one outreach worker who spent most of his time sitting at the local cemetery, which was the hangout for the kids who were getting high inhaling paint. Once they realized he wasn't an undercover cop, they began to talk. After a while he established a relationship with some of the kids and began to talk about alternatives.

Brief or Periodic Counseling

Periodic counseling involves from one to five counseling sessions to deal with the immediate issues and consequences of drug/alcohol use, dependence, and addiction. The client may periodically come back to counseling for the same or other drug/alcohol-related problems.

Short-Term Counseling

Short-term counseling emphasizes regularly established counseling appointments, and a shift away from the solution of immediate problems to more long-range treatment goals. Short-term counseling improves clients' ego strength, self-concept, and coping skills so that they can function more effectively and deal with issues and problems of drug/alcohol use in their lives.

Extended Individual Counseling

Extended individual counseling involves a year or more of weekly counseling sessions. The treatment methods and goals vary depending on the need of the patient and the framework in which the counselor works. There are various forms of counseling. Direct approaches provide suggestions and directives (i.e., tasks to be done outside of the counseling session), and therapeutic approaches focus more on the underlying motives.

The common goals of all counseling approaches are to educate, provide information and resources, catharsis (patients' release of emotion and feelings), connectedness and trust which facilitates disclosure of feelings and concerns, support for positive growth, awareness and insight, and personality change (reorganization). Counseling approaches explore both the conscious and the unconscious level of feelings. The Johari window in table 10.7 is a training model that describes the focus of counseling.

1. Public self: The public self includes all those aspects about the individual that are known by the individual and others close to the individual. (e.g., age, marital status, hobbies, job, interests, basic personality type, etc.)
2. Private self: The private self involves information that the individual is aware of but others don't know. (e.g., sexual practices, mistakes in the past or present, private feelings or thoughts, family of origin issues, etc.)
3. Blind self: The blind self includes those things the individual is not consciously aware of that others are aware of about the individual. (e.g., personality characteristics; denial about others' behavior or own behavior; lack of awareness of interpersonal, occupational, social, and marital issues.)
4. Discovery self: Discovery self is the category of the future. These things are not in the conscious awareness of the individual or others and will be discovered in the future. (e.g., the natural changes that occur in life's unexpected journey.)

TABLE 10.7
Johari Window

	Self	**Self**
	Things you know about self	*Things you don't know about self*
Others *Things they know about you*	1. Public	3. Blind
Others *Things they do not know about you*	2. Private	4. Discovery

Adapted from *Group Processes: An Introduction to Group Dynamics* by Joseph Luft by permission of Mayfield Publishing Company. Copyright © 1984, 1970, and 1963 by Joseph Luft.

Counseling focuses on all four of these areas of self. However, by placing a major emphasis in counseling on categories 2, the private self, and 3, the blind self, individuals can see changes in category 1, the public self, and category 4, the discovery self. When individuals are defensive or unwilling to deal with their feelings about their private selves and blind selves there are limitations to progress and personal change. Clients would do well to follow Louise Hay's (1984) advice: "If you think of the hardest thing for you to do and how much you resist it, then you're looking at your greatest lesson at the moment. Surrendering, giving up the resistance, and allowing yourself to learn what you need to learn, will make the next step easier."

Family Treatment

Peter Steinglass (1979) outlined five major family modalities for drug/alcohol treatment:

1. Pure family therapy is based on a family systems mode in which all family members are present at the same time in therapy sessions.
2. Individual or group treatment approaches fulfill specific criteria suggested by a family therapy theory of alcoholism, such as the concept of homeostasis.
3. Therapies involving concurrent therapeutic work with both the alcoholic and family members rely on a more traditional, individual, psychodynamic theoretical base.

4. Specific therapies designed for the spouses or partners of alcoholics.
5. Supportive treatments assist nonalcoholic family members in dealing with common problems related to having an alcoholic family member.

Some of the goals for the family treatment modality would be to

1. develop family commitment for recovery
2. identify enabling behaviors and counter them
3. encourage leveling or open communication
4. validate members reality and feelings regarding the chemical abusing member and the negative consequences of chemical abuse
5. educate the family to the family disease concept
6. elaborate concrete rules and consequences
7. plan and define family leisure activities
8. solidify the parental coalition
9. specify attitude and behavioral changes for each member
10. prepare relapse prevention guidelines and family response

According to Steinglass (1982), the advantages of a family systems approach are

1. It bridges the disparity between psychodynamic and stress reduction explanations of drinking.
2. It explains diversity in alcoholic families by redirecting the focus from finding common etiological characteristics in alcoholic families to the common function of alcohol to maintain imbalanced family systems.
3. It gives therapists an understanding of alcoholism as a total system's behavior.

Group Treatment

Educational Groups

Educational and study groups include any group activity focusing on education and information about drugs/alcohol, such as drug/alcohol prevention, parenting skills, self-discovery, family systems, classes on drug/alcohol intervention and treatment, or workshops and conferences.

Group Workshops

Group workshops are usually from one to five days long and focus on a particular skill, concept, or training to be developed or understood as a result of participation. Examples include workshops on drug/alcohol intervention, school-based drug prevention, drugs in the workplace, adolescent drug prevention, intervention and treatment strategies, or dual disorders.

Self-Help Groups

As we mentioned at the beginning of this chapter, self-help groups are modeled on Alcoholics Anonymous. Other groups include Narcotics Anonymous, Adult Children of Alcoholics, Co-Dependents Anonymous, and Al-Anon.

Peer-Led Support Groups

Peer-led support groups is a new and unique group modality. Usually, individuals who have gone through a common educational and/or training experience or counseling have discovered a common desire to continue working on these issues. They develop a peer-led support group. The major drawback to these groups in that expertise and leadership is peer-based making the group vulnerable to the strengths and weaknesses of the peer leader.

Educational/Therapeutic Groups

Educational/therapeutic groups are led by trained facilitators or counselors experienced in recovery issues. The group usually meets for one and a half hours, once a week. The group size can range from two to twenty members; their goal is to educate, counsel, and support one another for mutual recovery.

Group Therapy

Therapy groups have the same guidelines as individual counseling. Members adhere to strict confidentiality and do not socialize outside of group. The group's purpose is to provide a safe environment to explore individual and interpersonal issues.

Most therapy groups are led by professional counselors trained in group therapy and experienced in the dynamics of drug/alcohol recovery, family systems, and related areas of expertise. Some therapy groups have cotherapists, usually male-female counseling teams that colead and clarify issues in the group.

Most therapy groups focus around a specific recovery issue (e.g., adult children of alcoholics, recovery from drugs/alcohol, marital relationships, interpersonal issues, sexual violations). Most groups have from four to eight members to allow adequate opportunity for interaction by all group members.

Intensive Treatment

Intensive treatment modalities include intensive outpatient treatment, inpatient detoxification, and residential and inpatient treatment. These programs utilize a variety of treatment methods too lengthy to describe here.

Controlled Drinking

Widespread controversy has arisen over the issue of controlled drinking of alcohol. Controlled drinking has been defined as those experiencing problems with alcohol being taught to self-monitor their drinking and not returning to problem drinking. "With the trend has come a maelstrom of controversy. Many traditional figures in the alcoholism field have bitterly attacked the concept of controlled drinking, maintaining that a disease model and total abstinence represents the only true hope for alcoholics" (Miller 1980).

Ruth Fox (1967) has asserted that "Among my own approximately 3,000 patients, not one has been able to achieve moderate drinking, although almost every one of them has tried to."

Once someone has been diagnosed as being addicted to drugs/alcohol, experts would predominantly agree that a return to controlled drug or alcohol use is extremely difficult and could perhaps lead to a tragic outcome if pursued.

Proponents of controlled drinking agree with this position that controlled drinking is not a viable option for alcoholics, especially alcoholics already in successful abstinence recovery. They stress that controlled drinking is a viable treatment approach only for some problem drinkers.

Controlled drinking is only considered when individuals have a stable marital and occupational background and do not have a family history of alcoholism.

William Miller and G. R. Caddy (1977) identified controlled drinking as an appropriate treatment approach in situations involving resistant clients who view abstinence as unachievable or undesirable. The major criteria being (1) their refusal to consider abstinence as a goal; (2) their strong external demands to drink or lack of social support for abstinence; (3) an early-stage drinking problem without a history of physiological addiction; and (4) prior failure of competent abstinence-oriented treatment.

The problem with these criteria is that denial may be ignored. Almost every alcoholic/addict would like to continue using drugs/alcohol in a controlled fashion. Refusal to consider abstinence, failure in abstinence-oriented treatment, and preference for controlled drinking, may all be part of the addict/alcoholic's denial system.

Miller (1980) identified additional criteria that would favor choosing the abstinence model instead of moderation.

1. evidence of progressive liver disease or other medical problems
2. psychological problems of sufficient magnitude to render even moderate drinking harmful
3. a personal commitment to abstinence or strong external demands for abstinence
4. pathological intoxication
5. history of physiological addiction and severe withdrawal symptoms
6. use of medication considered dangerous when combined with alcohol
7. current successful abstinence following severe problem drinking
8. prior failure of competent moderation-oriented treatment.

Additional factors indicating at-risk factors for controlled drinking include addiction present, a family history of addiction, high-stress individual, high-stress life-style, inability to effectively cope with stress, and other relapse dynamics present, such as poor health, negative emotional states, or psychiatric problems.

Vernon Fox (1976) and others agree that abstinence remains the viable and conservative recommendation for alcohol/drug recovery while research and guidelines establish accurate means for identifying clients/patients appropriate for controlled drinking as an optimal treatment modality.

Relapse Prevention

In the 1970s, the issue of relapse—the addicts/alcoholics' return to drug/alcohol use—was not an integrated component of drug/alcohol treatment. The extremely high relapse rate was often justified as the client did not hit bottom or the patient wasn't ready for recovery. In many situations the relapse was in part due to the treatment program not giving adequate education, training, and counseling to prevent relapse.

The traditional inpatient, residential drug/alcohol treatment program has people leave the program after twenty-eight to thirty days. They leave because this is the usual time period that insurance companies have established as reimbursable. Unfortunately, the next 30 to 120 days is the time when alcoholics/addicts are most at risk for relapse. The initial glow of the alcoholics' first thirty days of recovery is soon

TABLE 10.8
Relapse Prone versus Recovery Prone

Denial and Evasion	**Recognition and Problem Solving**
Relapse Prone:	*Recovery Prone:*
Evade or deny the sticking point.	Recognize a problem exists.
Stress.	Accept that it is OK to have problems.
Compulsive behavior.	Detach to gain perspective.
Avoid others.	Ask for help.
Problems.	Respond with action when prepared.
Evade/deny new problems.	

Adapted with permission from Terence T. Gorski, *Counseling for Relapse Prevention.* Copyright © Independence Press, Division of Herald House, Independence, Missouri.

replaced with awareness of the reality of struggling to stay sober in the real world. After the first thirty days, the addict/alcoholic faces the first pivotal relapse point, or the wall. In the next ninety days, there are repeated situations that threaten the addicts' sobriety. "About two-thirds of relapses occur within the first 90 days following treatment" (i.e., between 30 and 120 days of sobriety) (Marlatt 1985).

Recognizing the Signs of Relapse

One must be trained to recognize the signs and problems that may cause relapse. (See table 10.8.) The defense mechanisms of denial (rationalization and minimization) may be invoked to avoid looking at the potential for relapse. Many addicts/alcoholics tend to discount stressful situations and distressful life-styles and behaviors that contribute to relapse. The addict/alcoholic trained in relapse prevention can recognize these problem areas and avoid being blindsided by high-risk relapse situations. (See table 10.9.)

Changing a Habit

Alan Marlatt (1985) decribed the following separate stages in changing a habit:

1. Preparation for change involves commitment, desire, and motivation to change.
2. Implementation of the specific behavioral change (e.g., such as to eat healthy, balanced meals or to stop using drugs/alcohol).
3. Maintenance of change in long-term goals.

TABLE 10.9
Analysis of Situations for Relapse

Situations	Example	n(sample)	Percent
Frustration/anger	Patient tried to call his wife (they were separated); she hung up on him; he became angry and took a drink.	14	29%
Social pressure	Patient went with the boys to a bar after work. They put pressure on him to join the crowd and he was unable to resist.	11	23
Intrapersonal temptation	Patient walked by a bar, and just unconsciously walked in for no real reason; could not resist the temptation to take a drink.	10	21
Negative emotional state	Patient living alone, no job; complained of feeling bored and useless; could see no reason why he should not take a drink.	5	10
Miscellaneous other situations	Patient reported that everything was going so well for him that he wanted to celebrate by having a drink.	5	10
No situation given or unable to remember		3	7

Source: (Marlatt 1985)

Marlatt quotes Mark Twain, who said, "Quitting smoking is easy, I've done it hundreds of times." Deciding to change a habit is easy. However, implementing the change is a bit more difficult, and maintaining change is the most difficult stage because it's an ongoing long-term goal.

For alcoholics/addicts the beginning step is admitting that they are powerless over drugs/alcohol and have the desire to stop using. Quitting is just the beginning of the journey while implementing the change by working a program of recovery is the next difficult step. Maintaining that program despite stressful situations and life events is the most difficult, day-at-a-time struggle for recovering addicts/alcoholics.

The first 120 days of drug/alcohol recovery are the most difficult because it is a significant period of time to establish a period of maintenance. Even after this primary period of maintenance, there is still no guarantee. Stressful situations, places, times, and interpersonal interactions may still cause a relapse. Even after one year of maintenance, there are

Drawing by Ed Arno; © 1980 The New Yorker Magazine, Inc.

Caution: relapse ahead

pressures as evidenced by the many addicts/alcoholics who have problems at their one-year anniversary of sobriety. After two to five years of maintaining sobriety, drug/alcohol use is not a choice for most, even during stressful periods.

Causes of Addict/ Alcoholic Relapses

A study by Marlatt (1985) identified three major categories that cause recovering alcoholics to be vulnerable to relapse:

1. Negative emotional states cause 35 percent of all relapses. In these situations, individuals experience negative or unpleasant emotional states, moods, or feelings such as frustration, anger, anxiety, depression, or boredom. (See table 10.10.)
2. Interpersonal conflict causes 16 percent of all relapses. These situations involve an ongoing or relatively recent conflict associated with any interpersonal relationship, such as marriage, friendship, family members, or employer-employee relations. Arguments and interpersonal confrontation occur frequently in this category. (See table 10.11.)
3. Social pressure causes 20 percent of all relapses. In these situations individuals respond to the influence of another person or group of people exerting pressure on them to engage in the taboo behavior. (See table 10.12.)

TABLE 10.10
Negative Emotional States

Difficulty Managing Negative Emotional States	Difficulty Effectively Managing Stress	Difficulty Dealing with Feelings from Family of Origin	Difficulty with Blocked Goal-Directed Activities	Physical States that Contribute to Negative Emotional States
Feelings of depression, anxiety, rage, and distress are exacerbated by feelings of shame and a poor sense of self	Feelings of confusion, and overreaction to problems and conflicts	Feelings of emotional pain, loss, grief, separation, abandonment, violation, rejection and isolation	Feelings of aggressiveness and rage Feeling hassled by normal daily living Feeling bored, lonely, isolated, useless, helpless, hopeless, or lacking purpose in life	Physical health problems, pain, illness, injury, fatigue, specific physical disorders (e.g., chronic or recurrent pain caused by headaches, menstrual cramps, back pain, etc.) Physical states associated with prior substance abuse

TABLE 10.11
Interpersonal Conflicts

Conflicts with Partner/Spouse	Conflicts with Family	Other Stressful Interpersonal Conflicts
Once sober, the recovering person begins to see dysfunctional aspects of the relationship Different stages of recovery: one person is working on her recovery program and the other is not actively working on his issues New adjustment in relationship due to recovery Fear that the relationship will not be maintained or improve	Recognition of family dysfunction may lead to unresolved feelings of loss, abandonment, violation, and rejection, then these issues are stuffed and not worked out Family system does not change or adapt to addict/alcoholic's recovery but maintains some dysfunctional patterns of communication and interaction	Separation; divorce; or continued physical, sexual, or emotional violations Conflicts with employer, employees, friends, and other social situations Pattern of excessive fighting, arguments, and conflicts that go unresolved, and are a repetitive cycle People pleasing, avoiding conflicts, not telling others how one feels, acquiescing, avoiding anger and other feelings associated with conflict.

TABLE 10.12
Social Pressure

Peer Group	Isolating
Return to old drug/alcohol using peer group Hanging out with drug/alcohol users	Withdrawal from friends who support recovery; nonattendance or passive involvement with support group such as AA or NA Not maintaining contact with sponsor, counselor, or aftercare program Emotionally shutting down, not sharing feelings with others who are trusted and supportive of recovery. AA's motto is "Silence is the enemy of recovery."

Inadequate Recovery Program

Sometimes recovering alcoholics/addicts do not develop or maintain all aspects of their recovery program. Table 10.13 lists some of the reasons certain persons are more prone to relapse. These reasons may lead to impulsive decisions to test their recovery by using drugs/alcohol. In effect, this testing of their willpower to go back to controlled drug/alcohol use frequently leads to relapse.

Cravings and Urges

Thoughts, desires, even dreams about using drugs/alcohol are very common in drug/alcohol recovery. A variety of things can trigger this craving for drugs/alcohol, and cravings acted on can lead to relapse. The most effective way of coping with cravings and urges is to detach from the craving. "Instead of identifying with the urge (e.g., I really want a cigarette right now) the client can be trained to monitor the urge or desire from the point of view of a detached observer (I am now experiencing the craving/urge to smoke). By externalizing and labeling the craving/urge and watching it come and go through the eyes of the observer, there will be a decreased tendency to identify with the urge and feel overwhelmed by its power" (Marlatt, 1985).

Triggers

Recovering addicts/alcoholics can identify triggers leading to cravings for drugs/alcohol and develop an awareness as to why cravings occur. Then the addicts/alcoholics can structure their lives to either avoid these triggers or desensitize themselves to the trigger.

TABLE 10.13
Other At-Risk Factors for Relapse

High-stress personality type Mood swings, temper, rage Shutting down, withdrawing emotionally Overseparation and overattachment Difficulty establishing intimacy and maintaining appropriate boundaries in relationships Personality disorders: narcissism, manic-depressive disorder, borderline personality, codependent personality, depression (affective disorder), anxiety disorders, obsessive compulsive disorders, and others High-risk life-style: constant changes, high-stress job (i.e., always wheeling and dealing), financial and employment roller coaster, partner/spouse relationship changes and/or conflicts, always around others who use drugs/alcohol (entertainment industry, business-related drinking, bars, nightclubs, etc.) Financial: problems in managing finances, inability to control spending, making inappropriate financial commitments and taking on inappropriate financial obligations Problems in employment, career change with poor planning Trouble with back taxes and the Internal Revenue Service or other previous debt
Thinking and Perceptual Problems
Self-defeating or self-sabotaging thoughts Painful memories and/or euphoric recall of drug/alcohol use Return of denial and inability to consciously recognize loss of control over drugs/alcohol Poor judgment and negative or grandiose thinking that leads to impulsive self-destructive decisions Overreaction, crisis building, and creating problems when things are beginning to go better
Spiritual
Feeling at a loss, not feeling that life has meaning Difficulty maintaining sobriety, or having a reason for staying sober Existential despair: not seeing a function or reason for living

A trigger is "a stimulus which has been repeatedly associated with the preparation for, anticipation of, or the actual use of drugs/alcohol. These stimuli include people, places, things, times of day, emotional states and drugs/alcohol" (Rawson 1989). The following lists of time, place, thing, and people triggers show how diverse triggers are.

Time triggers to using alcohol/drugs

- periods of idle or leisure time
- periods of extended stress
- payday, holidays, Fridays, and Saturdays
- birthdays and anniversaries
- specific times of the day or evening
- on vacation
- periods of unemployment, lack of or out of work

Place triggers to using alcohol/drugs

- drug dealers' home, bars, parties
- neighborhoods where drugs are dealt
- clubs, concerts, social events
- places where drugs/alcohol have been used before

Things that trigger using alcohol/drugs

- drug dealers' car, telephone number, name
- receiving large amounts of cash, $100 bills, bank machines
- paraphernalia: pipes, syringe, rolling papers
- movies, films, and television shows about drugs/alcohol and drug/alcohol life-style
- particular music
- alcohol and tobacco advertisements
- conferences, seminars on drugs/alcohol
- sexually explicit movies or magazines

People who trigger using alcohol/drugs

- alcohol/drug using friends
- drug dealer, bar maids, and bartenders
- partner/spouse, relatives, and family members who use drugs/alcohol
- sexual encounters
- groups of people talking about or using drugs/alcohol

Drug Relapse Induced by Alcohol Use

Some individuals in recovery test their recovery by using alcohol instead of drugs. They rationalize that they were addicted to drugs but never had a problem with alcohol. This rationalization is unfounded. Once addicted to drugs, people have an addiction potential to all drugs, including alcohol. It is only a matter of time before individuals build tolerance and become addicted to alcohol, or alcohol use impairs judgment and they return to drugs.

Case Study
Alcohol-Induced Relapse
Mary

Mary, forty-two years old, married with three children, was hospitalized for severe depression, panic reactions, and post-traumatic stress. She was also assessed as having an addiction to pain medication and tranquilizers. As part of her treatment plan, Mary worked with the dual disorders team (drug/alcohol and psychiatric problems) on her addiction to pills. Gradually she was physically withdrawn from the tranquilizers and pain medication, while she received individual and group counseling on alcoholism and drug addiction. Mary also attended AA meetings, and attended educational classes on various aspects of the disease model of alcoholism and drug addiction.

Approximately six weeks after her discharge from the hospital, Mary's aftercare nurse asked if it was appropriate for Mary to be drinking wine with dinner each evening. Despite inservice training on alcoholism and drug addiction with the hospital staff, Mary's psychiatrist had approved her use of wine with dinner. When asked about his counsel, the psychiatrist felt that Mary had no history of alcoholsim, and her problem was with drugs (medication).

Despite interventions by the treatment team, the psychiatrist insisted that Mary's use of alcohol with dinner was appropriate. Mary was only able to maintain this use of wine with dinner for a short time. Two weeks later, under the influence of alcohol, Mary tripped and broke her leg. She then lapsed back to using pain medication and alcohol. Six weeks later, she was readmitted to the hospital.

Unfortunately there are many Marys who continue on this revolving door cycle with treatment facilities.

Matrix Study, 1986	Percent Return to Regular Cocaine Use
Did return to alcohol use.	50%
Did not return to alcohol use.	6
Sierra Tucson, 1988	
Did return to alcohol use.	61
Did not return to alcohol use.	8

Two studies by Richard Rawson (1986, 1988) have established that a return to alcohol use by cocaine addicts increases their cocaine relapse vulnerability by an astounding 800 percent.

Relapse Prevention

Once recovering addicts/alcoholics understand which factors contribute to relapse, they can try to prevent relapses. Also, all drug/alcohol treatment programs have the responsibility to conduct relapse prevention to help maintain the client/patient's drug/alcohol recovery. Alan Marlatt has developed a very organized model of global self-control strategies in relapse prevention.

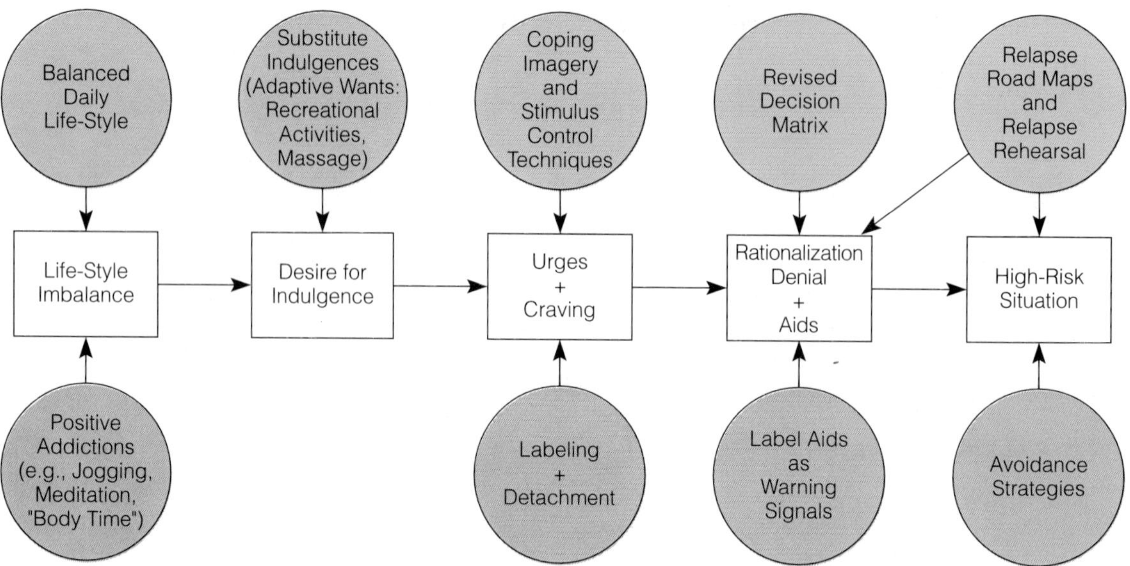

Relapse prevention: global self-control strategies

Life-Style Imbalance

Homeostasis is a term we borrow from science to describe the organism's natural tendency to seek a balanced state. If a life is imbalanced, the individual experiences too much or too little stress; eventually that results in a compensation in some area of life, or a breakdown. The imbalance can be evidenced by:

- too much work (workaholism) or overresponsibility resulting in a neglect of self
- difficulty relaxing, lack of spontaneity, and an inability to have fun, enjoy others, and most importantly feel emotions (shut down or emotionally unavailable to self or others, especially spouse and family) "too many shoulds, too many wants"
- too much play or irresponsibility resulting in procrastination, laziness, avoidance of conflicts and pain, and the avoidance of life-maintaining activities. (Passively forgetting or avoiding responsibilities.) "too many wants, not paying attention to needs"

Both workaholic and playaholic behavior have common root issues: the avoidance of taking up painful issues of self-concept interpersonal and life situation displeasure, and avoidance of recognizing and integrating true feelings. Usually some deeper family of origin issues that have not been worked through are recapitulated (duplicated) in present-day, here-and-now life situations.

Structure Creates Life-Style Balance

The addict/alcoholic has lived a life structured around alcohol or drugs. Drugs/alcohol have been the central organizing principle around which the addict/alcoholic and family members' lives have revolved. Removing the drugs/alcohol is a challenge to the individual and the family's systemic organization. Triggers for drug/alcohol cravings, and potential relapse, are frequently related to the lack of organization and structure in the newly sober addict/alcoholic and the family's life. Structure promotes a variety of important recovery functions. First, structure redirects idle time through time scheduling, goal setting, planning of activities. This includes work, play, vacation, recreation, and leisure time. Structured time maintains a focus on activities and is based on an integration of feelings. Second, structure teaches balance in daily activities, balance between work and play, balance in responsibility, balance in establishing effective boundaries in relationships. Third, structure promotes self-concept by placing emphasis on moving from passive dependence to proactive involvement in life. Structure reduces fears and anxieties, promotes self-reliance and preparedness. *Freedom* is a word often misused to represent lack of responsibility. Freedom is choosing your own version of responsibility to self and others, and the structure necessary to achieve such freedom.

Pitfalls to Structure

The following pitfalls to structure were adapted from Richard Rawson (1989):

- a rigid dysfunctional approach, overdoing, scheduling unrealistically
- burnout from workaholism and overextending of self
- neglecting recreation and leisure activity
- being perfectionistic and/or overly zealous about recovery
- talking a program, rather than working a program of recovery
- alienating others by preaching your program of recovery

- external control—structure that is not self-imposed; pleasing the counselor, sponsor, spouse, parent, instead of working a program for self; blind adherence without self-involvement in program
- failure to maintain spontaneously to others, and life in general

Areas of structure for the recovering addict/alcoholic include the following social, health, and cognitive facets of life.

Interpersonal and Social Recovery Support System

- drug-free friends who understand and support recovery from drugs/alcohol
- self-help groups such as Alcoholics Anonymous, Narcotics Anonymous, Adult Children of Alcoholics, and Co-Dependents Anonymous
- spouse/partner and family members who understand recovery and are involved in their own recovery and counseling
- support of an AA or NA sponsor; someone who has strong personal recovery, is available, and active in pointing out relapse vulnerability
- support from an aftercare program, group, or individual, and family counseling on a regular basis

Health and Physical Well-Being

- a regular program of exercise: athletic activities, long slow distance walking, or jogging/running, minimum three to five times per week.
- balanced, nutritionally sound, and structured diet
- adequate sleep, functional stress level, appropriate balance between work and play, activity and rest

Cognitive, Emotional, and Spiritual Self

- good sense of self, as a person (1) who is unique and worthwhile with emerging talents and skills; (2) who can accomplish things, has good decision-making and problem-solving skills—no self-sabotaging; (3) who can trust and be trusted while setting appropriate boundaries in relationships; and (4) who has the ability to

effectively resolve conflict and communicate feelings
- ability to be aware of feelings and thoughts and to integrate feelings and thoughts in taking appropriate action
- ability to adapt to life changes and stresses, and choose to grow emotionally, intellectually, occupationally, and interpersonally
- ability to achieve at work, school, home, and community
- spiritual orientation and growth with others and to life in general

Desire for Self-Indulgence

Frustration and anger are feelings that result from not attaining personal long-range goals. After losing hope and motivation, the recovering alcoholic/addict decides to take the short-range immediate relief by using drugs/alcohol.

The immediate gratification of drugs needs to be countered with the understanding that things change, feelings can be felt, and time changes the way one views things. The entire drug/alcohol recovery program is designed to get the person back on track by utilizing new recovery skills to instill feelings of hope. Those in recovery should follow the AA saying, "Take it one day at a time."

> Waiting is not mere empty hoping. It has the inner certainty of reaching a goal. Such certainty alone gives that light which leads to success. This leads to the perseverance that leads to good fortune and bestows power to cross the great water.
>
> One is faced with a danger that must be overcome. Weakness and impatience can do nothing. Only a strong man can stand up to his fate, for his inner security enables him to endure to the end. This strength shows itself in uncompromising truthfulness (with himself). It is only when we have the courage to face things exactly as they are, without any sort of self-deception or illusion, that a light will develop out of events, by which the path to success may be recognized. This recognition must be followed by resolute and persevering action. For only the man who goes to meet his fate resolutely is equipped to deal with it adequately. Then he will be able to cross the great water—that is to say, he will be capable of making the necessary decision and of surmounting the danger (*I Ching,* Hexagram 5).

Application of the Serenity Prayer

The serenity prayer of AA is a relapse prevention technique.

God grant me the serenity
To accept the things I cannot change,
Courage to change the things I can,
And wisdom to know the difference.

Accepting the things I cannot change means accepting what can't be controlled. Those in recovery need the skills to let go, to not control others, or project their wishes on others. As a result, recovering addicts/alcoholics avoid negative emotional feelings of anger, rage, anxiety, depression, and intolerable frustration.

Courage to change the things I can means controlling what can be controlled. Those in recovery need the skills to focus on today, to take action, and work on themselves. As a result, recovering addicts/alcoholics develop positive affirmations, progress toward long-term goals, and develop a stronger sense of self.

Wisdom to know the difference means learning to discriminate between the impossible and the possible. Those in recovery need the skills to talk about feelings, accept limits, and ask "Can I change this?" As a result, recovering addicts/alcoholics can achieve a balanced life-style, the ability to deal with urges and cravings, and avoid impulsive destructive decisions and destructive interactions.

An Effective Drug/Alcohol Treatment Strategy

The primary goal of recovery is complete abstinence from drugs/alcohol. The following steps can help those in recovery achieve their goal.

1. *Break the bonds of denial.* Recovery is an ongoing process often facilitated by the support of others—friends, others in recovery from drugs/alcohol, family, or a counselor. All of these people can help addicts/alcoholics work through their denial and maintain sobriety.
2. *Actively work and apply the twelve steps and other AA principles in recovery.* This provides guidelines, structure, and support for recovery efforts. Developing a relationship with an AA or NA sponsor is a key element in effectively helping the newly recovering person to understand and implement the principles of AA.

3. *Seek nonchemical altered states of consciousness.* The innate human drive to alter one's sense of consciousness can be attained through healthy and balanced activities, not the use of drugs/alcohol. These activities enhance the individual's sense of self and well-being.
4. *Working through negative emotional states and controlling destructive impulses.* Negative life experiences commonly result in emotions that get out of control and end up causing additional problems. The individual in recovery can learn new coping skills and gain support in working through impulses that may lead to destructive decisions and interactions.
5. *Move from passive to active choice making in all aspects of life.* Most addictive behaviors are passive, automatic, ritualistic, and habitual. This includes workaholism, gambling, eating disorders, and many other behaviors that fit our behavioral definition of addiction. Recovering individuals need to be involved and active in their recovery. Most learning comes from doing.
6. *Resist social or peer pressure.* When it endangers welfare or inhibits growth, peer pressure can cause those in recovery to make the wrong choices. Recovery is maintained by being and talking with others in recovery, rather than isolating. Associating with people who don't understand, or more importantly, don't respect the individual's recovery, could require changing relationships. Recovering addicts/alcoholics should develop and maintain relationships that support a healthy drug/alcohol-free life-style.
7. *Improve and continue to work on the sense of self.* Those in recovery need to be involved in activities and relationships that promote a positive sense of self. To develop a sense of self, they must believe they are unique, worthwhile individuals with emerging talents and skills; individuals who can accomplish things; individuals who can trust and be trusted while setting appropriate boundaries in relationships, and avoiding codependency and dysfunctionality.
8. *Deal more effectively with stress.* Recovering addicts/alcoholics must develop awareness in recognizing stressful situations and the need for support (attachments), coping skills, and resources to deal with or adapt to the stress.

9. *Maintain the structure of the recovery program.* Recovering alcoholics and addicts should consistently attend self-help meetings, aftercare, counseling sessions, and other elements of the recovery program.
10. *Have patience and direction.* Those in recovery must have a road map, while maintaining a day-at-a-time perspective in recovery.
11. *Learn how to enjoy life and others.* By developing the capacity to relax, enjoy, and have fun with others, recovering persons can establish leisure activities, hobbies, and explore personal interests.
12. *Maintain a sense of humor.* Those in recovery very much need to keep things in perspective, and remember, "I'm not OK. You're not OK. But that's OK."
13. *Take responsibility for self.* No matter what the event is, those in recovery have the freedom to choose their response to it. Taking responsibility for self leads to awareness, which in turn helps the individual to make effective choices.
14. *Maintain physical, emotional, and spiritual well-being.* Recovering alcoholics/addicts need regular exercise, balanced nutrition, adequate sleep and rest. Recovery also involves effective communication in relationships, especially intimate relationships. One must work on spiritual values in life and strive to experience the joy and creativity of life, while exploring your own sense of spirituality.
15. *Avoid shame.* Mistakes may occur but addicts/alcoholics can return to recovery without a burden of shame. Shame generated by others or themselves inhibits personal recovery and growth from situations that may be painful.
16. *Work on relapse prevention strategies.* Those in recovery need to deal with urges and cravings to use drugs/alcohol, imbalanced life-styles, negative emotional states, social pressures, high-risk situations, and other factors which may make them vulnerable to relapse.
17. *Adapt to changes in life.* Addicts/alcoholics can remind themselves that they are human and subject to human feelings and emotions. Life is not perfect and always involves change.

Recovery is facilitated by the individual's ability to adapt to change and integrate feelings related to change. Striving for progress rather than perfection is a healthy goal.

Summary

Self-help meetings are the most widely used and successful approach to alcohol and drug recovery. The advantages of AA and other self-help meetings are outlined as well as the drawbacks to give a clear, unbiased understanding of the role self-help can play in recovery. Richard Rawson's model describes the five stages of drug/alcohol recovery.

0–15 days—withdrawal
16–45 days—honeymoon
46–120 days—the wall
121–180 days—adjustment
181 + days—resolution

Each of these stages has its own behavioral, cognitive, emotional, and relational symptoms.

There is a tremendously high relapse rate following drug/alcohol treatment. Training patients in relapse prevention is an integral component of the recovery program; it was often neglected in early drug/alcohol treatment approaches.

Recognizing that specific times, places, things, and people, can trigger drug/alcohol cravings is an important component of drug/alcohol relapse training. It has also been demonstrated that drug relapse is induced by a return to alcohol use.

Two key points made in this chapter are first, that drug/alcohol recovery is an ongoing process and no one is cured due to the ongoing nature of the disease of alcoholism/drug addiction. And second, that drug/alcohol treatment is often as good as the counselor or treatment program itself, assuming that the patient is motivated to achieve recovery.

In the last 30 years there have been many changes in drug/alcohol treatment. The early days focused on therapeutic communities, methadone programs, outpatient community-based programs, and university-based research centers. In the 1980s there was a shift to inpatient residential and hospital-based twenty-eight to thirty-day programs. The rise in cocaine addiction also challenged these inpatient facilities to develop treatment appropriate to cocaine. The future trend in treatment tends to be toward intensive outpatient models. The increased cost of the 30-day inpatient model and research indicating similar success rates with outpatient treatment, makes intensive outpatient treatment a more viable and less costly option.

A variety of drug/alcohol treatment modalities are available from no treatment to structured day care. These modalities include no treatment, education and information, 24-hour helplines, crisis intervention, drop-in counseling services, brief or periodic counseling, short-term counseling, extended individual counseling, family treatment, group treatment, intensive outpatient, inpatient detoxification, residential and inpatient treatment.

A controversial treatment approach is the issue of controlled drinking. Despite opposition from most drug/alcohol treatment professionals, proponents of controlled drinking see it as a viable option for some problem drinkers. Most agree that abstinence from drugs/alcohol remains the viable option for recovery. However, others argue that for some problem drinkers with specific criteria, controlled drinking is possible. Certainly more controlled research is necessary because the risks involved are many and may be life threatening.

References

Armor, D. J., J. M. Polich, and H. B. Stambul. *Alcohol and Treatment.* New York: John Wiley & Sons, 1978.

Bateman, N. I. and D. M. Peterson. "Variables Related to Outcome of Treatment for Hospitalized Alcoholics." *International Journal of Addictions,* 1971, 215–24.

Brill, Leon. *The Clinical Treatment of Substance Abusers.* New York: Free Press, 1981.

Brill, Leon. *The Clinical Treatment of Substance Abusers.* New York: Free Press, 1981.

Browne-Mayers, A. N., E. E. Seeley, and D. E. Brown. "Reorganized Alcoholism Services: Two Years After." *Journal of American Medical Association,* 1973, 233–35.

Chafetz, Morris E., Howard T. Blane, and Marjorie Hill. *Frontiers of Alcoholism,* New York: Science House, 1970.

Cohen, Sidney. "The substance abuse problems." *New Issues for the 1980s,* 2. New York: Haworth Press, 1985.

Costello, R. M., M. B. Giffen, S. L. Schneider, P. W. Edgington, and K. R. Maders. "Comprehensive Alcohol Treatment Planning, Implementation, and Evaluation." *International Journal of the Addictions* 11, no. 4 (1976): 553–71.

Dole, V. P. and M. E. Nyswander. "A medical treatment of diacetylmorphine (herion) addiction." *Journal of American Medical Association* 193 (1965): 646–50.

Ford, B. with Chris Chase. *A Glad Awakening.* Garden City, N.Y.: Doubleday, 1987.

Fox, R. "Normal Drinking in Recovered Alcohol Addicts: Comment on the Article by D. L. Davies." *Quarterly Journal of Studies on Alcohol* 23 (1963): p. 117.

Fox, V. "The controlled drinking controversy." *Journal of American Medical Association* 236, (1976): p. 893.

Gold, Mark S. and Arnold M. Herman. *Cocaine: A Clinician's Handbook.* New York: Guilford Press, 1987.

Gorski, Terence T. *The Developmental Model of Recovery: The Recovery /Relapse Grid,* 1987.

Hay, Louise L. *You Can Heal Your Life.* Santa Monica, Calif.: Hay House, 1984.

Kish, G. B. and H. T. Herman. "The Fort Meade Alcoholism Treatment Program: A Follow Up Study." *Quarterly Journal of Studies on Alcohol* 32 (1971): 628–35.

Lawson, Gary, James S. Peterson, and Ann Lawson. *Alcoholism and the Family: A Guide to Treatment and Prevention.* Rockville, Md.: Aspen Publications, 1983.

Marks, S. J., L. Daroff, and S. Granick. "Basic Counseling for Drug Abusers." In *Treatment Services for Adolescent Substance Abusers.* U.S. Department of Health and Human Services, 1987.

Marlatt, Alan and Judith Gordon. *Relapse Prevention.* New York: Guilford Press, 1985.

Miller, W. R. and G. R. Caddy. "Abstinence and controlled drinking in the treatment of problem drinkers." *Journal of Studies of Alcohol* 38 (1977): 986–1003.

Miller, William R. *Addictive Behaviors—Treatment of Alcoholism, Drug Abuse, Smoking and Obesity.* New York: Pergamon Press, 1980.

Pittel, Stephen, et al. "Drug Abuse Treatment Modalities: An Overview, 1975." In *Facts About Drug Abuse.* Rockville, Md.: National Institute on Drug Abuse, 1976.

Rawson, R., J. Obert, M. McCann, and David Smith. *Treatment of Cocaine Dependence, A Neurobehavioral Approach.* Beverly Hills, Calif.: Matrix Institute on Addictions, 1988.

Rawson, Richard. "Chemical Dependency Treatment: The Integration of the Alcoholism and Drug Addiction Systems." *International Journal of Addictions,* 1991 in press.

Rawson, Richard. *Cocaine Recovery Issues: The Neurobehavioral Model.* Beverly Hills, Calif.: Matrix Institute on Addictions, 1989.

Ritson, E. B. "The Prognosis of Alcohol Addicts Treated by a Specialized Unit." *British Journal of Psychiatry* 114, (1968): pgs. 1019–29.

Robson, R. A., H. I. Paulus, and G. G. Clark. "An Evaluation of the Effect of a Clinic Treatment Program on the Rehabilitation of Alcoholic Patients." *Quarterly Journal of Studies on Alcohol* 26 (1965): pgs. 264–78.

Steinglass, Peter. "An Experimental Treatment Program for Alcoholic Couples." *Journal of Studies on Alcohol* 40 (1979): pgs. 159–82.

Zimberg, Sheldon, John Wallace, and Sheila Blume. eds. *Practical Approaches to Alcoholism Psychotherapy.* New York: Plenum Press, 1985.

CHAPTER 11

Drugs/Alcohol: The Modern Disease of Our American Society

At the start of this textbook we stated that there are no simple solutions to the problems of drug/alcohol dependence and addiction. Remember the wisdom of the philosopher H. L. Mencken, who said, "The solutions to big problems that are simple, are usually wrong."

Let us recognize that there will always be some level of drug/alcohol problem in the United States. Despite our best efforts, many people will still choose not to get help. This is not a war on drugs, but instead a crusade. A crusade to help those people who need and want drug and alcohol treatment. A crusade to prevent the next generation from developing drug/alcohol problems. A crusade to help those who care to intervene, when appropriate, on those who may benefit from drug/alcohol treatment.

Our efforts can help many people with drug/alcohol problems and prevent others from suffering the same devastating life of addiction. Most important, we can work on the current problems that make the next generation at risk for chemical dependency.

Chapter Goals

1. Identify some problems in our perception of drugs/alcohol and possible reforms.
2. Identify the problems associated with not adequately recognizing alcohol as a drug.
3. Describe the problems related to drug/alcohol use.
4. Describe the problem in adopting unhealthy U.S. life-styles.
5. Describe the impact of parental imbalance, shame, and imbalanced family systems on the development of drug/alcohol problems.
6. Clarify the importance of early diagnosis and at-risk factors for drug/alcohol dependence and addiction.
7. Explain the problem of using a supply side approach to the drug/alcohol problem while neglecting the demand side.
8. Describe the systemic problems of lack of cooperation and communication between the mental health and drug/alcohol fields.
9. Identify the importance of meeting the special drug/alcohol treatment needs of people of color and those suffering from systemic socioeconomic inequities.
10. Describe the impact of the failure of the educational system to motivate young people.

Problems in Perception

Recognizing Alcohol as a Drug Problem

The general tendency has been to emphasize the war on drugs and to exclude alcohol as a target of that war. Even in this time of developing awareness about drugs, many people fail to recognize alcohol as a drug. Many established institutions in the United States agree that we must do something about the drug problem, yet they deny, ignore, or neglect problems with alcohol and alcoholism. There is a double standard of talking about the problem with drugs but being quiet about alcohol and alcoholism.

Alcohol is integrated into the fabric of America's life-style, causing people to deny the impact it has on our society. The strong alcohol lobby and the economic realities created by our developed taste for alcohol, often blind our legislators to new and creative efforts in addressing the problems related to alcohol abuse and alcoholism.

Double standards for adults often give mixed messages to young people. The following comments were expressed by a tenth-grade psychology class:

- We don't understand why there is such a big deal about drugs, when alcohol is just as big a problem with kids.
- Our parents drink too much alcohol and then hypocritically talk about the dangers of drugs.
- Cigarette smoking is banned on all airline flights. Yet, alcohol is served in-flight, with double shots.
- The U.S. Navy provides an opportunity for those admitting they have an alcohol problem to receive alcohol treatment, but discharges anyone who admits to smoking marijuana or having a drug problem.
- We have a policy of zero tolerance for drugs, but not for alcohol. Driving under the influence of alcohol with a blood alcohol level of 0.10 is legal in most states even though this may impair judgment and one's capabilities to drive at the most efficient level. Why then is it legal to drink and drive at all?
- If alcohol is harmful, dangerous, and has a strong addiction potential, why isn't more done about prevention and treatment, instead of spending all the money on the busting of South American drug lords?

These issues are controversial and certainly require more discussion. They illustrate, however, the mixed and inconsistent messages we give young people about alcohol. Suggested reforms that address these perceptual problems with alcohol include:

1. All media, educational, and legislative communications or written material should not separate alcohol from drugs. References should be more consistently addressed as: alcohol/drug problem, alcohol/drug abuse, alcoholism/drug addiction, and so forth. The war on drugs is really the war on chemical dependency.
2. Treatment facilities for chemical dependency should train their staffs for both alcoholism and drug addiction. Educational instruction for patients should emphasize both alcohol and drugs because most patients are polydrug users who use alcohol and other drugs.
3. Separating federal, state, and local agencies into a department of alcoholism and a department of drug services perpetuates problems in communication, territorialism, lack of cooperation, and most important, costly duplication of services.
4. Parent education should focus on alcohol as a drug, and emphasize the negative impact of parents who model drug and alcohol abuse.

Failure to Recognize Alcohol Problems

Alcohol is the most devastating drug we know of today in the sheer number of people that it affects; estimates indicate more than 12 million alcoholics in the United States. This would also mean that there are more than 28 million children of alcoholics, who will suffer some form of dysfunction in their adult lives as a result of growing up in alcoholic family systems.

Child Abuse and Alcohol/Drugs

Families with alcohol and drug problems are involved in 90 percent of the cases of child abuse. The National Committee for the Prevention of Child Abuse 1990 reported that cases of child abuse in the United States rose 10 percent last year to 2.4 million. This increase is the largest since 1985 and is caused by parents' substance abuse, an increase in crack cocaine use, and changes in child abuse reporting requirements. Deaths due to child abuse were also up 3 percent to 1,237.

Homicides

More than 105,000 deaths occur each year directly related to alcoholism. Almost one-half of all homicides involve a murderer with a positive blood alcohol level.

Loss on the Job

Estimates are that more than $136 billion are lost each year in business and industry due to lost employment, reduced productivity, and health care costs related to alcohol.

Drinking and Driving

To give you a perspective on the United States' widespread problem with drinking alcohol and driving:

1. In the United States in 1989, more than 24,000 people died in alcohol-related traffic accidents. These deaths have affected approximately 100,000 immediate family members.
2. More than 1.8 million people are arrested for driving under the influence each year in the United States.
3. Alcohol use by drivers involved in fatal accidents has decreased from 43.8 percent in 1982 to 37.4 percent in 1988. Each of the fatally injured drivers was legally intoxicated with blood-alcohol levels of 0.10 percent or greater. This rate is still appreciably high considering the loss in human life and grief to the family and friends.
4. In 1988, drivers were legally intoxicated in 49 percent of all single vehicle accidents (U.S. Department of Transportation 1988).

Alcohol is still the number one drug of choice for most Americans. It is a drug that directly and indirectly affects the lives of millions of U.S. citizens. The recently reported decreases in patterns of alcohol use are significant but by no means indicate success. More needs to be done, much more. If more concerted efforts are not implemented on all fronts, these statistical trends may remain just that—trends that plateau at rates of alcohol abuse and alcoholism that are still appreciably high, with tremendous losses imparted on our society.

Possible Reforms

Former U.S. Surgeon General C. Everett Koop's last major initiative before leaving office was a campaign against drunken driving and alcohol abuse. Koop often emphasized that the American people tend to ignore the problems related to alcohol abuse and alcoholism.

In an attempt to reduce drinking and driving, Koop proposed the following plan:

1. Sharp restrictions on the advertising of alcohol, beer, and wine.
2. Tough new blood-alcohol standards for drivers driving under the influence of alcohol.

3. Higher taxes on beer, wine, and liquor. Until the 1991 federal tax increases on alcohol and cigarettes, taxes on beer and wine had not been raised since 1951.
4. Automatic suspensions of licenses for drivers testing above the legal blood-alcohol level.

An additional controversial aspect of Koop's proposal is the elimination of all happy hours and other common reductions in alcohol prices in bars, restaurants, and stadiums. These happy hours promote excessive drinking in short time spans, causing intoxication; in many situations, people then choose to drive under the influence.

Difficulty Recognizing Our Drug-Using Society

Many Americans seeking altered states of consciousness are drug users of some kind and/or have unhealthy life-styles. Americans use more than 20,000 tons of aspirin a day—that's the equivalent of every person in the whole country taking one aspirin each day. Americans smoke more than 600 million cigarettes per year. In addition, the coffee break is an integral feature of work, home, and play with Americans consuming approximately 16 pounds of coffee per person, each year.

Many Americans have gone beyond the normal seeking of altered states of consciousness. Our **pleasure lust** and avoidance of pain has resulted in a nation that is unhealthy, with drug-seeking behavior and addictive life-styles. Drug and alcohol use, abuse, and dependence are only one indicator of the problems in modern American society.

Often the seeking of pleasure at all costs creates problematic behaviors that can be destructive to individuals and their families. To avoid the painful issues of personal growth and the maintenance of healthy physical and psychological life-styles, individuals passively hang on to:

- addiction to cigarettes, caffeine, junk foods, drugs, alcohol, gambling
- a lack of balance and effectiveness in relationships with spouse, family, children, friends, coworkers
- a lack of balance in work, spending beyond one's need and means, high-risk ventures, and impulsive inappropriate business decisions
- general physical inactivity and lack of a balanced exercise program

- plug-in drugs, excessive time and energy spent on watching television, playing computer games, or other computer and media activities
- difficulty or inability to relax or enjoy natural things in life (e.g., nature, quiet meditative time, long walks)
- inactivity and lack of a proactive involvement in life-affirming activities that promote personal issues, values, and feelings
- difficulty in developing interests, hobbies, friendships, and positive nondrug altered states of consciousness
- inappropriate feelings of rage, anxiety, and/or depression without seeking help or treatment
- a lack of meaning in work, relationships, and leisure time, with a generalized feeling of existential despair (i.e., not knowing or pursuing or working on one's life).

All of these characteristics and many more have resulted in great numbers of people in the United States denying their unhappiness and feelings of personal ineffectiveness. The denial of this malaise can make a person at risk for developing problems with drugs/alcohol. The solution to this condition is too expansive to describe in this one chapter. There are many possible solutions and treatment strategies. A beginning step is to acknowledge that we as a society maintain unhealthy life-styles causing individuals and families to be at risk for problems with chemical dependency. We need more media, education, and training programs to emphasize positive alternatives and healthy life-styles. Most important, we need to care about ourselves, our children, our families, and friends and to respect one another's struggle with life's challenges.

Problems in the Family

Not Addressing Issues in Imbalanced Family Systems

The 1950s and 1960s gave us television programs such as "Father Knows Best," "My Three Sons," "The Donna Reed Show," "Lassie," "Leave It to Beaver," and others that extolled the virtues of the idealized American family system. This idealized system was in direct contrast to behavior in alcoholic/addict and imbalanced family systems. Because most dysfunctional behaviors were denied in the alcoholic/addict family system, family members deceived themselves into thinking that theirs was the normal behavior of most family systems. How many families are actually dysfunctional? It is estimated that 20 percent of American families are functional; 30 percent are dysfunctional; and 50 percent are extremely dysfunctional.

Awareness of the adult child of the alcoholic syndrome has spread like wildfire and focused public attention on the dysfunctional nature of alcoholic family systems. The generalization of this awareness to other imbalanced family systems has resulted in a significant public awareness that has become a kind of social movement.

Despite this movement, a proliferation of information, and treatment services for imbalanced families and adult children of alcoholics, there is still a widespread denial of dysfunction in most families. Parents with alcohol/drug problems often deny the impact of their dysfunctional behavior on their children. Also denied are feelings of shame, abandonment, and rejection experienced by family members.

In chapter 4, Carol L. Kempher identified various factors contributing to parenting dysfunction/imbalance. Chief among these factors was increased parental alcoholism, drug abuse, and nicotine dependence.

Chemically dependent and/or dysfunctional parents often lack knowledge and skills in parenting, as they, too, grew up in imbalanced family systems. These parents have unrealistic expectations because they do not know what is developmentally appropriate behavior for their child's age. Insensitive to the special needs of their children, they maintain inappropriate disciplining techniques, with inconsistent, rigid, or ambiguous boundaries.

In chapter 5, we discussed the impact of shame, abandonment, and rejection on the child in the imbalanced family system. The devastating and dramatic impact of shame is also perpetuated by peers, teachers, school systems, religious organizations, and other institutions.

Until there is a concerted and extensive emphasis on developing educational, preventive, and treatment approaches that promote healthy family systems, this cycle of abuse, shame, abandonment, rejection, and dysfunctional/imbalanced parenting will continue to be passed on from generation to generation.

Denial of Children's At-Risk Factors

The longer a family denies its drug/alcohol problem, the more vulnerable the family members become to experiencing the destructive consequences of drug/alcohol abuse. Early assessment of drug/alcohol problems and dysfunctional behavior may prevent a problem from getting out of control.

As outlined in earlier chapters, parental alcoholism and drug addiction make the children in that family four to eight times more likely to develop problems with alcohol/drugs. Children who grow up in families that exhibit dysfunctional behaviors such as physical and emotional abuse, sexual violation, and other traumas are at a greater risk for developing problems with drugs/alcohol.

Public media are beginning to address the issues of child abuse, sexual violation, and other abuses by parents. However, increased public awareness and multimedia programs need to be developed to address these issues, as well as information on early assessment and referral for treatment.

Systemic Problems

Before addressing these systemic problems, one must recognize that systems are often threatened by change, are resistant to change, or change too slowly. The pressures of public opinion and the influence of vested interests may cause systems to not respond to the need for change or to respond inappropriately in trying to solve the problem.

The Biggest Problems

Emphasis on Supply Side, Neglect of Demand Side of the Drug/Alcohol Problem in the United States

Approximately 70 percent or more of federal money available to fight the drug problem is being spent on programs and agencies who focus on reducing the supply of drugs in the United States. Despite these efforts, there appears to be no real reduction in the availability of drugs. The lucrative profits are such a strong incentive at every level of the illegal drug trade that government efforts to decrease drug trafficking have not been successful.

As a result, this strong emphasis on the supply side has caused a neglect in funding for demand-side programs of drug prevention, intervention, and treatment. The problem has escalated to such levels that respected government officials and other prominent individuals are considering the legalization of illicit drugs. In 1988, Mayor Kurt Schmoke of Baltimore, Maryland, asked for a "national debate on the question of decriminalizing drugs." Schmoke's suggestion was not well received by supply siders in the war on drugs, because it dramatically highlighted the ineffectiveness of the supply-side approach. Even considering legalizing drugs clearly points to the frustration of a segment of the American society with the lack of progress being made by the supply-side approach.

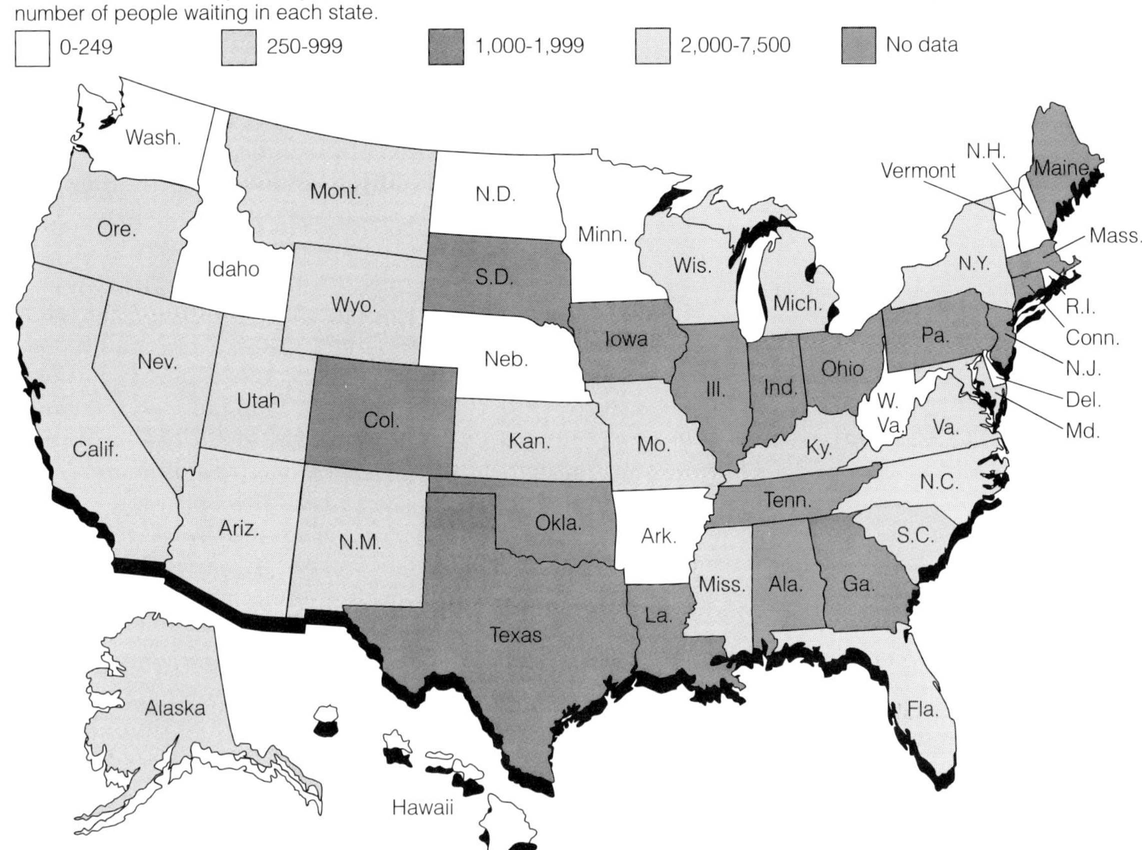

Treatment waiting list by states

Art reprinted by permission: Tribune Media Services. Data used with permission from National Association of State Alcohol and Drug Abuse Directors, Inc.

I would liken the supply-side approach without a significant emphasis on demand to parents who believe "If I keep my child away from drugs long enough, the child won't go back to using drugs." What the family fails to recognize, just as the current administration is failing to realize, is that regardless of all our efforts to cut off the supply of drugs, if the demand is not addressed, the child will find a way to get what he or she so strongly wants and craves.

As a result of this supply-side approach, less federal funding has been available for public alcohol and drug treatment programs. The March 1990 survey by the National Association of State Alcohol and Drug Abuse Directors indicated that publicly financed programs had long waiting lists for both inpatient and outpatient treatment services.

The average waiting time for publicly funded outpatient drug/alcohol treatment was 22 days. The average waiting time for publicly funded inpatient drug/alcohol treatment was 45 days. Nationally, more than 65,000 people are waiting to enter public drug/alcohol treatment programs. Once the addict/alcoholic is ready for treatment and breaks through denial, there is such a long waiting list, that relapse is inevitable. This costs taxpayers additional money in increased crime and public health care costs.

The same survey reported that in 1988, states outspent the federal government in supporting drug/alcohol treatment programs. Only 23 percent of the $2.1 billion spent on state-supported treatment programs comes from the federal government. In the 1991 federal budget, the $700 million in treatment grants represents only an 11 percent increase, despite backlogs in treatment services and dramatic funding needs to expand drug/alcohol treatment services.

Money alone cannot necessarily solve the problem. However, it can alleviate delays in providing treatment for those desperately seeking and needing drug/alcohol treatment.

Funding for innovative programs addressing the needs of the inner-city crack addict and programs for the prevention of addiction in pregnant women are high priorities. Funding is also needed for drug/alcohol prevention programs for high-risk youth, with a special early focus on kindergarten to sixth grade. To make a true impact, longitudinal prevention projects with funding for several years are needed. Innovative, yet realistic methods of funding are also necessary to effectively attract the support of big business.

Lack of Cooperation and Communication between the Various Perspectives Dealing with the Drug/Alcohol Problem

The four perspectives on drugs/alcohol outlined in chapter 2, moral-legal, medical, psychosocial, and social-cultural, need to communicate and cooperate with one another to effectively address the problems of drugs and alcohol and dependence and addiction. Biases, territorial issues, and an inability to trust and support one another has been the problem in establishing effective communication and cooperation between these perspectives.

Staff training, education, and workshops that facilitate various systems working more effectively with each other can clarify each perspective's role in addressing the drug/alcohol and mental health treatment needs of the clients/patients. Activities that promote cooperation and communication and build trust are essential for the various perspectives to work more effectively together.

Lack of Cooperation and Communication between the Drug/Alcohol and the Mental Health/Psychiatric Fields

Historically, the drug/alcohol treatment field and the mental health/psychiatric field, have not been able to overcome their biases to effectively develop trust and cooperation. Today, these biases still persist and prevent cooperation between two helping fields.

The persons most hurt by this lack of cooperation between the drug/alcohol and mental health/psychiatric fields are the clients/patients themselves. Their treatment plans often do not adequately address both their drug/alcohol and mental health recovery needs.

Illustration of the Problem The difficulty mental health and drug/alcohol experts have in cooperation is even further complicated by limited funding sources and high degrees of territorialism. This myopic survival perception is illustrated in the following story:

It came to be that a drug/alcohol specialist and a mental health worker decided to form a dual disorder team. They believed it was necessary to become familiar with each other's specialty to survive in competitive times.

To meld themselves into an effective team they decided to spend three weeks together in the wilderness of northern Alaska. They hoped that this experience would promote cooperation, understanding, effective team building, and mutual reliance on one another.

After initial adjustments during the first few days, they cooperated and got along quite well for the next two weeks. They learned from each other and respected each other's talents and skills. Throughout the day and night they had long talks about drug/alcohol recovery, the disease model and twelve steps of AA, and psychiatric diagnosis and treatment. They spent many hours reading the big book of AA as well as the *Diagnostic and Statistical Manual* (DSM-III-R). They spent much time discussing spirituality, philosophy, religion, their sense of a Higher Power, and other topics. They found themselves talking about family of origin issues, and shared their personal experiences of growing up in their families. Needless to say, they were beginning to trust one another and growing closer. Performing the daily chores to survive the weather and living conditions had become second nature as they could almost anticipate each other's needs.

One day, they wandered into a thicket inhabited by a big brown bear. Unfortunately for them, the brown bear got their scents and immediately charged them. It would be impossible to outrun the bear only 120 yards away, so the mental health worker sat down, took out the AA big book given to him by his new friend and began reading. He determined that the situation was beyond his control and up to the will of the Higher Power.

At the same time, the drug/alcohol specialist was frantically searching his backpack, looking for his spiked running shoes. He quickly took off his hiking boots and began feverishly putting on his running shoes. As he was doing this, the mental health worker looked at him and said, "There's no way you are going to outrun the bear." The drug/alcohol specialist finished tieing his shoes, looked the mental health worker square in the face, and said, "I don't have to outrun the bear, all I have to do is outrun you!"

This comical story fortunately isn't true but it does demonstrate that when the drug/alcohol specialist and mental health worker are threatened they see each other as adversaries not colleagues. In reality, each anticipates being one step ahead of the other for fear that they will lose their funding sources.

One of the most promising developments in the last few years is the concept of dual disorders, patients with psychiatric problems and drug/alcohol problems. The recognition that many patients are dual disordered has allowed communication and cooperation between the two systems in recognizing the need for education and training in each other's specialties. The exchange of information through conferences, workshops, and case consultation on dual disorder issues is a necessary and appropriate step in building bridges between the mental health/psychiatric field and the drug/alcohol treatment field.

If change is to occur in these systems, to better meet the needs of the client/patient, more people must speak out and address these issues. Those who choose to change and learn will be more sought after and provide better service to their clients/patients. This makes them more competent and secure for the future. Such a coalition is also necessary to adapt to the future trends in biological and genetic discoveries, and facilitates implementation of the future innovations in treatment program services.

Neglecting the Drug/Alcohol Treatment Needs of People of Color

Historically, we have seen prejudice and oppression of people of color, a scapegoating of minorities, and a neglect of drug/alcohol problems in the inner city. Legislation on drug policy was often formed more on racial scapegoating prejudices than a concern for the harmful impact of the drug on people. "People's attitudes toward a specific drug became inseparable from their feelings about that group of people with which the drug's use was associated" (White 1976).

In 1875, the goal of suppressing opium smoking or opium dens had little to do with the control of opium but more to do with the fear of interracial contact and a fear of interracial mixing of the Chinese with American women and the white working class.

> The Chinese question dominated California politics in the 1870s. The tremendous racial and class conflicts resulted in many racial riots, lynching and killing of Chinese, and burning of their dwellings, in numerous West Coast cities. The California Working Man's Party was organized under the cry of "The Chinese must go."
>
> The association between opium and the Chinese into the 1900s was part of the national legislation to prohibit opium smoking and opium dens, even though, at the time, opium was a primary ingredient in most over-the-counter medications and elixirs for physical ailments.
>
> *(White 1976)*

The same held true for the association between cocaine and blacks during the late 1800s and early 1900s. Hamilton Wright, a state department official considered by many as the father of American narcotics laws, went before Congress in 1910 and gave the following warning about cocaine.

> It has been authoritatively stated that cocaine is often the direct incentive to the crime of rape by the Negroes of the South and other sections of the country.
>
> Once the Negro has reached the stage of being a "dope taker" [dope here referring to cocaine] . . . he is a constant menace to his community until he is eliminated. . . . Sexual desires are increased and perverted, peaceful Negroes become quarrelsome, and timid Negroes develop a degree of "Dutch courage." The cocaine nigger is sure hard to kill . . . a fact that has been demonstrated so often that many of these officers in the South have increased the caliber of their guns for the express purpose of "stopping the cocaine fiend when he runs amuck."
>
> *(Williams 1914)*

These same racial associations with drugs were documented in a *New York Times* newspaper article that reflected the anti-Semitic feelings of the time: "There is little doubt that every Jew Peddler in the South carries the stuff (cocaine)."

This historical association of drugs with hated minority groups includes

- opium with the Chinese
- cocaine with the blacks
- alcohol with urban Catholic immigrants
- heroin with urban immigrants, blacks
- marijuana and PCP with latinos

The underlying assumption was that minorities were not able to control or tolerate use of alcohol and drugs because they were inherently lazy and physically, emotionally, and morally/ethically weak. Of course, most self-respecting white men could control their drug/alcohol use. This prejudice and association of drugs with hated minority subgroups caused politicians and others to use these emotional feelings in gaining support for antidrug legislation.

Unfortunately, as long as drugs were confined to minority populations, funding and treatment resources were limited. It wasn't until the 1960s, when white middle-to-upper class young adults and college students were using marijuana, hallucinogens, and other drugs that the modern drug war began.

Today, addiction to crack cocaine in the inner city is increasing despite the general decreasing trend of cocaine (cocaine hydrochloride) use in the general population. This dramatic increase in crack cocaine use in the inner city is recognized but there is very little action being taken or funding for treatment. Again, local communities are left to clean up their own neighborhoods with little assistance from outside sources. I would guess that if the crack epidemic would spread to the white suburban high school students we would see a different response by funding sources.

Until we resolve the more dramatic issues of socioeconomic inequities, racial prejudice and oppression of minorities, inequities in pay and occupational opportunities, and other related issues, the inner city will continue to be the breeding ground for drugs/alcohol.

Academic Failure and the Failure of the U.S. Educational System in Motivating and Educating Young People to Strive for Productive Lives

Academic failure lays the foundation for being at risk for antisocial behavior during adolescence. Research confirms that academic failure is strongly correlated with antisocial behavior. Too frequently, children fail to develop the skills necessary to effectively learn and succeed in school. Children's failure at school causes them to disregard school as a viable option for success in the real world. Drugs and alcohol are often the choice for these young people. Discouraged by their failure in school, the additional shame of being labeled poor learners leads dropouts to antisocial and rebellious behavior and alcohol/drug use.

In 1959, the U.S.S.R.'s launching of the first manned spacecraft caught the United States by surprise. As a result, the United States took up the challenge for space by rededicating energy and resources to emphasizing the importance of science and math as well as the general education of our young people. Perhaps, the current failure of the U.S. educational system and the high incidence of drug/alcohol use by young people will be the impetus to implement reform and innovation in school systems, much like that of the 1960s.

In the 1980s we have seen the educational system in the United States neglected to the point of an increasing level of academic failure and dropout rates. The academic standards for those students who do graduate is inferior. The ripple effect of this lowering of academic standards is also seen in colleges and education in general. Illiteracy has increased, and the quest for knowledge and general personal and intellectual improvement is a standard that is not emphasized or valued by the average American citizen. This complacency in education pervades other standards in American business and industry. Attitudes about doing high-quality work and performing with productive energy at work are diminished when the motivation for personal improvement is not there. The quality and pride in American workmanship is also decreased, resulting in inferior goods and services and a general public attitude that accepts these standards. The industries that employ individuals with good educational backgrounds and positive self-motivating attitudes tend to experience fewer of these problems.

The current failure of the educational systems of the United States is a result of a variety of problems. The biggest problems are poor administration, teacher burnout, lack of adequate funding, and a bureaucratic system that promotes complacency.

The factor that contributes the most to teacher burnout is the lack of support from the principal and school board. Innovation is threatening to some school administrations, and the fear of parents' complaints and litigation often results in a political administration that is more concerned with how parents and the school board may respond than the effective development and education of the child.

Another factor is the lack of incentives—other than the genuine desire to work with young people—for teachers to invest themselves in their profession. The teacher who repeats the same lesson plan over and over without making any investment in the job receives the same salary as the teacher who is attentive, involved, and spending time and energy in educating students.

The combination of inadequate pay, lack of support from administration, and no financial incentives or other motivations has resulted in dedicated and talented teachers leaving educational systems. This leaves students in the hands of teachers who often lack the talent or motivation to help them overcome academic failure and a poor sense of self.

Reforms such as site-based management, parent involvement, shared decision making, accountability, alternative schools, and other reforms have been successful in turning school systems around. We need to apply these principles in educational reform to provide children the opportunity for academic and personal success. The development of our children as a natural resource is essential in developing a future generation strong enough not to succumb to dependence and addiction to drugs/alcohol.

Socioeconomic Inequities Undermine the American Dream

The inequities in socioeconomic opportunities has created bitterness, racial conflict, and a general rebelliousness and hopelessness which fuels the desire to use drugs/alcohol. The American dream is a nightmare for those who are unable to develop feelings of competency and pride in their lives.

The reality is that hard work and dedication can be rewarded with the attainment of each person's American dream. Successful persons have refused to be limited by the color of their skin, their sex, their religious or ethnic background, or their lack of membership in the inner circles of our society. Many individuals positively strive to reach their full potentials by overcoming these limitations and work to correct these inequities when they have an opportunity to change them. Other individuals become so embittered by socioeconomic injustices that they give up, become alienated from society, and lack a personal commitment to strive for anything in life. Drugs/alcohol numb and shut down these feelings of embitterment, anger, and pain. Instead of working through these issues and resolving the conflict, a bitter hopelessness devours their meaningfulness in life.

Our American society needs to acknowledge and address these issues of disparity in opportunity. Other factors contributing to the drug/alcohol problem are the breakdown of the neighborhood, changes in the traditional nuclear and extended family system, limited support systems, stress, and trauma.

Summary

Although we are seeing improvements in some areas, the solution to the drug/alcohol problem is not simple and will always be with us to some degree. This chapter broadly explores three major areas, problems in perception, problems in the family, and systemic problems, while suggesting reforms and possible solutions.

There is still a tendency to deny, ignore, or minimize the problems of alcohol abuse and alcoholism. Expanded awareness of the costly impact of alcoholism on our society is needed through greater efforts in education. For example, more than 105,000 homicides occur each year directly related to alcoholism. Child abuse rose 10 percent last year to 2.4 million cases, with parental substance abuse as a leading cause. An estimated $136 billion are spent each year in business and industry due to lost employment, reduced productivity, and health care costs. More than 1.8 million people are arrested for driving under the influence each year in the United States. Another perceptual problem is the denial of the American pleasure lust (i.e., avoidance of painful growth issues, and maintenance of unhealthy, imbalanced life-styles). This is evidenced in problems not only to drugs/alcohol but also to food, spending beyond one's means, and codependency in relationships.

Family problems have been a major focus in this book due to the role imbalanced/dysfunctional families play in drug/alcohol addiction. It is estimated that 30 percent of all families are imbalanced/dysfunctional and 50 percent are extremely imbalanced/dysfunctional. The remaining 20 percent are functional.

The most dominant feature of dysfunctional/imbalanced parents and family systems is the devastating impact of shame, abandonment, and rejection on the children growing up in that system. Too frequently denial of drug/alcohol problems in the family is maintained for a long time resulting in extremely destructive consequences. Although public media programs are addressing the issues of child abuse, sexual abuse, and other parental and family imbalance, more needs to be done to create awareness, early assessment, and referral for treatment.

By far the biggest systemic problem has been the government's emphasis on the supply side of the drug/alcohol problem while not adequately addressing the demand side. A second systemic problem has been the lack of cooperation and communication between the mental health/psychiatric, and drug/alcohol treatment fields. A third systemic problem has been the historical neglect of the drug/alcohol prevention and treatment needs of people of color. The fourth systemic problem is the failure of the U.S. educational system to motivate and educate young people to strive for productive lives. The fifth problem is socioeconomic inequities that discourage the underclass from having the hope and means to attain the American Dream.

Final Note

Perhaps the problems that spawn drug/alcohol addiction may seem too difficult to overcome. The negative impact of these problems frequently gives rise to feelings of hopelessness that we can never adequately resolve these issues. There is however, positive and dramatic success: millions of Americans are in drug/alcohol recovery. Family members are changing their own codependent and enabling behavior in relationships. Adult children of alcoholics are overcoming the trauma of their childhoods. Most important, families are successfully developing more functional and healthy systems for the next generation of youngsters. Their children will be less vulnerable to the familial problems of drug/alcohol dependence and addiction.

There is something to be said for thinking small. Initially this might sound like strange advice. We each must think about our own small contribution to solving problems that seem large and insurmountable. Each of us needs to first think about our own behavior, our own family, and address growth and positive development in those areas. Then we can begin to address these same issues in our neighborhoods, communities, workplaces, and other interpersonal interactions. My hope is that we can each in our small way address the issue of drug/alcohol dependence and other issues in our society by endeavoring to focus on our own and our children's functional growth and development.

References

United States Department of Transportation, Fatal Accident Reporting System, 1988.

White, William. "Chemical Prohibition." In *Facts About Drug Abuse,* Participants' Manual, Rockville, Md.: National Institute on Drug Abuse, 1976.

Williams, Edward Huntington. Editorial in the *Medical Record Newspaper,* 1914. In *Facts About Drug Abuse,* Participants' Manual. Rockville, Md.: National Institute on Drug Abuse, 1976.

CREDITS

Photos

INTRODUCTION

Page xxiv: © Michael Siluk

CHAPTER 1

Page 5: © Jack Spratt/The Image Works, Inc.; **p. 7:** © Universal Studios. Photo courtesy of the Academy of Motion Picture Arts & Sciences; **p. 25:** © Dion Ogust/The Image Works, Inc.; **p. 27:** AP/Wide World Photos

CHAPTER 2

Page 44, 45: AP/Wide World Photos

CHAPTER 3

Page 71 top: © Rapho/Photo Researchers, Inc.; **p. 71 bottom left and right:** Drug Enforcement Agency; **pp. 72-73:** U.S. Department of Justice; **p. 77:** Drug Enforcement Agency; **p. 80:** © Michael Siluk; **p. 82:** The Bettmann Archive; **p. 83:** Dr. Ann P. Streissguth; **pp. 86, 87:** U.S. Department of Justice; **p. 100:** Courtesy of Wiener Presse Bilbbienst; **p. 102:** UPI/Bettmann Newsphotos; **p. 107:** U.S. Department of Justice; **p. 109:** © Michael Gadomski/National Audubon Society/Photo Researchers, Inc.; **pp. 110, 111, 113:** Drug Enforcement Agency; **p. 126:** UPI/Bettmann Newsphotos

CHAPTER 6

Page 202: © Michael Siluk; **p. 214:** © Paramount Pictures. Photo courtesy of the Academy of Motion Picture Arts & Sciences

CHAPTER 7

Page 246: © Mark Antman/The Image Works, Inc.

Text and illustrations

CHAPTER 2

Pages 46 and 47: Source: E. M. Jellinek, *The Disease Concept of Alcoholism.* Copyright © 1960 College and University Press, New Haven, Connecticut.

CHAPTER 3

Page 181: From American Psychiatric Association: *Diagnostic and Statistical Manual of Mental Disorders,* Third Edition, Revised. Washington, DC, American Psychiatric Association, 1987. Reprinted by permission.

CHAPTER 7

Page 237: From Jean E. Rhodes and Leonard A. Jason, *Preventing Substance Abuse Among Children and Adolescents.* Copyright © 1988 Pergamon Press, Oxford, England.

CHAPTER 9

Figures 9.1, 9.2, 9.4, 9.5, and 9.6: From American Psychiatric Association: *Diagnostic and Statistical Manual of Mental Disorders,* Third Edition, Revised. Washington, DC, American Psychiatric Association, 1987. Reprinted by permission.

CHAPTER 10

Page 316: Excerpted courtesy of Marcel Dekker, Inc., from Richard Rawson, "Chemical Dependency Treatment: The Integration of the Alcoholism and Drug Addiction Systems" in *International Journal of the Addictions,* 1990. Copyright © 1990 Marcel Dekker, Inc., New York; **p. 336:** From Alan Marlatt and Judith Gordon, *Relapse Prevention.* Copyright © 1985 Guilford Press, New York, New York. Reprinted by permission.

INDEX

A

B

C

D

E

F

G

H

I

L

M

N

O

P

R

S

T